DRIVING
TOWARD DESTINY

A NOVEL

TIM SCOTT

ISBN: 978-1-64314-771-0 (Paperback)

Library of Congress Control Number: 2022919228

AuthorsPress
California, USA
www.authorspress.com

BOOK 1

1

I Blow Up

IT WAS CHRISTMAS 1971. I was seven months out of college. I was in the draft pool for the army and had already taken a physical. I had little control over the course of my life. The lottery system would decide my fate. I believed that if I were drafted, I would die in Vietnam.

In the summer, I had driven across the country with my best friend, Chris Atwell, to see if I could find answers to my existential questions. I was looking for answers to these questions which were coursing through my brain. I needed to define: Who am I? What would be my future path in life?

We had fun in my VW bus, which I had converted to a camper. We were smoking dope, listening to tunes, and meeting a lot of people who were more out of it than I was. But the trip was a bust.

I had come back home to have my father insist that I take interviews with his business associates for a career-oriented job, which I would likely get drafted out of with my draft number of one hundred and sixty-six. Between the draft and my parents nagging at me to get a job, I was so frustrated I thought I would explode.

My college pal, Wild Bill Markus, had told me I had to learn about life through experience. He knew he had to gain this experience now while he was young. So he had moved to Berlin to get away from home and find a new perspective. He had asked me to come over and live with him in an apartment. At first I had said no, but now I knew I had to get far away from the United States and the confines I was in, especially from my parents.

On the afternoon of Christmas Eve, I went downstairs to talk to my parents, who were preparing to throw yet another cocktail party of their holiday season. My father had his business associates and clients to entertain, and my mother had to support my father's business with these affairs. They were replete with servants, a cook, and a bartender. Everything had to be perfect. They were engrossed in the preparations for the evening.

Although I wanted to be as dispassionate as I could be when I spoke to them, I could feel the fire behind my eyes.

I stepped into the living room. "I'm going to go to Berlin for a couple of months to live with my friend Bill from college," I said.

I watched as the parents turned to face me. Their facial expressions changed from the smiling gaiety of their social lives to the stern solemnity of parental authority.

After a moment of startled silence, my father was the first to speak. "You know you can't do that. The draft board has one Jack Higgins under notice. You've even taken a physical. And I won't give you any money for such a ridiculous adventure."

"How will you live over there, Jack?" my mother asked. "I thought your trip out West last summer was going to be your vacation."

"It's not a vacation!" I yelled at them. "Can't you see I'm going crazy here, waiting on the draft and doing meaningless interviews with your old college friends for jobs I don't want or understand? And if I took a job, I'd probably just get drafted away anyway. I've got to find out who I am and where I really belong in life. And to do that, I've got to get out of here. Both of you are driving me crazy with your constant nagging and insistence that I live my life the way you live yours. And that's never going to happen!"

My parents were shocked at my vehemence and repudiation of their lifestyle. My mother, the holder of the family's traditions, had to ask, "Are you saying that you want to leave our family forever?"

I was upset enough in having to take what I thought was a risky but necessary journey into the unknown. In having to explain my actions to two people whom I knew were incapable of understanding where I was at and what I felt had to do to break out of the challenging moment of life I was in, I lost it.

"You don't know me!" I shouted. "You don't know what I'm going through. I can't talk to you because you're so wrapped up in yourselves and your lifestyle. You think I can just do what you say and everything will come out all right. That's the way it was for you when you were my age, but things aren't like that now.

"Getting drafted could mean I'll be dead in a matter of months. What's the point of me in getting a job and starting to live your lives all over again? I'm not even going to try to do it. Don't you see what's going on all around you? There are millions of people my age out on the streets saying that your way, Nixon's way, doesn't work for them. I may not be out on the streets, but I'm screaming inside. Your life is wrong for me. Your cocktail parties and cozy business relationships are wrong for me. I have to find my own way!

"I've got to get away from all this. Going to San Francisco last summer was a joke. I never left this screwed-up country, so I never got my head straight to see things from a different perspective. I just saw how it's the same all over. I can't stay here, especially here at home with you two suffocating me. I'm going to Berlin, and that's that."

I saw my parents were in some state of shock or, likely, denial. They stared at me and then turned to look at each other but didn't say anything at first. I expected this. I knew from times past that when they had problems with my older sisters, they would clam up, circle the wagons, and take time to deliberate between themselves before making a parental pronouncement. My sisters had always been obedient to their dictum.

So to prod them, I said, "I'm going to see if I can be in Berlin just after New Year's."

My father didn't respond right away, but in closing the discussion, he said, "We're expecting guests, so we can discuss this later. In the meantime, why don't you think about what you'll do if your call-up notice comes here and you're in Berlin?"

Damn! I was so pissed off! The parents were doing it again. They were undermining my ideas and trying to shape me to their purpose by pulling my strings. And they did it subtly: no blow-ups, but just check and checkmate, using their repressive logic in calm maneuvers. I could never win at their game. I stormed up to my room and slammed the door.

When I got upstairs, I had to ask myself, *Why had I had allowed the parents to blow off my idea of going to Berlin so easily?* I had allowed them to rattle me. I didn't say I was going into permanent exile and ruin their social standing, so I wasn't going to feel bad for them. To hell with them.

I started to make concrete plans to go to Berlin. The first thing I had to do was to get in touch with Wild Bill in Berlin to let him know I'd like to come over to live with him for a few months. I was excited to call Bill, but it was nighttime in Berlin. I'd have to wait a few hours before placing the call since Berlin was six hours ahead of New York.

While I waited, I got a pad of paper and started to list the things I needed to ask Bill: How would I get to Berlin? What stuff would I need to do before I left so I could actually get there? I'm nothing if not organized.

I needed money. I could pull five hundred dollars from my savings and sell the VW bus. I should be able to get almost three thousand dollars for the bus, and thirty-five hundred dollars should be plenty for an extended trip. I'd buy American Express travelers' checks so I could keep the money safely on me.

I didn't want to carry around a dorky piece of luggage, so I would go to an army-navy store and get a duffle bag. I could get road clothes there too, like jeans, shirts, warm underwear, and maybe a quilted vest. I had my hiking boots and air force survival jacket, which had gotten me through frosty winters at college. The idea of planning out the journey as it took shape in my mind appealed to me.

By one thirty in the morning, my parents' party was over, and they had gone to bed. I went down to my father's study to call Wild Bill. It would be seven thirty in the morning on Christmas Day in Berlin. I dialed the operator and asked to make an international call. I was put through to the international operator, who asked for the country, city, and number. It seemed like a long time passed, but finally the line started ringing and ringing.

And then someone picked up. "Allo?" said a sleepy, accented voice. "Wer ist das?"

From the tone of voice, I figured that the man who answered was asking who was calling. "Hello. I'm Jack Higgins. I'm calling from the United States for Bill Markus. Is he there?"

There was a pause before the guy said, "Ja, er ist hier." Then there was a long wait.

Finally, another sleepy voice said, "Hello?"

"Bill, it's Jack. Merry Christmas, buddy! I'm coming over to see you. Can you put me up?"

"What? Jack? Are you shitting me? When are you coming?" Bill yelled into the phone, suddenly sounding wide awake.

"I'll be there as soon as I can, man. I've got to sell my bus to get up a stake, but I don't think that will take too long, maybe a week or so."

"Wow, man! That's great," Bill said. "Are you going to take Icelandic Air to Luxembourg from JFK like I did?"

"That's my plan. Can't beat that ninety-nine-dollar fare. But I'm going to need to know how to get from Luxembourg to Berlin."

"Ok. Got a pencil and paper?"

"Bill, this is an international call. It can't take too long."

"If I send you a letter, you might have to wait around for it to get there. You'd better take the basic info down now. It isn't too difficult."

I had my pad, thinking about how many fuses my father was going blow when he got the phone bill. Well, I wasn't going to be around when it came.

I took down the trains and the towns I'd go through before I got to Frankfurt and where I'd have to take a flight to Tempelhof in Berlin. It didn't sound very easy, but I wanted to get off the line, so I didn't ask questions.

At the end, Bill made sure I had his address correct and said, "It'll be great to have you here. I'll have a mattress ready for you in my room."

"It'll be great to see you," I replied and hung up.

I sat at my father's desk and thought about how I had just taken a step into the greater world of my future. Now I had to put my plans in motion.

The next day was Christmas, and there wasn't much I could do to further those plans, except to avoid a direct confrontation with the parents who wanted to pin me down as to what I meant about "going to Berlin." They acted as if I weren't serious, and I figured it was best to let them think just that. I owned up to having thought about taking a trip to visit my friend in Berlin for a couple of weeks as a vacation, but the parents came back at me that I had been on a permanent vacation since I graduated and it was time to get serious about planning for my future. My plans were set, so I didn't react.

I was up early the day after Christmas. I went to the bank and took out most of my savings. Then I went to the local newspaper where I placed a classified ad with a bold headline:

For Sale–1968 VW Bus/Camper
[exc. Cond., 54,000 miles, Blue w/ white roof,
Blaupunkt AM/FM radio, compl. serv. record; $2,800]

I also included my phone number. The paper was published twice a week, and I was lucky that it would be coming out the next day. I took the bus to the car wash to spruce it up for the sale.

Then I went to the army-navy store for road gear. As I walked around the random stacks of stuff, I picked out a green canvas duffle bag that had a strap I could sling over my shoulder. I thought that was perfect for my gear and it made a statement that I wasn't a typical American tourist.

I knew Germany was cold at this time of year, so I picked up two warm shirts, two pairs of jeans, and some heavy socks. That would give me a basis for warmth along with my air force survival jacket, hiking boots, scarf, and wool ski hat.

As I went up to the cashier, I passed a rack of blue jean jackets. My mother would hate these, so I put down the stuff I had collected, tried one on, and decided on the spot that was the look I wanted. Paired with the jeans pants, it made for a rugged look that suited my new mental image. I was pleased with the new look but was nagged by the thought that clothes do not make the man. I still had to go on the journey to find out what kind of man I really was.

When I got home, I washed all the new clothes three times using bleach to fade them and take out the stiffness. When they were done, I put on the jacket to see if it shrunk. It fit fine, but my mother saw me.

Horrified, she told me, "You look like a motorcycle outlaw. Get rid of it!"

This pissed me off for a moment, but I quickly realized that this was exactly the image I wanted to project, one that would piss off my mother. To placate her, I put the denim in the duffle bag and shoved that into the back of my closet.

By mentioning motorcycle outlaw, my mother had triggered an impulse in my teeming brain. I had a passport from a family trip, taken three years ago. But I might want to drive in Europe, and I didn't have an international driver's license. So I called the local AAA office to learn how I could get one. All I had to do was to come into the office with a valid state driver's license and a copy of my passport photo and pay ten dollars. *That's easy*, I thought.

I drove to the AAA office. I was issued a license, a very rudimentary document made of printed light cardboard showing five vehicle classes, which the AAA officer stamped corresponding to those vehicles I was listed as eligible to drive on my state license. I didn't have eligibility to drive a motorcycle on my state license, but I really wanted to have that, just for fun.

I asked the lady at the desk, "Could you please give me a stamp so that I can ride a motorcycle? I have experience riding a Honda 90."

"Absolutely not," she said. "If it wasn't on the state license, I cannot put it on the AAA license. We have a trust to uphold."

"But I'm only going to Europe. I doubt I'll ever get a chance to actually ride a motorcycle," I pleaded.

I could tell she was a hardened bureaucrat, and my appeals would get nowhere with her, so I looked carefully at the stamp she had used and made some mental notes. I saw a three-fourths-inch wide oval, a soft rubber stamp with AAA carved into it with a circle around the outside. *Why couldn't I make a copy of it and forge an entry on the motorcycle section of the license?* I thought. I didn't have any plans to drive a motorcycle in Europe, but this woman had pissed me off, just as my mother had. Motorcycle outlaw! Ha!

I went to the office supply shop and bought an ink pad, four medium-sized pink hand erasers with beveled ends, and a set of X-Acto knives with a dozen blades. When I got home, I got a small board from the garage, went up to my room, turned on some tunes, and spent the next couple of hours carving the AAA symbol with the circle around it on the ends of the erasers. When I thought I had a good match for the stamp on the license, I inked it on the pad and tried it out on a piece of cardboard. It was perfect.

Then I carefully touched the eraser to the ink again and stamped it on the license by the motorcycle designation. I looked it over and could not tell the real one from the forgery. Now I could drive a motorcycle if I wanted to, and I had created another pathway for myself as I was heading out on my journey.

2

Selling the Bus

I SLEPT LATE THE next day and went downstairs to find that the parents were not in the house. This was great. The paper with the ad for the bus was out, and I was the only one home to answer the phone. I fixed myself a large breakfast of two scrambled eggs, four strips of bacon, two English muffins, and two cups of coffee. I was putting the dishes in the washer when the phone rang. I picked up.

"I saw an ad in the paper for a VW bus for sale. Is it still for sale?"

I almost jumped. My first inquiry on the first day the ad was out! "Yes, it is. Would you like to see it?"

"Yeah. I would. Is it in good shape?"

"Absolutely. Why don't we meet and you can check it out for yourself?"

"Ok, cool," the guy said. "Where do we meet?"

I didn't want to have anyone over to my house during a potential sale in case my mother showed up.

"Meet me in the parking lot of the local diner in a half hour."

"I'll be there."

The guy was waiting for me when I got to the diner. It was a sunny day, not too cold. The guy was standing in front of the diner with his girlfriend. Both were smoking cigarettes. I liked the idea that the guy was early. He might be really interested.

I looked the guy over: he was tall and skinny with long, dark hair going down his back and tied at the neck to keep it under control. He was wearing embroidered bell-bottom jeans and a wild multicolored psychedelic jacket like I had seen in San Francisco last summer. The girlfriend was a long-haired, leggy blonde dressed in the same hippie style. Her over-the-knee, high-heel leather boots made her as tall as the guy.

I didn't have a favorable reaction to this pair. But I wanted to sell the bus, so I made nice. "How about getting in and taking a look around? I took the rear seat out and built the living quarters myself."

"Hey, the rear seat is really comfortable, the girl said.

"I used four-inch rubber foam," I said. "And see how the seat and table can be removed for a second bed, which is included."

"I want to hear the Blaupunkt," the guy said and turned the volume up all the way. I had put speakers in each corner for optimal sound, and we were nearly blown out the doors.

What a jerk, I said to myself. I turned the knob back to a reasonable volume.

"Wow! That's got a lot of power," he said.

"Blaupunkt is the best," I said. Then I offered to take them on a test drive.

The guy wanted to drive first, but the floor-mounted stick shift, which had a long throw to change gears, confused him, so I took the wheel and showed him how to do it.

After a while, I let the guy drive. He was a klutz at first and ground the gears, miss shifting several times, but he got the hang of it after a while. He said he loved sitting so far up front. I switched places with the girl on the fly through the passageway so she could get the feeling of sitting up front too. She loved it.

By the time we got back to the diner, it looked like a sale was imminent.

The guy looked the bus over again. "It's going to need new tires soon."

Ok, he's bargaining, I thought. *He's going to make an offer.*

The guy rubbed his chin a while. "So I'll give you twenty-five hundred for it. Whaddya say?"

I had determined that I was going to stand my ground. "I'm asking twenty-eight hundred when I could get three thousand easy. Besides, the three hundred-dollar difference for tires you want would be seventy-five dollars a tire. What are you going to get? Michelins? These are good for another twenty-five thousand miles anyway."

I realized I had a fish on the line, so after a pause, I made a concession. "Ok, I'll let you have it for twenty-seven hundred."

The guy stepped back and stroked his scraggly mustache as if considering a counteroffer The guy walked around the bus again. "Can you turn it on so I can see if all the lights work?"

I did what the guy asked. After I had turned on all the lights and the wipers and blown the horn, the guy took his babe aside and had a powwow.

The guy came up to me as I was leaning out the window of the driver's seat. "I'll give you a check for twenty-seven hundred for it right now. How about it?"

The red light went off in my head right away. "Sorry. This is strictly a cash deal. But I will give you fifty off and make it twenty-six fifty. But it's got to be cash or a bank check only."

"Hey," the hippie said. "I want to buy this bus, and I thought I could seal the deal right away. I don't have the cash on me. If I don't buy it now, you could sell it to someone else."

I certainly wasn't going to take a check from some hipster I'd never seen before, but I didn't want to lose a willing buyer. "Ok," I said, "how soon can you get the cash or a bank check?"

"Well, let's see. It's Wednesday afternoon. Can you give me until Friday morning?"

I was surprised he couldn't get the money by the next day. Then I thought ahead and realized that Friday was just before New Year's weekend. If other people called before Friday, I could say I was negotiating a deal, get their number, and call them back after New Year's, if this guy didn't come through. If I sold to this guy on Friday, Chris would be back from visiting his girlfriend, and he could give me a ride home.

"Ok, I'll hold the bus for you until Friday morning at ten. If you call me by then and you've got the cash, we can make a deal. Otherwise, the bus stays on the market."

"You got it, pal. You'll be hearing from me Friday morning." The hipster turned back to his babe, who jumped up and hugged him around the neck and gave him a big smooch. It was then that I saw the car they were driving. It was a hopeless, two-tone, late-fifties Ford Fairlane.

No wonder they want the bus so bad, I thought. *Pretty hard to be hip in that pile of junk.* I was wondering if they were going to be able to come up with the money, but I'd just have to hope for the best. They really wanted the bus.

------◆-◆◆-◆------

The next day I waited anxiously. Was there going to be another call from a potential buyer? My mother was home, so I had to stay near the phone so I could answer it before she did. I didn't want her to get any ideas about what I was doing. But the calls I answered were all for her.

In the late afternoon, the phone rang when I was listening to music on my headphones, so I didn't hear it. My mother opened the door to my room and gave me a fright.

"There's a call for you," she said. My mouth opened to say something, but before I could get anything out, she said, "It's Chris."

I let out a sigh of relief and picked up the phone in my room. "Hey, Chris. What are you up to? I was going to call, but I thought I'd wait to hear from you."

"I went to spend a couple of nights in the city with Amy. Took her to the airport. Just got back a few minutes ago. What's up with you?"

"I've been making some plans. Let's meet at the diner for some coffee and a piece of pie, and I'll tell you about them."

"Sounds great. See you in fifteen."

"Cool. You come over and pick me up. I'll tell you why later."

When Chris drove me to the diner, he told me about his adventures with Amy, his steady girlfriend he had met on our trip to San Francisco. I knew that Chris was totally smitten by the young, pretty, and seemingly innocent Amy. Chris had simply fallen under Amy's spell.

When we got to the diner, I dropped the bomb. "I'm virtually on my way to Berlin for several months."

"Holy shit," Chris yelled out when he heard the news. He then asked for the details.

I told him most of the preparations I had made, leaving out the AAA license forgery, which was my little secret. And I told him about the pending sale of the bus, which I was hoping would occur the next morning.

"So you're really going to sell the bus? Man, we've had a lot of fine times in that vehicle," Chris said.

"I've got to sell it to finance the trip. I've only got five hundred cash, and I don't know how long I'm going to be over there or how much it costs. I told the guy I want twenty-six fifty in cash, and he is supposed to call me by ten tomorrow if the deal is going through. The sale will take place here at the diner, so my mother won't catch wind of it. Now here's the thing: if this works out, I'm going to need you to be here at the diner to sort of ride shotgun for me and then drive me home after it's over. Can you do that?"

"Sure," Chris said. "That'll be cool. What time?"

"The guy is supposed to call me at home by ten. I'll call you right after, and then we can meet here."

So that was arranged. Chris took me home, and I found that there were no calls for me, so I had a sandwich and a beer and watched movies into the night before turning in. I remembered to set the alarm for eight so I could pick up any calls in the morning before the parents.

•——◆◄●►◆——•

I was having breakfast when the phone rang at nine thirty. I jumped for the phone and answered. "Hello."

"Hey, you the guy who's selling the bus? I've got the cash. Is it still for sale?"

"Yeah. Sure. You want to meet at the diner in an hour?"

"Yeah. That's cool. See you there."

I was ecstatic. I didn't finish my breakfast. Instead I called Chris to tell him the sale was on and to meet me at the diner in twenty minutes. That would give me time to get there and take the plates off the bus and empty all my stuff into Chris' car before the guy arrived. Then I checked the car's papers to see where the transfer signatures went. The insurance was under my father's policy, so I'd have to tell him to take the bus off the policy, but I could do that in a note when I left.

I gathered all the documents and headed to the diner. Chris was already there and very excited. It was another cool, clear day, which was great for showing the bus. The guy and his babe arrived around ten. The guy was all business, walking around the bus, checking for dents. He asked me to start it up and open the rear engine hood. He listened to the engine for a while. I figured that he had been talking to someone who knew something about engines.

"Ok. This bus is what I want, so let's make the deal. Think we can go inside and do the paperwork?"

We went into the diner, and I told the guy behind the counter that I was selling the bus so the guy wouldn't think there was a drug deal going down.

At the table, I told the guy that Chris was my buddy and my ride home. I put the papers on the table and asked to see the hippie's money. The girl pulled a wad of crumpled, greasy bills from her beaded hippie satchel.

"Could we count it together?" I asked.

I had seen pot deals before, so I knew that trust was not assumed by any party. There were a few hundreds, but mostly old twenties and tens. We both counted slowly, putting all the denominations in their respective piles. Then I counted each pile and asked the hippie to add up the total with him.

"If you were counting along with me, that comes to twenty-five fifty," I said.

"Yeah, I get twenty-five fifty too." The hipster shot a look at his girlfriend.

She turned slightly white, and her eyes bugged open. Then she started rummaging around in her satchel like crazy until she produced a crumpled hundred-dollar bill. The hipster snatched it from her and slapped it on the table.

"That's twenty-six fifty," he said.

"Right. Then you've got yourself a bus," I said.

I signed his copies of the papers and had the hipster sign mine. The guy seemed to be in a hurry to get this over with. When we had done the deal, I handed the guy the keys and said he'd gotten a great bus. The guy said "thanks" and just headed out. He got in the bus and drove off with the babe following in the piece-of-crap Ford.

"That was a little strange," Chris said.

"Yeah, I never like dealing with those guys. Well, goodbye bus, but I've got the cash. That's what matters."

We left the diner, and I got Chris to take me to the bank, where I bought three thousand dollars' worth of American Express travelers' checks. I now had the checks plus two hundred and fifty dollars in cash for the journey. The travelers' checks were safe money. They couldn't be stolen without a countersignature. I thought that $3,250 should be enough to last six months. I now had the stake I needed.

Chris and I went to the pub in town for a beer and a burger. I told Chris I was going to leave from JFK on Sunday morning, New Year's Day, because I thought there would be less people traveling then than at any other time. I didn't have an air reservation, so I'd have to get one at the gate, but there shouldn't be a problem there. I would be flying Icelandic Air. How crowded could it be?

"Hey, can you pick me up early and drive me to the train station, where I can catch the train into the city? Then I can take a cab from Grand Central."

Chris, who was still flabbergasted by what I was going to do, said, "No way! I'll drive you to JFK. I'd like to see you off."

"Hey, man. That's a real favor! I've got a lot of traveling ahead of me, and that'll give me a head start."

Chris left me off at the house, and I realized right away that my father was there, back from his business trip. So instead of making straight for my room, I went into the kitchen, where I heard the parents talking. I didn't think they had an inkling of my plans, but I wanted to make sure. If there were going to be a confrontation, it was going to be now. I was set for it.

"I see you got back for New Year's," I said, offhandedly.

"The Smiths are throwing their usual New Year's bash," my father said. "Everyone is going to be there."

Not me, I thought. *And maybe you'll be too hungover to notice I've left until tomorrow afternoon.*

"What are you doing for New Year's Eve?" my mother asked.

"No plans. New Year's Eve isn't my favorite."

"Well, don't wait up for us," my mother said with a coy smile.

"Don't worry," I said with a telling smile of my own.

Seeing that the parents weren't in a mood to hassle me, I went up to my room and took the time to write them a letter, telling them where I had gone (just to Berlin, no address or phone number), which I would leave on the hall table in the morning on my way out of the house heading for JFK. I mentioned that I had sold the bus to fund the trip and that it should be taken off the insurance. (I'd leave the license plates with it.) I said I didn't know when I'd be back, but I would contact them from time to time from the American Express office in Berlin. I thought that was adequate to keep them from freaking out. I couldn't help but reiterate my reasons for going away:

- I was being suffocated at home, listening to them try to direct my life.

- I needed to go places and talk to people who could help me find meaning in life.

- I was tired of all the noise on the streets, which was beamed into our living room on the TV news, which was riveted on the war and the body counts every night.

- I was going crazy with the draft hanging over me.

- I needed to put space between myself and the rabid dog that was America.

- The drive across the country last summer hadn't helped me resolve anything. It had turned out to be a lark. America was in the same mess everywhere. I needed a different perspective from a distance.

- If I were sent a call-up notice, I'd probably call them within a reasonable amount of time to respond. Honestly, I wasn't sure if I would come home to be drafted. (I put that in there because I really wasn't sure. I knew it would catch their attention too.)

I finished and reread the letter. I first saw it as a declaration of independence, but on reflection, before I put it in the envelope, I wondered about how I seemed to be cutting myself off from my past, and it gave me a pang of loneliness. I wasn't sure what my father's reaction to the letter was going to be, but I knew my mother would be really upset. I tried to figure out why they might be troubled, but I couldn't get into their heads, just like they couldn't get into mine. So I put the letter in the envelope, sealed it, and wrote "To Mom and Dad: IMPORTANT" on the front. I put it where I could grab it and put it on the hall table on my way out in the morning.

I lay back on my bed and put on Paul Butterfield's *In My Own Dream* album with the headphones and let the blues wash over me. "Everyone's got problems" was the message of the blues. I was going out to face my problems; the parents could face theirs here at home. When the music was done, I turned out the light.

3

Traveling to Berlin

NEW YEAR'S EVE DAY passed in a blur. I got up late and called Chris
to come over. We went to the diner and had brunch together. The
diner had great breakfasts as well as pies. After that, we cruised
around, smoking a couple of joints.

Nothing really mattered at home anymore. My head was in a
707 heading for a place I could only imagine. By the time Chris left
me back at the house, my parents had gone to their party. Chris said
he'd pick me up at 8:00 a.m. sharp the next morning.

Up in my room, I dumped the contents of the duffle bag on the
bed, taking out my passport, AAA license, travelers' checks, and
wallet. I stuffed them into the pockets of my Air Force survival
jacket and buttoned them down. I then repacked all the clothes in
the duffle, putting my copy of *The Odyssey*, my favorite novel, on
top along with *Sports Illustrated* to pass the time.

I couldn't sleep much that night. I was too restless. In my
wakefulness, I questioned myself: did I really have to make such a
wrenching break from home and my past to find my future? Was
there anything I would be leaving behind, which might be of value
to me on my journey?

When I left my room in the morning, I realized that what I was really leaving behind was my childhood, a part of myself that wasn't of use anymore, so I could find out who I was as a man in a larger world.

I clipped the strap of the duffle and left the letter and plates for the parents on the hall table before going into the kitchen to make breakfast. I had two English muffins with jam and coffee. I was wondering if the smell of coffee would wake up the parents when Chris pulled into the driveway.

Good old Chris, I thought as I put on my jacket and slung the duffle onto my shoulder. *Here I go.*

I got into Chris' car, and we headed for JFK. We didn't say much as we made our way quickly to the airport, encountering little traffic early on New Year's Day. Chris left me off at International Departures with a handshake and a "Good luck, buddy." I said I'd send him a postcard sometime.

I went into the terminal and found the Icelandic Airways desk. There was no one there, so I walked down to the KLM desk. The attendant told me that Icelandic flew at night, so the attendant usually didn't show up until after noon. It was just before 10:00 a.m., so I had to wait it out. I looked at the flight schedule behind the desk and saw there was just one flight that day to Reykjavik and Luxembourg, departing at 6:30 p.m.

I sat and waited, and finally, just before 2:00 p.m., a beautiful girl with silver-blonde hair, fair skin, and light-blue eyes, which matched her Icelandic Airways uniform, showed up behind the counter. I guessed she was about two years older than I was, but her uniform gave her a presence that made her look older. I couldn't help staring at her. She was a real knockout. Those types of girls always make me weak in the knees.

After a few minutes, she opened the desk and looked up at me. I had to get a ticket, which meant I had to talk to her. So I went over. "Can I get a ticket for tonight's flight to Luxembourg?"

She looked me hard in the eye as if to assert that she had seen me staring at her. At this point, I noticed that her eyes were bloodshot around the edges and figured that she had been partying hard last night, which was why she was late for work. *Hmm, maybe I don't have to take that cold look so seriously*, I thought. I smiled at her.

"Let me see if we have any seats available," she said in a voice that had a lilting Scandinavian accent. She looked down and busied herself with seating charts and schedules.

I thought she was taking a long time on all this when she could have easily told me if there were a single seat on the only flight of the day.

"That must have been some party you were at last night," I said to get her attention.

She immediately looked up at me with her eyes wide, showing even more how bloodshot they were. "Wh…Why do you say that?" she stammered.

"Well, the attendant down at KLM said you're usually here around noon, and it was New Year's Eve…"

"Oh, dear. Well, yes. It was crazy. I had some drinks and got into a fight with my boyfriend, and it turned into a bad time." She paused as she looked back at the seating chart. "I will get you a nice seat. There will be no problem. The flight is half empty to Reykjavik. A few more passengers will board there, but there will be plenty of room. Please don't complain to my supervisor."

I hadn't thought of complaining, but I realized that by being aggressive and playful at the same time had put me at an advantage. I liked the feeling of holding the upper hand. It was new to me with girls. She told me the fare was ninety-nine dollars, one way, as expected.

I paid for the ticket with an AMEX check, taking my reading material out of the duffle before checking it through to the flight. I went back to the waiting area and looked the ticket over, thinking it was the ticket to my journey of self-discovery. I looked over at the girl behind the counter and thought that maybe my interaction with her was a new beginning too, that my passage had begun right here where I had taken on a new, more assertive role with women to fit the man I was seeking to become.

Sitting on the bench, taking an occasional look at that beautiful girl, I thought of the circumstances that had trapped me in the indeterminate state between wanting to engage with girls but being prevented from doing so:

When I was born, I had two sisters who were eight and ten years older than I was. My father was thrilled to finally have a son, and he doted on me because, to him, having a son made him more of a man. This made my sisters wildly jealous. They bullied me psychologically for years, calling me by the pet name they had invented, Worm-Eaten, and performing continuing cruelties out of view of my parents.

I became wary of females and distrusted getting close to them. My sisters disappeared after a time, going to college and then getting married, but the damage they had inflicted lasted. My adolescence was torture.

Oh, how I would have liked to have just had a nice chat with that girl behind the counter! I didn't have anything to do, and I could see she really didn't either, but I was frozen in place and time. Deep down, I had to believe I was also looking for a solution to this dilemma in taking off on my journey.

I had to speak to the girl again to ask about doing some foreign exchange. She told me the Perera counter was near the end of the corridor, where I bought two hundred and fifty dollars' worth of German marks. I figured that would get me to Wild Bill's place, what with train tickets, the flight from Frankfurt, and food.

I went back and sat near the Icelandic counter. I really was geared for the future. I stretched out my legs on the bench to wait for the flight and thought about how I had come to be here:

In senior year, I spent more time with Wild Bill, needing a guide, a support, someone who could help me take my next step toward my future. Bill, with his Harley Sportster, was an enigmatic figure on campus, given to pulling off antics, who had become my friend over time, a big man who commanded respect, despite his oddities. I guess I looked up to him.

One day in April, a few weeks before graduation, as we were throwing a Frisbee on the college green, Wild Bill shouted, "Hey, Jack! Come to Berlin with me!"

I stared at Bill as the Frisbee sailed over my head, and some people watching us laughed. So did Bill. I retrieved the disc, went over to Bill, and asked, "What the hell are you talking about?"

Bill told me he was going to sow his wild oats in the year after graduation and then settle down, go to law school, and become corporate counsel for a big company.

The fact that Wild Bill had opened up to me surprised me with his maturity. Bill had told me he'd come from a large, third-generation Latvian-American family. He said he wanted to get married, have lots of children, and support his parents in their old age because they had sent him to college.

"After commencement, I'm going to ride home on my bike, help my dad around the house for a few weeks, and then go to Berlin. I'm going to enroll in some law courses at the Frei University of Berlin. It actually is free to go there because the West Berlin government wants people to stay in Berlin. If too many people leave the city, the Soviets might try to take it over like they did in 1948. I know a guy who lives in an apartment. Why don't you come along with me? It'll be a gas."

I was floored. The idea of hitting the road in the United States in my VW bus had been percolating in the back of my mind for a while, but I hadn't formed up any plans to go. Just taking off to Europe with a crazy guy like Wild Bill wasn't on my scope at all.

"Bill," I asked, "you're really doing this?"

"Sure," Bill said. "I speak German and Latvian. If I get good grades over there, I can transfer the courses to my first year at law school here in the States. The Frei University is a very good school. I've spoken to my friend on the phone. If you haven't figured out what you're doing by then or you aren't in the army, come on over. You can bunk out in my room."

I thanked Bill for the offer but said I was considering taking a cross-country trip in the summer if I could find someone to go with me. I'd been thinking of asking Bill, but that just faded out.

Wild Bill said he wanted to get away from the United States entirely, and Berlin was unique, an island of the West inside the Soviet Bloc. The tensions of the past twenty years had become muted. The East Germans had effectively stopped their people from making the headline-grabbing escapes to the West over and under the Wall, so there was little to rattle sabers about except policies and procedures.

"You've done some homework on Berlin," I said.

"I am definitely taking some time after school to see something of the world, something that's long term, not just a vacation, and something that's affordable. I want to live in a place where I can immerse myself. Berlin fits perfectly."

Again I was left wide-eyed. I was seeing a Bill Markus who was more mature than I was. The old Wild Bill seemed to have crossed the threshold out of adolescence I had been standing on for so long. Bill knew where he was going and what path he wanted to follow, and most importantly, he knew who he was.

I looked at Bill differently as we left the green and walked back to my apartment for a joint. I wanted to query Bill as to how he had put together his plans, how he had come to find out so much about himself that he could see a path ahead, and how he seemed to calmly have learned who he was in a world made up of so much chaos. I needed to put a voice to some of my deepest concerns, and I thought I might talk about the more fundamental aspects of life with Wild Bill.

I asked Bill, "In listening to your plans, I think you may have figured out what the direction of your life is."

Bill thought about it and said, "No, I'm just making a plan to find out what it is. I think direction is something everyone has to discover for himself."

I accepted that but persisted, "How do you discover it?"

"I think you have to go out and gain experience of life. That's where the meaning is, in experience. I'm going to go to Berlin to find experience for myself. You should come along."

I remembered this exchange and smiled. Back then, while we were still in school, I couldn't have imagined flying to Europe to live for several months.

The trip out West was occupying my mind. I thought the answers were on the road, and I thought the road was anywhere you found it. Why not stay in the United States? How wrong I was! Growing up was not a condition of my generation here. Too many kids seemed likely to be adult/children all their lives. If I wanted to find deeper meaning in life, I'd have to go further afield. Bill was providing the place; I was taking the leap.

When I heard the call for my flight, I'd been lying on the bench in the terminal for nearly six hours with occasional walks down the corridors and a stop at a stand-up bar for a sandwich and a Coke.

I boarded the 707 and asked the flight attendant, "Can I sit in a row where I could stretch out?"

She told me, "Pick your own seat."

It was six and a half hours to Reykjavik with a two-hour layover. When we arrived there, it was snowing so hard I couldn't see out the window. The pilot pulled off a perfect landing, though. I guessed they must have lots of practice with Iceland as a home airport. We took off an hour late because the plane had to be shoveled off and de-iced. Then it was another six hours to Luxembourg.

When we arrived in Luxembourg, I went through passport control and customs in a daze of jet lag and sleeplessness. I saw that it was 1630 local time (4:30 p.m. my time) and realized I'd better get used to being on the metric system. I'd been on the move for twenty-five hours and still had a long way to go, so I stopped at the airport coffee shop for a mug of coffee and a pastry.

Following Bill's instructions, I then took a cab to the Bahnhof and bought a second-class rail ticket to Frankfurt. The train was leaving in twenty minutes. There was a change at Mannheim, and I asked the conductor to remind me when it came up. I then went back to my compartment and fell deeply asleep.

At Mannheim, I got off the train and stood on the platform to wait for the train to Frankfurt. I had been asleep in the warm compartment and realized it was cold outside. I looked at a thermometer, which said it was minus three degrees. I was freaked out until I remembered that the temperature was on the metric system too, which meant it was just a little below freezing. Changes of all types were coming at me quickly. *I'd adjust*, I told myself as I walked into the station waiting room to get warm.

It was almost an hour before the train, so I went to the Bahnhof café to get something to eat. I had no idea if it were breakfast, lunch, or dinner, but I sure was hungry. I had coffee and rolls with preserves. I was congratulating myself on having made it this far, when I saw that it was time to get ready for my train. I realized that I should relieve myself before doing anything else, so I stood up, but a little too quickly.

I didn't think that I may have been dehydrated by the long flight and disoriented by lack of sleep. My head spun, and I almost fell, bumping the corner of the table and knocking the coffee mug to the floor where it shattered. The waiter came over and gave me a stern look. I said I was sorry in English. The waiter pointed to the floor as he wrote out my bill, which included the cost of the mug. I paid and included a tip. I then headed for the toilet, which was marked WC–Herren and Damen. There were pictures so I didn't have a problem there.

I caught the train to Frankfurt, which took less than an hour, and then got a cab for the airport. I was in luck. The last flight for Berlin was in thirty-five minutes. It was a seventy-five-minute flight, which got into Tempelhof at 9:25 p.m. I was truly wiped out and needed to crash. When they called the flight, I had to walk out on the tarmac and mount a rolling staircase to board the plane, a four-engine prop plane of indeterminate vintage. *Great*, I thought. *I hope I'm seated near the front away from those noisy engines.*

In fact, the seat was just behind the engines. But the old plane had a redeeming feature: the seats were wide and comfortable. I settled down and started to doze off even as the plane taxied to the runway. My eyelids involuntarily closed just after takeoff.

Landing in West Berlin, there were no customs because we were coming from West Germany and West Berlin was part of West Germany. I looked at the clock over the exit to the terminal, which said 2140, or 9:40 p.m. I found a phone booth and called Wild Bill.

As I waited for someone to answer the phone, I tried to think what day it was. I had left late on New Year's Day in New York but had traveled more than thirty-six hours. Berlin was six hours ahead of New York, so I guessed it might be 9:40 p.m. on January 2, but in my state of fatigue, I really couldn't be sure.

"Allo?" someone finally said.

"Is Bill there?" I asked.

"Please wait."

And then there was Bill. "Jack? Jack, is that you?"

"Yeah, or what's left of me after more than a day and half's worth of travel by everything except boat. I'm at Tempelhof. Any chance you could swing by and lead me to a bed?"

"Hey, Jack. No sense in taking two cabs. Just go out the front and get a cab at the taxi stand. Tell the guy 38 Hubertusallee. You'll be here in fifteen minutes. Cost you twenty marks."

"Just be at the front door in case there's any hassle. I'm not up for that at this point. Ok?"

Bill said he'd be there, so I lugged the duffle out and got a cab. It appeared to me that we drove right thought the heart of the city. The taxi driver called out that this was the "Ku'damm." I saw the ruins of a big church that was all lit up just before we tuned down Hubertusallee. The cabbie said it was the Kaiser-Wilhelm Church.

In a few minutes, we were at 38 Hubertusallee. I paid the twenty-mark fare and got out. As soon as I did, I saw Bill open the door of the four-story building and come rushing down the front stoop to give me a big hug. He then took my duffle and wrapped me up around his shoulder with his massive right arm and ushered me inside out of the cold Berlin night.

Bill brought me to his room without introductions to some of the people I saw in the living room down the hallway. They appeared to me as shadowy because my vision had started to blur as the adrenaline of travel passed out of my body and sleep became imperative. He showed me where I'd be sleeping.

I just wanted to use the bathroom and to brush my teeth before sleep. Bill said that bathrooms were called WCs in Europe and showed me where it was. He told me that this was actually a commune that was shared with five other people, but I didn't care at the moment. The WC was unoccupied, so I took care of my business and went back to Bill's room, where I lay down on the mattress in my clothes and passed out.

4

The Commune

When I woke up, it was bright daylight. The clock on the table read two thirty. I did a quick calculation and figured I'd slept about seventeen hours and noticed that someone had put a blanket over me during the night. That wasn't like Bill. I wondered whose blanket it was and thought that this might not be a bad place to have landed. I was hungry, but I really wanted to get out of my traveling clothes and take a shower. So I got up and scouted around the apartment. No one was there. I took a towel from a drawer in Bill's armoire, showered, and changed.

I combed my hair in the WC and saw that I needed a haircut and a shave. "No, I don't," I said out loud and determined to let my hair grow to a length that had become the hallmark of my generation. "And a beard too," I said to myself. No more being cowed by my parents' ways and outdated *Weltanschauung*, a good German word I'd learned in English class. It meant "worldview," and it was a fundamental component of what I needed to discover in my own character. I could use it in discussions about the questions I had about life. Germans would surely know about a concept they had invented a term for.

I looked around the quarters a little more closely, even opening the refrigerator, but I figured it would be better not to touch anything, especially food, until I got to know what the people who lived here were like and what the ground rules were for interacting.

A *commune*? I'd heard about these in the states and was not thrilled about it—but here I was. This deliberation did nothing to assuage my hunger, so I went for a walk up Hubertusallee in the direction of the Ku'damm. I could tell where it was because I could see the shell of the Kaiser-Wilhelm Church, which had been left as a war memorial of bombed-out Berlin right in the heart of the Ku'damm. There were lots of stores and bars there, as I remembered, so there should be somewhere I could find something to eat.

But first I needed cash, so I found a bank and changed two hundred dollars into eight hundred marks. The marks I'd bought at JFK had just gotten me here. Now I was staked for a while. I walked further down the avenue to find some food, and I came to a café, which had a menu in the window that listed something called *goulashsuppe mit ei*. That sounded like some sort of soup with eggs, probably on the side, which would do me for breakfast.

I went in and ordered from a buxom waitress in a peasant dress. When she placed a large bowl in front of me, I saw a raw egg floating on top of a dozen unidentifiable objects partially hidden in the deep-crimson murk. I stared at it a moment and was about to refuse it, but the waitress caught me up and said, as she stood over me with her arms folded across her ample bosom, "Es its Sehr gut!"

She was an intimidating figure, so I smelled the soup, and it seemed tasty. I gave a half-smile to the waitress as I turned to take a spoonful of soup and discovered it was delicious. I smiled at the waitress again, and she gave me a basket of black bread and indicated I should dip it in the soup as I was eating. I mixed the raw egg in with the rest and finished the bowl and two pieces of bread, after which my hunger was sated.

I walked further down the Ku'damm and saw office buildings, fancy women's clothing shops, auto dealerships, strip clubs, hookers, and movie theaters, all packed into a ten-to twelve-block jumble of commerce. There were panhandlers by the score, several with Middle Eastern-looking faces. I saw at least one drug deal going down right on the sidewalk.

Man, this place is crazy, I thought. It seemed as though it was a city without rules, without a sense of a future, just living for the moment. And then I was struck by the reality that Berlin was, in fact, living for the moment. It was surrounded by the Soviet Bloc, which could cut it off from the rest of the world in a moment of communist displeasure.

In 1948, Stalin had tried to do just that; only the Berlin Airlift had saved it. But the commies had gone further, and in 1961, they had walled off West Berlin to keep East Germans from escaping into the West. So West Berlin had become an island of Western hedonist, capitalist culture surrounded by East German/Soviet communist authoritarian dictatorship and a thousand Russian T-80 tanks. The Ku'damm was a catch basin for enterprise of all sorts, licit and illicit. I figured that this island city had to make many adaptations to world politics. After all, it was run by four separate countries: the United States, Britain, and France in the West and the USSR in the East.

It was past six when I got back the house. Not having a key, I had to ring the bell. The door was opened by a tall, skinny, bearded man with long, blond hair tied in a ponytail. The man's skin was as fair as his hair and tight around the eyes, giving his head the appearance of a skull. I guessed that he was a Nordic-type.

He just stood in the doorway looking at me. Finally he asked, "What do you want?"

"I'm staying here with Bill Markus. Is he here?"

"So you are Bill's American friend come from the States?"

"Yes. I just got here last night."

"Well, commen sie in," the man said and stepped aside.

I could hear that there were a number of people in the back rooms as I walked through the doorway. I could smell a meal being prepared in the kitchen too. And there was Wild Bill in his room, who yelled out, "Hey, man! Where have you been? I was thinking you beat it back home." And he grabbed me around the shoulders with his right arm in his familiar grasp.

"Not a chance," I said through a toothy grin. "No one was here when I woke up around two thirty, so I got cleaned up and walked up to the Ku'damm to get something to eat and learn the lay of the land."

"Way to go. Very enterprising of you. We're just fixing up our occasional communal dinner here if you're still hungry. It's how we keep everyone in touch. We've got people here who are working, going to school, and bumming around. We even have a commie activist, but no one pays attention to him. This is a good chance for you to meet everyone."

I was ready for a real dinner after the *goulashsuppe* appetizer. Bill and I went into the dining room where the table had been set, and a pretty, young blonde woman was telling everyone what to do in German, so I just stood and waited for cues from Bill. I was told to stand behind a chair between Bill and the tall, blond man who had opened the door for me earlier. Everyone sat, and the bread was passed around.

Then the blonde girl asked me, "Why have you come to Berlin? It is cold here in winter."

"I am on a quest for self-knowledge," I said. Everyone laughed and applauded.

Someone said, "That's why most of us are here!" And everyone laughed again.

The blonde went back into the kitchen.

I figured that the others would introduce themselves, but they didn't. I got the impression that despite what might have been a common bond in living together, these people were all walking down their own paths and the house was just shelter. I wasn't necessarily an interloper; I was sharing the roof.

The door from the kitchen burst open, and the German girl and another woman came out bearing trays with the meal. There was a bowl full of bratwurst, a large plate with pieces of schnitzel, and bowls of home fries and steamed cabbage. Everyone had a bottle of beer except Bill and me, so Bill went into the kitchen to get one for both of us. One of the men said I could make a contribution to the community pot after the meal.

The girls sat down, and conversation softly mulled around the table as everyone ate. I took a schnitzel and squeezed lemon onto the breaded veal chop. It was really good. I was happy to join in. As I sipped on the beer, I had a chance to look around the table and see the people I would be living with for the foreseeable future.

I glanced at the fair, apparition-like man to my left who had opened the door for me. I learned his name was Piet. I looked next at the young woman who had brought in the meal. She was blonde, but full-figured with red, rounded lips and rosy cheeks. It seemed like she took up twice the space of the gaunt man next to her. I heard that her name was Trudi. She smiled a lot, especially at the guy on her other side whom she called Wolfgang several times. Wolfgang had black hair, wildly unkempt, and a full black beard, trimmed to a ragged four inches. His eyes shone brightly, and he talked incessantly, emphasizing points by gesticulating with his hands, sometimes while holding a fork full of food. I was sorry I couldn't understand a word he said because he looked very entertaining.

As I watched Wolfgang, I noticed he was paying a lot more attention to the other woman sitting on the opposite side from Trudi. I also couldn't fail to notice that while Trudi was making an effort to engage with Wolfgang, the other woman was purposely remaining aloof from him, keeping her head bowed over the meal, allowing her long, golden-red hair to shield her eyes from Wolfgang's probing.

Something's going on here, I thought. It was easy to see why Wolfgang was so interested when she looked up to take some bread from the board. She gave me a furtive look in the eye before going back into her seclusion.

She was gorgeous, maybe mid-twenties. Her hair was parted in the middle and cascaded down over her slender shoulders. Her long arms were slim, and her hands were somewhat large. Her face was permanently wrapped in semi-secrecy by her beautiful hair, but I could see that her eyes were turned down at the corners, sloe-eyed, I recalled from my reading. They made her look both sad and appealing. *Whoa!* I thought. *One look at that one and she's got you thinking. You're going to be here a while, and you can see this other guy is making a move. You better steer clear of her.*

I turned to Wild Bill, who saw me looking at him. "I see you've noticed Eva," Bill said as he leaned over to talk into my ear.

"I've just been looking around," I said a little sheepishly.

"Not a problem," Bill said. "We can go for a walk after dinner and talk."

When Bill and I got outside, I asked Bill, "How well does everyone here speak English?"

"Most of the people I've run into in Berlin all speak English very well," Bill said. "Even the Turkish guest workers speak some English. You'll pick up some street German easy enough, but you'll get by on English."

"How did you come to be at this commune?" I asked Bill. "I thought you said you knew someone who had an apartment."

"I knew a guy in an apartment when I applied to the Frei University, but the guy left before I got here," Bill said. "I asked the university for housing options, and they sent me a list of five places, which had posted vacancies for tenants. I chose 38 Hubertusallee because it was in the center of town and on a bus route that would take me to the university."

Then he laughed. "I didn't know that the apartment was really a commune. I found out that this is the way people like to live in Berlin and in cities around Europe pretty much," he said. "It's a really unusual scene. These guys and girls are as diverse as can be. Take Wolfgang. He's our resident commie-activist. He's not just anti-American, but because of Vietnam, he's actually pro-Viet Cong. He's got a big Viet Cong flag on the wall in his room and a poster of Che Guevara."

"I saw Trudi had an eye for Wolfgang," I said.

"Oh, yes. Trudi is head over heels for Wolfgang. She's only twenty-one, and he's twenty-nine. He gets drunk sometimes and screws her, but otherwise he doesn't pay attention to her. She's good-looking but not too bright. She's a waitress at a restaurant in the KaDeWe. I don't get how she lets herself be treated that way, but it's her business. And there's Wolfgang trying to make the moves on Eva at the table tonight right in front of Trudi. Like I said, not too bright."

"And what about Eva anyways," I asked, pleased that Bill had been the one who brought her up.

"Yeah, Eva. She's really something. So fucking gorgeous you'd never think that she's thirty-six. She looks twenty-two. She's French from Algeria. Her father was in the French military there while Algeria was a colony. She had a blow-up with her family, and she's been floating around Europe for the past dozen years or so. She learned to be a bartender, and with her looks, she gets plenty of tips, but she also has to duck guys all the time. She's a pro at ducking guys. I know. I tried to hit on her once. Really dumb. I lost her trust." Bill paused and looked down at the ground. "Wolfgang is too stupid and keeps trying. He'll never get anywhere with her."

"Boy, that's a sad story," I said, thinking about Eva's troubles and mentally distancing myself from her, while at the same time having been drawn to her beauty and vulnerability.

We walked a little further and found ourselves in front of 38 Hubertusallee. I was reminded that I needed to knock on the door the last time I stood here and also who it was who let me in.

"What about Piet?" he asked. "What's his story?"

"Piet is Dutch," Bill said. "Early thirties. He's a student. I see him at the university sometimes, but I don't know what he's studying. He pretty much stays to himself in the house."

I made a note to say hi to Piet sometime to see what he was about.

Bill pulled out his keys to open the door.

"Can I get a key tomorrow?" I asked.

"Tomorrow is your day, old buddy." Bill wrapped his arm around my shoulders and swept me in the door. "I'm off classes, and we're going to get you fixed up to be a real Berliner. I'll show you around town. Then we've got to get you outfitted with a sleeping bag and pillow and go to the KaDeWe for whatever else you might need and get some food. The KaDeWe has everything. It's the biggest department store in all of Europe. It even has five restaurants in it."

As we walked the hall to Bill's room, I thought it was nice of Bill to take an interest in me. Sure, we were friends, and I could see that Bill was happy that I had come over to be with him. Bill probably appreciated the company from home. At the same time, I looked back on some of Bill's first thoughts when he spoke about going to Berlin, and I wondered if Bill weren't calling on me to come too, way back in school, as some sort of herald. But I surely wasn't ready then.

Time and events had made me ready, and here I was flopping on a lumpy mattress on the floor of Bill's room in Berlin using my rolled-up duffle as a pillow and a blanket someone had covered me with in the middle of the night for warmth. My time for discovery had come along and overtaken me.

In the morning, I found that Bill wasn't in the house again. When I checked my watch, it was ten thirty. I'd slept another eleven hours. I looked around and didn't see Bill, and I was concerned because Bill had said this was to be my day. I got up to brush my teeth, only to find that the bathroom was occupied. I went into the kitchen and saw Wolfgang draining a beer and chewing on some salami while reading a tabloid newspaper.

"Och! Dus ist neist!" he yelled out, obviously skulking about something in the paper since he hadn't noticed my appearance.

I didn't want to disturb him, but I did want to know where Bill went, so I asked, "Excuse me, but do you know where Bill went?"

Wolfgang didn't look up, but he did say something about *frustuck* and went back to reading his paper. *Great help*, I thought as I went to wait by the bathroom door.

Momentarily, the door opened, and Trudi came out, all decked up in traditional German peasant clothing for her waitress job, I supposed. She was in a rush, but I asked her what *frustuck* meant, not wanting to take much of her time.

"Ach! Frustuck! Das ist der breakfast. You want breakfast, yes? We have breakfast at my restaurant. Commen sie mit me."

I figured if Bill had skipped out on me to get breakfast, I might as well do the same to him. Breakfast was an essential part of my day. But I did need to catch up with Bill at some point to get the stuff I needed.

"Ok," I said to Trudi, "give me a minute to get cleaned up and dressed."

I went into the bathroom to brush my teeth. When I came out of the bathroom, I heard Trudi clapping her hands and laughing and turned to see her and Bill in the kitchen. Bill was taking one thing after another out of a large bag and laying them on the table.

Trudi pointed at the stuff and said, "Frustuck! Frustuck!"

Bill had gone out to get breakfast at some store and was laying it out in all its glory on the table. There were rolls and sliced thick bread, a couple of pastries, a jar of butter, a jar of jam, some cold cuts, sliced cheese, and a bag of small oranges.

"We don't have to eat all this today. Thought we should have a reserve. I've got coffee in the room," Bill said. "Put the kettle on the stove."

We discussed the day's itinerary. Bill wanted me to be able to get around the major parts of the city by myself, so we would take the yellow, double-decker buses around the Wilimersdorf, Schoenberg, and Charlottenberg areas, ending at the Tiergarten, the Central Park of the city. From there, we could walk to the Brandenburg Gate and see the Wall. Then we'd head back to the Ku'damm before going shopping to get my stuff. We could stop at one of the several restaurants in KaDeWe, grab a beer, and get dinner before heading home.

I asked Bill, "How are we going to do all that in a day?"

Bill laughed. "What you're going to find out is how small this city really is. There are some woods on the west side and a few factories in Spandau, which take up about a third of the city. There are two lakes. The rest is just a small island surrounded by the Wall, really small. You can't go in any direction more than a few miles before you run into that damn Wall. After you've been here any length of time, the Wall starts to close in on you. It's a bad vibe. I don't know how people deal with it year after year."

"Man, I can see it's got you bugged, and you've only been here a few months."

"Well, I don't like being hammed in. Back home, if I'm stressed out, I just get on my Harley and go. Nothing like the freedom of riding a bike down the open road with the wind in your hair. To tell you the truth, I hadn't thought about giving that up when I came to this political postage stamp of a city." Bill paused and shook his head. "Still, the idea was a good one. It'll work out. The courses are good and will be useful when I get back. And now that you're here, it will be fun for both of us. I'll make sure of that!"

After breakfast, we went out and took a bus around the Tiergarten to get a perspective of the inner city. The bus rounded the Plaza der Republik with the two hundred-foot-tall Victory Pillar and the golden statue on top, and we got off on the Strasse de 17 Juni to walk to the Brandenburg Gate. The Gate comprised six columns on each side with a charioteer driving four horses on top on the East Berlin side of the Wall. The East Germans had closed off access to it from the west by building a six-foot concrete wall at the actual border.

Further back, at the gate, there were sentry boxes and more than twenty Volks Polizei, or Vopos, as the East German border police were called, armed with machine guns, patrolling the area tirelessly. Beyond the Gate, I could see a high wall built of concrete blocks and topped with barbed wire. We then turned to follow Tiergarten Strasse, which bordered the park, and then to Budapester Strasse, which connected to the Ku'damm.

Bill had scouted out an army-navy type store on a small street just off the Ku'damm when he first got to Berlin. I bought a sleeping bag and a small pillow, which suited my immediate needs. Then we went to Tauentzien Strasse to KaDeWe.

At first, I thought the enormous building was a government facility or maybe a massive university building, but as we approached the entrance, we were soon under the KaDeWe sign and a huge illuminated, revolving advertising poster, which at the moment showed a supermodel wearing a Bulgari necklace.

There were five restaurants, and we were famished. We went into one on the first floor, as it was nearest. Bill ordered two beers, schnitzel plates, and bread. I got the drift of the order, and that sounded fine. I took large gulps of the rich beer I had already come to love. The waitress brought the meal, and Bill ordered two more steins.

"This is the biggest department store in Europe," Bill said. "Takes up several blocks. This is where everybody shops for groceries. There are a dozen markets in here, plus everything from clothing to Christmas ornaments. There's even a glassed-in restaurant on the entire top floor. It's amazing. But right now, we need to get food for the week, so grab a basket and let's go."

We shopped a half-dozen markets on several floors with Bill pointing out things he had discovered since he had been there and items I could best store and cook in the apartment with the space and kitchenware available. We lugged it all back to 38 Hubertusallee, put the stuff away, and collapsed on the mattresses. It was well after dark.

"It may be a small city," I said, "but if you walk it, it's big enough to tire you out."

"Today was an exception," Bill said. "Mostly I take the bus to school or walk to the Ku'damm or Grunewald. There isn't too much else to see. I've been to a couple of museums and a few movies. It gets pretty monotonous after a while."

"Well, it doesn't need to be so monotonous. I brought the Frisbee," I said.

"Holy shit! You're kidding?! No, you better not be! Where is it?" Bill yelled.

I dug into the duffle and pulled out the red-and-white flying disk we had passed so much time bonding over at college.

Bill grabbed the Frisbee with delight, a wide grin on his face. "C'mon. Let's give it a spin."

"Hey, let's do it tomorrow. I'm beat."

"Don't wimp out on me. This is something I really need! We can do it on the sidewalk in front of the house. Just a few tosses."

I couldn't refuse, so I forced myself up and went out to toss the Frisbee with Bill. After a few throws and behind-the-head catches, I got into the rhythm. The game was lit by the streetlights along the street, and every once and a while, a car would stop in the middle of the street, and the driver would stare out his window at us.

When we came in, I unzipped my new sleeping bag, which I was looking forward to using. I folded the blanket and put in outside the door. Then I undressed and for the first time in several days climbed into what approximated a bed. I luxuriated in the moment before falling deeply asleep.

5

Piet and Siddhartha

THE NEXT MORNING I got up and noticed that Bill and everyone except Piet were either gone or in their rooms, likely asleep. Bill was at class in the mornings, Trudi was waitressing, Wolfgang was probably sleeping off a drunk, Eva had been up late bartending so no one ever saw her before noon, and Piet was on the couch in the living room in a lotus position I recognized as meditation, so I left him alone.

I went into the kitchen and made breakfast as quietly as I could and thought about where I was at and how far I had come. I knew I had broken the bonds of home and hearth. I hadn't just run away from my parents and what they said was my responsibility to myself. I was on a journey of discovery.

Now that I was removed from the toxicity of my former life, I had breathing room. My thoughts, which had formerly sprung back on one another in self-reinforcing negative spirals, seemed to have attained a simplicity and clarity I hadn't experienced in a long time. What I saw that lay ahead could be reckoned in days or even hours. I didn't know what was going to happen next, but whatever it was, I knew it didn't have to impact the rest of my life unless I wanted it to. Coming to Europe had given me room to maneuver. I felt released.

As I sat sipping the last of my coffee, I was warmed by my thoughts, but I also realized that I didn't know what my path would be. Now that I was free to choose, how would I resolve my issues by finding the answers to the fundamental questions? Bill had called me to Berlin in what I was beginning to realize was a spiritual fashion, like a herald. I had been forced by my circumstances to follow him. I had separated myself from my childhood home because of that call, and I knew I had been set on a new course. But what was the next step? And how did I develop outcomes?

Piet got up and reached into the fridge and poured himself a glass of orange juice. I thought I'd take a chance and see what Piet knew that might help me in my quest.

"Bill tells me you are at the Frei University. What are you studying?" I asked.

"Supposedly Eastern philosophy," Piet said. "But I know more about it than the professor. I go over to listen in class sometimes, but mostly to meet up with my friends for discussion groups. We are far advanced from the class. Of course, we are much older than most of the students. I have my degree from Erasmus University College, Rotterdam."

"Why did you learn meditation?"

"I must admit I was swept up in the movement during the late sixties." He paused a moment and then said, "For most, it was just a fad. They didn't learn how to do it properly. No patience. I kept at it and learned how to allow the meditative technique to penetrate my consciousness and reach my soul. It brings me inner peace."

Looking at Piet's somewhat hollowed-out face with the deeply recessed eyes and sunken cheeks, I wondered if Piet spent too much time meditating and too little time eating. But what Piet said struck a chord in my newly liberated consciousness, and the way he said it, with the conviction of a true believer, stimulated my imagination. *Maybe this guy can give me some answers*, I thought, seeing in Piet someone who could possibly make a spiritual guide.

"I don't know much about Eastern philosophy. I guess meditation is pretty much a part of it, though," I said.

"Meditation is a means of leaving the world behind. The world is full of words. In meditation, there is just one word, *Om*, and *Om* becomes the unity of the world. Once you reach that unity, you are at peace."

This statement left me far behind. I could see that Piet had an understanding of the concepts of unity and peace, but how he got there through *Om* was incomprehensible to me. Further, I just wanted to understand more about looking into my soul because that was where I figured the answer to "Who I Am?" might be.

I decided to approach Piet from that direction. "When you have found unity and are at peace, do you know who you are and why you are here?"

"Ah, this is what you said you were looking for at dinner the other night. You are a seeker of knowledge of the world." Piet appraised me with a somber expression. "I sense your impatience, but it will only hinder you. There are no easy answers, no shortcuts. You must have experience of the world, which will finally release you from seeking your destiny and conquering time if you want your soul to be at peace."

Piet then softened his tone. "You are at a commencement. You seek knowledge, which is a good beginning. Read *Siddhartha* by Herman Hesse. It's a story of a young man who leaves his home to seek knowledge and finds much more. You know this book?"

I said, "I know of it, but I have not read it."

" Read *Siddhartha* with care, remembering what he learns at each step of his journey. Perhaps you should take notes of what you didn't understand or want to discuss. Then we would get together for another talk." Piet suggested.

"That would be great. I have always wanted to know what *Siddhartha* was about. A lot of people at college had the book in their apartments, but I thought it was just a hippie thing."

"I think you will find some profound meaning there if you apply yourself," Piet said."

I was excited about this prospect. The way Piet had presented it, it might help me develop answers for my questions.

When Wild Bill came back from his class in the afternoon, I asked, "Do you know of a bookstore where I could get a copy of *Siddhartha* and a notebook?"

"We can go to KaDeWe. They've got books in all languages, stationery, everything you need," Bill said.

"'Everything you need.' That should be their slogan," I said.

Bill laughed in agreement as we headed toward the huge department store. We stopped into two of the bookstores in

KaDeWe to get what I wanted and also splurged at a Backerei for some tortes and cookies. By the time we left the store, it was snowing hard, but we decided we could get home quicker by walking than waiting for a bus.

Bill said the Germans were very regimented. Everything ran on schedule, especially transportation. If we missed a bus, there would certainly be another coming along, but the schedule said it would be twenty-three minutes so that's how long we'd have to wait. We didn't want to wait in the snow, so we hoofed it.

When we got back, we were covered in thick, damp snow, and our shoes and socks were soaked. Bill said I could take the first shower if I made it quick. I said I'd make hot chocolate while he was in the shower and warm up the pastries. We put our clothes on the radiator in the bedroom to dry. I was really glad I had brought the wool socks, a warm benison after the slog through the city snow. Then we settled in for coffee and warm pastries, German style, and watched the snow fall from the kitchen window.

Eva stopped by on her way to her job at the bar, and we gave her a cookie.

"I got my blanket back. Merci," she said.

Bill and I looked at each other, not knowing what she meant. Then I figured it out. "Oh, it was you! I should be thanking you. That was kind of you. I really needed to sleep."

"I could see that. I have to go now." She hurried out into the snow.

"What was that all about?" Bill said.

I told Bill about waking up the day after I arrived and finding that someone had put a blanket over me in the night.

"Hmm, maybe she likes you," Bill leered.

"Get out!" I growled. "She's the last thing I need."

"You might be looking at things backward," Bill suggested with a smile.

It snowed on and off for three days, but I could care less. I had discovered that 38 Hubertusallee was a warm haven. It had thick walls to defend against North German winters, and they had not been blown apart by Allied bombs twenty-five years ago. I was reminded of my apartment at college in the Northeastern United States where I been warm up under the eaves. I opened *Siddhartha* with an agreeable feeling of going back into a familiar space where I could exercise my intellect on something new and compelling.

I set myself in a routine where I settled on the sofa by the lamp. I put the spiral notebook on my knee and tucked the pen down the spiral within easy reach. When I began to read the book, I found it to be relaxing reading with a pleasant flow. I learned that Siddhartha, despite being the son of a rich man of high caste, was unhappy, had many questions about life, and did not know how to find answers to his questions.

Immediately I identified with Siddhartha's struggle. I was happy to be digging into material that spoke to me of my own general condition. By the time I finished the first chapter, when Siddhartha left his father to join the ascetic Samana group, I realized that the story was not just about Eastern religion. It was about a young man's voyage of self-discovery, and I was hooked. *Siddhartha* would be my guidebook.

January in Berlin was cold and damp, sometimes with snow or cold rain, frequently with leaden clouds barring any sunshine, so I didn't go out much. I decided I would read *Siddhartha* through before taking notes and then go back to the beginning and start again, marking passages I wanted to talk to Piet about. I spent a lot of time on the sofa during the day; sometimes Piet would come in to meditate, but we would only smile at each other and return to our respective preoccupations.

Bill told me that the weather got better later in March and we could get out more, but the next day he wanted to get tickets for the Elton John concert on March 19, which should be a smash. He was a particular fan of Elton.

"My courses end in early April, so there will be lots of recreational time after that," he said.

"I'm having fun now," I told him. "I'm on a voyage of self-discovery using *Siddhartha* as a guide, and Piet is helping me translate it to my own experience."

"If you say so, but Piet sure looks the part of an ascetic, if that's where you want to go," Bill said with a wink.

The next day we went to the Deutschland Halle to get the tickets to see the Elton John concert. I was surprised the tickets cost thirty dollars each for seats in the nosebleed section, but I had plenty of money since all I had spent it on was food in Berlin. Sitting at home studying *Siddhartha* had residual benefits.

I continued to study *Siddhartha* though the cold of late January and February. I did not understand all the nuances of Hesse's creation, so I wrote things down in the notebook to ask Piet. *I'm up to my ears in this stuff,* I thought, but I wasn't put off. I was happy to be digging into material that spoke to me of my general condition, even though *Siddhartha* was steeped in religion and I had none. I understood the timeline of the journey Siddhartha was on, but I was confused with the steps Siddhartha took as he went forward. In the story, Siddhartha had left his former life completely behind. After speaking with the Buddha, he felt he no longer needed to have teachers and to listen to their teachings.

I read those words over and tried to apply them to myself, but I could not. I knew I had more to learn. I was, after all, reading *Siddhartha* to discuss it with Piet, who would guide me through it as a teacher. But then I read that the reason Siddhartha had left his teachers was that they could not teach him about the Self. He had wanted to learn about the Self.

> *The reason why I do not know anything about myself, the reason why Siddhartha has remained alive and unknown to myself, is due to one thing, to one single thing—I was afraid of myself. I was fleeing from myself.*

"I was afraid of myself," I said aloud. "I am afraid of myself."

Then I put down the book to reflect on the times in my life when I had been a follower or an observer and had never taken responsibility for standing up for being myself. I understood that my awareness of my inner fears was a step toward resolving them. I knew instinctively that I couldn't live my life with these fears. The realization of the trauma my sisters had caused me might be the motivating force to shut myself in for so many years, and now to travel, to break away from my past, my home life, and to prove myself, to find out who I was.

I reflected that there had been circumstances where I never fully enjoyed time with women. It depressed me to think of my times with women, and it frustrated me because I could not say why. Was it because of the fear of women my sisters had engendered in me as a little boy? In the past, I had only understood it as my being shy and inexperienced, but I realized that if it were fear and I never conquered it, I would never gain the experience of them.

When I started reading again, Siddhartha had come to the garden of Kamala, the courtesan, and I read how Siddhartha's blood had been stirred by Kamala's beauty. She smiled as she passed by and gave Siddhartha the courage to clean himself up so he could approach her the next day. She gave him his first kiss as a token. She also found him a job with a rich merchant with whom he could make money so he could come back and pay her to learn the arts of love.

Confidence and money, I thought, *the keys to a woman's heart and her sexual favors*. Without confidence, I was a boy. I needed to gain confidence to become a man. I had come on this journey to gain confidence through experience, and as I continued reading, I found that Siddhartha had done the same thing.

By learning how to be a businessman, Siddhartha made lots of money, and he and Kamala became friends and lovers over time. Then the story turned in a way I didn't understand. Siddhartha made money so easily that he didn't value it. Instead it gave him a sickening of the soul. Siddhartha had the experience of being born rich and then became an ascetic who had nothing. I had always been a rich boy, a materialist at heart and in practice, but I wasn't going to give everything up to become a monk. Siddhartha left Kamala and all his wealth behind because he ceased to experience joy in the very experiences I thought that if I experienced them, they would make me a man.

In his past, Siddhartha had felt in his heart, "A path lies before you which you are called to follow. The gods await you." But he had left that path and become an ordinary person in the world, and it no longer satisfied him. I felt I was searching for a path too, but I wasn't expecting to find any gods at the end of it. I just wanted to know who I was in the world.

To me, Siddhartha's life with Kamala and as a rich man of the world seemed to validate that what one needed to become a man was experience of the world. In reading further, I discovered that Siddhartha had learned the opposite. For him, the pleasures of the world and riches were not good. They had robbed him of his happiness.

I had difficulty with this philosophy. Why would someone who had gained everything to become a man renounce it all and be happier as an ingénue? This was the Eastern way that was alien to me. I had to put the book down. Although Siddhartha had renounced his worldly acquisitions and adventures to find his bliss, I saw that those worldly experiences were what he needed to acquire to ultimately define himself.

One particular worldly delight I needed desperately was sex. Siddhartha had attained that. And although I didn't yet have the confidence to reach for it, in reading about Siddhartha's experience in the touching and smelling and tasting of life, I felt I had to get there soon because the urge was building in me.

———•◦◦◦•———

Days passed, and I didn't have the chance to discuss *Siddhartha* with Piet. I wasn't sure what the point of the discussion would be after I had finished the book and read of Siddhartha's final days as a ferryman and did not comprehend the meaning of his final, peaceful smile, which his friend, Govinda, had wept over.

I left vindicated in my views by invoking the disconnect between Siddhartha, the mystic, and his son, who was an ordinary person. I could not emulate Siddhartha because Siddhartha did not want to be a man in this world, which was what I wanted to be, so any discussion with Piet was likely to be barren.

———•◦◦◦•———

On a rainy day at the beginning of March, I went into the living room. Piet was sitting on the couch meditating. I decided to wait until he had finished and come back later, but as I was leaving, Piet called to me, "So have you finished with *Siddhartha*?"

"Yes, I finished it," I said. "Up to a point. I mean, I read the whole book, but I didn't get why he left Kamala and all the money he made and went and became a ferryman. So I sort of glossed over the end. What was his fascination with the river? He said it has no beginning and no ending, but all rivers do. I mean this is the Eastern philosophy stuff I don't understand. I don't see myself in it at all."

"You do understand that he was on a journey of self-discovery?" Piet asked.

"Yeah. I get that. But once he had Kamala and all his riches, he gave them up. I wouldn't have done that. He found love and created what should have been his legacy, and he walked out on it."

"But the journey is to discover one's soul. Siddhartha could not find his soul as an ordinary person. He had to experience what ordinary people experience, to know what they feel, in order to transcend this life and find the unity of all things."

"That's what I don't get about Eastern philosophy," I said. "I think you have to live your life here and now and not worry about unity, Nirvana, or even an afterlife. People in medieval times spent too much time worrying about heaven and hell and didn't take pleasure in living life day to day. Of course, they were under the thumb of the church, but that's another story."

"But that's a cop-out for your soul," Piet said.

"You've got to live your life," I repeated. "I agreed with Siddhartha about going out on your path to gain experience. Beyond that, we came to a parting of the ways."

"This is a journey we all must make and travel through to the end. I think you'll find that there are no shortcuts. But I suppose everyone reaches the end by taking his own path. I wish you luck," Piet said.

Although I had come away from *Siddhartha* with an increased awareness of how another person had discovered himself by taking a journey through life, I was disappointed that the ending of the story hadn't resonated with me more completely. I thought that

Piet was pretty smug sometimes, but he may have been right when he said that there are no shortcuts if you want to find the true answers. Anyway, I was down after giving up on *Siddhartha*.

I told Wild Bill about my situation, and he came up with the perfect answer. "How long has it been since you got stoned?" he asked me.

"Too long," I said.

"Why don't we see if we can't find my friend Adnan and score some hash? Can we put together about thirty marks for a couple of grams?"

I was more than agreeable, feeling the need for a breakout. I gave Bill fifteen marks, and we went up to the Ku'damm to look for Adnan, the Turkish hashish dealer. Bill had bought hash from Adnan before and knew his usual hangout. He told me to keep my distance while he made the deal.

"No sense in spooking him," Bill said.

When we found him, I saw another Turkish guy standing near Adnan, but things looked friendly enough once Bill started talking with Adnan. Then Adnan motioned to the other guy who came over and pulled something out of his pocket. It was something shiny, and I was ready to start running. But they kept talking, and Bill bent over and stuck his nose near the shiny thing. He then nodded his head and pulled out the money. Adnan gave Bill the shiny thing and the high-five sign as they parted.

"What went on over there?" I asked.

"Oh, Adnan has his pal keep the hash on him while he does the deal. Plausible deniability, I guess. I wanted them to open the package so I could smell the hash. I trust Adnan more or less, but the Turks can be a little shifty. I will tell you that this hash is primo, very fresh."

Bill had a shit-eating grin on his face as we headed back to the house to alter our realities. Enough studying of *Siddhartha* and contemplating the future for me. Bill got his hash pipe out of a drawer in the room, and we sat on the couch while he placed a small ball of hash in the bowl. I could smell the sweet, pungent aroma of the hash from three feet away. I never experienced that before. Even the wicked Egyptian hash we'd smoked on the trip out West last summer hadn't smelled like that.

Bill lit a match and held it over the pipe while he said, "We're not going to need more than one or two puffs of this shit. It's really strong." Then he lit the bowl, took a drag, and passed it over.

I took a puff and held it in. It was very fine smoke, tasting sweet and resinous. I tried to hold it in, but I couldn't. I went into a coughing fit that lasted a minute.

Bill did better and laughed at me after he exhaled. "Man, you're an amateur," he guffawed as he pointed at me.

"I need a beer to cool this off." I went into the kitchen, feeling a little light-headed. Having taken a long swig of beer, I sat back down on the couch and ordered up another puff of hash.

"You sure you can handle it?" Bill said.

"Up yours."

Bill lit the hash, took a puff, and handed the pipe to me with a wisp of smoke ascending from the bowl. I took a quick sip of beer and then sucked firmly on the pipe, drawing the smoke smoothly back into my throat. *Much better technique*, I thought to myself as I sat back to digest the hash before exhaling.

I looked at Bill who was, in turn, looking at me after putting the pipe on the coffee table. It was a moment frozen in time before I began to feel the need for more breath. I thought my eyes were letting in more light than they had moments before. Then I felt as though the back of my head was expanding. I needed more air. I felt wobbly. I tried to say something to Bill, but I couldn't mouth the words. I saw Bill on the couch, but he looked farther away than before. The room moved around me. I wasn't sure if I were sitting on the couch so I tried to stand up but couldn't and fell back on the couch.

At this point, I heard laughter and saw Bill pointing at me and saying, "Nothing like fresh hash! Ha, ha, ha!"

Hearing this, I backed down from what I thought was some kind of hallucinating panic attack and realized that I was totally stoned in a way I'd never been before. *On just a couple of hits of Turkish hash*, I thought.

I finally got words out. "That stuff is dynamite!"

"Yeah. It's because it's so fresh," Bill said as he lay back looking at the ceiling. "The hash we get in the States is a month or more old, and it's all dried out. It'll get you high, but this stuff is a week old at most. It's still all gooey with resin. That's why it's got such a kick. You really can't take more than two hits or you'll be crawling under the carpet."

We sat and contemplated our newly ordered states of mind for a while until I realized there was something missing. "What kind of music have we got around here?" I asked.

"We're woefully short on tunes unfortunately. We've got Trudi's stereo, but nobody's got the money to buy the latest tunes."

"Ouch!" I said, reflecting on the over three hundred albums in my collection back home. "What's getting stoned with no music?"

At the moment, I was too wiped out to care. I sat back on the couch and closed my eyes as the hash meandered through my brain and central nervous system, provoking indescribable visions and colors. After a while, I heard a voice from far away. I opened my eyes to see Wolfgang standing in front of me.

"Ach, so. You guys been smoking hash, eh? You know Helmut doesn't like drugs in the house."

Bill shrugged off his drug-induced lethargy. "Helmut doesn't have to know about it, does he? Especially if you would like to join us, hmm?"

My reasoning powers were pretty dull at the moment, but I did ask myself, *Who the hell is Helmut?*

Wolfgang was quick to accept the offer, so Bill put another ball of hash in the pipe and handed it to Wolfgang. He had his own lighter, so he did the honors, but instead of passing the pipe around, he kept it and smoked the whole bowl, taking at least four hits. He was standing up while he smoked, but just after his last puff, he dropped the pipe and fell over on his side on the floor.

"Schieisse!" he said as he tried to crawl over to a chair. "Was ist das fur en Gift?" he said as he gave up trying to get on the chair and lay flat on his back on the floor.

Bill started laughing and couldn't stop. Wolfgang was clearly having difficulty. I knew he had pigged out on the hash, but it was his fault, so I just watched as he tried to make some sense out of what had happened to him.

I was thinking that this was getting scary when Bill stopped laughing and had a conversation with Wolfgang in German.

Wolfgang slowly nodded his head and began to take some deep breaths, which calmed him down.

I asked Bill, "What was the conversation about?"

Bill told me, "Wolfgang thought we had poisoned him. I told him it was just superior stuff and he had taken too much. He should just lie still, and it will pass. I didn't tell him he was a stupid hog, though."

Wolfgang's antics had taken us down from our initial highs, so we went out for a walk.

"How can we get to listen to some tunes when we smoke that stuff? That would be unreal," I asked Bill.

Bill said, "There are listening rooms at the KaDeWe. We could have a puff and then go in and listen to any number of records."

"That sounds cool."

"But don't forget about the Elton John concert," he said. "That's next week. We are going to get high for that."

"Oh, absolutely." But then I asked him, "Who is Helmut?"

"He's the landlord. Best to stay away from him." And that was all he said about Helmut.

* * *

We got really stoned before the Elton John concert and had to mellow out before we took the bus to the Deutchelandhalle. It was a trip just getting there and navigating through the crowd. Not many big-name acts came to Berlin, so the people turned out to see them when they played here.

When we got to our seats, Bill was very unhappy. The seats were on the third level and behind the keyboard. He liked Elton and wanted to see him play the piano and do his antics, but we were too far away for a decent view. He got up and said, "Come with me."

I didn't like his tone of voice, but I was in a totally stoned state and a willing follower. We went all the way down to the orchestra level where he found an usher. He was an old guy, who Bill accosted by wrapping his big right arm around his shoulders and giving him one of his patented grins. Then he spoke quickly to him, pointing once to where our seats were and telling him they obviously would not do. He then shoved a wad of mark notes into the guy's hand and gave his shoulders a big squeeze, from which the guy actually winced. He then grinned again and looked straight into the guy's eyes. The guy was pretty freaked out from what I could see, but he pocketed the bills and said, "Folge mir."

We walked around the stage, which was in the middle of the auditorium, to two seats where we would be able to see old Elton pounding the keyboard up close, I mean forty feet away. Bill smiled at the usher, and we sat down.

It was a hell of a concert, great music for stoned heads, and Elton was berserk, but the most I remember of it was what Bill had pulled off with the seats.

6

Me and Eva

Soon it was the end of March, and the temperature broke fifty degrees and stayed there for days. The dank north wind had softened to a breeze, and it actually seemed warm. Bill and I went into the Grunewald to throw the Frisbee and always attracted a small crowd by flying the disc for long distances and making acrobatic catches behind our backs or between our legs, and the people would clap.

But I was bored. All I'd been doing was studying *Siddhartha* for five weeks, sometimes playing Frisbee with Bill, taking contemplative walks through Wilmersdorf, Charlottenberg and Dahlem, and being pursued by the questions of life, which I realized were as pressing now as they were when I was at home.

One afternoon I came in from a walk and passed Eva's room on his way to the kitchen. Her door was open, so I stopped and tentatively stuck my head in to see her sitting on her bed, reading.

"I never thanked you for putting your blanket over me when I first got here," I told her. "That was nice of you."

"C'est rien," she said. "You looked exhausted and needed sleep."

"Yeah, I was." I paused, not sure of how to go on, but feeling very much like I wanted to.

Eva sat up and asked me, "What are you going to do here? I mean, if you want to stay, how long will you stay?"

"I don't know the answer to either of those questions," I admitted. "What I know is that I came over here to find out things about life that I wasn't able to back home. Things are really screwed up in the States right now with the war going on and everybody choosing sides and screaming at each other. I had to get away."

"What things about life do you need to find out about?" Eva asked playfully. "Life is pretty much the same everywhere. People are people, you know."

I looked directly at Eva and saw she was smiling at me. I couldn't fathom her thoughts, but I decided that this might be a chance to get out of the rut I'd been in trying to engage with women and move forward.

"Well, I guess I'm sort of tied up in knots about some things. There's the draft for the army. There isn't much I can do about that but wait and see." I hung my head and didn't look at Eva as I continued, "And I've always been shy with girls. I can never get anywhere with them, you know?" That was as far as I'd ever gotten, in fact, so I let the subject hang.

Eva looked me over intently, appraising my words and demeanor carefully. Then she said, "Tu ne m'a jamais avance. J'aime bien cela."

"What do you mean?" I asked, afraid that I'd said something wrong.

"Oh, I'm sorry. I was sort of thinking aloud in French. What I mean is that you have been here for three months and you have never made a pass or dirty suggestion to me. I'm not used to this from men. I get it every night at the bar and in here from that couchon, Wolfgang. Even your friend Bill, but I cooled him off."

I couldn't think of anything to say so I just sat there. Eva's experiences were off my radar screen, and I'd never seriously tried to get a woman to go to bed with me. But sex was a life experience I sorely needed to have, so I hung in to see where this was going.

Eva went on, "I have been mistreated by men too. They can be kind, especially when they want something, but then they can be couchons afterward."

"What's a couchon?"

"That's a pig," Eva said, "a man-pig who has no culture."

I just sat there and blinked, trying to understand that Eva was opening up her emotions to me in her own words.

"I grow tired of men," she said after a while but still looking at me intently. "They just want one thing, and when they've had it, poof! They're gone. So I keep them away." She smiled sadly.

I remained silent. I reasoned that from what Eva had said, she wanted to be left alone, and if she thought of me as a good guy because I hadn't gone after her, I'd best keep it that way, so I started to get up.

"Wait. Don't go," Eva said. "Tell me more about yourself."

I had wanted to have a real conversation with a girl, a woman, a female for a long time, seemingly forever, so I sat back down on the mattress, facing Eva and feeling more relaxed since it was she who had asked the questions.

"Well, I'm from New York. I was brought up there ..."

"No, no," Eva said. "How old are you? Did you go to university? How do you get the money to just come to Europe to lay around with no job?"

I was a little startled by her direct questioning, but I told her I was twenty-three, I had just graduated from college, and my parents were well-off, but I was using my own money to make this trip.

"Why didn't you get a job coming out of university?" Eva asked. "People over here go to university so they can begin careers."

"Generally, that is true in the States," I said. "But right now colleges are sort of like entrenched camps for dissent against the Vietnam War. People spend most of their time protesting against Nixon and the war.

"Not too many people I know are serious about careers. They are mostly all waiting to hear if they were going to be drafted into the army, like me. So what's the sense in making future plans?"

"Merde on Nixon and the war," Eva said. "But how do you get away and come over here? Won't you have to go back?"

"Well, I was thinking the other day that I wouldn't go back if I got drafted, but I'm not sure how that would work out. I don't think I'd ever be able to go back to the States again," I said wistfully. "I'd be arrested."

I watched Eva's eyes as they shifted from the piercing look of a questioner to the warm, sympathetic gaze of a comforting soul. Then she slid over next to me on the mattress and put her hand on my cheek. It was warm and soft. I was surprised and excited that she would do that.

"Poor boy," she said. "I know what it means not to be able to go home."

Then Eva put both her hands on my cheeks and then reached over and kissed me full on the lips. She lingered there and moved her body against mine. I was stunned, aroused, and yet not certain how to behave. I thought about pulling away, but she clutched me tighter, opening my mouth with her tongue. I responded. I'd been in make-out sessions before, but this was more profound.

Eva stroked the back of my neck with one hand and ran her other hand up and down my chest. She broke away from my tongue and kissed my lips over and under. Then she sat slightly back and looked at my face. I looked at her presence in a flush of wonder and at her face, which was partially hidden by her long, auburn locks, which had fallen in from the sides. She parted her hair away from her face deftly with her hands and then leaned forward and kissed me first under my right eye and then under my left eye. It was the sexiest moment of my life.

"You should close the door," she told me.

———◆●◆———

For the next few days, I felt like I was walking on clouds. I felt a glowing sensation all over, a release from a tension I had always carried but was now dispelled. I had an awareness of my body that I had never experienced or imagined before. Senses pulsed through my nerves that I couldn't describe. It was magical, yet I realized it was something that everyone else experienced daily. Where had I been all this time?

I was living this sex schedule that Eva had presented me with, "If you like," as she put it. This meant I could knock on her door around three in the afternoon before she got ready to go to work. "Now we can discuss more about life," she said.

At first, the discussions were mostly conducted in the passionate, unreasoned language of lovemaking. It became apparent to me that Eva was as needful of my body, as I was of hers. But I had no skills, so I let her lead and take her pleasure as she wanted. And she never left me wanting, so I didn't care.

After a while, things cooled off enough for me to collect my thoughts. I remembered what Kamala had said about lovers not parting from each other after making love without admiring one another so that neither one would feel used. I told this to Eva, wanting to know how I should admire her, but as she heard these words, she jumped on me and began smothering me in kisses. As she kissed my face, I felt the tears streaming from her eyes. I figured I had said something right, something that had touched a nerve. Then she took my cock in her mouth, and I stopped thinking for a long time.

7

Buying the Bike

IT WASN'T TOO LONG before there was a different vibe circulating in the commune. Trudi had picked up on it during a communal dinner when Eva had kept looking at me and blatantly ignoring Wolfgang, who was still trying to assault her beachhead. Wolfgang was becoming annoyed at being ignored but hadn't figured out the reason yet. Piet watched all the interaction in his detached way, summing up his conclusions only with an opaque half-smile, which resembled those on statues of the Buddha.

Bill had felt the vibe too and confronted me after dinner that night in our room. He put it to me directly. "So is there something going on between you and Eva?"

"What do you mean?" I snapped, a bit too quickly and defensively.

"Yeah? Yeah? I thought so!" Bill said, smiling broadly. "You're screwing Eva! How the hell did you manage that? Hahaha!" Bill grabbed me around the shoulders with his big right arm and punched me playfully on the chest with his left. "Man, that's a major score. I'm proud of you!"

I smiled as broadly as Bill, but I felt a little sheepish. I didn't want to be boastful of what Bill saw as a conquest. I saw it as something private. But the cat was out of the bag now.

"Do you think everyone else knows?"

"It was all over the table tonight just like the tablecloth," Bill said. "No one could miss it, except maybe that dunce, Wolfgang.

He's still trying to get in the door, but he's been shut out." Bill paused a moment and looked me over. "So now you've got a lover and a French beauty at that. Well, well. What's she like in the sack?"

"C'mon, man. That's personal. I don't want to talk about it."

"Shit, I'd tell you."

"Well, I wouldn't want to hear about it, so let's drop it, ok?"

"After you've had a couple more girls, you won't be so touchy," Bill needled.

"Fuck you."

"Well, at least let's celebrate with a beer. I'm buying."

We headed out to a nearby biergarten on the corner of the Ku'damm and Hubertusallee. I thought Bill was pretty impressed. He said he blew his chance with Eva, so now I guessed he was looking at me as some kind of conquering hero. It's a good thing he didn't know how things really happened.

Still smiling, Bill said, "I'm proud of you, and you should be proud of yourself. I mean it's not every guy who gets his first lay with a thirty-six-year-old French beauty. I mean mine was in the back seat of my dad's Oldsmobile, parked next to a lumberyard outside of town. It was sex, but it sure wasn't sexy. Had to have it, though. It was my time, and she wasn't any virgin. Oh well, past history, although you never forget the first time." Bill paused and took a few gulps of beer.

"So I guess this will have to go down as one of those experiences of life you've been looking for. Hahaha! And you've got a regular thing going with her, too? Holy cow! How did you swing that? Never mind. Enjoy yourself, but be careful not to let Wolfgang in on it. He could get sore and get you in trouble with Helmut."

"Who the hell is Helmut?" I asked again.

"He's the landlord," Bill said. "And Wolfgang is in tight with him."

"How could Wolfgang get us in trouble with the landlord?"

"Because Wolfgang can be a pain in the ass, that's all. Just have your fun and keep your game with Eva to yourself. Now, let's have another beer. I want to show you something that will fit in with your newfound manhood. Hahaha!"

I was getting sick of all this, so I told Bill to "fuck off!" But we had another beer, got a bit tipsy, and left the biergarten heading for the traffic circle with the victory column rising from the center and two avenues heading 180 degrees from each other. One avenue led to the Ku'damm where we turned to see a brightly lit row of auto showrooms: Mercedes, DKW Auto Union, Volkswagen, and Opel. The last one we came to was a BMW motorcycle showroom.

Bill stuck his face up close to the glass, staring approvingly at the machines on display. "So what do you think?" he said.

"Whaddya mean what do I think?" I gazed at the gleaming new motorcycles with a strange desire in my heart.

"Look, I have a Harley Sportster back home. I may not be the biggest ladies' man around, but the girls flip out for a ride on my bike. It's the big bike, man. It turns you into a king, a lady-slayer. Having all that horsepower between your legs reminds you of who you are too. Listen, man," Bill continued, "you've got this thing going with Eva, and that's great. But she's a lot older than you. She could dump you and move on to someone more her own age, who knows. If you had a bike, you'd keep her longer. Plus, if you split up, you could just ride down the road and see the girls waiting for you to pick them up. No shit. The bike makes you the man."

I was feeling the effects of a couple of large mugs of heady German beer, and the rush of wild ideas that Bill was throwing at me was making my head spin. A small, dreamy voice inside myself kept saying, *Those sure are beautiful bikes* ... But I had no way to attach any cogent reality to the dreams I saw through the glass. Besides, the showroom was closed, so we could only gaze and then walk home.

But Wild Bill wasn't done. "You know, BMW makes those bikes right here in Berlin. The factory is over in Spandau. We could take a tour of it, like, tomorrow."

"Yeah, that would be something to do," I said. "A field trip would be cool."

Bill grabbed me around the shoulder with his big right arm. "We're there."

So the next day, Bill and I hopped on the S-Bahn subway, which took us to the Spandau industrial section of West Berlin. Needing directions to BMW, Bill went into the front office of a building to ask. It only took a minute, and then we were standing in the factory showroom surrounded by a dozen of the latest models produced by one of the great motorcycle manufacturers in the world.

When I saw the motorcycles, I noticed that the motors looked odd, weirdly shaped, compared with the motorcycles I'd seen in the States. But before I could mention it to Bill, a salesman came up to us and asked a question in German. Bill answered in German but pointed to me, and the man immediately started speaking perfect English.

"So you are Americans. Welcome to BMW. You want to take a tour of the factory? Yes, we give tours at one every day, so you are two hours early. But you are the only people here, so it would be my pleasure to answer any questions you might have."

I asked him about the motors. "Why do they have the two bread loaf-sized things sticking out the side with pipes connected to the front?"

Bill started laughing at my ignorance, but the salesman said, "That's a good question because this configuration for a motorcycle engine is unique to BMW and always has been. These things that stick out are the cylinders that drive the drive shaft, which is another unique feature of the BMW.

"Having opposed cylinders down low makes the motorcycle very stable on the road. Having a drive shaft means much less maintenance than on other motorcycles that have chain drives. The chains get dirty, you see," the salesman said. "You need only to change the oil every five thousand kilometers to keep a BMW running smoothly.

"And there is another nice thing about the drive shaft design." Here he motioned to me to get on a black R60/5 standing in the middle of the showroom.

"Just mount the seat and put your feet on the pedals, no need to work them. The clutch is the handle on the left. Pull it in. Now turn the key and push the electric starter. We added that this year. It eliminates the need to kick-start, which can be cumbersome. Of course, there is still the kick-starter if you prefer to use it."

I had never driven or even sat on a big bike before, and I was afraid of embarrassing myself. I had driven a Honda 90 at home and knew the basics, but this felt like I was trying out a semi-trailer for the first time. I positioned myself on the bike as instructed. I noted it was very steady, standing on its parking stand so I didn't think it would fall over. Then I remembered how loud Bill's Harley Sportster was, a great *vroom* followed by decreasing volume of burbling exhaust roar whenever Bill fired it up.

"Won't it be a little loud to turn on in here?" I asked the salesman. I looked over to see Bill grinning broadly.

"Please, no one will mind," the salesman said. "Just start the engine."

Ok, you asked for it, I thought to myself as I turned the key, pushed the starter, and slowly rolled my right wrist to give it some gas. I could feel the motor come to life between my legs with a smooth, steady beat, but I was amazed I didn't hear an engine roar. What I heard was the solid sound of a motor murmuring beneath me, passing the low purr it made out through the exhausts. It was smooth and seductive, seeming to await my pleasure as to where and when to take me on my journey like a magic carpet.

I rolled my wrist over to give it some more gas, and the volume barely rose even though we were indoors. This was stunning. I had always thought of Harleys as the only road bikes, and they weren't my style at all, both loud and brassy and for guys who wanted to project an outlaw image. As I sat on the BMW, I could see myself riding this classy machine down the road. I was dreaming about it right there in the showroom.

When the salesman reached over and turned off the motor, I was shaken from my reverie. I looked up at the salesman, who had a particularly satisfied smile on his face. Bill had his customary shit-eating grin on his face. The salesman just continued his patter as I slung my leg off the saddle of the bike.

"This is the fiftieth year of BMW motorcycle manufacture. There is no machine like it for durability, reliability, or stability. And as you can see, it is very civilized in its attitude and sound. A truly great touring machine."

"I thought you'd like it," Bill said, somewhat sheepishly.

I frowned at Bill and drew him aside, away from the salesman. "What are you talking about? You think I'm going to buy one or something? How do you know how much it costs or if I could afford it? Man, you're nuts."

"I just thought you should see this bike. I already told you how I thought it could fit your new lifestyle with Eva and all or whatever chick you want. Man, you need to project your image, and a bike is a man's way to go."

"Bill, you've got to back off. I don't want to get tied to something like this. I've only got so much money. This thing costs plenty, and it will need to be serviced. And where can you go on it in this walled-in city? I'd do better buying a bicycle."

"Listen, there's more to it. I have a plan," Bill said.

"Oh wow! Just what I need. Another Wild Bill plan, and this one involves me buying an expensive motorcycle. Leave me out!" I headed out the door of the salesroom.

I had to wait a few minutes for Bill to follow because Bill was involved in a discussion with the salesman. I figured he was mollifying him because the salesman was likely counting my money already.

When Bill came out, he was smiling. "Everything's cool. The guy said we can come back anytime."

"But I don't want to come back anytime. Did you tell him that?"

"Ok, Ok. Look, let's get a beer and something to eat. The guy said there's a place down by the river where he goes for lunch sometimes."

We started walking down the street lined with industrial shops and small factories. "Boy, you got kinda chummy with him in there," I said.

"Hey, I was just being friendly. You blew out of there kind of abruptly."

"Things were moving a little fast for me, that's all."

"No problem. Hey, here's the place. I could use some food."

We went into the small restaurant that overlooked the Hovel River, which wasn't exactly a tourist spot. The river was greenish-brown from the industrial waste that came from the factories. We both ordered steins of beer and bratwurst with boiled potatoes. The meal came with sauerkraut, which I couldn't stand. Bill loved it and ate all of mine.

As we sat and finished our beers, Bill quietly proposed, "I know you're not interested, but could I just tell you what I was thinking about as far as my post-Berlin planning goes?"

I was hoisting a red flag when Bill started talking, thinking he was going to start pitching me on the BMW again, but when I heard "post-Berlin," I had to admit an interest.

"Post-Berlin? I thought you were going back home and to law school, post-Berlin."

"And I am," Bill said, "but I didn't say exactly when, did I?"

"I suppose not, but I figure we're going to have to go back sooner or later."

"Absolutely, but we're here now, and we should use our time to the utmost. I mean, when's the next time you're going to be able to spend a few months in Europe? It'll be a long time for me, and I'll probably be too old to enjoy it. So listen to my plan. It's just an idea. If you don't like it, say so, ok?"

I figured I'd heard a dozen crazy plans from Bill, most of them pure fantasy, but here I was in Berlin living out one of those plans because it corresponded to my own needs, my circumstances, and my time of life. And this current Berlin plan of Bill's had provided benefits, which I hadn't been able to gain for myself at home, like getting laid for the first time. Bill had called me here in that strange way. Since he was the only link I had with my old life, I was loathe to sever the bond, so I asked Bill what he was thinking post-Berlin.

"I've always thought that Istanbul, Beirut, and Cairo were three of the coolest cities I can think of," he said. "The Middle East, mystery, intrigue, and ancient history are all there and had been for more than eight thousand years. I want to see those places and experience them.

"Sure, I came to Berlin to get some courses under my belt, but I have three more months to hit the road and explore. And I'm sick of being cooped up in Berlin. So here's my plan:

"I can get a used motorcycle here in Berlin and drive to Istanbul, Beirut, and Cairo. I've looked up the trip in the library at the university. It's about five thousand kilometers, or thirty-five hundred miles. If I spend a week in each of the three cities, the whole trip will take six or seven weeks.

"If you get a bike, you could join me!"

I was stunned by the scope of Bill's imaginings. He wasn't called Wild Bill for nothing. Two guys on motorcycles heading into what were to me alien lands. It might as well be the wild blue yonder. I shook my head. Jesus, it was crazy. Bill was a biker to his soul; I understood this now.

"Bill, count me out. This isn't what I came over here for. Besides, if there were any place I'd like to go, it would be Greece. I want to see the Acropolis sometime. Also Eva told me about this place on the south coast of Crete she went to once called Aigia Galini, which sounds cool. She went there herself and told me that there is something mystical about the place. She said she felt there was something there for me too. Knossos is on Crete. I'd love to see that. But your trip is way too much for me. And you're talking about biking in the Middle East in summer? The temperatures get up to a hundred and twenty degrees there. You'd be fried."

"I'd travel at night," Bill said without a pause. He had it all figured out. "But maybe we could still ride together. I wouldn't mind seeing Athens, which isn't too far from Istanbul."

"There's that *we* again, Bill. I don't know about this whole idea. I'll tell you the truth. The idea of driving a bike like the BMW is something I might see myself doing. It's a rush. But your trip is way out of my league."

"I understand," Bill said, dismissing my excuses. "But you just said that a bike is something that you'd like to do. And for a beginner, the BMW is the most forgiving, easy-riding machine out there. You saw how it sits. Smooth and easy and it never breaks down. Why don't we go back and see what it would cost to get you on the road?"

Maybe it was the beer, but more likely it was my own desire to place myself in an unanticipated future and distance myself from a conventional past, so I agreed to take another look at the bike. As we walked back to the showroom, I was nonetheless clouded with doubts despite a longing to be a man on a motorcycle. Naturally, I was worried about the cost. If it were over a certain amount, the whole thing would be out of the question. There was driving the machine itself, which was large and heavy, and getting caught with my fake motorcycle license, along with what it would be like if I got caught in a rainstorm.

By the time we reached the showroom, I was a jumble of nerves. As soon as we went in the door, the salesman, who had been at his desk, got up to greet us with a big smile on his face. That made me even more nervous and a little angry. I felt as though I was being cornered, despite the contrary feeling that I actually wanted to buy the bike.

"Did you find the restaurant?" the salesman asked.

"Good bratwurst and sauerkraut," Bill said.

"And you still have an interest in the motorcycle?"

"I think he does," Bill said. "A good stein of beer always helps stiffen the resolve."

"Bill, come over here. We've got to talk," I said. "I don't want you to push me into this. This is way more than I thought about when I came over here. I don't know if I want to handle this. You've got your big biker plans, but I don't."

"You know you want this, so why bitch so much? Anything you need to know about the bike I can show you."

"Holy shit! You're talking like you've already conned me into doing this. This is nuts. And it probably costs a fortune. I didn't come over here to get tied to a motorcycle."

The salesman had retreated while Bill and I had our discussion. He chose this moment to come forward. "So I understand that you are the one who has an interest in the motorcycle," he said to me.

"I have to say it's a beautiful machine," I told him. "But my friend here has made some assumptions that I'm not sure are going to work for me."

"What I last heard was that you were concerned about the cost, am I correct?"

"That's certainly a big part of it," I said, staring at Bill.

The salesman deftly took over the conversation. "Consider you are standing in the factory, the point of manufacture. You realize that a purchase at this point is at the lowest possible cost because there is no shipping, marketing, or dealer costs or, because you are not German citizens, even taxes to pay. Further, if you order directly from me, I can have your machine customized with accessories you may want at minimal cost because I can specify it should come off the line that way."

Both Bill and I were listening to this obviously very experienced salesman with our mouths slightly agape. He had us in thrall, withholding just one piece of information until the right moment. "I believe that this BMW R60/5 motorcycle would sell for approximately twenty-five hundred dollars in the United States, which I believe is more than a comparable Harley Davidson."

"That's true," Bill said glumly, knowing what he had paid for his Sportster.

"And that's way out of my league," I said as I shook my head emphatically.

"But please remember you are at the point of origin," the salesman smoothly continued. "There are so many costs added to bring the product to market. Well, let me be direct. The BMW R60/5, which you just sat on and were so pleasantly surprised to find fit your style, as you said, has a price of fifty-two hundred marks from point of origin, which would make thirteen hundred American dollars. And if you are really interested, I can show you some basic but essential accessories, which we can put on for very little more. Would you like to see?"

Bill and I were both speechless in the wake of this withering display of sales expertise. I looked at Bill and could see that he was dumbfounded by the price of this great, pedigreed machine, which he knew, as an avid cyclist, was a great value. Bill then looked at me, saying nothing, widening his eyes in a "this is too good to be true" expression.

The salesman said nothing, standing between us and slowly rubbing his hands together. "You can take one for a test drive, if you like."

Although I knew in my heart that I had been sold on this bike, I felt in the moment that I had been trapped to some degree by Bill and his crazy motorcycle passion from way back in college, by this circumstance of being at "the point of origin" where I could actually buy a BMW for a price I couldn't afford anywhere else, and by this slick salesman who seemed to know exactly how to push my buttons.

But there it was. I still had almost three thousand dollars on me because I hadn't any place to spend the money I came over with. The Elton John tickets, some books, and a few dinners were the most I'd spent on anything, and they weren't going to take me where I needed to go. The motorcycle provided the transportation, the boost to my ego, and the freedom to open my horizons. And I'd still have seventeen hundred dollars left after buying the bike, which should last a while and maybe take me somewhere like Crete.

The test drive was just a formality. When we went out into the street, the salesman wheeled an R60/5 out from the garage. When he handled me the handlebars, I could feel how well-balanced the bike was. It was a little heavy; the salesman said it weighed around two hundred kilograms, which was over four hundred pounds, but I didn't have a problem handling it. The salesman went over the starting sequence again. The electric starter was a breeze, and he told me how the gears worked, all with the right foot. The left foot was for the brakes. The left hand was for the clutch lever; the right hand was for the accelerator.

"Alles gut?" he said.

I said "sure" and turned on the bike. I gave it a little gas, popped the clutch lever, and stalled it out, causing me to fall to the right, but I managed to catch myself before letting the cylinder head hit the ground.

The salesman came over and said, "It is a matter of timing, you know. I think a little more of the accelerator and feel when to engage the clutch."

"Right," I said, feeling very embarrassed. But I was going to make it happen.

On my second try, I gave the bike a bit too much gas and popped the clutch a little too quickly, causing the rear of the bike to spin out slightly, but I caught the bike with my right leg, straightened it out, and zoomed down the street at forty miles per hour in first gear before I remembered to clutch and flip up my right foot to get into second gear. It was exhilarating, a total trip. I didn't want to stop.

But I did reach the end of the street in one piece and braked, remembering to clutch and gear down by pressing on the gears with my foot. I stood in the middle of the street with the bike between my legs and said out loud, "I've got this!" before repeating the mechanics to get back to the waiting salesman and Wild Bill.

Bill was grinning from ear to ear, but he didn't say anything. The salesman asked, "Shall we go inside to make up an order form?"

I thought things were moving very quickly, but I had no doubt in my mind that I wanted this bike. I had a feeling it was predetermined as part of my journey. I thought about forging the AAA license. Why would I have done that unless there was a reason beyond tweaking my mother and that bureaucrat?

Back in the showroom, Bill pulled me aside and said, "Look, better let me do the negotiating with this guy. I've bought a bike before and I want to pin the salesman down on the price and the accessories he mentioned."

"Good idea, I said. "I'm too keyed up to get into details at the moment."

When we sat at the desk, Bill started talking, and the salesman switched to German. Bill caught on fast. The salesman knew it was my money, so he wanted me out of the conversation.

"Could you please speak in English so that my friend can understand the details of the transaction?" Bill asked.

The salesman quickly started talking in English again. "Of course. Here is a book with the accessories you might be interested in."

Bill flipped through the accessories book quickly, dismissing most of them as frivolous toys.

Bill had been riding for years so he knew what was additive to the experience and what wasn't. He didn't like windshields; you couldn't feel the wind in your face. He didn't like helmets either for the same reasons. He loved the electric starter, but that was now standard. He stopped at the last page and pointed to something he said was a "Gepacktrager," which retailed at 275 marks.

I looked at it and couldn't tell what it was. Bill told the salesman that if they installed this thing as a part of the deal for fifty-two hundred marks, he had a deal.

"What is that thing?" I asked.

"It's a luggage rack. You hang your saddlebags off it, and there's more room on the rear for a sleeping bag. They're great." I could feel the thirteen hundred marks trying to bust out of my billfold of travelers' checks. I was set on this course now.

The salesman looked hard at Bill. It was plain that he was ready to deal. "All right, gentlemen, we shall put on a Gepacktrager at no additional cost," he said.

"Mr. Higgins." He looked at me, remembering the name from the license. "I congratulate you on your purchase of the finest motorcycle in the world." We shook hands. "I also congratulate you on being so smart as to bring a very experienced negotiator as your companion." He shook Bill's hand. "Now I must collect the paperwork. You understand that we do not keep a stock of inventory here. You will make an order, and you will come back to pick up your motorcycle in approximately one week when it comes off the line and has been tuned up. At that time, you will have to pay for registration and insurance, which I will set up for you. This is in addition, of course."

I understood. It was more money, but that went with driving anything. Then the salesman gave me a sheet that had the color options on it and said I should choose one while he got the papers. I choose silver fenders and tank with black pinstripes instead of the traditional black fenders with white stripes. When he came back, I signed over thirteen hundred dollars in travelers' checks.

The next thing I knew, I was out on the street with Wild Bill squeezing me hard around my shoulders with his big right arm, saying, "Man, I knew you'd do it. You've really got balls. You know there aren't that many guys who are willing to put it on the line like you just did."

Having extracted myself from Bill's grip, I looked over at the big, friendly guy and said, "Although I think this is going to work out to be really cool, I get the feeling that you've been thinking more about this than I have and for quite a while."

Wild Bill took on a look of feigned surprise. "Listen, man. You're the one who ditched everything and came over here to find yourself. That's what you said. I think I can tell you that having a bike will get you further along and faster down that road than sitting on a couch reading *Siddhartha*.

"Now I've got to say you pulled off a major score by getting Eva, but that's just a breakthrough, your first woman. There will be others. The bike will bring them to you. And it will take you to places and in a way that can't be compared with others. It's a ticket and a passport to bigger things, man, so don't say I've been manipulating you or anything. You were ready for this as soon as you saw the bike and figured out you could pay for it."

I had nothing to say. Bill was right. I wanted the bike in my imagination even before I saw it, even before I came to Europe. I had felt the wind in my hair on the short test drive, and although I was concentrating hard not to crash in front of the salesman, the feeling had been intoxicating. And now having to wait a week to get the bike was going to be painful.

I patted Bill on the back. "You're right, buddy. Let's go back and get shit-faced out of our minds."

8

Setting Up the Bike

THE ANTICIPATION OF WAITING for the motorcycle reminded me of when I was a little kid waiting for Christmas. I knew it was coming, but it never came. It was like my life was on pause, yet I realized it wasn't something that was planned. It was more of a mystical happening, gestated by Wild Bill.

"It's coming," I kept telling myself and did things to distract myself from thinking about it.

Fortunately, there was Eva. We had been making love in the afternoons before she went to work for several weeks. She seemed to be happy with me; I was delighted with her, of course, but I didn't think we were in love or anything. We were doing what Siddhartha and Kamala had done, pleasing each other. She taught me how to please her; I found that her pleasures were more complicated than mine, although she showed me some ways I could be pleased that I could never have imagined.

I didn't think Eva was in love with me. She treated me as someone special as far as I could see. We were lovers, a couple, but Eva always played a game where she would hold me in suspense, at arms' length, and then pull me to her when she wanted it. She was in control, and she was comfortable with that. I had never been in this place before, so I accepted it and the pleasures it conferred on me without questioning her motives. I figured she needed sex as much as I did, and I just took what I got willingly.

I told Eva right away about buying the motorcycle. She was thrilled. I caught a gleam in her eye that told me she thought I was more of a man for doing it. She wanted to see it right away and was disappointed when I said I was waiting for it to come out of the factory. But she insisted that I take her on drives every day, to which I readily consented.

Then she went into a sort of reverie about when she was in her early teens. She and a girlfriend had taken a summer trip from Algiers to Crete by ferry boat. They had gone to the south coast of Crete, where there was a small town called Aigia Galini over the mountains from Heraklion. It was a beautiful little town with a mystic air to it. The soft wind blew across the Mediterranean from Africa, and there was no one on the beach they had found so they could swim and tan in the nude. One evening the two girls went for a swim and made love on the beach. Eva felt that she had entered another world and never wanted to leave. She thought there was an ancient presence there that had reached her inner soul, but she had to leave before she could discover its true meaning.

When they got back home, they learned that her girlfriend's father had been transferred to the main office of his company in France taking his family with him. Eva felt abandoned. Her father was in the military and so was very strict. He had not wanted her to go to Greece and had sensed a change in her when she returned. She told him she had come to an understanding of her inner self in Crete. He said that was nonsense. She began to flout his authority and annoyed him greatly. That was when she got into trouble, she said.

She looked at me wistfully. "I wish I could go back to Aigia Galini," she said very softly. "I left part of my soul there."

I didn't have a response to this. Was she looking for a ride to the south coast of Crete on a motorcycle? How many kilometers? Twenty-five hundred? I just said that I'd have to learn to ride the bike first, hoping she was just musing. But she grabbed the sides of my head with her hands and kissed me all over, maybe to encourage me. But it turned into some serious encouragement, if that's what it was, as she taught me some new sex positions for the next hour. I heard Bill's words about women and motorcycles confirmed in my ears that afternoon, even before I took delivery of the bike.

A few days later, Bill woke me up and told me BMW had called to say that the bike was ready. Bill and I scarfed down coffee, rolls, and strawberry preserves and the last measure of anticipation of this momentous event and headed to Spandau.

Soon we were passing through the door of the factory showroom, where the salesman came over to shake our hands. He led us through the back door of the showroom into a large garage. There, standing on its parking stand, was a gleaming silver R60/5 BWM motorcycle. The gas tank had a chrome facing with the BMW blue-and-white propeller symbol on it. The seat was a double bench in black for two riders. Everything else was silver with a thin, black pinstripe highlight, just as I had hoped, the perfect charger for a knight of the road.

We walked around the bike a couple of times, examining every detail. I checked the speedometer, which was calibrated to 160 kilometers per hour, and the fuel gauge, both of which were recessed into the top of the headlight, an eight-inch glass circle on a black mounting between the handgrips. Bill checked the luggage rack and showed me how bags and gear could be hung over or strapped onto them. The salesman said there was a full tank of gas, compliments of the management.

Bill asked, "How far can it go on a full tank?"

The salesman said, "About three hundred and thirty kilometers, which is a long way in Berlin, ya?"

We all laughed at that because of the irony that no one could drive more than twenty-five kilometers in one direction in Berlin before hitting the Wall and having to turn around.

The salesman showed me the license plate, a black square on the rear with silver lettering "ST-467," and there was a lone "B" underneath in the middle.

"The B is for Berlin. Wherever you go, people will know you are from Berlin. Now let us finish the papers and sign your insurance. You can finish your payment and be on your way."

The registration and insurance cost 380 marks, which set me back, but it was all required, and the insurance was from Allianz, which was a global name if I wanted to travel out of Berlin. Then he handed me the keys and the papers along with a street map of Berlin and went back out to the garage and opened the door.

"Gentlemen, your adventure awaits you. Auf Wiedersehen."

I looked at Bill. I wasn't sure I wanted to drive with someone else on the bike for my first ride in traffic, especially someone the size of Bill, so I tossed the key to Bill and told him to drive, which Bill quickly acceded to, grinning broadly. He swung his leg over and onto the driver's position. I hopped on the back and flipped down the passenger footholds. I felt a bit mortified as I looked at the salesman, who had an incredulous look on his face. I consoled myself that I could get in a lot of practice on my own starting when we got back to the house, but for now, I didn't want to crash with Bill on the back just because I didn't know what the hell I was doing.

I put my hands on Bill's waist as he started the bike using the kick-starter, which I saw required a major effort by the big man. I'd leave that alone and use the electric starter. Then Bill gunned the gas and took off, deftly slipping through the gears before heeling the bike over as we passed through an intersection and around a traffic circle.

Bill let out a "Wahoo!" as we shot down Charlottenburger Strasse, going much too fast from what I could tell, feeling the wind in my hair, watching the trees of the Tiergarten zip past on either side, and seeing the road fly by underneath. But I quickly dismissed the notion of *too fast* because at this moment, the speed and the sensation of being free on the road was the very feeling of being truly alive that I craved.

"Wahoo!" I yelled.

We were home in a moment. Bill pulled the bike up onto its parking stand rather than using the kickstand, which may have been sexier, but the parking stand gave the bike much better stability.

"Thanks for letting me drive it," Bill said.

"I'd like to get the feel of it before taking passengers."

"That's what I figured. Boy, it sure is a beauty, although I'll take my Sportster any day."

"Well, I'm going to get some miles under my belt right now."

"Not surprised to hear you say that. That map should come in handy."

"Yeah. That salesman was pretty slick, but I think he gave me a good deal overall. I'm glad you were there to keep him in line."

Bill grinned. "What are friends for? I couldn't let you get fleeced. Look, you paid fifty-two hundred marks for the bike and three hundred and eighty for the registration and insurance. That's a little over fourteen hundred dollars. Man, I'll say that's a good deal! You'd pay double that in the States. And BMWs can last fifty years. Hahaha! Fantastic! Go forth and conquer the road! I'll see ya back for dinner."

I needed no encouragement. I pulled the bike off the stand, swung myself into position, and took off up Hubertusallee to the Ku'damm, weaving my way through the traffic to Budapester Strasse and from there to the Victory Column in Koenig Platz on the 17 Juni Strasse. I was getting the feel of the machine. I found it to be responsive, not explosive, in its ability to accelerate. It was easy to coordinate my left hand on the clutch with my right foot on the gears. And the gears made a satisfying *klunk* when I shifted properly so I knew I was doing it right. The brakes were good, but there was no place I could go more than eighty kilometers per hour, so I had no way of telling how good they'd be at speed.

I'd been driving around for nearly an hour in a blissful, dreamlike state, thinking only of how to work the bike and soaking in the feeling of floating through the atmosphere as if I were detached from the world and all its problems, when I realized I was getting cold. I stopped and zipped up the Air Force survival jacket, which provided warmth, but I realized that with its fur-lined hood, it was hardly the biker image I wanted to project. It was more like Nanook of the North. I'd have to find leather or an equivalent, probably an equivalent because leather was expensive. Bill's jacket cost around four hundred dollars.

I'd also need sunglasses because my eyes were watering from the wind. I wiped the tears from around my eyes to check the map. I had no idea where I'd gotten to; I was so enthralled with the experience. The map I had was not very detailed, just a free advertising handout from BMW. I'd have to get a better one. But

I could see how to get back to the Brandenburg Gate and then retrace the route home.

The route took me along the Wall on my left where I could see the ends of bricked-up streets that I passed, which were the ends of hope for the people who were walled up on the other side in the East. They were supposed to think that I was imprisoned in West Berlin, but everyone knew by now that it was the other way around. That was why the guard towers faced toward the East. *Fuck the commies*, I thought.

When I got back, my cheeks were cherry red, and a grin was spread across my face. I went into the bedroom and stood next to the radiator to warm up. I told Bill I needed to get some biker gear for the road at a reasonable cost. Bill was right on it, telling me that he had seen a military surplus store down by the university that sold the kind of gear I'd need. The students were always in there because the stuff was cheap.

In the morning, I drove Bill to Dahlem, where the university was. I found that I could manage the bike even with the 220 pounds of Wild Bill on the back. Bill made it easy for me to ride with him. I figured that this was because Bill knew how to lean into curves and follow the motion of the bike because of his own experience.

When we found the store, Bill immediately showed me a rack of surplus German army boots, which he said were indispensable for bikers, especially BMWs where the cylinders jutted out right in front of the rider's shins. I put on a pair and found that the dull, black leather boots, which rode halfway up the calves, would do the job perfectly. Bill said they were also essential for deflecting road debris.

We next went hunting for a jacket. The leather jackets were all new and too expensive at around a thousand marks, which was what I figured. We looked everywhere, but in the end, I had to settle on a lined denim jacket. Bill said I'd be sorry if I got caught out in the rain, but I wasn't going to spend money on the leather. I found a canvas poncho, which I thought might be useful in the rain, but Bill said it would be too dangerous because it blew around too much. I picked up a canteen, which had a case and a strap. That made 215 marks, or $55, and I figured that would be it.

But Bill had found something else, and he signaled me to come over and take a look. At the bottom of a shelf of shirts, there was a pair of black leather German army dispatch rider's saddlebags that closed with two buckles in front and two clips on the back that Bill was sure would clip onto the luggage rack on the bike. They looked old-fashioned, but when I touched the leather, I could feel that it was still soft and supple. They were beautiful.

Bill took one of the bags up front and talked to the clerk. He then went out and tried to attach the bag to the rack on the bike. I went up to the front to pay for the stuff I had gathered and watched with the clerk as Bill worked on the bike. Bill came back after a while looking downcast.

"Well, these could work if we did some modifications," he said to me, winking so the clerk wouldn't see.

He had a lengthy discussion with the clerk in German, frequently shaking his head. The clerk was somewhat dumbfounded by everything Bill was saying, but I got the idea that Bill was trying to talk the guy into selling the saddlebags for cheap, figuring that they were something that I might not actually use, but still knowing how fine they really were.

Finally, Bill asked me, "Are you willing to part with a hundred and eighty marks for these bags? Let me tell you that they are worth a whole lot more and you need saddlebags."

That was another forty-five dollars, but I could see that I would need a place to carry stuff, and those old bags had a pedigree to them I liked, so I said, "Go for it," realizing that the cost of the bike was now approaching fifteen hundred dollars, leaving me with around fifteen hundred cash. Given my expenses so far, excluding the bike, I guessed I could live with that, but I was going to have to start keeping a close watch on the outflow.

A few minutes later, we were headed home, saddlebags attached to the rack and filled with my new gear, except the boots, which I wore self-importantly. We stopped for a beer and sat in the window of the café looking out and admiring the bike with the old saddlebags on it. It looked terrific.

"I'll bet those saddlebags are forty years old," Bill said. "They were probably made before the war and never used. Somehow they wound up in that shop and were buried under merchandise until we found them. They've got to be worth two hundred dollars each, maybe more."

Because we had taken longer than I thought, Eva was waiting for us when we got back to the house, standing in the hall in one of her dark moods. "Where have you been, Jack?" she snapped. "You said you'd give me a ride today. I was looking forward to it."

"Eva, I'm sorry. We had to get some stuff for the bike, like these boots and a pair of saddlebags. It just took longer than we thought," I said, knowing I had forgotten all about Eva.

"Well, as you can see, I have to get ready to go to work now, so you can just prepare to take me."

"Will you ride without a helmet?"

"I will wear a scarf."

I wasn't thrilled by Eva's peremptory command, but I knew I was at fault, so rather than get into an argument with her, I went out and took the saddlebags off the bike and brought them back to the room. When I got there, Bill was laughing uproariously, calling me "pussy-whipped." I gave him the finger and went out to the bike to wait for Eva.

As I sat on the bike, I mused that I didn't want the bike to become a taxi or carnival ride for Eva at her leisure. I'd have to see where that went. As a reflection of my mood, as much as my growing confidence in mastering the bike, I determined to deliver Eva to work in half the time as the prior night. That should put me squarely in the driver's seat.

She came out and hopped aboard as casually as last night. As soon as she was settled, I gunned the bike down Hubertusallee and blew past a red light onto the Ku'damm. I zipped through the traffic and heeled the bike over hard on two turns so that Eva gripped onto me like death was imminent.

When we arrived at the bar, she got off and looked at me with her eyes wide. She touched her lips with her hand and then touched my cheek. "A demain," she said as I sped away. I felt that I had made a statement of my independence, using the bike as an exclamation point.

9

To East Berlin

Spring in Berlin unfolded like the leaves on the trees and the flowers in the Tiergarten, slowly, hesitatingly, but ultimately colorfully and beautifully. By the beginning of April, the temperature had reached the upper sixties, and biking around town was a lark. Eva and I went for picnics by the Havel, and as I had figured, she roped me into providing her a regular ride to work. We had grown friendly beyond the sex, and I had learned to loosen up with her. I learned that she was a survivor and took her pleasure where she could find it. I wondered if most women were like that.

Certainly a lot of people just lived day to day, I thought. I had a feeling I might be falling into the same trap now that I had a girlfriend and a new toy. Is this what happens to people when they get satisfied? I didn't want this to happen to me. I was on a mission.

But I shook off this scenario as it might apply to me because at the moment I was living a lie, having no job, and living for free on Wild Bill's floor. Bill had never asked me to contribute to the rent, so I bought most of the beers when we went out and a substantial portion of the food. As a result, I still had lots of cash, despite buying the bike. Still, I woke up to the fact that my quest for greater meaning in my life had stalled as I lived my existence on Easy Street in the warming spring of Berlin.

I mentioned this to Bill one evening, who replied, "Listen, Jack, you've been here four months or so. You've hit on and gotten laid off the hottest woman I've seen in years, one who actually shot me down! I mean she's thirty-six and looks younger than you! You've read *Siddhartha* and actually had an intelligent discussion about it with a thirty-year-old PhD philosophy student who lives and breathes this stuff. You've bought one of the world's best motorcycles and have learned to ride it pretty damn well, despite having no experience and holding a license, which you forged yourself. You're living in a crazy, fucked-up city surrounded by a thousand Russian tanks and you act like a native. And you're complaining that your life is stalled?!"

Bill was really rolling, so he continued, "Shit, man. You've lived a whole lifetime compared to some of those shitbirds back home and all in four months! And why? Because you dared to make the move! Don't be greedy. Don't be impatient. You're moving at close to light speed. You just don't see it. I see you changing, but I'm on the outside. Give yourself time to pick up some perspective."

"I guess so," I said. "I've put some of my hang-ups behind me. I couldn't have done that unless I had come here and had you to push me along.

"Still, I've got the draft to worry about, and if I get out of that one way or another, I need a path to follow, and I've got a life ahead of me ,which I haven't got a clue of yet. We've been having fun, and I have been doing some catching up on things. But where are my answers? You're figuring on becoming a lawyer, so you're on your path, way ahead of me."

Bill had spoken his piece for now, and I could see he wasn't interested in being a life coach anymore. He confirmed this, "Hey, screw all this shit. We're here now, so let's act on what we've got. There are cool things we haven't done yet, and I've got one that will truly blow your mind for tomorrow."

I wanted to know what it was before being led into something potentially costly, illegal, or dangerous, which was what Wild Bill seemed to be all about at his core. But when Bill told me what he had in mind, I was all-in on the idea from the beginning.

The next morning we went to the KaDeWe to buy a detailed map of Berlin, which included both the Eastern and Western zones. Then we went to a currency exchange shop on the Ku'damm, where we changed one hundred sixty West German marks for nine hundred sixty East German marks, which were worth the same in East Berlin because the East Germans refused to recognize that the West mark was more valuable than the East mark. The world pegged the exchange rate at one West mark to six East marks.

The forty dollars we each spent on East marks would buy us six times the goods in East Berlin as in West Berlin. The dealer advised us that it was illegal to bring East marks into East Germany because the East Germans didn't like people bringing their currency into the country in a devalued state.

I saw that Bill had worked out another illegal scheme, but the fact that we could change forty dollars into two hundred and forty dollars for one day's spending money was just too good to pass up. And there were some once-in-a-lifetime things to see in East Berlin that sealed the deal. Besides, East-West relations were at a thaw, and we knew there was actual tourism between East and West Berlin these days, although it was mostly in tourist buses. Bill joked that the Vopos weren't likely to strip search people at the checkpoint, so we were on our way.

The only passage through the Wall into the East was through Checkpoint Charlie, which was in the American sector. All the attributes of the Wall ran right up to the gates on the Eastern side. As I drove the bike up to the line of cars entering the checkpoint, I could see guard towers in the East with machine gun-toting, helmeted Vopos patrolling on the balconies that surrounded them. The Americans just had shacks that had red-and-white diagonal striping on them. No one was interested in escaping from the West to the East.

I inched the bike forward as the American guards checked everyone's papers. When it was our turn, one of the MPs, who looked about our age, smiled at us and asked, "What're you boys doin' today? Thinkin' about defecting? Ha, ha!"

"To that shithole over there?" Bill said. "Not on your life."

The MP waved us through the gate and told us to take care.

Bill leaned forward and said in my ear, "Let me do the talking with the Vopos, ok?"

I nodded, as if I had anything to say to the commies.

I drove up to the huge watchtower and thick gate where three Vopos were waiting, two of them brandishing machine guns. I just saw the guns; the Vopo without the gun walked over and put out his hand for our papers. Then to my horror, the other Vopos started circling around the bike, staring at it and talking to each other. I thought we were doomed, but Bill picked up on their conversation, and the Vopos asked him a few questions, which he answered, and they smiled. Apparently the guards were more interested in the bike than its passengers. The Vopo passed back the papers, said something to Bill, and then had the gate lifted and waved us through into the communist East zone.

"We have to cross back to the West by six," Bill said.

"Wow. I thought they were going to run us in."

"Nah. They've never seen a bike like this before, especially a brand-new one. They don't have anything like this in the East."

Bill had checked the map and told me to head straight ahead toward our first stop, the Pergamon Museum on the Unter den Linden. He said this museum had been damaged in WWII and that the Russians had looted a lot of the artifacts, but there were some amazing things from the ancient Middle East still here because the Russians couldn't get the largest ones out, like the altar of the gods from the city of Pergamon or the blue-tiled gates from the city of Nineveh. Bill said these were wonders of the world, but no one could get to see them anymore because they were behind the Iron Curtain.

I parked the bike right out in front of the museum as there were no other cars. We paid ten East marks to enter what was a deserted museum. As soon as we passed the atrium, we encountered the altar of Pergamon. It was staggering in its size and design, the more so because it was indoors. German archeologists had dismantled it brick by brick and moved it to Berlin in 1871.

Bill read from the brochure that the altar was likely built in the fifth century BC, and then we climbed forty feet up the stairs. The altar was only part of the entire structure, which was 115 feet wide, 110 feet deep, and 65 feet tall. I was fascinated by the life-sized friezes of the history of the Greek gods that circled the base of the altar. I wished that I'd had brought my book about the wars between the Giants and the Titans and the final victory of Zeus because I could see some of the depictions of the titanic struggle in the marble carvings on the friezes. I'd been interested in ancient Greek history ever since I took a course on Greek gods and heroes in sixth grade. We were blown away by this enormous piece of architecture. I didn't know of Bill's interest in antiquities, but clearly he was impressed by the scale of it.

"I knew that the Russians had left some of the loot here, but now I can see why. Look at the size of this mother!" Bill said. "But the Germans were lucky they got to keep any. After all, they were the original thieves. Ha!"

Bill's interest in the altar certainly had a different spin on it than mine, but it was time to move to the next room, where we came upon an even more incredible sight, the Ishtar gate of the city of Nineveh. While the gate was only a part of the original, it still stood fifty feet high and was ninety feet wide. It too had been dismantled brick by brick by the Germans and brought to Berlin.

It captured one's eye immediately because of its colors, dark-blue glazed brick with many golden animals in glazed brick spread all over the wall. Bill read that this gate was just one of eight gates that King Nebuchadnezzar had built as a processional into his capital around 575 BC. I couldn't imagine what the whole array must have looked like blazing in line in the desert sunlight.

Next, we saw the market gate from the island of Miletus, built around 200 AD. It wasn't in as good condition as the other structures, but it was a hundred feet long and thirty feet high. Miletus was an important trading center in ancient history.

Then I spotted the Meissner fragment of the *Epic of Gilgamesh* in a small case as we were leaving the museum. This was a real gem.

"What are you wasting your time with over there?" Bill said.

"Oh, nothing really," I said. "This little piece of stone writing is from a poem that predates the *Odyssey* by about a thousand years, that's all."

Bill didn't get it, but the whole experience had taken me back to class trips to the Metropolitan Museum of Art in New York when we were studying ancient Egypt. The museum in New York had some pieces of ancient Egyptian art that looked gigantic to a small boy, but none of those rivaled what I'd had seen today.

As we went out to the bike, I said, "Bill, you chose a great spot to start off. That was terrific. Where to next?"

"We should probably start looking for some lunch. It's almost one."

We drove further up Unter den Linden until we came to Alexander Platz, a large square that had been concreted over. There was a large radio tower on one corner and an administrative building on another.

Bill looked it over and said, "I'll bet this whole area was bombed out and the commies just leveled it and poured concrete on it."

"They do seem to do as little as possible when it comes to being decorative or using their imagination," I said.

"You're right," Bill replied. "Let's bring a little life to this wasteland." He dug into my saddlebag and pulled out the Frisbee.

"Holy cow! You brought the Frisbee!?" I said. "Don't you think the Vopos will get riled by a couple of tourists frolicking in their commie paradise?"

"How could anyone complain about a Frisbee? It's even more innocuous than a hula hoop," Bill said as he put thirty yards between us and sent the disc sailing over my head so I had to sprint to pick it off before it hit the ground.

The Alexander Platz was a perfect Frisbee ground, a hundred yards square and completely flat. We could really air it out, soon getting into a rhythm with our patented catches and finger twirls. Out of the corner of my eye, I could see that a small crowd was gathering around the edges of the square to watch us. We drew some "Ooo's" and "Ahh's" at our best efforts, but that was usual.

And all of a sudden, the crowd disappeared, suddenly and silently as if a wind had blown the people away like dried leaves.

Bill held onto the Frisbee looking past me, shaking his head. As I stood looking over the deserted expanse of the square, I turned to see behind me two Vopos marching toward me. One looked like an officer from his bearing and his pair of shiny jackboots; the other was a trooper who was carrying a sub-machine gun at the ready.

The officer came up to me and said, "Papers, please."

Bill came over, and we quickly produced our passports, which the officer scrutinized and handed back. "Americans," he said. "On a tourist visit to see how well we have rebuilt the Eastern section?"

"We have just come from the Pergamon museum, which is magnificent," he said. "And then we stopped to see the Alexander Platz, which we thought was a perfect place to take a little exercise."

"So you Americans thought of it as a playground," the officer said, putting out his hand to examine the Frisbee. "What is this toy?"

"This is a flying disk called a Frisbee. We are on the on the Frisbee team at our university in the States. We like to stay in practice."

"Practice elsewhere. We have more serious sports here," the officer said and gave the Frisbee back to Bill. "And keep to the tourist attractions if you want to stay out of trouble.

Bill assured him we would, and I muttered "asshole" as we got back on the bike and drove to see the Reichstag, which was under construction after it had been destroyed in the war. Then we went to the Soviet Memorial in Treptower Park, which was on a huge mound. Bill said this Soviet monument was built like this because there were five thousand Russian soldiers buried under it from when the Russians captured Berlin in the war.

We needed lunch and found a cafe with outdoor tables. There were no other patrons, but as soon as we sat down, a waiter came rushing out to ask if he could be of service. Bill asked for two beers and the menu.

"I'll bet this place has good food, which costs money—that's why there's no one here," Bill said.

The menu proved Bill to be correct. We both chose the Weiner Schnitzel with roast potatoes, beans and for dessert, Baumkuchen, a layered chocolate cake. The food was great, and the cost of each meal, plus the beer, was eighty East marks, which made it especially delicious because we knew we were paying around five dollars each. We left a ten East mark tip.

"Good thing we don't have a community dinner tonight. I'm stuffed," I said.

As we headed back toward Checkpoint Charlie, Bill saw a department store and said we should go in and buy me some gloves for riding the bike because they'd be really cheap. I said it was warming up, but he said gloves were essential for bike riding at any time, so in we went.

The interior of the store was like going back in time, like maybe the late 1930s in the States. The floors were just unvarnished boards, and the display cases were ancient, some with broken glass sides. There wasn't much merchandise either as I could see from the fact that the shelves on the walls were mostly empty. This was where you could see that the East German economy was in shambles. Bill asked a saleslady if we could see some gloves, and she pulled out a few pair of cheap knitted mittens, which would be useless on a bike.

Bill asked for leather ones, and the lady took out two pairs of leather gloves, which she said were the most expensive ones in the store, figuring we wouldn't be interested, I guessed. One pair fit pretty well, so I bought them for one hundred forty East marks, or six dollars. They were nice gloves, and I got a steal.

We headed back toward Checkpoint Charlie so we wouldn't be late, but on the way, Bill spotted a sign for a cigar store.

"I'll bet they have real Cuban cigars in there," Bill said. "We've still got a bunch of these useless East marks, and I want some!"

"Aren't they illegal in the West?" I asked, but Bill had already gone into the store.

I followed him in. It was a world filled with the aroma of tobacco and the stench of men puffing on cigars of all sizes and shapes. Smoking turned me off, but cigar smoke was the limit. I peered through the haze toward the back of the store and saw men in business suits and a few Vopos sampling the wares, trying to look cool by taking a long drag on the cigars and slowly letting out the smoke to pick up on the taste and then commenting to the men around them how delicious it was, I supposed.

Bill had cornered a fat, sweaty German whose sleeves were rolled up to his elbows, in a conversation about something I couldn't figure. I just wanted to get out of there. The smoke was getting to me, so I went out to wait by the bike.

When Bill came out, he was carrying two boxes wrapped in plain brown paper, which he stuffed into my saddlebags, and his pockets were stuffed with cigars. I started to tell him again that the Cubans were illegal in the West, but he told me that the Vopos wouldn't care what we took out of the Eastern sector. It was the MPs we had to worry about.

"If we give the MPs a few of the Cubans, they will most likely forget about the saddlebags where the boxes of cigars are," Bill said. I was skeptical, but time was pressing so we had to scoot for Checkpoint Charlie.

We got to Checkpoint Charlie with little time to spare. The Vopos were already starting to close up for the night, so we were waved through fairly quickly after a passport inspection.

When we came up to the MPs, one of them said, "You guys just made it. You could have spent the night in an East German prison if they didn't let you through." He looked at us as if we really didn't get it that the East Germans were serious assholes when it came to the rules. He asked for our passports.

"Hey, sorry about that," Bill said. "We went all over the place. East Berlin is bigger than West Berlin, and we didn't know our way around. We figured you guys might like a souvenir." He gave the MP a handful of Havanans as he got back the passports.

The MP's eyes opened wide. "Hoo boy! These are genuine Havanans. We hardly ever see them over here. They are illegal, you know," he said as he winked at Bill. "The guys and I will sure enjoy them. Have a good night, boys."

Bill did it again, I thought as we drove back to 38 Hubertusallee after spending a crazy day in Communist territory, being accosted by the Vopos, bribing our own border guards, and living to tell about it. *How does he find the confidence to pull off the shit he does?*

As soon as we got back to the house, Wolfgang confronted me in the front hall. "Eva was looking for you. She was upset. She said you take her to work every night, but not tonight. How is it you take her to work every night? How is it she spends so much time with you? Just because you have a new motorcycle? Is it something more, yah?"

I was taken aback by Wolfgang's hostility. Bill had told me that Wolfgang was interested in Eva, but I hadn't known Wolfgang had figured out what was going on or that Wolfgang would clash with me directly. Eva was right: Wolfgang was a pig.

"When I got the bike, Eva asked me if I would ride her to work. It is no big deal, only fifteen minutes. I'm just helping her out," I said as nonchalantly as I could.

"And she disappears in the afternoons these days. Do you help her out with that too?" Wolfgang was getting belligerent.

Bill heard the argument and stuck his head out of his room. "Wolfgang, Eva is her own person. She's the oldest person in the house. I'm sure she can do what she wants. Back off!"

"Schieze!" Wolfgang spat out and went into his own room and slammed the door.

I went into Bill's room and closed the door. "Looks like Wolfgang has figured it out about Eva and me."

"He'd be incredibly dense not to. Everybody else figured it out a month ago. Eva doesn't hide her emotions. She's French."

"So what do I do now? Wolfgang was ready to slug it out with me just now. I mean he's positively primitive."

"Tell Eva what happened. If she thinks he needs to have his jets cooled, she can take care of it. If I were you, I'd give Wolfgang a wide berth for a while."

"How about I give him a couple of those Havanans of yours as a peace offering?"

"Why not? What've you got to lose? I'll go with you."

I grabbed three of the Cuban cigars and knocked on Wolfgang's door. He opened it, looking as pissed off as before. "We just smuggled these Havanans across from the Eastern sector. We thought you might enjoy them."

Wolfgang looked at the cigars for a moment in some bewilderment. Then he took one and ran it under his nose. He managed a weak smile, took all the cigars, said a weak "Danke," and closed his door.

"That went well," I said ruefully.

"Looks like he's really hung up on Eva. You'd better cool it with her or change your modus operandi for a while."

"This is over my head. I'll talk to Eva about it tomorrow."

———————◆──◆◆◆──◆———————

I knocked on Eva's door at the usual time the following afternoon. I could tell she was in a foul mood when she asked "Ou'est-ce qui se passe?" through the door before I opened it. I knew that meant roughly "What do you want?" which was not her usual greeting for me. I cautiously opened the door and saw her sitting on her mattress with her legs folded up so her chin was resting on her knees and her arms were wrapped around her shins.

"Bonsoir," I said sheepishly.

"Bonsoir, scheize!" Eva spat back at me. "Where were you yesterday all day that you could not tell me?"

"Bill and I went to East Berlin for the day," I volunteered, not wanting to provoke her further.

"East Berlin! *East* Berlin?! Qu' est-ce que c'est que ca? What is East Berlin? We were going to picnic in Grunewald, did you forget? Yes. And then this couchon Wolfgang is hanging around trying to chat me up all afternoon. And then I have to take the bus to work. And then my boss is giving me a hard time. And then I have to walk home in the cold. This is not nice, Jack."

I hung my head and said that Bill and I had acted on impulse. I told her about the money exchange and the cigar smuggling, but she wasn't interested in our adventure. She had not had a good day, and she was going to let me know about it.

Eva went on and on, venting her emotional state all over me. I was bewildered by her litany of hard feelings and bad times. Finally, knowing that I was not well-versed in dealing with a woman who was expressing her angst, I said, "Eva, I can see that my not letting you know about our going to East Berlin for the day and not telling you has upset you, and I'm really sorry about that, but I have to believe that there is something more going on here for you to be so upset. Like, for instance, what has Wolfgang been doing that's bugging you? Isn't there something we can do to get him off your case?"

Eva, who had risen and was pacing slowly up and down her room, heard me say this and turned to me and put her hand on my cheek. "You are a nice boy. If only things were so simple." She then returned to her pacing with her arms folded across her chest and one hand up at her lips where she was biting her finger.

I now saw that Wolfgang was just part of Eva's trouble. I had a sudden dread that maybe she was pregnant or had a sexually transmitted disease, but I knew she took the pill and was scrupulous in her sexual hygiene. She had insisted that I learn how to take care of myself too. So what could be eating at her? I was unsure what to say, but my impulse was to wait and see if she said anything that would explain things.

After pacing a couple more minutes, Eva asked, "Will you ride me to work?" She then came over and hugged me and buried her head in the crook of my shoulder and began to sob.

I felt awkward in this position. This was a new place for me, but I instinctively knew I had to step up. I lifted Eva's chin and gave her a quick kiss on the lips.

"Listen, there's plenty of time for us to go out to dinner before you have to go to work," I said. "So why don't you get dressed? Then we can eat and talk, and I can take you to work from there."

That made her smile, and she gave me a nice kiss. "I'll be ready in a few minutes," she said.

I went into the room to get a clean shirt. I had to wait for Eva to get out of the bathroom before I could wash up. My mind was in turmoil. Yesterday Bill and I had been having some good times, and then I came back and caught shit from Wolfgang, of all people. And today Eva was bent out of shape, partly because of Wolfgang, partly because of me, but there was something else. My good times had hit the Berlin Wall of reality, and I wanted to know what had happened. Eva was part of my good times, so I wanted to learn what was going on with her.

Bill came into the room with a beer in one hand and holding a Havana in the other, occasionally gazing at it as if were a rare metal.

"Boy, those things stink," I said.

Bill ignored my distaste for the world's finest cigar. "Got some problems with Eva, huh?"

"I don't know. I'll have to see." I grabbed the beer from Bill and took a large swig.

"Got to fortify yourself. Must be bad." Bill laughed.

I gave him the finger, saw that the bathroom was vacant, and went in to clean up. I just took a minute, and when I came out, Eva was waiting in the hall.

10

Eva's Troubles

I DROVE SLOWLY TO a quiet Italian restaurant Eva knew about that had red-and-white checkered tablecloths and lights strung from the ceiling beams above the tables. Eva wanted Chianti, so I ordered a bottle. Eva had pasta puttanesca; I got spaghetti Bolognese, my favorite pasta dish.

While we waited for the food, I came right out and asked Eva, "What is bothering you?"

She looked away at first, but then she turned to me and said, "Thank you for bringing me to dinner. It is very considerate. I can see that you have been well brought up by your parents."

I squirmed when she said that, as it emphasized the difference in age between us, but I took it as a complimentary remark about my background. As far as my parents were concerned, I was still chafing from the past year's treatment they had imposed upon me.

"I was perhaps not so lucky since my father was in the military and always posted to foreign assignments. I grew up in Algeria and fell in love with a Moroccan man. He was a Muslim. When my father found out, he was furious and told me to break it off, but I was young and in love, so I ran away and married this man and converted to Islam. I haven't seen my parents since." Eva paused to sip at her Chianti.

I saw her eyes grow sad and wistful. "Look, you don't have to tell me this," I said.

"Yes, I must because my past is part of my problem now." Eva gathered herself and pushed her hair back away from her face. "In 1962, the French gave Algeria its independence, and most French people, including my parents, left. My husband felt that he and the Muslims had been liberated, and he became like a mad sheik around the house. He ordered me about and beat me when I didn't do what he said. After about two years, I could take no more, so I stole money from him and took a boat to Marseilles. When I got off the boat, I considered myself no longer married or a Muslim. But I was afraid that my husband might come looking for me in a place as near as Marseilles, so I thought to go to Paris where I might get lost and maybe get a job.

"I was completely alone for the first time in my life, and I was scared. I had enough money to take the train, and I sat in a compartment with a man who managed a cabaret in Paris. He said he liked my looks; they would do me well in a cabaret as a waitress. I could make good money on tips. I told him I had never been a waitress, but he assured me it was the easiest thing in the world. He was quite charming. He told me that a waitress makes money with her smile and that I have a very nice one. When we got to Paris, we went to the cabaret, and I was hired right away. I had no place to sleep, so he offered to put me up until I could find a place.

"Well, you know how that goes," she said, not seeing that I just shrugged my unknowing, inexperienced shoulders. "He was a heavy drinker and had many women, sometimes when I was in the apartment. I finally left Denys after a year and moved in with one of the other waitresses. The bartender at the cabaret quit at this time, so I asked the owner if I could take that job. I knew all the drinks by then, and I wanted to get off the floor where I get my ass pinched every few minutes.

"So the owner gives me an audition. He tells me to mix this drink and that drink and pour from this bottle and that bottle, and I do it. He drinks them all and gets drunk, and he hires me. 'Can't waste good liquor,' he says. Then he asks if I want to sleep with him, but I tell him he is drunk and to go home to his wife. He thinks that is funny and says that is what I have to say to the customers.

"'Exactement!' I tell him, and he says he will pay me fifty francs per week, and I get tips from the customers and 10 percent of the tips from the waitresses. I tell him I was a waitress and I know that game. I'm lucky to get 5 percent. He laughs again. Then he stumbles out, saying, 'And make sure you don't steal from me!'"

Eva looked plaintively at me. "But after I had been a bartender for six months, I knew I could not stay there. It was a bad scene. Denys would show up and tell stories about me. The owner became more lecherous. I needed money to make a getaway, so I started skimming money from the register, knowing I would get caught if I did it for too long. I got just enough for transport and a start here in Berlin where I didn't think they would come looking for me. I ran away early one morning and somehow made it here. I found this commune in a post in the newspaper, and then I went searching for bartender work and I found a job. And so it has been for the past three and a half years."

She stopped and sighed deeply. I noticed that she hadn't touched her food, although I'd finished mine and most of the Chianti. I said, "You should have something to eat before you go to work." And then I said, "So now you have a problem with Wolfgang. I would think you could handle him pretty easily."

"It's not just Wolfgang, who is a couchon. I am having trouble at work." She put her hand over her eyes and let out a small sob. "I am not stealing. I should not be the cause even. But my boss is getting into the business of making what he calls soft-porn movies, and he wants me to be in them! I ran from Algeria. I ran from Paris. I have been a little happy here, but now I fear that I must run again."

And she broke down in sobs. I was horrified to hear that she might be forced into performing in sex movies. I didn't understand how this could happen. I needed a minute to respond. "Can't you just get another bartending job at another cabaret?"

"That's not possible. Here in Berlin, it is a small community of nightclub and cabaret owners. They all know each other. Some own several clubs. If one of them blackballs someone, that person is finished. You can't work in any of them. They run things their way."

Eva's chin was on her breast, which drooped her hair over her face so I couldn't see her eyes. But her tone was woeful, bereft of hope. I could think of nothing to say. I just sat and thought that my first girl had turned to be very different than the one whom I had known just a few weeks ago. She had been my sex teacher, for God's sake. There had been a few bike rides around the city and some picnics in Grunewald, which made it seem like she was something like a girlfriend, but in fact, she was older, harder, and far removed from what I expected or wanted, having heard about her past and current circumstances.

I didn't want to hurt her. She was suffering enough as it was, but I started thinking that I should probably start distancing myself from her for self-preservation. She was trouble. But then she looked up at me, and I saw real sorrow in her eyes. I realized that where I came from, people didn't experience that kind of pain in life. I sort of had to stick with her, as best I could.

"Are you going to go to work tonight?" I asked.

She took a moment to answer. "Yes, I must." She got up and went to the ladies' room while I paid the tab. Then we got on the bike for the short ride to the club. She kissed me lightly on the cheek when she got off.

"Thanks for listening and being a friend," she said.

When I got back to the house, I told Bill everything Eva had said. Bill confirmed that what she had told me about her background was what she had told him, although I had gotten more details. He also told me that there was an active sex trade in Berlin as well as in West Germany where prostitution was legal. He said that he was surprised that a good-looking, unattached female like Eva hadn't been caught up in it sooner.

I asked him, "What should I do?"

"What can you do, man?" he asked. "Things are as they are. If you want to protect her, you think you should marry her and take back home to the States? Hah! Yeah, right. Your parents would disown you. She's got to work this out for herself. She most likely will have to run again. Anyway, there isn't anything you can do. Have some more fun with her, and there will be an end to it, probably sooner rather than later."

I felt that this wasn't enough, but I couldn't think of anything else.

For the next couple of days, Eva kept to her room. I didn't want to intrude, or more truthfully, I didn't want to get ensnared in her problems. I continued to drive her to work, but we didn't say much to each other.

11

Unravelings

Daytimes, Bill and I would drive around Berlin exploring the whole city. I'd let Bill drive sometimes, and he would show me the finer points of driving a motorcycle. The problem with driving a true road bike like the BMW in West Berlin was that sooner or later you were going to run into the Wall. The Wall suffocated us. It impinged on the very freedom that a motorcycle confers on the cyclist. We could go only so far in any direction and then *wham!* Cinder blocks, barbed wire, guard towers, and Vopos.

One day we were riding on Bernhauer Strasse, which paralleled the Wall and ran next to it in places. Bill was driving. Suddenly he stopped the bike, got off, and said to me, "C'mon, here's your chance to show the commies what you think of them."

And he walked right over next to the Wall. I wanted no part of this craziness. I slid up onto the driver's seat in case bullets started flying. But nothing happened. I watched as Bill pulled down his fly and took a leisurely piss all over the Wall.

He zipped up and walked back to the bike. "Your turn," he said.

I hesitated and shook my head, telling myself I didn't believe this was happening. But then, realizing that I really would like to piss on the commies, I walked over to the Wall and made my statement in urine.

When we got back to the house, Bill found a note pinned on his door telling him that he should call home right away. Bill placed the call and started talking in Latvian with a worried expression on his face. I understood that he must be talking to someone in his family. I was concerned about his tone of voice. Bill talked for a long time, at least for an international call. When he was done, he went into the room and closed the door.

I talked with Eva for a while and then drove her to work. By the time I got back, Bill was still in the room with the door closed. I needed to know what was going on, so I knocked on the door, and Bill came to open it. His face was contorted into a kind of mask by a tight, mishapen smile he sometimes fixed upon it. He was obviously in distress. But before I could ask what was troubling him, I saw that Bill had packed all his things into two large suitcases and a satchel.

I looked wide-eyed at Bill. "You're leaving. Now?!"

"Got to go. My father had a heart attack, and my mother needs me to come back and help her take care of him when he gets out of the hospital."

"Wow. I'm really sorry, Bill," I said. "I hope things work out all right." I paused before saying, "Thanks for inviting me to come over to stay with you. It's really meant a lot to me."

"Hey, I was happy to have you room with me, but it was your decision to come to Berlin and break out of your rut back home. You made the move and bought the bike. Now you're on your way. Keep going."

"I'm on my way because of you. And I will keep going. Do you think there's any chance you'll be coming back?"

"There's no way to tell. Here's my number. Give me a call in a week or so. I'll know better then. I ordered a cab," he said. He picked up his bags and headed toward the front hall. Then he turned and said, "You're going to have to negotiate the rent with Helmut, and he can be a real bastard."

That jolted me. I'd just bought the bike and had not given a thought to paying rent. I didn't even know how much it was, but I only had half as much money as I had started out with. I certainly didn't want to be tied to paying rent every month. It would drain my resources to no real purpose except to stay in a place where I didn't know anybody except Eva, and she was proving to be a real wild card. This was not a space I wanted to be in.

"I'm taking the eight o'clock flight from Tempelhof to Frankfurt. I'll get a plane to the States from there," Bill said. "Listen, man, I'm sorry to leave you in the lurch like this, but these things happen. My father hasn't been well lately, so I'm not really surprised. It always gets you when it does happen, though. While I was packing, I was thinking that if my father isn't in too bad shape and recovers well, I could come back, and we could drive to Athens or Istanbul. I probably won't get any further, but we could try for that."

I said, "I understand. I'll call you."

The taxi came, and Bill loaded his stuff and waved goodbye out the window.

I watched the cab disappear down Hubertusallee with an empty feeling inside. The emptiness encompassed not just the loss of my friend and companion, but also the untethering of my spiritual guide. Bill had called me to come to Berlin, but I hadn't listened at first. When I did, I embraced the adventure, and it was proving itself out. Bill had given me shelter, been my translator, led me through the city, put me together with Eva, however indirectly, and insisted that I be a man by buying the bike.

Now I was standing in the street by myself, suddenly knowing that my fate was in my hands alone. I needed to process this new reality, so I walked over to the Grunewald and continued to walk until well after dark before returning to the commune without a clue as to what my next move was going to be.

I started seeing Eva again every afternoon after Bill left. I was feeling lonely, although I wouldn't admit it to myself. Eva was needful of my company with the situation she was in. We leaned on each other for support, and the sex felt more intense to me. I sensed that I could give more freely of myself now that I needed support and had a partner who was in a similar state. We talked afterwards, and while I didn't have any particular focus, Eva spoke mostly of her youth and her girlfriend and the things they did together when she was young. She always choked up when she got to the point in her life when she went to Crete with her friend. It was a special time for her.

It wasn't hard for me to see that she regretted screwing up by marrying the Moroccan guy and losing touch with her parents. She wanted an escape, so that's why she dwelt on her past. We could best communicate in intimacy where we could assuage these deep-set anxieties in the primal medium of sex.

I still drove her to work every night, but I could feel that she dreaded going more and more. I lost track of time in this floating world. The end of April neared, and Eva reminded me that the rent for May on Bill's room was coming due. Bill had paid for April, and he had left after the first of the month, so I had inherited it for April. But I didn't want to pay rent for May. I felt trapped in this circumstance. I didn't know what I was going to do on April 30 when I would have to pay up. But that afternoon the decision was made for me.

Wolfgang saw me coming out of Eva's room partially dressed and yelled, "Hey, what you been doing in there? Sleeping with Eva, no?"

"Fuck off, Wolfgang!" I yelled back at him.

Wolfgang exploded. "I will go to Helmut about everything!" he screamed, and stormed out of the house.

I couldn't figure out what he meant by that. What would the landlord care about the sleeping arrangements in the house? After all, Wolfgang was banging Trudi occasionally.

I thought that was the end of it, but Eva had heard the confrontation.

"You shouldn't have antagonized him, she said. "Wolfgang is insanely jealous and he will figure out a way to hurt you."

"I've never been involved in such a situation before," I said. "But what is done is done. So what? He doesn't hold anything over me."

Eva looked me in the eyes, and said, "The world works in nasty ways, cheri. I don't think you have been around long enough to know what can happen." She touched my cheek and went back into her room.

An hour later Wolfgang returned to the house with a man dressed in a suit. He introduced himself to me as Helmut Schroeder, the owner of the house.

"So," he said. "Wolfgang tells me that you have been living at the house for several months without paying rent."

"Oh, no," I said. "I have been living in Bill's room as a guest and Bill has been paying the rent, but Bill has been called home suddenly due to an illness in the family. It is my understanding that Bill has paid rent through April. I am prepared to pay rent for May."

"No, you are mistaken," Helmut said. "Everyone who lives in the house pays full rent of three hundred marks per month. If two people share a room, then both people pay full rent of three hundred marks per month each. Wolfgang advised me that you have been living in the house since January, so you owe twelve hundred marks back rent, plus three hundred marks rent for May. *Fifteen hundred marks.*"

He was very specific.

I felt a constriction in my throat. This was out of the question, but I was stuck. My mind started to race. Did Bill know this was the case? It was too late to worry about that. Helmut probably had a contract Bill signed, so he had the law on his side. There wasn't going to be any negotiating here. I had to think fast.

"I'm sorry that I wasn't made aware of the lease provisions, Herr Schroeder," I said. "I will certainly pay what I owe you. However, I do not have the cash on hand tonight. If you can give me until tomorrow at ten when I can go to American Express to get the money, I will come back to meet you here and pay you then."

Herr Schroeder was pleased by my attitude. He shook my hand, saying he would at the house at ten sharp and patted Wolfgang's shoulder on his way out the door. Wolfgang turned and gave me an evil look as he went out with Helmut. Obviously, he had hoped to be rid of me entirely and would have to scheme some more to chase me from the premises so he could move in on Eva.

I was dazed from the clash. I had to climb out of the emotional shell hole I had been blasted into and review my position. I was amazed that I had figured out an escape path so glibly. Maybe some of Bill's liar's magic had rubbed off on me. But the fact was that I wasn't going to fork over fifteen hundred marks to Helmut, if I had it. That was my driving force. Now I had to get out of 38 Hubertusallee before ten tomorrow. In fact, I couldn't stay in West Berlin either. I remembered what Eva had said about the city being a closed community. Either the landlords or the cops would come after me for running out on the rent. I had to hit the road tomorrow, early.

These thoughts filled my mind as I went back to the room to pack my gear.

Eva was there. She had heard the conversation between Helmut and me. "What are you going to do?"

"That, I can't tell you because I *just don't know*." I said. "All I know is I can't pay that guy fifteen hundred marks. I'm going to have to hit the road." I looked at her, hoping I hadn't reminded her of her past.

"Maybe I can help," Eva offered. "Would you like that?"

"I'm not sure what you can do. I can't see you coming up with fifteen hundred marks, and honestly, I wouldn't ask you for them, but any ideas you might have would be helpful." I looked at her. "But please stay with me for a bit. I feel a little shaky right now."

"Of course, mon cheri. But if you are going to run, you will need a place to run to, n' es-c'est pas? A destination. And you will need to know how to get there. I can help you with that."

Eva said she would call in sick at work tonight. We could go to KaDeWe and buy maps and plan a route for me to take while we had dinner in the store. This was an emotional lifeline being offered to me at a moment when I was struggling to recover my mental balance after a brief but devastating encounter with an endgame to my journey. I asked her to call her boss right away so we could get down to planning the next few days of my life, which I saw through a haze at the moment.

As we drove to KaDeWe, it seemed to me as if Eva were clinging to my waist particularly ardently, but I was so keyed up from the encounter with Helmut and my own decision to skip out on the rent that I wasn't sure. My mind and body were almost vibrating from the tension.

We went into one of the bookstores in KaDeWe, and Eva started pulling maps out of the rack one after another as if she had my trip planned out in advance. A Michelin map of Germany and Austria (which made sense), a very detailed Hallweg (Swiss) map of Vienna, a Hallweg map of Yugoslavia (not in English), a Hallweg map of Greece (with an inset map of Crete), and a Hallweg map of Athens, entirely in Greek, were stuffed into my arms as I followed her past rack after rack of maps of every country in Europe and the Middle East.

When Eva was satisfied she had the route picked out, I complimented her on her knowledge of geography. She said I should buy some markers, a notebook, and some pencils. Then we would go to one of the restaurants and make a plan. I said we should watch out for Trudi because she worked in one of the restaurants in the store. Eva said she had seen Trudi in the house, so she must be finished for the day.

So we went up to the top-floor restaurant where there was lots of room. Eva asked a waiter if we could push two tables together so we could spread out the maps and work while we ate. Food wasn't the main consideration, but I found that the stress had made me hungry, so I ordered a beer and a bratwurst. Eva had a glass of wine and a German cucumber salad.

I said to Eva, "This might be my last bratwurst."

But she laughed at me. "You could get another in Austria. I've never been there, but if they speak German, they must eat bratwurst."

We both laughed at that.

The food came, and we spread out the maps, making it a working dinner. Germany/Austria was first. Eva said I should take the southern autobahn from Berlin through East Germany toward Nurnberg. The map had markers and was very detailed as to kilometers between places on every road, so we could add up the mileage I would have to ride between any set of markers.

I could tell that the first day was going to be a long ride because I had to drive all the way from Berlin to the West German border to get through East Germany. It was over 290 kilometers to the border and would take over three hours, longer because of the border checks and the fact that speeding was closely regulated. I had never been on the bike nonstop for more than an hour and at slow speeds. There were no rest stops in East Germany. It was a straight shot. I would be tested, but there was no choice.

I knew I'd have to leave early in the morning to have the whole day to get there. Eva marked off that I could stop in Bayreuth for the night instead of going to Nurnberg to save an hour. I resolved to do that, but I saw what I was facing and thought about the next leg of the journey.

"Where next?" I said, letting her keep the lead.

"You should go to Vienna. It's beautiful there, and then you can go south."

Without thinking about it, I said, "That might be a good idea." Then I asked, "Why did you pick out the maps for Yugoslavia and Greece?"

She simply replied, "Because you have to go to Crete, and that's how you will get there. Jack, there is something special waiting for you in Crete. It is a magical land, I know it."

I shook my head. *How does she know that? And why Crete? Because that's where she went with her girlfriend? She didn't fully discover what was there for her. Is that what she wants for me?* I wasn't of a mind to delve into Eva's musings at this point. She had shown me an immediate path out of Berlin, and it seemed to be a reasonable one, so I settled on it, figuring a trip to Vienna would get me far enough away from Germany to avoid any problems I would be leaving behind.

The maps weren't expensive, so I bought them all. They were maps, symbolic of direction and right now I was in desperate need of direction. We drove back to 38 Hubertusallee for the last time, and I went into my room to finish packing.

Once again Eva came in and interrupted, "I see you are almost finished. When you are done, you should bring your packs to my room so Wolfgang won't see them. Then we can spend some time together."

I was exhausted, and my mind was not centered on lovemaking. I finished packing and brought all my stuff into Eva's room, closing my door to my room to keep Wolfgang's nose out of it. *Not a bad precaution*, I thought.

I made Eva set the alarm for six and let her make passionate love to me until I fell into a deep sleep. When Eva woke me up, I saw it was six thirty. She told me that she thought I needed as much sleep as I could get.

She had gotten up to prepare breakfast. I thanked her by giving her a hug and a kiss. I told her it was nice of her to do that before sitting down and tearing into the pumpernickel bread and jam and coffee. I knew I would need the breakfast for sustenance on the road.

I took the rest of the loaf, cut off four thick slices, and stuffed slices of salami and cheese between them for road sandwiches, which I wrapped in wax paper. I had a second mug of coffee while I did this, before taking the sandwiches to Eva's room where I placed them on top of one of the saddlebags. The maps were on top of the other bag.

I went to the bathroom and doused my head in cold water and toweled off. As I did this, I felt as if the wind were already blowing through my hair because of the jolt the caffeine had given my system. I dressed in my riding gear, putting all my papers in my jacket pocket, and buttoned it down, finishing by pulling on my boots. I had found some foot pads at KaDeWe, which had made them really comfortable. I figured I was set for the road.

It was almost seven thirty. I had to get moving in case Wolfgang woke up and saw what I was doing or Helmut decided to come early. I brought the saddlebags out and clipped them on the bike. Then I tied the sleeping bag on the back.

I wouldn't be sad to leave the commune behind. Eva was the only attachment I had left in Berlin, and I was sorry to leave her alone, especially with the troubles she was facing. But there was no way I could help her now, no matter what she had done for me. She was up against the institution. I had to save my own skin.

I had to admit I was pissed that Bill had left me in this situation. "Just stay away from Helmut," he'd said. I'd become another milestone in Bill's course of deceptions, although Bill had got caught unawares by his situation at home and so hadn't had a chance to cover himself as he usually did. Still, it was my ass that was hanging in the breeze, and I didn't like it. But Bill had given me the call to come to Berlin to begin my life's quest, so how much shit could I lay on him?

Bill was the last contact I'd had with what I was becoming aware of as being a past life where there was always someone near whom I could turn to. Once I drove the bike out of West Berlin and over the border into East Germany and beyond into places I'd had never been, I'd be truly on my own. It was a daunting prospect, so I fussed with the bike, trying to take every precaution, mulling over all these thoughts while muttering to myself.

Once before I had driven down to the control point at Kol-Drielinden, the southern exit from West Berlin onto the main autobahn to Nurnberg, so I knew where I was heading. But I knew I was just winging it as far as riding the bike the whole 293 kilometers to the East-West German border. That damn Wall had limited me to forty kilometers maximum range in Berlin at eighty kilometers per hour, which was only fifty miles per hour, so I lacked the experience of a real road trip that I needed. *Damn.* I'd just have to get on with it.

I paused a moment and looked up and down Hubertusallee, which was just beginning to show signs of a typical morning's activity. I realized I'd been daydreaming, probably putting off the final moment that would take me out of the familiar and into the unknown. I had a thought about how this could be another step on my path to self-knowledge like Siddhartha had made.

I shook my head at these familiar-sounding thoughts, orienting myself for my coming ordeal, when I saw Eva standing in the doorway of the house, staring at me with her huge brown eyes and long, dark-red hair cascading over her shoulders, down her breasts to her waist. She had allowed some of her hair to mask her face so I couldn't see her expression. *Wow*, I thought. *That woman really fascinates me. She gave me my manhood, and I owe her, but I can't do anything but leave her behind now.*

"So you are leaving without saying goodbye," she said.

I gave her a hangdog look. "I was coming back inside. I'm still packing up."

"But you were just going to make a show of it," she said, pouting.

"No, I wasn't. We talked all this over last night. I've got to get out of here now. I don't have time for delays."

"But you leave me with the couchon, Wolfgang. And what about Fritz?"

"You can handle Wolfgang, I'm sure. I simply can't do anything about Fritz. You're going to have to make a move on that yourself."

I didn't mean to dismiss her, but I was getting edgy about hitting the road. Eva was holding me back by going over all her stuff again, and I couldn't let Wolfgang see me all packed up ready to take off.

"Salut," Eva spat out. "You men are all couchons!" She went back into the house and slammed the door.

I wasn't wise to the ways of women, but I should have seen that coming. I owed her a better *au revoir* than that. I checked the street to see if there were anyone around who might snatch something off the bike and ran quickly up the front stairs and into Eva's room.

Eva was sitting on her mattress on the floor, hugging her knees. I knew this was her position of defense and deliberation. She gave me an evil look when I came in.

"I don't want to leave it this way," I said. "I would be staying if it weren't for Helmut. We've had some great times, and I'm sorry they're over, but what do you want me to do?"

She didn't say anything, but she looked up, and her face had softened. I fidgeted, thinking about the loaded-up bike on the street.

"I know you have to go. I was thinking maybe you could take me with you," she said with a look of desperation on her face.

My eyes popped wide open. I managed not to say anything, but my face must have clearly shown that this was out of the question. While I wouldn't mind her company, especially at night, I had precious little time to get out of town, and she had a ton of crap that wouldn't fit on the bike anyway.

"No way," I said. "Can't do it. And I've got to go. Now!"

She continued to look me in the eyes, but I turned toward the door. "I may not be safe here," she said very softly.

I felt her desperation. It wasn't just a justification. She might be right. "Here's what we'll do. I'm going to Vienna, and I should be there in three days. When I get there, I'll call you, ok?"

Her eyes didn't like what I said, but she asked, "Do you have the number of the phone in the hall? No? I'll write down for you." She did that and put the paper in my jacket pocket.

"Ok. I'll call." I only wanted to get outside and on the road at this point. Eva stood up, put her arms around my neck, and kissed me on the mouth. I kissed her back and then pried myself loose and went out the front door. Eva let me go. She didn't follow.

I saw that no one had disturbed the carefully packed bike. Swinging my right leg over the seat and settling into the saddle, I took it off the parking stand, placed my feet firmly on the ground on each side of the bike, and shifted the bike from side to side so I could feel its heft. As I did this, I squeezed on the brake and clutch levers to accustom myself for the ride.

The mechanics of bike riding came naturally to me by now, even though I'd only been riding for two months. But as I stood on the avenue, preparing to embark on my longest journey, I didn't feel like a real biker.

Memories of my childhood arose and were entwined with a feeling of emptiness, but now I realized that the future was in my hands. I could feel a yearning within, a desire to fill the void with knowledge of who I was and what I could do. I was in charge, and the bike was my power, my means to access the greater world to discover these things.

I had never been able to break away from home and parents and family before. I had considered myself too soft, too comfortable. Now there was no backing out. My ties had been cut. For the first time in my life I thought, *Now I have myself.*

With this thought in mind, I pushed the starter button, and the bike purred to life. I really liked that the piston-driven BMW was almost silent. It matched the quiet confidence I was gaining in myself.

As I settled the sunglasses on my face, I glanced over at the front of the commune for the last time and saw Eva standing in the front doorway. She looked sad, but she swept the hair away from her face so I could see her mouth the words "bon voyage." I waved and then flicked my right wrist, accelerating down Hubertusallee toward Teplizer Strasse.

I was really doing it. I was becoming more than what I had been, but I wasn't sure what that was yet. I knew I had made strides toward becoming a man. Going to Berlin had given me my independence, my first woman, and a motorcycle that would carry me on the twentieth-century path that Siddhartha had traveled in sandals in his era.

I would remember to call Eva when I got to Vienna to see how she was coping. It would be a relief to have a few hundred kilometers between us. Still, she had been my first girl, and that was something we'd have between us forever. Maybe Crete would be something else.

Enough daydreaming, I thought. I had to concentrate on the task at hand, driving the machine for three hours through communist territory to get away from what was certainly going to be a very angry landlord.

BOOK II

12

Leaving Berlin

My sudden departure bewildered me. I am an organized person, and I usually have a plan for major adventures, but this was strictly improvised. I was sure I could escape Helmut, but I had no landing zone except for points on a map. I was alone on the road with no counsel, only maps to guide me.

The traffic was heavy on Potsdamer Strasse because it was the major artery leading to the Kol Drellinden control point for the highways through East Germany. People wanted to leave plenty of time to travel the road through the communist country.

I pulled into one of the lines where first the Americans and then the Vopos would check my papers. It was going to be a long wait, and there is nothing more frustrating for a biker than getting stuck in traffic. I waited nervously, shifting the bike from side to side, foot to foot, occasionally flipping my wrist to rev the engine and walking the bike slowly forward without dismounting, as the traffic inched toward the border.

Finally I came to the American gate. The MP stepped up and said, "Papiers, bitte."

I guessed the MP wasn't much older than I was. Lucky guy, he didn't get sent to Vietnam. I took my passport and bike papers out and handed them to him.

The MP took a look, looked back at me, surprised, and said, "You American?"

"Always have been," I said.

"With the German army boots and the Berlin registration I wasn't sure, but the jeans give you away. German bikers wear leather."

"I'm not trying to fool anyone."

The MP checked the passport and the papers. "Ok," he said as he gave them back. "Which road are you going down?"

"I'm heading for the E6 to Nurnberg."

"Ever been out on these roads before?"

"No, but I've heard there's no stopping all the way."

"For the record, the East Germans built a rest stop last year because of breakdowns in the winter, but we tell people not to stop because the Vopos can cause them a lot of grief if they do. And be sure to stick to the speed limit. There are speed traps everywhere."

"Thanks for letting me know."

"You got a full tank of gas?"

"Yeah, I do."

"Have a good ride," the MP said and waved me through.

I engaged the gear and rolled slowly toward the East German gate, where I saw that I would have to wait again. I was waved into the line of cars to the left, away from the line of trucks. The trucks were pulled into a covered area where, I guessed, potential escapees couldn't jump on top of them.

All around the Eastern gate, there were fifteen-foot-high cinder block walls topped with rolls of barbed wire. I inched closer to the gates where the Vopos were scrutinizing papers closely and having people open the trunks of their cars.

Then I was the next one in line. A steel-helmeted Vopo came up to me. "Papiers, bitte."

I gave the Vopo my passport and bike papers. The Vopo looked at the passport and my face carefully. I didn't have the beard in the passport photo, so the Vopo took his time looking me over. Then the Vopo walked around to the back of the bike to check out the license plate. He didn't ask me to open the saddlebags though.

"Wohin gehst du?" the Vopo asked.

I knew what he meant. "I'm going to Nurnberg," I said, wondering what business it was of this guy. But the guy just gave me back the papers and motioned me through the gate.

I tucked the papers back into my jacket pocket, engaged the gear, and slowly accelerated away from the fearsome border post.

I had been standing in the gate traffic for a half hour and would really have liked to have gotten off the bike and stretched, but as I pulled away from the station, I saw more rolls of barbed wire and a two-story concrete guard tower with a Vopo patrolling on the balcony and a slit for a machine gun at the first level. Jesus, it was a pillbox! This was no time to stop.

I adjusted my sunglasses, so they were ready to take on the speed. I realized I wasn't going to need the map for this trip. It was a straight shot. There was only one road, an autobahn, which headed south for twenty-nine kilometers toward the junction of two autobahns, the E6, which went south to Nurnberg, and the E8, which went west to Hannover. I had to get on the E6.

As I drove away from the control point, I realized I was lucky that the timing of my enforced departure from Berlin had happened in late-April and not sooner when it could be really cold on the road.

The traffic was heavy heading toward the junction where I hoped it would thin out. I was crawling along at fifty kilometers per hour, surrounded by cars and trucks that didn't dare speed up to pass because of the East German restrictions. I was impatient to get to the junction because I figured I could put on more speed at that point.

Wild Bill had kept telling me how cool it was to get the bike up to eighty or ninety miles per hour with the wind in your hair and the skin on your face being pushed back by the airflow. I didn't like sunglasses, generally, but Bill had convinced me that they were a necessity when you rode a bike to protect your eyes from too much wind or in case a pebble or a bug hit you in the face at speed.

As the line of traffic was plodding along, I looked left and right to see double lines of barbed wire fencing with occasional guard towers on either side of the road. It was dispiriting to see what lengths the commies would go to lock up their own people.

My thoughts were still wandering when I neared the junction, and I didn't see the sign for the E6. This gave me a shock until I remembered from the map that I had to take the E8 east for two kilometers before I could pick up the E6 going south.

I gathered myself as I refocused on driving the bike. That was something the bike did to you. *You can't space out while you're riding a 594-cc, 30-horsepower, 430-pound motorcycle, or you'll be roadkill. You really have you keep it together. So forget all that other shit,* I told myself.

This being my first road trip on the BMW, I could see that the bike behaved beautifully. It sat on the road like a Rolls and was totally responsive to my commands. *I'd better be worthy of it,* I thought as I reached down and patted the BMW insignia on the gas tank and managed a half-smile.

I looked up to the right and saw the sign for the E6 to Nurnberg, and I leaned the bike over and gunned it in front of a car, which blew its horn at me. "Tough shit," I said to the other driver as I leaned the bike left up the overpass and down onto the E6.

When I got to the big road, I was happy to see that at least half the Berlin traffic had gone to Hannover and that I would be able to open up the bike a bit. Fortunately, I saw a speed limit sign right away, ninety kilometers per hour, which was fifty-six miles per hour, so I wouldn't exceed the commie speed limit. But still, it was faster than I had gone before. I cranked it up and was rewarded with a portion of that blast of wind which Wild Bill had been talking about. I checked the speedometer and was glad I had opted for a dial in kilometers per hour instead of miles per hour because it matched the road signs. I figured it would make driving in Europe a lot easier, and it was proving so.

I pulled out into the passing lane to pass a slow-moving car when I heard a blast from a big horn behind me. In the mirror, I saw a truck bearing down on me, so I lowered my right shoulder and leaned the bike back into the right lane. The truck inched by, buffeting me with its draft. Never having experienced anything like this on the bike before, I struggled to maintain control of the bike as well as my composure.

I wasn't fifty kilometers into the trip, and I was quickly learning what I didn't know. I figured if the truck could go faster, I could too, so I sped up to ninety-five kilometers per hour and found that I could leave the cars behind more easily. It seemed that family cars were more obedient to the laws. I learned that this regular traffic stayed in the right lane. You only went into the passing lane to pass. *They ought to make that a law in the States*, I thought.

My hair was flying back, and the wind rushed around my sunglasses. I could feel the wind penetrate my blue jeans and jeans jacket. I suddenly wished I had my Air Force survival jacket and realized why bikers wear leathers. I didn't want to spend the money on leather, but now I saw that the cold could be a problem. Spring in Berlin had been mild for short drives, but high-speed travel was going to require some adjustments.

I stayed in the slow lane to see if the reduced speed would help, but by now I was getting chilled, and it didn't. Then I had an idea. I had all the maps and my new gloves in the saddlebags. I could stuff the maps into my jacket arms and across my chest and stomach to deflect the wind. But I would need to pull over and stop to do this, and I was concerned about the Vopo patrols.

"To hell with it." I pulled the bike onto the shoulder, hopped off the bike, and quickly pulled the maps out of the top of the saddlebag. I unbuttoned my jacket and shoved a folded map up over each of my biceps. I unfolded two maps, plastered them onto my front, and buttoned up the jacket. Then I put on my gloves, jumped onto the bike, and gunned it up to ninety kilometers per hour, revived from the few minutes of rest. No Vopos had taken notice.

I noted the shielding effect of the maps right away, and my hands were blissfully warm. I would keep the bike at ninety kilometers per hour, which would help too. I smiled because I knew I had a knack for ingenuity and improvising, but I admitted a hope that that the sun would stay out to warm things up.

I saw a sign that read Rudolphstein-Hirshberg Kontrollpunkt, 182 kilometers. I made a quick calculation, which told me I had about two hours to go until the border. I checked my watch, eleven thirty, so I'd get to the border around two o'clock and have one of my sandwiches then. Two hours with no stops would be a stretch, but there was nothing for it. I wondered what I'd be feeling like after that much time in the saddle.

The autobahn followed a rise in the ground so I could see over the wire to the countryside, which was gently rolling farmland and woods all around. I passed a gated exit, which was closed to traffic. A sign said "Dessau."

Another half hour went by, and the autobahn rose on an overpass over another autobahn where I could see the cities of Halle on the right and Leipzig on the left in the distance. I'd been sticking to ninety-five kilometers per hour for about an hour, quickly darting out into the passing lane to pass trucks and slow cars, making excellent time. The seat was comfortable, obviously set up for distance riding. The sun was out, and it was warming me. The wind was in my hair. This was biking. What could be better?

With nothing to do but keep the bike rolling forward, it wasn't long before my thoughts returned to Eva. I could see her standing in the front door and wishing me 'bon voyage', and I felt empty in my heart. Instead of Wild Bill, she had been my last contact with anything approximating hearth and home. Did she really want to come with me? She had hatched the plan for my escape with a sureness that only could have come with some pre-plotting. But she didn't understand the management of the two of us on the bike with all our gear. Impossible.

She was a problem for me. She was fourteen years older, and I didn't know how to handle her moods. She was so contradictory, changeable, and emotional. I couldn't read her, and yet she could roil my passions at will. When I was with her, she could make me feel like a man above men by what she said and did. Sometimes it was just a gesture, a glance toward another man or woman or the way she touched me that made me feel like her king. She was fond of saying that, although after a while I got the idea that she had practice in saying it to other men before me.

Other times, when she was out of sorts, she could be short, cross, and self-absorbed. I didn't know how to approach her then so I kept my distance, which didn't improve her mood. I sensed that she needed to be stroked constantly like a cat, but I didn't have the experience to keep her purring. I felt that she could manipulate me, but I didn't fully realize how she used her sex and what she knew about lovemaking to pull my strings. I wished she had more time to instruct me in this art, like Kamala had done for Siddhartha.

I remembered what she had told me about her strict upbringing. I knew quite a few kids in college whose parents had screwed them up by being too strict. When they got out from under the parents' thumbs, they just exploded, especially these days with the world changing so fast. I felt Eva's pain in that she had been controlled for so long that she just rebelled. It had really cost her.

I smiled as I thought that Eva had been my first lover. I didn't gloat. I just realized that she was someone I had innocently bumped into with out of mutual need. She had taught me about lovemaking on different levels, but she had also imparted to me some of the subtleties of how a woman appreciates being treated as a lover. I didn't think an American woman would have done this for me. My experience of them was that they were too haughty and distant. I didn't think I could ever get close to one of them.

I had been hunched over the handlebars for quite a while and was getting stiff. How long until the border? I looked at the watch, one thirty. Wow, only a half hour to go. I dialed the bike down to seventy-five kilometers per hour and did what I could to stretch myself while riding. Once I'd gotten a few kinks out, I accelerated back up to ninety-five kilometers per hour to get to the border fast. I started to think about how hungry I was.

I came over a rise and saw signs for the border straddling the autobahn in four languages:

ACHTUNG—KONTROLLPUNKT—20km

Meaning the border was just a matter of minutes away. As I drew nearer to the buildings and gates, I noticed how the barbed wire was funneled inward toward the border post. There were the two large towers with the machine-gun slits on the bottom level funneling out toward East Germany, just like in Berlin.

I slowed the bike quickly as I saw that the traffic was backed up at the crossing. The road widened so there were two lanes for cars and two for trucks. The trucks went under a roof. All the car drivers were out of their cars opening doors and trunks, which Vopos were inspecting. The trucks had more Vopos circling around them, several with machine guns. Paperwork was being examined to the point that it was being brought into the offices for added scrutiny.

I figured it would be quite a while before I'd be called up to the gate, so I parked the bike and reached into a saddlebag to grab a sandwich. I hopped back on the bike and had eaten the whole sandwich before I was called up to the gate. It had taken a good twenty minutes, and my crotch, arms, and legs were sore from walking the bike. The only thing I was thinking about was having a beer as soon as I got across the border.

Suddenly a Vopo waving a machine gun came up to me and motioned with the gun that I had to get out of the line and go to an area where three Vopos were waiting. *What the hell?* I said to myself. *What's the problem? Maybe they don't like bikers.*

I rolled up to the three Vopos, and an officer said, " Vom Motorrad absteigen!" He motioned twice with his hand to emphasize the point that he wanted me to get off the bike. The other Vopos stepped up at the same time. I turned off the engine, quickly hopped off the bike, and pulled it onto the kickstand. The officer stuck out his hand and ordered me to produce my papers, which I did readily.

"Ah, Amerikaner," the Vopo said, giving me a sharp look.

I was getting more and more concerned. What had I done wrong? Or were these people just making up something they could detain me on? I knew the commies could do anything they wanted. The officer took his time going through my papers. Did they detect my fake motorcycle stamp?

Then he said, "Open the saddlebags."

I complied by unclipping the buckles on each bag. The Vopo bent down and methodically emptied the contents of each bag on the ground, examining each article as he took it out. There wasn't anything I could do about it, but what had I done? And why me?

The Vopo looked at the sleeping bag on the back of the bike and poked at it with his hand. He ordered me to take it off and unroll it. Then he slowly walked around the bike, examining everything before stopping face-to-face in front of me. "Why did you stop and get off up there?" he said, pointing back up the autobahn.

"I wanted to get out a sandwich to eat."

"It is forbidden to stop and get out on the autobahn!" the Vopo said in his most overbearing, bureaucratic voice. He waited until that pronouncement had sunk into my brain. Then he said, "Pack your bags and proceed to the control point."

This encounter unnerved me. I realized I was shaking a bit, but at the same time, I cursed under my breath the dark forces of the communist mindset as I shoved my stuff back into the saddlebags as best I could. I'd had encounters with police before, especially my speeding escapades, and there was that time I'd almost walked into a pot bust, but the cops had worked within legal boundaries. Here, I had just gotten off my bike to get a sandwich, and I'd gotten the third degree.

"Fuck these guys!" I muttered.

I folded my stuff into the bags and then got back on the bike and walked it over to the line of cars looking for an opening. A guy in a grey Opel leaned out his window and waved me in front of him. I figured he had seen what the Vopos had done to me, so he was offering a kindness. I waved back my thanks and moved into the line.

When I came up to the East German border guards, they thoroughly examined my papers as though they had never seen me before. I kept saying "Fuck these guys!" to myself but maintained a smile on my face. I got the papers back, started up the bike, and headed for West Germany.

At the border, a huge West German border guard in a forest-green uniform came up to ask for my papers. He was so big that he didn't need to carry a machine gun to be as intimidating as the Vopos.

"Papiers, bitte."

"Here you go," I said as I handed them over.

"Ah. American. So you are the motorcyclist we saw the Vopos giving such trouble to. What was the cause?"

"I stopped to get a sandwich out of my saddlebag."

"Ach, so. That is against the rules over there, and they love their rules. I see that your bags are in something of a mess. Where are you going?"

"I'm headed to Vienna."

"You should spend the night near here. Vienna is a long ride. Maybe two days by motorcycle."

"That's a good idea. I was planning on going to Bayreuth, but that's an hour away. Do you know of someplace closer?"

"You could try Munchberg, about forty kilometers down the road. There are a couple of Gasthofs there."

"Danke. I'm quite tired. I will go there."

The guard gave me back my papers and waved me through the gate. I couldn't help but be struck by the difference in the attitudes of the Eastern and the Western German guards. Those people who escaped communism after the war sure made the right choice.

I got the bike up to ninety kilometers per hour before I realized that some of my stuff was hanging out of the saddlebags and I only had forty kilometers to go to get to Munchberg. That was only twenty minutes or so. Boy, could I use a shower and a beer!

I looked around as I drove into West Germany and saw that something was missing: the fences! Without them, I could see as far as I could see. The colors of the West German countryside seemed to be brighter, as if the fences cast a specter over the landscape the way the communist government cast the shadow of repression over their peoples' spirit.

I checked again to see if it were my imagination, but no, the ride through East Germany had shown me an entire country that was dirty in a way the sun itself couldn't show as being clean. In the West, everything seemed to be brighter, cleaner, and more robust. Here were sun-dappled fields and woods in honest greens, browns, and yellows. In the distance, I saw wood-beamed, white-and-brown houses and red barns.

I came up to the exit sign for Munchberg and turned left, entering by the main street, slowly passing a few shops and a market. I drove down the street until I found a gas station that had a restroom. The mechanic who came to fill out to fill the tank was very impressed by the bike. I let him ogle it while I went to wash up. When I paid the guy, I asked him where I could find a gasthof, and he told me that there was one just a kilometer down the road.

I drove into the small parking lot in front of the gasthof, which looked like it was taken from a travel poster of Germany. It was a large white house with wood beams and a sharply pitched roof that had a gable with two small windows in it. There were four windows on the ground floor, two on each side of the large-beamed wooden front door and four windows on the second floor. The windows all had flower boxes in them with colorful flowers spilling out of them. I wondered if this picture-perfect place would take in a grimy American biker, but I was tired and hungry enough to give it a shot.

I walked up the front steps and knocked on the door. No one came so I opened the door and found myself in a room with winter gear and coats hanging on hooks. I went through another door and was in a large living room with stuffed sofas and chairs surrounding a fireplace on one side and a dining area with a table and chairs on the other side. There was a fireplace on that side as well. A flight of stairs led to the upper floors in front of me. I realized that I was actually in someone's home and felt I was an intruder.

I was about to go back outside when I heard a woman's voice calling out from behind the dining area, "Wer its da? Ich komme!"

The voice had a pleasant lilt to it. Little bells rang in the vowels, and I knew that "Ich komme" meant "I'm coming" as an innkeeper would welcome a guest.

The woman appeared from behind a swinging door into the dining room, and as soon as she saw me, her hand flashed up to her mouth, and her eyes opened wide. I recognized that she was shocked by my filthy appearance, but I managed to ask if she had a room for the night.

The woman, who looked to be about fifty and was dressed in a white blouse and a flower-patterned skirt of traditional German country style, gathered herself by using her hands to smooth her skirt. She calmly looked me over and asked, "Motoradderfahrer?"

"Yes. I just drove my motorcycle down from Berlin. It was my first long ride, and I'm quite tired. I could use dinner and a bed for the night."

She brightened up and said, "Ah. Amerikaner. Motoradderfahrer. Sehr gut. Comme. Comme." She gestured for me to come into the dining room and sit at the table. I was surprised that she actually seemed pleased at my arrival.

The woman said, "I speak a little English, yes? But my husband, he speaks good English. He will be back soon, and you can speak English with him. So you want a room for the night?"

"Yes, one night, please."

"Sehr gut," she said and brought the guest log over for me to sign and asked for my papers.

I gave her my passport and bike papers, and she entered the number in the box next to my name. Then she looked at the bike's papers, and her eye grew wide.

"BMW Motorrad?" she asked.

"Yes, it's a BMW."

"Wunderbar!" Then she put my papers in the sideboard. I figured that was customary in country inns to ensure payment. "You wish to eat?"

"Yes, please," I said. I was starving.

The woman motioned for me to come upstairs to see the room, but I gestured that I needed to get my bags from the bike. She waited while I brought all my stuff, which had been disordered by the Vopos. I hoped it was all still there.

I was led up a flight of stairs, where there were four doors. The woman opened one and ushered me into one of them, a small room with a nicely made bed with a duvet on it and a crucifix over it. There was a table, chair, and standing lamp. The window had ruffled white curtains and looked out over the parking lot, where I could see the bike.

"Ist es gut?" she asked.

"Ya, ist gut."

The woman made some gestures, which I understood to mean washing up, and she handed me a towel from a hook behind the door. She led me across the hall and showed me the bathroom and the WC and indicated that dinner would be ready soon. I thanked her and went into the bathroom and showered, gratefully. I went up and dressed in a clean pair of jeans and a sports shirt and repacked my bags. I then went downstairs to wait for dinner, which smelled deliciously all over the house. I could hardly wait.

I sat in one of the stuffed chairs and thought that this had been a unique day for me, and that my plans going forward had to be flexible as far as details were concerned. Bill's father had been a wild card. And what about Helmut? He had almost closed me out. Driving that distance on the bike wasn't easy, but I'd taken care of it, although the Vopos had scared the shit out of me. But I had moved past those obstacles. I needed the challenge of gaining experience of the world on my own, and I was creating solutions for myself.

13

Hans' Story

THE SMELL OF THE dinner was making my mouth water so I decided to go out and check on the bike. When I opened the front door, I saw a man walking around the bike, examining it intently. He was dressed in a grey suit with green lapel stripes of German provincial fashion. His long grey pants had a thin, green stripe down the outer seam. He had on a white shirt with a dark-green tie.

He turned toward me as I approached him, and I saw that he appeared much older than I might have thought, yet he appeared very fit. His face was deeply tanned with many creases and wrinkles in it. The wrinkles came into full play as the man smiled, put out his hand, and said, "Ist dis dein Motorrad?"

"Yes, it's mine," Jack said.

"Ah. You speak English. Are you British or American?"

"I'm American."

"Very good. Where have you come from?"

"I just drove down from Berlin."

"That would be a pleasant ride if it weren't for the Vopos."

"That's true. They gave me a hard time at the border."

"Really. For what reason?"

"I stopped to take a sandwich out of my pack."

"Ha! That would set them off. I'm sorry you had to endure that. Are you staying here for the night?"

"Yes, I am."

"Well then, you must have met my wife, Lisa. She has settled you in your room?"

"Yes, I'm just waiting for dinner."

"As I am. Lisa is an excellent cook. Come let us go in."

As we went into the gasthof, the man introduced himself as Hans, and I introduced myself. Hans seated me at the dinner table and went to the kitchen through the swinging door. When he returned, he was holding two large crockery steins and two bottles of Psorrbrau beer. He gave me one and proceeded to pour his own. I did the same.

He then stood up and said, "Welcome to my guest and fellow motorcyclist. Please drink with me. I'm sure your ride has made you thirsty."

I needed no encouragement. I lifted my stein and said, "Prost."

Hans said "Prost" and drained off half his stein. He smiled, and the cracks and wrinkles animated his face like a small tremor would have moved a dry riverbed.

"So, my friend, you have a brand-new BMW R60/5, which you must have bought at the factory in Spandau. I saw from that odometer that you haven't driven enough kilometers to have left Berlin except this one time. You must be on your first journey on this machine. Where are you going to?"

"I am on my way to Vienna; but after that I'm not certain. I'd like go to Athens and then to Crete," I said.

"How did you know where I have been just by looking at my bike.?" I asked.

Hans didn't say anything. His eyes took on a faraway look for a minute. Finally, he broke out of his trance and said, "Crete. I lost some fine friends on Crete."

He guzzled the rest of his beer and went to get another for both him and me, although I hadn't finished half of mine.

He came back and said, "Please excuse my questions, but you see, I am a motorcycle rider myself. I have a motorcycle in my barn, which I have journeyed far on. Would you like to see it?"

I was hoping to get to bed soon after dinner, but here was a guy who must have had motorcycle adventures, and he wanted to talk with me, so I said, "Sure. That would be great."

"Well then, drink up. I hear my wife coming with the dinner."

Lisa brought out a tray, piled high with various sausages, home fries, and cucumber salad. Hans had his plate filled while Lisa spoke with him before Hans started to eat. Lisa looked at me and patted me on the shoulder as she served me. I recognized the bratwurst but couldn't identify the other meats. They were all good. I wasn't sure about the cucumber salad, but at least it wasn't sauerkraut.

Hans said, "I have been saying to Lisa that you are starting on an adventure on your BMW. She says to me that I should tell you about my adventures, which started my love of motorcycles. I don't like to talk about it, but she says it would be good for me, and you might learn something, so I tonight I will make the exception, if you want to listen."

I was more than willing, and I told Hans so. We finished our dinner and moved into the stuffed chairs in the living room. Lisa brought Hans another beer, but I declined.

"How many years have you? How old?" Hans asked me.

"Twenty-three."

Hans began,

> *My adventure began in the Hitler Youth when I was fourteen. This was 1935. I was a flag-bearer in the games in the Olympiastadion in 1936. It was very exciting time for a young person. The Hitler Youth began to train more in 1937 as if we were Wehrmacht. I was a good athlete, so I stood out and was given more difficult training like mountain climbing. I still like to climb mountains, although I am getting too old for the higher peaks.*

> *In 1939, I was assigned to a motorcycle unit because I was strong and could handle the machine. When war began, I was a courier for a headquarters unit in Poland. It was an easy time except for when it rained because Poland had mostly dirt roads. I had to be strong to make the machine go in the mud. That's not something you will have to worry about, ya?*

Hans smiled at me and gulped some more beer. He continued,

> *That part of the war was over fast, so then they sent me to parachute school. That was a crazy time, but we were young and had many good times with the jumping and the training. The officers let us 'sich austoben', how you say, 'blow off steam.' We were young and training as an elite group.*

Hans paused again, and I could see his eyes take on a look that saw well past the walls of the gasthof. He took a sip of beer and continued,

> *My Fliger attacked and captured Fort Eben-Email in Belgium on the day the Western war began. It was a great coup for us, and we received citations. I won an Iron Cross. This war was over fairly quickly as well. We were on top of the world. I was your age, a decorated veteran soldier.*
>
> *From there we went back into training, but now I was an instructor. The army was building parachute divisions, and the old hands had to teach the new boys how to jump and fight. Half the new men were older than I was, but I had more than a hundred jumps, so I was a man for them, and they were eager to learn from me. There is something about jumping out of an airplane that hardens the hoden, ya? Ha, ha, ha!*

I looked at Hans, not understanding his last remark. Hans reached down and grabbed his crotch and jerked up on it. I got the message.

"Have you ever jumped?" he asked me. I shook my head no.

"You should try it once at least. It will steel your nerves. But riding a Motorrad from Berlin to Crete for your first ride is a fair proxy, I think, ya?" Hans reached over to smack the back of my hand as he said this.

I could see that Hans was a little lit up from the beer and that he was really into the old times. I thought it was fantastic I had run into a guy who had these stories and could actually tell them in English. I wondered why Hans needed a nudge from his wife to tell his war stories because it seemed to have been a great time in his youth. It had made him a man. I found myself staring at Hans in admiration.

Hans saw my look. "I see you have some interest in my story, so I will continue, but maybe without so much beer. Lisa! Bring out the dessert, so I can eat and finish my story without being confused in the head."

Hans sat back in his chair as Lisa brought out the Obstkaltschale, which I discovered was a fabulous fruit pudding we could eat from bowls while sitting in our chairs. We enjoyed the pudding in silence for a while before Hans picked up his story again.

So I was promoted to lieutenant and made a jump-instructor in charge of a Flieger of men although I was just twenty-two years old. There was no fighting for us for the rest of 1940. I think those were the best times of my life. We trained, we jumped, and we had girls and kamerades. Then Hitler decided to invade Greece, which the army did, and the British retreated from Greece into Crete. So Crete had to be taken, and it was decided that the paratroops could do its best.

It was May 1941. Germany was winning the war everywhere. We owned Europe. Rommel had taken the Afrika Corps almost to Cairo. We were invincible. The army did not suffer many losses in Greece, until we dropped into Crete.

Hans paused, and his eyes grew misty. His wrinkled face exhibited the effect of a slow-motion landslide, as his features turned downward at the corners of the eyes and the mouth, pulling the face into a wizened grimace.

We dropped into Crete: nine thousand paratroops and five thousand glider-borne troops. The British and the partisans were waiting for us. They cut us to pieces. We regrouped and called for reinforcements. My unit took an airfield near Heraklion, which allowed for reinforcements to come in. Once we had the men, we chased the British over the mountains to the east.

Hans paused for a moment.

You know Crete is very mountainous. Some peaks reach twenty-four hundred meters, and the roads there are more like goat tracks. You must be very careful if you ride a Motorrad there.

I thought for a moment and realized that twenty-four hundred meters was eight thousand feet. I hadn't thought about facing that kind of a challenge on the road.

Once we had cleared the enemy off the island, we counted our dead. My Flieger had suffered 70 percent casualties. Others had suffered the same. The high command decided that paratroops would not be used again because of the cost, so they broke up our units. Most went to invade Russia with the army. Of my friends who went there, I never saw any again.

Hans dropped his head and shook it slowly side to side. I could see that his memories deeply affected him. I thought that Lisa might have nudged him to tell the stories to get the pain out of his system. I was young and just starting out on a motorcycle with no war stories of my own to relate to. Or maybe there weren't too many Germans who wanted to listen to old war stories the way things turned out for Germany.

Hans continued,

> *If I had been sent to the Eastern front, I would not be telling any stories today, but because I had been a motorcyclist, I was sent to join the Afrika Corps as a headquarters liaison officer. Rommel had requested motorcycle troops because of the constant movement in the front. There were no real roads. The sand was hard in some places; in others, it had been blown away from the rock underneath, but if you went into deep sand, you could be in trouble. I had to haul my Motorrad back to a place where I could ride it several times.*

> *We had a good time of it until El Alamein. That battle was a nightmare. It lasted ten days. The heat, the smoke, the noise, and the bugs were maddening. In the end, the British had too many tanks, and they broke through our lines. Hitler told Rommel to stand until the last man, but Rommel wouldn't sacrifice his army for a strip of desert, so he retreated.*

> *Unfortunately, not everyone got the message, and some units were left surrounded. A British tanker captured me. It was not easy for a German officer to surrender, I assure you, but there it was. I was shipped to Canada for internment, so the war was definitely over for me.*

He smiled a bit ruefully as he stood up, indicating that his story had come to an end. "That's where I learned to speak English. Danke for listening to my story. It relieves my mind. Now, come. I will show you why I have told you my story."

He led me outside to the back of the house, where there was a barn with a light on over the double doors. Hans opened one of the doors, led me inside, and turned on the lights, and I saw that we were in a full-scale garage.

There were two BMW cars of indeterminate vintage, but I could see that they were in pristine condition. I saw that on one wall there were automotive tools of all descriptions hanging in neatly over workbenches, which were clear of any debris.

Hans stood between the two cars. "These are my kamerades of my later years. I drive this one, and Lisa drives that one. If I don't let her have one to drive, she won't cook for me, ya? Ha! Ha! But over here is why I brought you out."

Hans went to the side of the garage, where I saw something covered by a tarp. He turned on a light and lifted the tarp to reveal an older-model BMW motorcycle. Like the cars, it was in pristine condition. I saw that it was longer and lower than my bike, but there were the telltale BMW dual-protruding cylinders and the signature BMW shaft drive. The paint job was vintage BMW black with white pinstripes.

"Wow. She's a beauty," I said.

"This is the R75 model, which I had in the desert. Of course, it is not the same Motorrad. I found this one after I returned from the war and restored it using parts. This model was made before or during the war because the factory was bombed, and production was prohibited for a time after the war."

He swung his leg over the bike and settled in the saddle. "This is a great machine. It could go all day on the desert and not overheat. Very little maintenance, although we'd have to beg a liter of oil from the tankers from time to time, but that was all. Would you like to climb on?"

I nodded, and Hans made way to trade places. I kept my feet spread apart as I put my hands on the handlebars. Right away I could tell that this bike was heavier than mine. I looked back to check the length. Steering would be a problem too, especially off-road. Did Hans say he had to carry the bike out of the sand? Holy shit. Hans must be a moose.

"This bike is pretty heavy," I said.

"Ya, ya. That's because this one has a steel frame. Yours has aluminum. I take it out for a ride from time to time, sometimes on the autobahn to Nurnberg for speed, sometimes for a ride on the country roads along the Czech border where there is little traffic.

Riding this machine on pavement is like riding a car for me. It is so stable, but I have much practice, no? Ha! Ha!"

I had nothing to say to that. I'd ridden a total of six hundred or so kilometers total in my life, and here I was sitting on a bike that could have seen action in WWII and listening to a veteran who had logged thousands of kilometers on BMWs. I was regressing to feeling small and boyish. I had nothing to say to Hans, so I swung my leg off the bike and backed away while looking at it with a combination of admiration and awe.

Hans saw the look on my face and clapped me on the shoulder. "Enough of my stories, eh? I think maybe you want some sleep. You have to get up early if you are going to make Vienna tomorrow."

He led me back to the house and wished me a good sleep. I went upstairs and undressed. It had been a long day on the road. Those commie bastards had pissed me off, but I'd made it to a nice place to crash. I really enjoyed Hans' stories, but they had tired me out, too. I set the alarm for seven, crawled under the heavy duvet, and was quickly enveloped by an all-consuming sleep.

14

I Ride with Hans

I SLEPT SO SOUNDLY that I barely heard the alarm. I opened my eyes and looked up to see the sharply angled ceiling of the dormer in my room and thought for a moment I was in my apartment in college. But I quickly figured out that I was in a different place and time. I looked out the window to see my bike in the driveway to confirm my thought. I also saw that it was past dawn, and I had to get moving if I were going to get to Vienna today. It was almost five hundred kilometers, a longer trip than I drove yesterday, and that one had been an effort. Well, at least I wouldn't have to deal with the commies today.

I got dressed and looked in the mirror. I wanted to see a man standing there, but after listening to Hans' story, I knew I had to experience more of the world before I had the *hoden*, the manliness, which would bring me to that point. Having had a woman was a vital step, but gaining more experience of the world was essential.

It was amazing to hear all the things Hans had done by the time he was my age. Of course, history had thrust Hans into his part, and I couldn't equate WWII with Vietnam, if that were to be my proving ground.

It's too early to be thinking like this, I said to myself as I finished packing the saddlebags. I went downstairs and smelled sausages frying and coffee brewing. Lisa had heard me clomping down the stairs and poked her head out of the kitchen to say "frustuck kommt" as she pointed to the table for me to sit.

I sat, but before Lisa came out with the breakfast, Hans came in from outside. "Guten morgen," he said. "You slept well."

"Yes, I did. Very well."

"Very good. Let us eat our breakfast. I have decided that the R75 needs some exercise. And I need some fresh air today. I will accompany you to Passau. Lisa! Wo ist das frustuck?"

Lisa quickly appeared carrying a large tray with plates of sausage and scrambled eggs, a basket of bread, a crock of butter, and a pot of jam, which she left for Hans to distribute while she went back to the kitchen for the coffee.

I was thrilled to have a companion to ride with on the road, especially a biker who knew the back roads in the region. I could learn from Hans' biking experience too. It was 160 kilometers to Passau, so that was no short round trip for Hans, but I figured Hans would just enjoy himself on a day's outing.

We ate our breakfast in silence but with relish. Lisa could really cook. When we were done, I called to Lisa to ask how much I owed for the night and the meals. She looked at Hans and then back at me and asked for forty marks.

I paid Lisa and thanked her very much. She gave me a peck on the cheek and said, "Gute Reise."

Hans said that meant "bon voyage" in German.

I picked up my gear and went outside to see that Hans had been up early getting the R75 ready for the road. It was gleaming in the sunshine. I thought the black paint gave it a look of greater bulk than the silver of my bike, but it definitely was longer. I clipped my gear on the bike, put on my sunglasses and gloves, swung my leg over the seat, and settled into position.

Hans was on his bike already, wearing an old pair of goggles. He gave the kick-starter a hefty shove, and the engine purred to life. I pushed the electric starter to turn on my bike. It galled me to see Hans use his strength to fire up his machine while I only needed to push a button. I thought there was something of the wuss in it next to Hans.

Hans was watching me and guessed at my thoughts. "The electric starter is a nice innovation. I would like one of those in future years. Ha! Ha! Come, we are off!"

He pulled away from the gasthof, heading south out of Munchberg. I followed behind, but Hans waved at me to come up and ride alongside.

"Always ride together, in tandem," Hans shouted. "It lets the auto drivers know who's boss. Ha! Ha! Now we go to Bayreuth. Stay close as we pass through the city. Then we go on Route 22 in open country. Very nice ride."

I had thought of going to Vienna solely on the autobahns so I wouldn't get lost, so it was great to have the chance to see the countryside on secondary roads and with a guide. I gave Hans the thumbs-up sign. Hans smiled and increased his speed; I followed suit. We passed through Bayreuth and took a short stretch of autobahn before turning off onto Route 22.

We motored along at seventy kilometers per hour in the warming sunshine of early morning. It was a glorious day. We passed small farms where I could see men working in the fields, with their tractors plowing up the soil. The fields being tilled gave off the pungent aroma of receptive earth.

We passed through stands of woods, which separated the open farmland. The woods were cool with the scent of pine and cedar being held in the air by the morning moisture. Some woods were several kilometers long, and these made it appear as if we were in a broken tunnel of green.

We rode through several hamlets, the names of which were marked by signs, but we were traveling too fast for me to pick up the long German names. The road wound lazily through the countryside, allowing us to softly roll our machines from side to side to make the turns, hardly using the handlebars. This technique wasn't new to me, but I improved by watching Hans who barely moved when navigating a curve.

I loved being totally out in the open on the bike. Without having to worry about traffic like on the autobahn, I was less tense, yet I could remain focused. I saw that Hans was concentrating on driving, but he was comfortable as well and enjoying the experience. I thought about how wearing a helmet would deaden the experience. I looked over at Hans, who didn't wear a helmet either, as a reassurance of my thought.

I noticed that the air had warmed, and the sun was topping out over the trees in the wooded areas we drove through. I looked at my watch. We'd been driving for almost an hour and a half, yet I wasn't tired at all. This kind of cruising was really a pleasure.

Hans waved his hand, signaling we should pull into a turnoff ahead. When we stopped and got off the bikes, Hans took off his goggles and ran his fingers through his hair. He didn't look as if he'd had any more exercise than if he'd walked across the street.

"You like the ride?" he asked.

"It was fantastic."

"Very good. I see that you have begun to relax. Young drivers always seem to be tense. They want to control the motion of the Motorrad, especially with their hands and arms. You must allow your legs and lower body to control the direction of the machine, especially with a BMW. You have good coordination, so practice this."

I couldn't figure out how Hans could have observed me so well because I never saw him look over at me, but I understood what Hans was saying, so I took it to heart.

"So in a few minutes, we will pass into the village of Chem. The streets are not wide, so follow behind me. From Chem, we will go to Passau, about an hour's ride, through forests and up and down hills. A wunderbar drive! Then we will have lunch in Passau, and I will leave you to your journey."

We passed through Chem, where I saw old houses with tall ornamentation over the upper windows that looked like whipped cream on top of cakes. We went over the river Regen bridge, and then we were on the open road again when Hans motioned for me to come back alongside him.

There were more woods, and the sun was fully overhead, casting dappled shadows onto the road like I had never seen while riding in a car. Greens, yellows, and browns surrounded us on the ground, while blues, whites, and greys popped out from between black branches above. The experience was totally immersive at the leisurely pace of seventy kilometers per hour, which Hans had set. I noted that Hans was looking around at the scenery, too.

This is what biking was all about! It was glorious! Without Hans, I wouldn't have seen it. I felt happy in the moment and reflected that Wild Bill had told me how cool it was out on his Sportster. But Bill hadn't told me about the sensory experience. Maybe he couldn't express it in words. Or maybe the American road had an element of danger to it for bikers that Bill didn't want to admit, especially considering *Easy Rider*.

Bill was a born biker, tall and muscular, as well as a born risk-taker, so I figured it wouldn't have mattered to him. He just kept his thoughts on those subjects from me if he had any. I had let Bill talk me into buying the bike, which was going to be my proving ground where I would separate myself from my uncertainty, my insecurity, and my inner fears, and today's experience made me think it was going to work out.

At this point, I realized, despite my newly relaxed attitude on the bike, that biking was work, and I was getting hungry. About twenty minutes or so from Passau, we began a descent from the hills and entered a town called Tiefenbach. Hans motioned to me to fall in behind him until we had gone through the town. When we formed up again, we passed downhill through woods for a few kilometers, and suddenly there was a broad river in front of us. I knew this was the Danube, but it wasn't blue like in Strauss' waltz. It was grey-green, flowing powerfully from west to east. Across the river was the city of Passau.

Hans took the road along the north bank of the river into the town of Hecklberg where he turned off into a parking lot in front of a biergarten. We got off the bikes, and Hans came over and put his arm around my shoulders.

"That was a fine ride, yes? I haven't come through the Bavarian National Forest in some time, but I don't forget how beautiful it is. The air cleans the senses, yes?"

He led me through a darkened entryway into the main hall where there were long tables and benches set up parallel to each other and a bandstand at the end of the hall. The ceiling was high, under a pitched roof. I could imagine some roaring, beer-swilling evenings in here with an oomp-pa-pa band blowing and everyone singing, but at lunchtime the hall was empty.

Hans went up a staircase at the far side of the hall and opened a pair of double doors. I followed, and there, below us, was the Danube flowing under our feet. We were standing on a balcony that overhung the river. People were having lunch at a dozen tables, which were set near the railing. It was a spectacular scene with the river below, stretching toward the city, which angled upwards on a series of hills.

Hans found a waitress and ordered beer and sausage for two and plopped down on a chair and motioned for me to join him. When he sat down, he checked the time, one fifteen. "We made good time, considering I wanted to go slow enough to take in the scenery."

"It was a beautiful ride."

"Yes. But I will go a little faster on the way back. I want to be home before dark, and more speed will remind me of my youth. Ha! Ha!"

I smiled. Speed was one of the things youth was all about. I certainly liked to speed in cars. But why? With speed, you just got from one place where you didn't know what was going on to another where you didn't know what was going on, only faster. What was the point? And I was always speeding. My car was just an extension of my thought process. I wanted to get away from uncertain ground as fast as possible but never could find the solid ground. While I was driving, I was in control of the mode of transport, but when I arrived, I always found that I had found nothing new.

It took me a number of years and a lot of frustration to glean that the change of scene wasn't the answer. I had come to Europe using that same old formula, but this time I was determined I would find experiences that were new and would prove that I could grow into a man.

Hans hadn't heard anything from me for a couple of minutes so he said, "You are having some deep thoughts."

"Yeah, I guess so. I was thinking that I've been traveling a lot, especially since I got out of college last year. I'm looking for something, some set of answers about life, but I'm not sure if I even know the right questions. I thought that if I came over here to Europe, I might find a new perspective and some answers about life, like 'Who I Am?' and 'What is my place in the world?' I read *Siddhartha*, which was written by Herman Hesse, who was a German, but I didn't get all of it because he wrote about Eastern philosophy. Do you know what I mean?"

I had the feeling that I had gone too far, spilling my innermost thoughts to a guy I had known for less than twenty-four hours. Hans had turned to look at the river with the faraway look in his eyes from last evening. He continued to watch the water move with its unending force, sometimes revealing its strength in a swirl or an eddy.

Finally, he said, "Last evening I told you something of my youth, which was directed at every turn by the Nazi state. My brothers and sisters in the Hitler Youth pledged our lives to Hitler. By the time I was your age, my kamerades in the paratroops were dying for Hitler, but we were also fighting to save ourselves. We were not individuals with time to think of such questions. We did what the state told us and did not question. Of course, we look back now and see that we should have questioned many things, but then it was not possible. What you speak of is philosophy, which I missed in my youth. I came to it later in life, which may be better because it is profound and requires experience and understanding.

"There was a man who lived in Constantinople in the sixth century, a general named Boethius, who fell from grace and was imprisoned and executed. While he was in prison, he wrote *The Consolation of Philosophy*, in which he said that suffering was a necessary step in forming one's own philosophy. That spoke to me. And I have read Kant, Schopenhauer, and Hegel, and yes, I have read Hesse also. And I have lived through good times and terrible days, so I have found a philosophy for myself." He looked me straight in the eye. "So I know very well what you are talking about."

He made me feel quite small as he said this, but he did not say it unkindly.

"Because of the circumstances of our lives, we have had to find our paths at different times, which will cause a necessary divergence. I am settled on my path, but you are just in the process of finding yours. I think you have made a good decision to take this motorcycle trip. The experiences you will encounter will help you form your philosophy. Everyone should go on such a journey of the soul, but not many do. You should not complain that the story of Siddhartha is an Eastern tale. The point is that Siddhartha passes through many phases of experience, always searching, until he finds what he needs. It is a universal story, which is what makes it so powerful."

I listened to Hans intently, hearing what I knew were truths about life from a man who had experienced much of it. I felt Hans' words penetrate my consciousness and wished I could hear more, but I knew it was to be short-lived. We had talked through lunch, and now Hans finished his beer, wiped his mouth on the back of his sleeve, and then motioned for the waitress to bring the bill.

"My young friend, I must go home, or Lisa will think I have gone to Crete with you. Ha! Ha! Now here's what you should do. You should take the route that follows the Danube to Vienna. It is Route 150, a small road that borders the river all the way to Vienna. It is a beautiful ride! You can join it just north of Hecklberg. It is too late for you to reach Vienna before dark in any case, and you don't want to take the autobahn at night. When you get to Linz, take Route 3 to Perg, where there is a nice gasthof and biergarten. The next day you can reach Vienna in three hours easily."

Hans got up and left money for lunch on the table, as I did. When we got to the bikes, Hans reached out to shake my hand, smiling broadly with all the wrinkles on his face in motion. He held my hand as he said, "I have enjoyed meeting you and riding with you. You make a fine Kamerade. Our riding together has brought me back to the best days of my youth. As for you, I would suggest that you do not think so much about yourself or seek the answers so hard. Siddhartha found that in seeking, one focuses too much on one thing and misses everything else around him. You must find the unity in all things. Then your path will be clear. But I bore you! I must go. Danke for your pleasant company and much success on your journey. Gut Reise."

Hans swung his right leg onto the R75 and stomped down hard with his left leg on the kick-starter. The bike purred to life. Hans gunned the engine a couple of times and then waved as he shot off down the road, and he was gone around a curve in a moment.

15

To Vienna

I watched Hans disappear down the road, feeling that I had lost something unique, a lifelong friend I had known for less than a day, a guide into the world I must now discover for myself. Hans knew the questions and the answers. I stood alone; empty despite having been filled with the richness of Hans' wisdom.

I got on the bike, wishing I had taken notes over lunch, and started it up, remembering that Hans had told me to go to Linz and then find a gasthof in Perg. I was feeling satisfied that Hans had told me that I had made the right decision in coming to Europe to prove myself. All the people back home just hung around and talked about life. Out on the road, life happened. I wouldn't have found anything if I had stayed home.

It had been a real boost to have run into Hans, not just because Hans had been so kind, but because of what Hans had revealed about his thoughts. From what Hans said, I could make the inference that, despite all the disconnects I had with others at college and with Piet, there was a pattern to the lives of people of my age, and there was something universal about Siddhartha's journey. Those who chose to go on the journey were searching for a Truth, exactly what I couldn't tell yet, but it was out there on the road, waiting for me to find it.

I realized I was getting ahead of myself. I'd only been on the road for two days, and while Hans had clarified various lines of thought I'd been pursuing, I knew inside that I was still the same old Jack until I could build more self-esteem for myself. Hans had laid some more bricks on that foundation for me, but I needed to add experience to put myself together as a man.

The fact that I wasn't sure where I'd be sleeping that night got me moving. I looked at the map and saw that I would have to follow Route 150, as Hans had said, and then cross the German-Austrian border by the river in twenty kilometers. After that, I'd go to Linz, which was about eighty kilometers. Then I'd pick up Route 3 to Perg, which was another thirty kilometers.

As I drove along with the smooth-flowing, grey-green river on my right, I saw that the woods came down to the edge of the road, making green walls of the hills, which formed the riverbanks. The two-lane road had been cut into the bank and was shored up in places with boulders, which the water caressed as it flowed past. I had a leisurely ride with slow curves following the course of the river. The sun cast shadows from behind as the afternoon progressed.

As I took a curve at sixty kilometers per hour, I passed into the hamlet of Jochenstein, which was at a chokepoint between the hills and the river. When I came out into the open again, I saw a sign that said the Austrian border was two hundred meters ahead. I approached it and was surprised to see that there was just one guardhouse on one side of the road with a single white metal swinging fence blocking the road.

I pulled up to the fence and waited and waited. Then I saw two uniformed men walking down a dirt path from a larger house about thirty yards up the hill. One was dressed in the green of the German border police; the other was in a brown uniform. I supposed he must be his Austrian counterpart. The Austrian had a kepi on his head with a clutch of three-inch hair bristles sticking up at the front. I thought they looked ridiculous, but I knew better than to antagonize border guards after my run-in with the Vopos yesterday.

However, I could see right away that this was going to be a completely different kind of encounter. As the guards approached, the two guards were bantering with each other. One would shout something, and the other would laugh and return the favor. Strolling down the hill in this jocular manner, they showed themselves to be friends.

As they approached me, I expected the usual "papiers, bitte," but the German took one look at the bike and started to wax eloquent over it. His pal was equally enthusiastic and began to ask me questions in German. I had to pull out my passport and tell them I was an American and didn't speak much German.

Neither of the guards spoke passable English, so they had to use sign language and pidgin English. They wanted to know where I had come from.

"Berlin."

"Zehr gut."

"Wo hast du das Motorrad gekauft?"

"In the BMW factory in Spandau."

"Zehr gut."

"Wohin gehst du?"

"Vienna and then to Athens."

"Wunderbar!"

By pointing at his watch, the Austrian indicated that Vienna was a long way and that I should stop for the night. I said "Ya," knowing that Hans had advised me to stop in Perg.

The sun was going down, and here I was being lectured to by a couple of bumbling border guards who reminded me of Laurel and Hardy and realizing that I was in the middle of nowhere and needed a bed and a meal. The thought of using my sleeping bag outdoors for the first time crossed my mind, so I pulled the map out of my waistband.

At the sight of the map, the Austrian brightened and held out his hand to see it. When I handed it over, the guard pointed to Linz and said "gasthof" while pointing to the far side of the city. He explained it was just past the Bahnhof, which was marked on the map. I said again that Perg was where I wanted to go, but he was insistent that I should go to Linz, and he kept pointing at his watch, indicating that Perg was too far at this time of day.

Finally, I gave in and said, "Danke," to him. I was about to drive on as the German and opened the gate for me to cross the border, but before I started up the bike, the Austrian shouted, "Halt! Papiers, bitte!"

In trying to help me out with my accommodations, these clowns had forgotten to stamp my passport with an entry to Austria. I knew that this was an essential to foreign travel, so I quickly handed over the passport, which the Austrian took to the guardhouse to stamp. He returned the document with a sheepish grin on his face.

As I left the border, the shadow I cast on the road was lengthening in front of me as the sun went down at my back. I had to continue to take the river road because it was the only road to get to Linz from where I was, although it was slow and winding. I figured I'd make it to Linz just before sunset.

The hills cast darker and deeper shadows as I progressed, so as I came closer to Linz and noticed that there were more cars on the road, I turned on my headlamp to make myself seen in the gloaming. I didn't think biking at night in the country was going to be a good idea going forward.

There were streetlights in Linz, so it was easy to find the bridge to cross the river. I had to go through the main square, a large rectangle with a tall, elaborate column in the center with a gold-plated sun on top. The sun on the column reflected the last rays of the setting sun as I drove past it and saw a sign that pointed the way to the Bahnhof on the far side of the square. I passed the Bahnhof and found the gasthof three blocks further down the street.

I knocked on the door and said when it was opened, "Ich bin Jack, Amerikanisher Motorradfahrer." I produced my passport. "Have you a room for the night?"

"Willkommen bien Amerikanisher Motorradfahrer! Ich bin Hilda. Commen sie."

Hilda, a very large lady, made me sign the guest book and led me into the main room on the first floor, which had a couch and chairs around a TV set and a dining table on the other side. She let me know that dinner was ready, but I wanted to go get my gear from the bike first, so she came out with me and told me to park the bike in the garage in the back of the house. She carried one of my saddlebags in for me too.

Hilda brought dinner, a bowl filled with a dark, red-brown stew-like concoction that had pieces of meat and potatoes floating in it. I was reminded of the *goulaschsuppe* I had in Berlin. She also gave me a basket of bread and a bottle of Gemeidebrau, an Austrian brew. She stood and watched as I tasted the soup, which I found to be very spicy but delicious. I would have appreciated any kind of food at that moment, but the Austrian *goulaschsuppe* really lit me up. As I got down to the bottom of the bowl, Hilda told me to use the bread to wipe up the rest of the soup.

When I finished, I sat back and had an uncontrollable urge to belch, which I did. Hilda started laughing and bent over and slapped her knees, as if she knew it was going to happen. I felt my stomach burning and realized that the Austrian version of *goulaschsuppe* was much spicier than the German kind.

All I could do was wash it down with the rest of the beer and hope my insides could handle it. Hilda took pity on me and got me another beer. As I sipped on it, I understood how tired I was. I sat back in the chair and thought about my second full day on the road, wondering if it were going to be like this the whole way. I would have to chop up the journey into more manageable segments somehow. At least Vienna was only four hours from here.

Hilda had taken away the dishes. She then told me that the rate for room and board was 140 schillings. I had no idea what the conversion rate was in dollars. In any case, I had forgotten to convert money from German marks to Austrian schillings, so I didn't have any.

I didn't want to get into an argument with Hilda, who was nice, but she was also the size of a linebacker for any NFL team. I decided to approach the subject honestly.

"I don't have any Austrian Schillings," I said. "Will you take German marks?"

"Ya, forty-five German marks, bitte."

I had paid Lisa forty marks for last night so that seemed reasonable.

"Does that include frustuck?"

"Ya, und der goulaschsuppe."

I asked to see my room, and she led me upstairs where she showed me my room, the bathroom, and the WC.

I said good night, washed up, and plunged into the bed, which was too soft, but I hardly noticed. I slept soundly until in the middle of the night when my stomach growled loudly, and I knew that the goulaschsuppe had come to take its revenge. I ducked quickly into the WC where I spent a fiery fifteen minutes on the toilet voiding my insides. As if the bike ride hadn't tired me out enough, I had to go back to bed with a burning asshole. I downed a full glass of water so I wouldn't be dehydrated later and slid under the duvet and fell asleep.

———◆◗●◖◆———

I hadn't set the alarm because I knew this was going to be a short day on the road, but I knew it was late when I woke up. I had a burning, empty feeling in my stomach from my WC episode in the night. I wished I had some Pepto Bismol, but I had no idea of where to get anything resembling that.

The long sleep had refreshed me, but when I saw that it was ten twenty, I realized my plans for the day would have to be accelerated. I hoped Hilda could provide something light for breakfast. I dressed quickly, packed my gear, and headed downstairs. Hilda heard me on the stairs and gave me a sympathetic look.

"Goulaschsuppe zu scharf?" she asked.

"Ya, ya. Too spicy." I said, rubbing my stomach.

"Komme. Frustuck," she said.

I didn't know if I were ready for some stomach repair job made by the massive Hilda, but I did need something in my belly, so I sat at the table to see what she had in store. To my surprise, she came out with some toasted white bread, butter, a pot of honey, and a large glass of milk.

"Danke, Hilda," I said as I slowly reconstructed my digestive tract with the light fare.

When I had had enough to make me feel normal enough to hit the road, I asked her if I could have an extra piece of bread for the road, and she gave me two. I got up and thanked her again.

I went to pick up my gear to go out the front door, and I found that Hilda had already taken half of it. We went out to the garage together, and she said she had locked the bike in the garage as a precaution against theft. I clipped on the bags and tied the sleeping bag on the back, swung my leg over the saddle, and pushed the starter.

I waved at Hilda as she went back into the house. Then I thought I'd better check the gas, so I popped the cap and sloshed the tank to find that it was almost empty. *Damn!* I'd have to do better with keeping tabs on the gas level as I went into Yugoslavia and Greece where I guessed that gas stations would be few and far between. For now, I remembered that there was a gas station on Bahnhofstrasse a couple of blocks away, so I headed there and filled up.

I also got directions to get on the autobahn for Vienna. I checked the time, eleven forty-five. I had to go 194 kilometers, which would be one and three-quarters hours at a hundred kilometers per hour. I figured I could cut it to one and a quarter hours at 125 kilometers per hour, which would be around eighty miles per hour. That would be cool, to open up the bike on the autobahn. If I could do that, I'd get to Vienna by four, and I needed time to find a place to stay.

When I got on the autobahn, I juiced the bike to 110 kilometers per hour right away as I gauged the speed of the traffic. This was the main autobahn in the country, going west to east, Innsbruck, Salzburg, Linz, and Vienna, so there was quite a bit of traffic. I soon judged that the drivers adhered to the system of autobahn traffic, normal speed cars staying in the right lane while the unlimited speed lane was left open for faster cars. Most of the cars and trucks stayed in the right lane at about 110 kilometers per hour.

I moved quickly from the normal lane to the unlimited speed lane and gunned the bike up to 125 kilometers per hour, almost 80 miles per hour, which was faster than I had ever driven the bike before.

Wow! This is fantastic! I thought. My beard and sunglasses were plastered to my face, while my hair was streaming back off my head. I was really glad I had gotten the gloves in East Berlin because they helped me hold onto the handlebars. But sitting up in the saddle, I realized that my body was acting as a wind break.

While I was sorting out this problem, a car behind me beeped twice. I found a spot in the slow lane and leaned over into it to let the car pass. It was a red Porsche 911S Turbo, which quickly zoomed past. It disappeared so fast that I figured it could have been going 240 kilometers per hour, or 150 miles per hour. I'd better keep an eye on the rearview mirror when I went into the unlimited lane.

I adjusted my body to reduce wind resistance and pulled back out into the fast lane at 125 kilometers per hour. I pressed my chest down as near the gas tank as far as I could and folded my elbows down toward my knees, which I bent up by lifting my heels so only my toes were on the struts for the gears and the brake. Although I wasn't very comfortable, I didn't feel nearly as much wind resistance as before. I put my face down as far behind the headlamp as I could and pushed the bike up to 140 kilometers per hour. I kept checking the rearview mirror, but no one came up to challenge me.

What a rush! 140 kilometers per hour was almost 90 miles per hour. If I could maintain this speed, I'd be in Vienna by three thirty. I didn't really care about the time; the speed was what mattered. The wind tearing past my body made me feel as if I were part of a natural power, which emanated from my will. The wind was the only sound I heard. The blur of the concrete of the road beneath me, and the kilometers of road racing toward me were all I saw as my mind fixated on how fast I was going.

On the bike, my body was speed itself. It was intoxicating. Speed seemed to have conquered time. What passed for a moment of time was translated into a rush of air swirling around my sunglasses and pressing the skin of my cheeks. I wanted to go faster to have the speed embrace me more completely, to sweep me from this world where thought had to be deliberated upon. I just wanted to go *fast* and nothing else.

A quick check of the speedometer showed that I was going 155 kilometers per hour, over 90 miles per hour, which was the top end of the bike. I noticed that I had screwed the accelerator all the way around with my right hand. It was like an addiction.

I had an uneasy awareness overtake me. I dropped down to 130 kilometers per hour, which was a bit deflating compared to having lost myself to my sensations. I would have to guard against my habit of speeding when on the bike. What if a stone hit me in the face or I hit a pothole? Being on a bike could wind up being a lot more dangerous than being in a car. Still, the sensation was incomparable.

16

In Vienna: Plans

I HAD SLOWED DOWN to 125 kilometers per hour, but it was only a couple of kilometers before I saw a sign that straddled the autobahn:

ACHTUNG! Autobahn Ende! WIEN—10 kilometers

I had to slow to eighty kilometers per hour and began to readjust myself out of my egg-shaped speed position into a posture from which I could steer more easily. As I did, I felt the painful effects of the tension in my muscles relax in my shoulders, arms, and back. I figured that professional motorcycle racers must have a better way to position themselves than this. In any case, I thought I should do some work on my upper body, which I had neglected since college.

I drove with the Danube on my right until I came to a large bridge. From there, I could see the taller buildings and church spires of Vienna in the distance, and I followed Karnter Strasse toward the center of the city, where I saw the Opera House. And in a stroke of luck, I looked across the street and saw the American Express office. I checked my watch, three forty-five. The office was still open. I turned around in a traffic circle and parked in front of the AMEX building, opened the large glass door, and strode inside.

The AMEX office projected a presence of American capitalist hegemony. The vestibule had a high ceiling with another set of glass doors leading into the main office, which was spacious. There was a concierge in the vestibule who asked my business in German. I told him I was an American tourist, and he looked at a dirty, windblown biker with a look of disdain and queried me as to how he could be of help.

I had a map of the city but needed a guidebook, which would tell me where I could find hotels and Gasthofs. The concierge pointed toward a rack of printed material on a wall. I went through the second set of doors into an enormous old-fashioned banking floor with caged tellers on one wall, stand-up writing desks for customers to use in the middle of the floor, and a section for customer managers' desks, which was partitioned off by a thirty-inch-high polished wood divider.

There were managers talking across their desks with tourist types who reminded me of my parents. I avoided looking at them as I went over to the rack of pamphlets and searched for what I wanted. I came away with a booklet, which listed mid- to small-priced hotels. On my way out, I saw where the bank of phone booths was. I'd call Eva tomorrow.

The guidebook was in German so it was fairly useless. I stood outside examining my map and had an idea. The Technical University of Vienna was only a few blocks down the street from where I was standing. There was likely to be inexpensive housing for students in the area, so I drove down to the university, passed it, and started to circle the streets looking for a youth hostel or something equivalent. I came to a small street named Walter Gasse and saw a sign in a window of a house, which said, "Zimmer fur Lassen." I knew that meant "room for rent," so I pulled the bike into a spot directly in front of the building and went up the stairs to knock on the door.

I was greeted by a short, white-haired man with rosy cheeks, whom I thought resembled a garden gnome from people's gardens back home but without the red hat. He wore a broad smile on his thick lips. I asked about the room for rent.

The man nodded. "Ya, Ya. Fur vie viele?"

"Just for me," I said, pointing to myself.

"Bist du ein student?"

"Yes," I lied.

"Wie Lange?

I didn't get that, so I said, "I am an American student."

"Ah, Amerikaner. Zehr gut." And he switched seamlessly into English. "My wife and I own this building for many years. We rent rooms to students at the university. We are old and like to have younger people around. They come and go, but they brighten our days. I ask you how long you will stay."

I had to think fast. I didn't want to get into a situation like the one with Helmut where I had to commit to staying for more than a few days. How to do that?

"I have just finished taking classes at the Frei University in Berlin, and I have driven here by motorcycle. The Frei University offered a number of classes in English. I want to see if the Technical University here offers English language classes which I could take."

"We have had Americans stay with us before. Perhaps you will find something. As for now, two young people have just left a room on the ground floor. Would you like to see it?"

"Yes, please," I said, hoping this would work out because otherwise I'd have to spend the night in a relatively expensive hotel and resume the search in the morning.

The old man introduced himself as Max when he asked for my name as we went down a flight of stairs. He showed me the room, which had two beds, two small tables with chairs, an armoire, a sink, and a small cooking area with a hot plate and a coffee pot. I pulled back the curtains on a set of French doors, which led out onto a well-tended garden.

"Ah, you see my Heidi's garden. She has the Gruner Daunen, what you call the 'green thumb, yes?"

I was impressed and told him so. Max was pleased by my reaction.

Max thought a moment and said, "I usually rent the room by the month for two thousand schillings. Two people pay a thousand each, but since you are not sure of your situation, I can rent to you for four hundred schillings for five days. That should give you time to see what is available at the university, and then you can let me know. Is that satisfactory?"

I did a quick calculation to find that four hundred schillings were only about ten dollars per day. I figured I couldn't beat that in the city. I'd have to add food, but that would fit my budget.

I told Max, "That will be fine. Can I pay you tomorrow when I could do a money exchange?"

Max smiled and put his hand on my shoulder, saying, "I never knew a student who had cash on hand."

We went upstairs, and I signed the guest log. Max gave me the key to the house and the room, but didn't take my passport. He showed me to the shower and WC, which were on the floor above, and told me there were towels in the armoire. Then he smiled at me and left me to myself.

I was delighted at my good fortune. Five nights for fifty dollars! I offloaded the bike, brought everything to the room, unpacked, showered, changed clothes, and started to unwind from the day on the road. I'd gone over ninety miles per hour on the bike. Whoa! I'd been flying, but I'd have to watch that. You never knew what could be the end of everything.

I didn't want to think about it. It was time to eat, so I got on the bike and motored back up to the center of town. I seemed to get hungry a lot from riding the bike. Maybe it was the wind, but it was work. It was also the essence of my newfound sense of freedom, and both these senses had to be fed. I looked around and saw that I was now living in Vienna, Austria. I had complete freedom of movement. I was tied to nothing, so I drove with my eyes wide open to the possibilities for adventure, knowledge, and experience that might come my way.

However, Vienna at this time of day was closing down. People were heading home from work, it appeared, so adventure would have to wait until tomorrow. I passed a couple of huge churches. What little I knew about Austrian history was that it had been locked at the hip for centuries with the Roman Catholic Church through the ruling Hapsburg emperors. I looked at these buildings as monuments to both the spiritual and temporal power over the people; the emperors held the power over the peoples' daily lives, and the church held the power over their souls. In this life and the afterlife, they had you coming and going. I thought it was bullshit; I wasn't into religion. I could see this all the more clearly being out on the road as a free spirit.

I was happy to be shaken out of this mood when I saw a neon sign that said "pizza" in the window of a small café. I had three slices and a Coke. Then I found my way back to my room on

Walter Gasse. I went outside into the garden and sat on the bench and smelled the flowers.

"This is living free," I said to myself as if to put a punctuation mark on the day and my accumulation of thoughts. I went to bed knowing I had things to do tomorrow, but allowing them to settle in the back of my mind.

I woke up after having a good sleep, washed and put on clean clothes. My hair was down to my shoulders, long enough to be a mess, especially when riding the bike, but not long enough to put in a ponytail. I combed it out and wet it down so I could get some respect in the AMEX office where I had business to do. Then I went to find some breakfast. It was nine thirty, which I thought might be late. This wasn't New York, after all.

I drove around the university area and found a coffee shop, where I had rolls, preserves, and excellent coffee. There were students having a lively argument about something and cursing at each other. It reminded me of the student union at college.

After breakfast, I went to the AMEX office, where I had three things to do. First, I had change money to pay Max to carry me through five nights in Vienna. Second, I had to call Wild Bill to tell him I was now in Vienna and find out when he was coming back. Third, I had to call Eva, as I had promised.

After changing money, I checked the time. It was ten forty-five, which would be the same time in Berlin. Eva would be asleep, so I'd call Bill because it would be four forty-five on the East Coast. I would call Bill collect because he had screwed me over with Helmut, so he owed me, and if he didn't accept the charges, that would be the end of that.

I went to a booth and placed the call. A woman answered, and the international operator told her it was a collect call for Bill Markus from Jack Higgins in Vienna. I figured it was Bill's mother. She hesitated a couple of moments before calling out for Bill. The operator asked again if she would accept the call. She said yes, as she turned the phone over to Bill.

"Jack! How are you doing? Are still with Eva? How're things at 38 Hubertusallee?"

"Hey, man! I am definitely *not* at 38 Hubertusallee!" I really lit into him for asking that.

"You screwed me over about the rent. Wolfgang caught me coming out of Eva's room with my pants off one afternoon and flipped out.

"He went straight to Helmut, who came over demanding that I pay four months back rent plus the rent for May. That would have been fifteen hundred marks! I spent that money on the bike. I sure as hell didn't want to spend it on rent—which I couldn't at that point, anyway.

"I lied to him and told him I'd give him the money the next morning.

"Eva and I went to KaDeWe and bought maps to give me a route out of the city. So I fled the city in the early morning a couple of days ago and I'm now in Vienna as a result."

Bill started laughing and said, when he caught his breath, "I told you to stay away from Helmut. That included keeping Wolfgang appeased, but you got into Eva's pants and screwed up the whole arrangement. Well, that's split milk. How did you like riding the bike on the open road?"

"The bike is amazing. Everything you said it would be. I got it up over ninety coming into Vienna. What a trip."

I was not amused at Bill's laughing off the predicament he'd gotten me into, but I glossed that aside and asked him, "When do you think you might be coming back to Europe?"

Bill paused. Then he said, "My father had a bad heart attack. I have to stay home to help my mother care for him and run the house for the foreseeable future. I won't be coming back."

"At all?!" I said.

"No. Not at all. I just can't," Bill replied. "I'm sorry, but sometimes dreams run into reality. That's what's happened to me. But you're out there on the road. Go for it! I wish I could come, but it ain't gonna happen. Good luck." And he hung up.

I sat in the booth not thinking because I didn't know what to think. Then I felt the awareness of my situation wash over me like a large wave at the beach that I wasn't prepared for. First, I felt its power as it knocked me down. Then I felt its strength as its undertow wouldn't let me regain my footing. Before I could shake off the feeling, I heard a knock on the door. My time was up, and I had to get out of the booth.

I stood in the middle of the AMEX office by the standing tables and realized that I was as far from home as I had ever been and now I was totally on my own. What had been a pleasurable feeling of freedom yesterday, I was now obliged to embrace as complete autonomy. All right, Bill had said "Go for it!" And that was what I was going to do. I was going to go to Athens and Crete on my own.

That reminded me of Eva, who had helped me get away from Helmut and down to Vienna. I had to call her, but I wasn't thrilled about it. Eva had been great for me, but she weighed me down. Bill bombing out on me had dissipated some of the freedom I had felt yesterday. Reconnecting with Eva would be a mixed blessing: she was a straw to clutch onto, but she was fraught with troubles. *Damn!* Women are complicated, I thought.

But first, I thought that since I was in an AMEX office, I should speak with a travel agent to get some more advice as to the best way to go to Greece by motorcycle. I asked the concierge and was told I would need to make an appointment, which I did for two o'clock.

I decided to call Eva during the day because I wanted to get it over with. She wanted me to call, so I would, on my schedule. I realized I'd need a fistful of coins to make the call because no one at the commune would accept a collect call, so I went back to the teller.

When someone answered the phone at the commune, it was a male voice, and I recognized Piet. Thank God it wasn't Wolfgang. I asked for Eva.

"Kleine moment," Piet said.

And then Eva was on the line. "Jack, is that you?"

"Yeah, it's me. I made it to Vienna. Biking on the road is fantastic. How are you doing?"

"Oh, Jack. I'm so glad you called. Things are terrible here. As soon as you left, Wolfgang starts grabbing at me. Then when I go to work, Fritz insists that if I want to keep my job, I have to start working in his porno films. When I tell him I won't do it, he slaps me in the face. I can cover it with makeup, but it hurts." She stopped talking and sobbed.

"I'm afraid to go out of my room because of Wolfgang. I sneak out to go to the WC or at night sometimes to get food. I haven't been back to work because I am afraid of what Fritz will do next. I have been hoping you would call for three days. Oh, Jack! What can I do?"

I was flabbergasted. This morning I had been as free and independent as a person could be. In the last hour, Bill had dumped me onto my own resources, which I figured I could manage, but now Eva was looking to cling to me for her salvation. That was a stretch. I didn't know what I could do. The operator told me to put more coins into the phone.

"Jack, are you still there?" Eva said.

"I'm here. I just had to feed the phone some more coins. Listen, don't you have someone you could stay with for a few days?"

"You know I don't! I have my room and my job only. My room is now a hateful place. I don't know when Wolfgang just decides to come in here and takes what he wants. I told you how the bar owners are here. I am finished. Alles kaput!"

I could hear her totally break down at this point. "Eva, listen to me. Do you have any cash? Like enough to buy a train ticket to Vienna? You could come here, and I could help you plan something like you did for me when we were at KaDeWe."

Eva didn't answer for a minute. Then she said, "I have about nine hundred marks I have saved. Do you think it would be enough?"

"I'm at American Express. I can find out schedules and ticket costs here. Let me do that, and I'll call you back in a few minutes."

I hung up and went to the rack of materials I had seen yesterday. I found the Deutche Bundesbahn timetable and found trains and ticket prices. Then I called Eva back.

"Eva, I've found a train for you, and it only costs six hundred and twenty marks for second class. It leaves from Berlin this afternoon at four forty-five. It goes to Nurnberg, where you change for Vienna. It's a twenty-two-hour trip. You'll have to pack quickly and take the bus to the station. Can you do that?"

"Jack, I can't get out of here fast enough. I'll manage. Merci."

"I'll meet you at the station here at two tomorrow afternoon. Bonne chance."

I hung up the phone and shook my head. I couldn't understand why I had been so quick to get myself involved with Eva again. Yeah, she was in a real jam, but she was just a magnet for trouble, and now I had saddled myself with her again. Still, I couldn't leave her in the position she was in. It just wasn't in me. I stuffed the train schedule in my pocket and left the AMEX office. I needed some air and lunch. I walked the streets behind the AMEX and found a café where I sat at an outdoor table and had a sandwich and a Coke.

By the time I returned to the AMEX for my two o'clock appointment, I had decided I was going to Greece, come hell or high water. I got my maps out of my saddlebag and went into the office to talk to the travel agent about the best way to get there.

When my turn came up, I went inside the polished wooden cubicle, plopped the maps down on the guy's desk, and told him I wanted to go to Greece. "Could you please advise me of the best way to get to Greece by motorcycle?" I asked the guy.

The young man, who was dressed in a jacket and tie, didn't seem to be offended by my brusqueness. Maybe he was used to it from American tourists.

He stood up and said, "My name is Alex Morgen. I am a travel advisor for American Express. How can I help you?"

"I'm sorry I was so brusque," I said. "I've had some bad news on the phone a little while ago which upset me."

"I saw you going go in and out of the phone booths, and each time you had looked worse coming out."

I had to laugh. With all the crap hitting the fan around me, I forgot there were other people in the world, and what I might look like to them as I was weathering my shitstorm. I sat at Alex's desk and gave him the short version of my time in Europe, the commune, the buying of the bike, and my desire to get to Greece. I opened up the maps and asked Alex what he thought of the route I had planned.

Alex pondered over the maps for a few minutes. "You are an experienced rider on the motorcycle?"

"Not really. Actually, this is my first long road trip. Why do you ask?"

"You will be exposing yourself to riding the mountains in northern Yugoslavia, and they are not good for motorcycling, especially for inexperienced riders. You are going to have to go through the mountains in southern Yugoslavia to get to Greece no matter what, and they are dangerous too, so you would do better to drive to Belgrade, which is halfway down the country on the eastern plain before the road goes into the mountains in the south."

"I don't see from the maps how I could do that."

Alex took a map of Hungary out of his desk and opened it. "You go through Hungary. That way you can bypass the northern mountains in Yugoslavia."

"But Hungary is behind the Iron Curtain!" I said, horrified at the suggestion.

"Yes, but you can get a forty-eight-hour transit visa."

I related the troubles I had at the East German border. "I'm not interested in going into communist territory again."

"I have driven through Yugoslavia several times to get to the Dalmatian coast. My wife and I love Dubrovnik. But the drive is arduous in a car where you must go through the northern mountains. I could not recommend it on a motorcycle. You can avoid the northern mountains by going to Budapest and down the eastern side of Yugoslavia to Belgrade."

"How bad are the roads really?" I asked.

"They pass through peaks that go up to six thousand feet on one-lane roads that have no guardrails where there are drop-offs of two hundred feet or more. They are quite primitive compared to roads in the West. And, here, you can see that the distance to drive from Vienna to Budapest and then to Belgrade is only a few kilometers longer than driving direct from Vienna to Belgrade, but it is much safer."

"If you don't get arrested by the commies," I said.

"If you go to InTourist, the government travel bureau in Budapest, they will take you to your accommodations. You spend the night, and the next morning you leave. We have never had anyone arrested. Just leave Hungary within forty-eight hours."

"What are the accommodations like?"

"You will be assigned to stay in someone's apartment. The Party requests that the comrades provide this service. We pay them, of course, and they pass some of that money to the people who board you. They need the money, so they don't complain."

"If they complained, they'd probably lose their accommodations," I said.

"Be that as it may, our clients can say they have spent the night in Budapest, and that has enhanced their travel experience."

I was not thrilled with what Alex was proposing, but it made sense if the driving were going to be easier. Whichever way I went, Belgrade was over six hundred kilometers from Vienna, so I'd have to spend the night somewhere on the route. This was the third crazy thing that had happened to me in the last couple of hours if I decided to do it.

"How much is this going to cost?"

"There are border fees, the InTourist fee, the fee for the room, and our fee. It usually comes to around thirty-five dollars per person."

Wow! Going to Budapest. Even Wild Bill wouldn't have thought of that, I thought. Then I thought of Eva. I bet she would be angling to go to Crete with me, but this excursion would completely dash that idea. I'd have to help her get along by herself somehow.

"Ok." I said. "So you can make all the arrangements for the trip to Budapest, spend the night, and handle paperwork and everything for thirty-five dollars?"

"Yes. Leave me five hundred schillings and your passport for the visa. InTourist requires three days' notice, so come back then for your papers and be prepared to leave the following day."

I had to get more money changed at the teller's window, and I gave that and my passport to Alex, thanked him for his help, folded up the maps, and left the office. I stood outside next to the bike and lifted my face into the sunshine and asked the world at large, "What next?"

I drove back to the house, where I found Max and paid him. He was pleased. He seemed to be a trusting soul, and by paying him when I said I would, I confirmed his faith. However, under the arrangements I had just made, I knew that the money I had given

Max was just going to cover my stay without accounting for the fact that Eva would be spending three nights undercover. I wasn't sure if she'd be under *my* covers, but I wasn't counting on it. I would be leaving early in the morning of the day after I had paid for, so technically I'd owe Max for a night, but it couldn't be helped. Max wouldn't be chasing me behind the Iron Curtain for the rest.

I lay on the bed and looked back at the events of the day. I thought about how free I had felt yesterday. I went from being contentedly on my own when I got up this morning to being totally cut off from my former life by Wild Bill to being saddled with the responsibility of saving Eva from her foibles all in a moment. And I'd be driving behind the Iron Curtain for two days. Wow.

Was this the way it worked? Could someone be truly free, or was the world structured to make you run through mazes like a rat? Or was it the people you were associated with? My parents' expectations of me forced me to behave in certain ways because their class demanded it of them. I got that, but I saw that many of my contemporaries had broken free of their parents. I thought I'd done that too, but feeling alone after Will Bill pulled out on me and then offering to help Eva made me see that I might never break completely away. I was what I was raised to be.

Still, I was here to find out more about myself and my capacities. As the nagging questions came back to me, I realized that today had presented me with life challenges I had to face in rapid succession, and I had worked through them in a fairly competent manner.

I was on my own, all alone, and that's where I should be to gain the most experience of life. Eva was in trouble. She was my friend, and I could help her, but only so far. She'd have to take it from there, and then I would move on, going into the lion's mouth with Alex Morgen's plan as my guide, hoping to reach Athens and Crete after a dangerous ride through communist territory and the mountains of Yugoslavia.

I sat up and laughed. All this started to sound like a movie with a runaway plot and with me cast as the lead, but I didn't want it to be that way. In Berlin, I had been living day to day, adapting to a different environment, and trying to study and think myself into an independent way of life. That didn't work out. I had slept with

Eva, which was progress. I'd gotten the best of Helmut, but that was too easy.

Now I was on the road in Europe. Hans had given me pieces of priceless wisdom to carry forward. Alex had presented me a real plan, not just maps, to get to Greece, which I had started to think of as my way to destiny. And I had to gain experience all along the way if I were going to transform myself.

My reading of *The Odyssey* and studying the gods and heroes of ancient Greece had been one of the favorite parts of my early education. One of the best things about the story was how Odysseus had worked through all his problems to return to his old life. I felt I needed to overcome my obstacles and get to Greece where my world would fall into symmetry. I couldn't define it any further than that. I'd just have to go and find out how things worked out. I went to bed content with that thought.

17

In Vienna with Eva

THE NEXT DAY, I got up and shaved off my beard. I remembered how it had picked up bugs on the road, and I didn't like the way the straightlaced citizens of Vienna looked at me as I cruised around their city. I also thought Eva might appreciate the gesture. I had breakfast and motored around aimlessly, waiting for Eva's train to arrive that afternoon. I was floating, my ideas scattered between settling on a plan for Eva and thinking about driving to Budapest. I wished that going through communist territory hadn't struck me as being sensible, compared to driving through the mountains. Well, I was in for it now.

I drove past the Nordbahn and quickly came up to the giant Ferris wheel, which had been a landmark in Vienna for ages. It was located in the Volksprater, a large permanent carnival where all the Viennese came after work or on weekends to relax. There were cafés, rides, and walks down tree-lined streets. Some were closed during the day, but I could see that the park would look really cool at night when it was lit up and a lot of people were having fun. I figured Eva would like to come here in the evening. I found a wurst stand and bought a bratwurst on a roll and a beer for lunch and sat down to work out what I was going to do with Eva.

I had to tell her that I was driving to Budapest through the Iron Curtain in a few days and obviously she couldn't come with me. That got me out of any entanglement with her. I knew how much money I had left, and that certainly wasn't taking two people anywhere. She had helped me figure out how to get out of my trouble in Berlin, and I had done the same for her, so we were even there. But now she was coming to Vienna: was she expecting me to be her king again? At the least, she'd be depending on me to take care of her for a while. I could put her up for a few nights for free, stretch my food budget, and do some sightseeing with her, and then I'd be gone. What would become of her then?

I wracked my brain trying to come up with a solution that would leave Eva in a better spot than what she had left in Berlin and one I could live with myself. I was stumped. In the end, I decided I would hold off telling her about my plans for a day or so and let het her get her bearings after Berlin before pulling the rug out from under her again so soon.

I went back to the bike to pick Eva up. I was thinking, *How did life get to be so full of obstacles and hard choices?* I reflected that I had come to Europe to free myself from these conditions so I could find my own place, and yet obstacles and choices followed me as if they were conditions of life itself.

I drove back to the Nordbahn and waited for Eva's train. When it got to be a half hour late, I asked at the kiosk when they expected the train from Nurnberg, and the agent told me in halting English that trains from Berlin were frequently delayed due to the communists checking them at the border. I was sick of that story, but there was nothing I could do but sit on a bench and wait.

Eva's train came in ninety minutes late. When I saw her walking down the platform, I'd forgotten what a knockout she was, as I watched her lugging her bags in a pair of tight jeans with brown, knee-length, high-heel leather boots, a paisley blouse, and a waist-length tan leather jacket and all that auburn hair flowing from side to side as she moved. She looked fabulous, and she'd been on the train for a whole day. My attention quickly shifted from her looks to the two suitcases, each of which was nearly twice the size of my saddlebags. *Holy cow! How do I get those on the bike with her too?* I thought.

She came up to me and was about to put her arms around my neck when she saw the expression on my face. "What? You are not pleased to see me? After that awful train ride and those couchon border guards who hold up the train for so long? And I am starving. Oh, Jack. What is the matter?"

"Eva, I'm sorry. Of course I'm happy to see you. I just saw your bags, and I don't know how we are going to get them back to my room."

"This is everything I own. I left some clothes behind because they wouldn't fit. What could I do?"

"We'll figure something out. If you're hungry, we can pile everything on the bike and walk it over to the Volksprater. It should be opening about now. There are cafés over there. And I really want to hear about what happened after I left 38 Hubertusallee."

We found an outdoor table at a café where I could leave the bike with all Eva's things in sight. Eva ordered wine with a schnitzel. I had a schnitzel as well, but with beer. Before the meal came, Eva tore into the rolls. I figured she might have skipped lunch to save money.

She talked a blue streak. "Helmut was furious that you skipped out on the rent. Wolfgang accused me of helping you. There was nothing that couchon wouldn't do to get at me.

"Helmut called the West Berlin police from the house at ten-thirty, seeing that you must have run out on him. I was certain that you had gone through the border by then."

"I was halfway to West Germany at ten-thirty," I said. We had a laugh at that.

"How did you make your escape?" I asked her. "Surely Wolfgang was watching you like a hawk."

"Oh, yes, he was, but he couldn't watch every minute.," she said. "I packed everything and waited my chance. I had told Helmut that I had not been able to get to work to pick up my paycheck, so he had given me two extra days to pay for May. He was going to come the morning after I left to collect. When I had a chance, I called for a taxi to make a faster getaway. Wolfgang was in the WC when I put my bags out on the street to wait for it to come."

We laughed again.

We finished our meal, and some of Eva's nervous excitement had dissipated. I told her about the situation at Max's house. She would have to be quiet, and I'd have to stand guard while she used the facilities. She said they were still being outlaws, and we both laughed once more.

I still needed a way to get Eva and all her stuff on the bike, and I figured a way to do it. We walked back to the Nordbahn, where I went into the package room to ask if I could have a couple of lengths of string. The clerk gave me what I needed.

When I went back outside, Eva asked, "Q'est-ce que c'est, cheri?"

"You'll see."

I went to the bike and eyed the baggage holder to figure the best way to tie the bags on and still leave room for Eva. I tried a few configurations, but finally gave up on that idea. I looked around the streets and saw that the traffic was fairly light, so I just tied the bags on the back seat, using the string to tie them to the holder.

"But where do I sit?" Eva asked anxiously when I was finished.

I got on the bike and pulled it off the kickstand. "Here." I pointed to the gas tank in front of me.

She stared at me but did what I asked. I told her to keep her feet up away from the cylinders and to lean back into me so I could see to steer. I said we didn't have far to go and took off in first gear where I figured to leave it the whole way. I found that braking was difficult, so I slid through a couple of red lights and made it to the house without mishap.

I snuck Eva downstairs into the room and told her I would come back with her bags. Then she could go to the WC and shower upstairs. By the time I had come back to the room, I found that Eva had washed herself in the sink, stripped down to her underwear, and folded up in her bed, asleep. I figured she was done in after what she'd been through the last twenty-four hours, so I put the duvet over her and wished her pleasant dreams.

She was still asleep after I came back from breakfast the next morning and having picked up some supplies at a grocery store. I waited until noon to wake her, feeling the clock ticking on my departure in three days. I gave her a shove, but she cursed in her sleep and rolled over. I went out to sit on the bench in the garden to mull over how the plan I had finally thought out for her was going to flesh out.

She came out into the garden at two. I jumped up and put her in a bear hug and carried her back into the room. She protested, but I reminded her that she wasn't supposed to be there. She reluctantly acquiesced. Then she said she needed a shower. Another problem. I said she could shower now when most of the other residents were out, but not later. It would be too risky. She said we could shower together. I had to say maybe to that, but wound up standing guard as she showered alone.

And she took forever to shower! I led her back to the room while I watched her dry her hair as best she could and then dress in another pair of tight-fitting jeans and high-heeled boots. She put on a purple blouse and shook that auburn hair out over it, all the while saying that she didn't like sneaking around the house.

"Too bad," I said. "It is the way it is."

When she had prepared herself, she turned to show herself off to me, and I just stared, thinking, *She is a fabulous-looking babe. How can she get into such jams with those looks? She's too old and fiery for me, but I'd like to have a girl who looks like that.*

Eva must have sensed my admiration because she stepped up to me, radiant and beautiful, kissed me on the lips, and said, "My savior. My king."

I smiled self-consciously. *Oh, brother,* I thought. She took one of the rolls I had bought and munched on it.

It was past three, so we discussed what to do with the rest of the day. I said that the palaces and museums closed at four, so we might drive around and check out the inner city, which was a sight itself. Then we could go to the Prater for dinner and attractions. Eva said that sounded like fun, so we headed out for a drive.

As we motored slowly through the inner ring of the city, I noticed that people, particularly men, were staring at us. When we stopped at a light, some guys would just stand on the curb and stare, forgetting to cross the street. Women would take a quick, sharp look, raise their chins, and march ahead with their eyes directed forward.

I hadn't experienced these reactions while I was tooling around Berlin with Eva on the bike. I wondered if the straightlaced Viennese were more uptight about the sight of a beautiful woman with her hair streaming out behind her, riding through their streets on a motorcycle than the denizens of Berlin, which was a free-wheeling mixture of nationalities and races. I was certainly enjoying the ego-stroke.

Eva saw the Ferris wheel before we got to the Prater and said she wanted to ride it right away. As we went up, Eva put her arms around me and gave me a long, sexy kiss, which embarrassed the people in the car with us. When we came down, we walked through the chestnut trees in the park, which were in full apple-green spring leaf. It was a lovely late afternoon, but I was not happy. I was playing with Eva in her lighthearted, newly liberated mood, and inside I felt terrible for what I was going to have to tell her.

We found an Italian restaurant with checkered tablecloths and candles in used bottles of Chianti on the tables. I asked Eva if she wanted Chianti, and when she said yes, I said I'd join her and ordered a bottle. I'd decided I couldn't keep the secret any longer, so I wanted to smooth the waters as much as I could. I figured the best way would be to approach the subject from her standpoint.

"Eva, how long were you in Berlin?"

"Almost six years."

"And how long in Paris?"

"About five years."

"And how long were you living, married, in Algeria?"

"A little more than two years. Why are you asking me these questions, Jack?" she demanded.

"Well, I've been thinking what it must be like to be on the run," I lied. "You see, that's pretty much what I've been doing since I graduated from college, but that's only a year and a half. If I get called for the draft, I might continue to be on the run for a lot longer, but I was thinking about you. You've been on the run for almost fourteen years, and you burn your bridges behind you. I was wondering how that feels."

Eva held her wine glass in both hands with the rim just under her nose. Her eyelids were tightened in concentration, and her gaze was fixed on my eyes. She said nothing for some time. Finally, she disengaged her stare, took a sip of wine, and put the glass on the table.

"For a moment, I thought you were going to propose to me, but, of course, that is impossible. Just three days ago you drove off on your little boy's adventure and left me in a horrible situation surrounded by les couchons. No, there must be another reason you ask me these things. Do you mind telling me what it is?" Eva looked intently at me as she tapped her index finger on the table. Her long fingernail made the sound menacing even through the tablecloth.

I knew I had made a mistake. I had wanted to do a little probing to see if the strategy I had come up with would pan out. Instead, I had opened the door to my thinking, and Eva was standing on the threshold, insisting that I reveal what was inside.

I tried to prevaricate. "I was just trying to get a feel for what you thought of your situation, given that you've gone from one bad situation to another over the course of fourteen years."

"So? You have only known me for four months. Why this concern for my life all of a sudden?"

I knew the moment of truth had arrived. I was truly sad when I said, "Eva, in two days I'm going to the AMEX office. They have arranged passage for me through Budapest on my way to Greece. I leave early the following morning. There's no way I can take you with me. I'm sorry."

Eva's mouth dropped open, and her eyes widened to an extent I thought impossible. She was speechless. Then she realized how what I had said impacted her. "But you will leave me in Vienna with no money, no bed, no food. How can this be?" Tears started to well up in her eyes and then run one by one down her cheeks. She made no move to wipe them away. She was shattered.

I looked at my friend, my first girl, and was melted inside by what I felt was my callousness. But I did have the strategy I had thought out, so I spelled it out as rationally as I could, so it would make sense to Eva as well as relieve me of my guilt.

"Listen, I was *not* planning to just drive away and leave you on your own. I have been thinking about you a lot. Like, what about if I hadn't bothered to call you when I got here? You'd be in that nasty mess in Berlin with no way out. I gave you a way out, and you took it. But it's only temporary. I've got to move on. So do you if you'll hear me out."

167

Eva recovered her composure slowly, keeping a wary eye on me as she wiped the tears away off her face with her finger. "You have an idea for me?" she asked tentatively.

"Well, it's one idea with two possible outcomes you could choose from. The main idea is that I'll buy you a train ticket to France, which is where I think you should be. You are French after all. In one case, the ticket could be to Paris where you could start over as a bartender. Paris is a big city. After six years, I'm sure you could start with a clean slate. And you know the job better now, so maybe that could work out. That's one outcome."

I saw that Eva was listening attentively. It was evident to her that I wasn't just going to dump her in Vienna on her own.

"And the other outcome?"

"Because I have to go to AMEX, I was thinking I might give my parents a call to let them know I'm on the move. I left them a note when I left for Berlin and haven't contacted them since. That was over four months ago. I guess they might like to hear from me.

"Well, the idea is the same for you. I don't know how long it's been since you spoke with your parents, but you haven't seen them in fifteen years. You said they moved to Provence. Are they still there? If you can reach them, maybe they'd like to see you, and you could get back together with them. After fifteen years and the fact that you left your husband, your father might have softened up a bit. It would give you a home base, you know? Well, that's what I was thinking about for you. I couldn't leave you here with nothing. We had a great time, and you showed me a lot that I needed to know, but this is the end of the line for us. The guy at the AMEX office told me that the roads through Yugoslavia are dangerous, and we can't both can't fit on the bike anyway…"

"Oh, shut up, Jack!" Eva said, freezing me in mid-sentence.

I looked quickly at Eva to see if she were angry with me, but to my surprise, her expression had softened, and she had a half-smile on her lips. I noticed that there were tears on her cheeks again. I was unsure of myself and off-base as to where Eva's emotions were at. I watched as Eva tossed her head and brushed her hair away from her face with her hands. She nonchalantly dabbed away the tears from her cheeks with the napkin as if they were nothing more than raindrops.

Then she had a sip of wine and addressed me. "Jack, you really have thought about me. I have known few men who have cared enough to do that. I will have to think about what you have said—your plans, as you say—but you have touched me."

I was relieved that Eva hadn't blown a fuse and pleased with myself for having averted a crisis, although in the back of my mind, I figured it wasn't really *my* crisis. We finished dinner in relative silence. I figured that Eva was deliberating on her options; for all I knew, she might decide to get some money off me and get a bartending job here in Vienna. *No, I don't think she wants to keep running. Tomorrow will tell*, I thought.

I paid the check, and we walked out into a mild evening, The Prater was in full swing with people promenading along the broad walkways bordered by the chestnut trees, the lights lit festively, and the attractions and games each drawing small crowds. Eva had taken my arm, and we strolled without saying anything. It was a poignant moment, and I was sad that this was going to be a long goodbye. We went back to the bike, and I drove back to the house. We skipped our showers and went to sleep in our separate beds.

We had breakfast in the room. Eva wanted to shower, so I did a recon of the upstairs until I was sure she could shower undisturbed. She took her usual time about it. When she was done and dressed, I said that my first stop for the day would be the AMEX office to check on my papers and call my parents. It would be five o'clock in New York, so I stood a chance of reaching them.

Eva was noncommittal as to her thinking, so I had to remind her that I was leaving in two days. She said she was coming with me to the AMEX office.

At AMEX, I made an appointment with Alex Morgen but was told I would have to wait until he finished his business with an American couple who looked like they just got off the boat from Honolulu. *What costumes*, I thought to myself. Just as I thought this, Eva nudged me in the ribs, looking at the couple and holding her hand in front of her mouth to keep from laughing out loud.

When Alex was done, he motioned me to come to his desk. He handed me my passport, the forty-eight-hour InTourist transit visa, which was effective at 12:01 a.m. the day after tomorrow, and the voucher with the address of the house I would be staying in.

"You should be on the road at sunrise to make sure you have plenty of time to get to the InTourist office in Budapest to check in. You must check out the following morning with InTourist and then get to the Yugoslav border before the forty-eight-hour visa expires. The Hungarian authorities are very strict about this," he said.

He gave me a detailed map of Budapest and showed me where the InTourist office was.

"Food is included in the bill, but don't expect much. I would bring my own food if I were you, and a pack of American cigarettes as a gratuity for the host. The cost is five hundred schillings, as projected. Gute Reise."

I thanked him for his services.

Eva had been watching Alex and me dispassionately.

When I was done, she told me, "I want to make a phone call to France. Could you pay for it?"

I wondered which outcome she had chosen, but I said she knew I'd pay. I went to get coins from the teller. I figured she'd need a lot; women talk forever on the phone.

I stood outside the booth as Eva called the international operator. She asked for directory assistance for France. There was a long pause. Then Eva asked the operator to make the connection and stuffed half the coins into the phone. Then there was another long pause, and I heard Eva say, "Maman? C'est Eva ici."

Then there was a pause and a lot of "Oui, Oui!" and "Moi aussi." Tears were falling down Eva's cheeks like a waterfall. Then Eva put the rest of the coins in and said nothing for a while. She opened the door to the booth and asked me if I could get more coins and a pencil, so I dug in my pockets and pulled out what I had and gave them to her. She shoved them in the slots and rattled off a few sentences in rapid-fire French, ending with "A bientot, Maman." She wrote down her mother's address and hung up.

I looked at Eva, expecting her to stand up and leave the booth, but she just sat there, fixed to the seat, staring as if in a trance. *That was some phone call*, I thought. *She looks pretty shaken up.*

Other people were waiting to use the booth, so I touched Eva on the shoulder to stir her. She looked up at me and said, "Mon papa, il est mort."

I knew that meant that her father had died. I took her by the elbow and walked her to the middle of the office by the standing desks and wrapped my arms around her. She was weeping softly with her head against my chest. I looked around and saw people staring at us, including Alex Morgen. *Boy, what a spectacle,* I thought.

But my heart went out to Eva, whose emotions were being transmitted to me through direct body contact. I figured the best thing to do was to postpone my call until Eva could tell me what her call was all about. I led Eva out of AMEX and down the street to a Konditorei where we could have a cup of coffee and a linser torte.

Eva just wanted coffee, but I ordered the torte in case she changed her mind. I'd eat it anyway. Eva slowly unwound and told me what she had learned on the phone. She started by saying that she was lucky to have reached her mother, who still lived in the house in Aix-en-Provence. It was only because she hadn't moved after her father had died that there was a listing.

Her mother was becoming hard of hearing, so she didn't understand it was Eva on the phone at first. When she did, she was very emotional. The first thing she told Eva was that her father had died of cancer two years ago. He had words for Eva before he died, but he never really forgave her. Eva choked up when she said this.

Her mother then said that she was in good health and living fairly well on her father's pension, but she was lonely and finding it difficult to get things done on a daily basis. She wished she could see her daughter again. Eva said she understood and asked her mother if she could come stay with her for a while. Her mother was overjoyed. Eva told her where she was and that she would be coming to Aix soon by train. It might take two or three days, but she would be there soon. Then the operator asked for more coins, so she was cut off.

I smiled at Eva and said that while I was sorry about her father, I thought she had made the right choice. Eva nodded her agreement. We finished our coffee, and I drove to the Nordbahn to buy Eva's ticket to Aix-en-Provence. The clerk was helpful. It was a complicated journey, involving four changes of trains, and he seemed to enjoy the task of putting it all together. The train would leave Vienna at ten tomorrow with changes in Munich, Zurich, Geneva, and Lyon. Eva would get to Aix-en-Provence at one the next day, twenty-seven hours later. The cost of a second-class ticket was 1,189 schillings.

When I heard that, I sucked in my breath. That was eighty-five dollars, and Eva would need some money for food, so I'd have to fork over a hundred dollars to get her home. I shook my head and asked the clerk if he would take AMEX travelers' checks. The clerk said that would be fine. The clerk proceeded to print out the various tickets and put them in a small portfolio while I signed over the checks. Eva gave me a kiss and a quiet "merci."

Thinking about my shrinking wad of travelers' checks, I realized I was going to need more cash, not just for the next two days in Vienna, but for gas in Hungary, Yugoslavia, and Greece and food and lodging in Yugoslavia and Greece. I'd have to go back to AMEX to get more money changed. I told Eva to get on the bike, and we went to get the money.

At the teller's booth, I counted out what I had left: $1,160 in AMEX checks. I did a backward calculation, and it came to $2,550, which meant I'd spent $650 of my original $3,200 in almost five months, not including the cost of the bike, but including airfare to Berlin. Whew! It was a good thing I'd gotten out of paying rent in Berlin, or I'd be broke.

I bought some Hungarian forints, some Yugoslavian dinars, and fifty dollars' worth of Greek drachmae to get me through Salonika to Athens. I'd buy more drachmae in Athens to get me to Crete. I also bought thirty dollars' worth of schillings for the last two days in Austria. That reminded me to buy twenty dollars of French francs to give to Eva for her trip. She was really happy when I gave her the money. Her eyes lit up like sparklers.

I didn't like carrying cash on the road, but there was no choice where I was going. I buttoned the bills in my jacket pocket with my passport. Then I suggested to Eva that we return to the house so she could pack up and be ready to get to the train in the morning. Then we could go to the Prater and walk until the park got going in the evening and we were ready for dinner. Eva said that would be fine.

We went to a biergarten in the Prater, which reminded us of Berlin. We each had a stein of beer and laughed at how we had hoodwinked Helmut out of his rent. I told Eva that paying the rent would have wiped me out. Eva said, "Couchon!" when I mentioned his name. She then said "Wolfgang, couchon!" and "Fritz, couchon!" and made a face each time. I didn't laugh because I knew how much she hated these people.

But Eva just said, "They are behind me now, thanks to you."

"They're behind me, too, thank goodness," and we both smiled and guzzled some beer. We reminded each other of rides around Berlin and how confining the city felt after I bought the bike. That damn Wall always stopped us from going anywhere. I told Eva how Bill and I had pissed on the Wall one day, and Eva started laughing so hard she had to find the ladies' room.

When she got back, I ordered another stein apiece. After a while, being tipsy, I asked Eva if we would ever meet up again, although I couldn't imagine how. She was equally unsteady, and she said I could call her if I ever got to Aix-en-Provence. She wrote her mother's number on a piece of paper and gave it to me, leaning over the table to give me a kiss and knocking over her beer.

That straightened me up enough to realize that she had been through an emotional roller coaster of a day and we should call it a night. I paid the bill and put the phone number in my jacket pocket. We stumbled back to the bike, and Eva gripped me like a vise as I slowly navigated the nighttime streets of the city. I half-carried her to the room where she collapsed face-first on her bed.

I went over to my bed to take off my boots and clothes, not noticing that she had stripped off her top in the meantime, and there she was with her arms locked around my neck from behind, pressing her naked tits against me in a ferocious embrace. In case I had any doubt of what she wanted, she bit me on the shoulder, which caused me to yell, "Ouch!"

I backed her up to her bed where I deposited her on her back and spun around to get out of her grip. I grabbed her wrists as I hovered over her for a moment. Her wicked smile let me know she was getting exactly what she wanted, so I kissed her fiercely and pulled off her boots and her pants. Then I finished stripping myself, and she wound herself around me again. We made love until we were spent.

———•◆•———

Morning and silky light streamed through the lace curtains on the French doors. I checked my watch. It was eight twenty. *Eva's train!* But we hadn't slept too late. I woke Eva. She wanted to wash up, but I told her she'd have to do it in the room. She wasn't happy.

I put some coffee on the hot plate and got out the rolls and jam while I thought about last night's lovemaking *in extremis,* as I called it. It was savage. I couldn't remember all the things we did, but I'd never forget the intensity of the feeling.

Once Eva was dressed and had some breakfast, I took her bags and tied them onto the bike as far back as I could. Eva could sit in front of them, and I'd have to cram myself up over the tank. I drove slowly to the Nordbahn and got there in plenty of time. I parked and carried Eva's bags down the platform to the Munich train. The conductor stopped us at the carriage where Eva showed her ticket. She reached up and kissed me, saying, "Au revoir, mon cheri," in my ear. Then she carried her bags onto the train, and I walked back up the platform.

I felt a sense of loneliness as I drove away from the station. The last few days had been a whirlwind of activity, coming from the sedentary life I had spent in the commune behind the Wall; to fleeing the landlord; being searched at the border; meeting Hans; getting Eva to Vienna and hopefully putting her on a sustainable path in her life; and me about to continue on my path, heading behind the Iron Curtain as a "safety measure." All this was on me, but I figured I should call the parents, so someone would know of my last whereabouts should I get chewed up in the lion's mouth.

It was noon, six o'clock in New York. I drove back to the AMEX office and placed a collect call. There was the usual wait for an international connection. Then someone picked up, and the operator said, "I have a collect call from a Jack Higgins in Vienna, Austria. Will you accept the charges?"

"Oh, yes!" It was my mother.

"Go ahead, please," said the operator.

"Oh, Jack! I can't believe it! You're in Vienna. You said you were going to Berlin. Are you all right?"

I explained my circumstances, leaving out details that would upset her. I asked about my father. He was away on business. *Figures*, I thought. I decided to tell my mother about the bike to let her know how I was getting about, although she'd probably freak out.

"Oh my God, those things are so dangerous," she said.

I'll be leaving Vienna in the morning for Athens and get there in a week or so. I'll send a postcard when I get there."

"Do let us know how you are, Jack. You can't imagine how worried we've been. And leaving a note like that—it was cruel."

I'm sorry about that, but I'd made all my plans and I knew you were against it. I didn't want to have a scene, so I just left. I'll call again sometime." Then I hung up.

Talking with my mother was something I would have preferred to avoid, but after four months, I felt it was a duty of sorts. She was so clingy, like scotch tape all over me. I couldn't imagine myself as a parent, but if I ever were one, I sure as hell wasn't going to suffocate my kids with my emotional and societal hang-ups.

I went to a café for a cup of coffee to clear my head. I still had that feeling of loneliness. The last twenty-four hours had taken something out of my spirit. I wanted to have something I could connect myself to.

I figured a new book might be something that would help me as I went further into the unknown tomorrow. I drove around the university and saw a bookstore that advertised English-language books. I went in and browsed, letting my eyes wander the shelves. I noted that most of the English-language authors were Americans like Hemingway, Fitzgerald, and Jack London or British classics like Dickens, Huxley, and Virginia Woolf. There was *1984* too, but I'd read many of those. I wanted a road story or one by an ex-pat.

Then I saw *The Tropic of Cancer* by Henry Miller. This was forbidden fruit in the world back home. My teachers called it smut, but I'd learned that it was about Miller's life as an expatriate in Paris in the 1930s and there was a lot of sex in it. It sounded like it fit my current life on the road and was exactly what I wanted.

I bought it and then drove to the grocery store to buy sandwich food for my trip through Hungary, not forgetting the pack of Marlboros for my host. I then went back to the house to pack. I had to get on the road by sunrise, so I'd turn in early. I wasn't sure if I'd say anything to Max or just leave.

When I got back to the house, it started to rain.

18

Into the Lion's Mouth

I DID NOT SLEEP well, thinking about going into communist territory and wondering how Eva was faring, although I was sure she could get to Aix alright and hoped things would finally come together for her.

I got up and had breakfast before dawn, downing two cups of coffee while I dressed. In the end, I decided to leave a note for Max, telling him I couldn't find the courses I was looking for. The old guy had an illusion of friendly students. Why pop his bubble?

Then I remembered the rain from last night. I looked out through the curtains into the garden, and it was still raining. It looked like it had been raining all night from the puddles on the pathways. *Damn!* The weather had been perfect up till now. All I needed was rain on a trip to a place where I was on an unforgiving schedule. It was 243 kilometers to Budapest, and in the rain, this was going to be a really hellish drive. Well, I'd signed up for this, and I had to go.

I went out and clipped my bags onto the bike. They were made with flaps that were designed to keep dirt and hopefully rain out. It was too early in the morning to find any store where I could find something to protect me. Just standing around the bike I was getting wet, so I hopped on and got going.

As soon as I was moving, I discovered that the water distorted my vision on the sunglasses, but if I took them off, the rain would go straight into my eyes, so I left them on. I went about twenty kilometers out of the city and realized how soaked my arms and legs were. Another 220 kilometers of this might catch me pneumonia, but then I saw the airport and had an idea.

I pulled into the main terminal and saw an open newsstand. I bought six of the thickest magazines I could find and went into the men's room to strip off my wet clothes and wring them out as best I could and then put them back on with the magazines inside my arms and my thighs and across my chest. My underwear was only damp, so I left it on. I actually felt drier, but I wondered how long the magazines would hold out. My feet were all right in the boots because I had pulled my jeans over the tops, but my head was totally exposed.

When I got back out to the bike, the rain had let up a bit, but it was still coming down. The Austrian-Hungarian border was only sixty kilometers, so I figured to get there and see if I could go any further. I couldn't go any faster than eighty kilometers per hour as long as it was raining, and I started thinking about turning around and heading back to Vienna because I'd never get to Budapest in time to check in with InTourist. I went into my speed crouch on the bike to keep from having the rain pelt me directly. The magazines were keeping me from freezing, but they were getting heavy as they soaked up the moisture. I couldn't believe the difference between driving in the sunshine and in the wet, but I didn't see how leathers would help in these conditions, so I congratulated myself on not having spent the money.

The few cars ahead of me caused excess water to come up off the road, and once a big truck barreled past, splashing water all over me, but I was far too drenched to care.

It took forty-five minutes to get to the Austrian border post, and by then the rain had stopped, but I was soaked, and the magazines were bloated from the water. I must have looked like the Michelin Man.

I pulled into the Austrian border post, dripping from every inch of my frame. I went to pull out my passport and papers and got a shock when I saw they were mostly dry, as was the cash I had tucked in with them in my jacket pockets. I figured that my crouched speed position must have shielded them from the water, but the pockets were double-lined as well.

There was no waiting line at the Austrian border, so I got off the bike under the toll booth-style post and went up to the window to hand my papers to the guard. He took my papers, looked at them, and then looked at me in dismay. I could understand that I was a mess, but why should he get upset?

He stepped out of the booth and motioned for me to park the bike next to the booth and follow him. I was alarmed. I'd had enough trouble at border crossings, and that was from the commies. I was going to have to face more of them just up the road. What was this about? He led me to a two-story concrete building and motioned me to come inside where we went to a room where an officer was sitting behind a desk. The guard spoke to the officer in German, and I could pick out the words, 'American' and 'Budapest' from what he was saying. I looked down and saw that I had created a small pond at my feet in the officer's office. That would make him happy.

The guard left, and the officer stood up and said in perfect English, "Ludwig tells me you have come from Vienna and got caught in the rain on your motorcycle. I can see you are all wet and still have to get to Budapest, probably on a forty-eight-hour transit visa. I believe the rain has stopped, or I would tell you to go back to Vienna. But since it has, I think we can help you, if you would like."

"I sure would. How could you do that?"

"We have to spend weeklong shifts here at the border, sometimes longer, so things are made as comfortable as possible for us. We have living quarters, showers, a kitchen, laundry, and a half-football field for exercise. If you have a change of clothes, you can shower, change, and dry your wet clothes while you wait, and then go on your way."

"Wow! That would be terrific! Thank you! I mean Danke! I'll get my bags from my bike."

I went down to get the bags. When I got back inside, the bags had proved their worth. Almost everything was perfectly dry. Wild Bill had really spotted a gem in that store. I took out all my dry clothes and started to get out of my wet ones. As I did, the magazines fell out on the floor.

The officer came over and picked up a magazine gingerly by the corner. "What is this?" he asked. "You were going to bring these into Hungary?"

I told him, "I just used them to deflect water away from me as I was driving."

The officer shook his head, ruefully. "These are magazines that our communist friends think glorify Western culture at their expense. You could have gotten into a lot of trouble for smuggling these into the East. I think you don't want them anymore; you can throw them in that trash can." Then he went back to his office. "When you are done, I will be at my desk."

He had pointed out where the showers were, along with the laundry room. I put all my wet clothes in the dryer and took a hot shower before getting dressed in dry clothes. The shower felt almost as good as sex after that cold ride from Vienna. I had to wait an hour for the wet clothes to dry because I wasn't going to pack anything wet in the bags. I ate half a sandwich while I waited. When they were done, I packed the bags and went to thank the officer again.

"You have lodging in Budapest tonight?" he asked.

"Yes, I do, from InTourist."

"Be sure to go to InTourist to check in before you go to your lodging. InTourist is a part of the state police. They will want to know where you are all the time."

I thanked him for his hospitality and cursed Alex Morgen under my breath for setting me up with the commie police.

"Gute Reise," the officer said.

When I left the building, I saw that the rain had indeed stopped. *If only it will stay that way*, I said to myself. I clipped the bags onto the bike and went to see Ludwig, who stamped my passport. I thanked him warmly for his help. He looked like a good guy.

I drove to the Hungarian crossing, which was more formidable than the Austrian one. There were two gates in between, which drivers were being made to get out of cars, and mirrors were being used to look under their cars. All this took time, which I was short on. I kept my eye on the sky, but it remained overcast. When it was my turn, the guards made me open my saddlebags but didn't inspect them. The Marlboros were in a sock at the bottom of one of the bags. Then they opened the gate and let me through.

I remembered from my conversation with Alex that I had to follow the M1 highway all the way to Budapest. It was about 190 kilometers and should take around one and a half hours at the speed limit, which I intended to stick to.

I drove at ninety kilometers per hour and looked around for speed traps, but all I saw was flat, open farmland. The road was remarkably straight, lined with trees that were spaced like telephone poles. I guessed they had been planted after the war. The surface was poorly maintained with potholes and inadequately engineered shoulders. I didn't want to go faster. At least it wasn't raining, and there were few cars, so water coming up off the road wasn't a problem. I had seen the same thing in East Berlin: The average communist worker didn't have the money to buy a car. *The Peoples' Paradise*, I thought.

After a boring hour, the M1 passed by a town in a valley and went through a woods. I checked my watch, three fifty-five. I was in the suburbs of the city, and in ten minutes, I was going over the Danube on the bridge, which was my landmark. I slowed on the bridge to look at the ornate Hungarian Parliament buildings, but I had to get to the InTourist office so I kept going and found the sign on an office building on the right in a couple of blocks.

I parked the bike and went into the office. Right away I was struck by the contrast between the splendor of the AMEX office in Vienna and this dump of officialdom, which reminded me of a rundown big city police station on a TV show back home. The walls were painted grey/green to match the furniture, or was it the other way around? The Austrian officer had said that InTourist was a part of the state police. I believed him.

I walked up to the desk where a woman in an olive-colored military uniform with a Sam Browne belt was sorting papers. She looked up at me without saying anything, so I pulled out my passport, transit visa, and InTourist papers and handed them over, figuring that she could figure out for herself what I was doing there.

She scrutinized them carefully. She asked me a question in Hungarian, but I just shrugged my shoulders. *How many Americans speak Hungarian?* I asked myself.

She turned away in disgust and went to one of the desks in the office and gave my papers to another uniformed official. The guy made an entry in a ledger and came to the front and said, "I will take you to the place you are staying for the night."

I was relieved that someone spoke English. I went out and got on the bike. When the guy followed me, he stopped at the bike and looked at it with an amazed look on his face. He walked all around it. I got off so he could get a good view.

"This is a wonderful machine," the guy said. "We never see such machines here, except the military, and those are Russian-made. No good."

I didn't say anything because I thought it might be provocative. I was feeling paranoid in this place where the government could tell an ordinary citizen to put up a tourist for the night without their consent. I wondered again why I had let Alex Morgen talk me into this.

The guy got in a little box of a car across the street and told me to follow him. We re-crossed the Danube, drove over an island in the river, and went up a few hilly streets until we came to an apartment block that was identical to many we passed on the hill. We parked in front of one building, and the guy waited for me to unclip the bags and get my sleeping bag. Then we went inside.

I was struck by the odor of disinfectant in the hallway and the even stronger aromas of spicy cooking as we went up the stairs to a fourth-floor apartment. A woman opened the door when the guy knocked and said a few words and handed her my accommodation slip. Then he turned to go and told me to report to his office before I left the city in the morning.

There I was with my host. I noticed that she looked scared of me. She was kind of skinny, as if she didn't eat enough, and her skin was pallid as if she didn't get enough sun or exercise. She could be thirty or fifty, I couldn't tell.

To brighten things up, I patted myself on the chest and said, "I'm Jack."

That certainly didn't spark a conversation. I was tired and didn't want to spend time trying to figure out her problems, so I picked up my bags and motioned that I'd like to see my room.

She led me to a curtained-off alcove, which was part of the kitchen. It had a cot and a small table with a lamp and a wooden chair. There was hardly enough room for me and my stuff. I cursed Alex Morgen again for having soaked me thirty-five dollars for the privilege of staying in this rattrap. Well, I was here, and it was all part of the adventure, I mumbled, as I laid out my food on the table, deciding between dinner sandwich and breakfast sandwich. From what I smelled of the cooking in the building, I sure as hell wasn't eating anything produced in here.

I needed water, so I went to the kitchen to ask for a glass. The woman was chopping up some vegetables in the sink and didn't hear me coming. I cleared my throat, and she jumped around, eyes wide. I pantomimed that I wanted a drink of water. She settled down and got me a glass, never taking her eyes off me. I used the tap to fill it, hoping I wasn't going to get some dread disease.

I went back to the alcove and ate my dinner sandwich, figuring I'd turn in early so I could get out of this country as quickly as I could tomorrow. I finished the sandwich and opened the curtain to the alcove to see if the woman were still in the kitchen. She wasn't. I needed to wash up, so I did that at the kitchen sink, but I also needed to use the WC and couldn't find it. I guessed that there might be a communal one in the hall, so I went out and saw a guy coming out of a doorway buckling his belt. That must be it.

I went to the door and discovered why there was such a strong odor of disinfectant in the hallway. There was a squat-down toilet with a hole in the floor and a box of rags in place of a roll of toilet paper. I was appalled. No wonder commies tried to escape to the West. This was reason enough!

I did my business Hungarian-style and returned to the apartment, where I rewashed my hands and got on the cot to get my bearings for the next day's ride. I opened up the Hallweg map of Yugoslavia, which included the eastern half of Hungary, all of Yugoslavia, and northern Greece all the way to Salonika. It was 180 kilometers to Szeged, the last city in Hungary, about fourteen miles from the Yugoslav border. (I'd need gas at this point.) That should take about two hours. From there, it was two hundred kilometers to Belgrade, another two hours. The map showed flat land and a four-lane highway, so I could make good time to Belgrade. I hoped Alex was right for once.

I took off my boots to let them air out. They were a little damp inside, and I spread my jeans and jacket out under the cot so they would be dry in the morning. I got into my sleeping bag, which had a waterproof shell on the outside, and it was warm and dry inside. I used the threadbare blanket from the cot as a pillow. I turned out the light, listening to the woman shuffling around the kitchen.

I tried to sleep, but I kept thinking of my surroundings and the way the people were treated by the communists. Was it really so different from back home? I fell lightly asleep and dreamed about the nightmare of the American landscape as I perceived it.

There were signs everywhere, moving and pointing in opposite directions and none showing me my way. I lifted my head, and my eyes searched. I saw the crowd, divided by barriers. "Police line: do not cross."

On one side, the crowd was colorful with song and laughter; on the other side, the mob was dark-hued with shouting and hatred. Suddenly, out of the darkness, the dark-hued mob broke through the barriers, huge, shouting, and ugly. I turned to run. I was alone, and they were upon me.

I tried to defend myself, but I was struck down. I lay on my back as they surged around me, shouting and fists striking. I tried to move, but I could not. A boot appeared above my head, so big that I could see nothing but its huge sole and heel. And slowly it came toward my face, blackening all light and deadening all sound, bigger and bigger.

I wanted to scream, no, No, NO! But I began to suffocate.

I woke up sweating. I looked through the curtain, but I was alone in the kitchen.

I woke and peered out of the alcove to see that the sun had risen outside the dirty window over the sink. It was seven thirty, and the woman was puttering away at the sink already. I got up, went to the WC, and washed my hands in the kitchen sink, sort of barging the woman out of the way. She seemed to accept this behavior as if she'd been conditioned to it. I ate my breakfast sandwich, packed up the bags, and said goodbye. I figured I had to give her something for her trouble, so I handed her the pack of Marlboros on the way out, to no response. I was surprised. The commies must have snuffed the spirit out of her.

I loaded up the bike and went down the hill, reaching the Danube and pulling up in front of the InTourist office, but it hadn't opened yet, so I drove across the river where I could get a good view of the parliament buildings. They were really beautiful, shining white in the morning sunlight with a large dome on top, spires, and arches floating in reflection on the river. I couldn't tell what period they were from, but I knew they weren't being used for anything like a representative parliament in these days of communist repression.

I watched a few boats making their way slowly up and down the river. Then I decided to see if InTourist were open. I drove over the bridge, saw the lights on, and went in to get my pass stamped and to ask the best way out of the city. No one wanted to help me with that, so I looked carefully at the map Alex had given me and saw that all I had to do was follow the river west and take the fourth left, and I'd be on the M5, which would take me to Yugoslavia.

When I got to the M5, I put on my sunglasses and opened the bike up to the ninety-kilometers-per-hour speed limit. The sun was coming up, and the wind was in my hair again. I was feeling like I was in my element. But I soon found that this road was in no better shape than the M1 from Vienna, so I had to watch out for potholes and stones. However, I had plenty of time to get to the border on the transit visa.

I had checked the tank before leaving the InTourist office, and it was half full. It took a little over an hour to get to Szeged, where I pulled into a gas station. When the attendant came out, he immediately started looking at the bike and making comments, but I wanted to get moving, so I popped the cap on the tank and pointed to it. The guy filled it up with eighteen liters. I couldn't remember what the exchange rate was to forints, but I'd bought

$10 worth of them. Figuring that should more than do it, I gave him the entire wad of them. The guy went to get change, but I got on the bike and took off. I'd never need the forints again. It was the attendant's lucky day.

It was forty kilometers to the border, and I had almost two hours to get there. I relaxed on the seat and stretched my arms away from the handlebars as far as I could, remembering Peter Fonda with his ape-hangers in *Easy Rider*, although there was no realistic comparison. Still, I was riding easy, happy to be on my way out from behind the Iron Curtain. This was one place I never dreamed my journey would take me, and I'd made it, unlike *Easy Rider* in the good old USA.

I got to the border to find a typical toll booth arrangement and pulled out my passport and transit visa when it was my turn. The guard checked the time on the visa against the clock in the booth and filed the visa. He looked me over, stamped the passport, and came out of the booth to look in my saddlebags. He poked around in my clothes but couldn't find anything incriminating, so he waved me through, a last bit of commie bluster.

It was much easier getting into Yugoslavia, and as soon as I was through the crossing, I was on a four-lane highway with a speed limit of 110 kilometers per hour. I could be in Belgrade in one and a half hours. That was good, but I was still a long way from Athens. The forty-eight hours in Commie Land had left me feeling alone and separated from the realities I had always known.

Driving on a decent road, I began to feel that it was like a spool of ribbon unraveling without an end, having solidity only in its asphalt and concrete, but with no meaning for my soul. The road was just a blur beneath my feet. My life was just a speck, at this moment being blown down that road at 110 kilometers per hour. I searched my memory for times when I was more connected, but I had always distanced myself from people.

Riding in the sunshine, I was reminded of my connection to Eva. I figured she should have made it to Aix by now. She'd have a big-time reunion with her mother. Maybe she would get settled for a while. I wondered if I would get settled at some point; well, not before I'd gotten some answers to my questions. I'd guard my money and just keep going. The answers had to be out there in the realm of experience.

Love was a means of connecting I had read about in books, seen in movies, and heard about incessantly in songs, but I had never experienced any real element of it until Eva. Was that love or just sex? I had experienced sex now, and it tied me to Eva in some primal way I didn't understand. It was mostly sex, so where did love come into it? Weren't there supposed to be feelings attached to it?

The girls I knew back home never pressed for sex. They sort of gave subtle signals, which confused me. As a result, I'd be left asking questions as to their motivations, and I'd never make the move. Because of the psychological battering my sisters had given me when I was little, I never wanted to get too close to women anyway. That had to be why I'd never gotten laid before.

Now that Eva had initiated me, I had a basis of knowledge to move forward with sex. Who knew? Maybe sex and love would come together at some point. I didn't think I was going to figure this out by myself. I'd need to find a woman who would help me make it happen, but I didn't know how to love women.

It had turned into a beautiful spring day, and I wanted to enjoy the physical sensations of the ride. I took the bike up to 120 kilometers per hour and felt the pull from the wind on my face and body. I was a part of the ride every time I rode the bike, it was an intimate experience of my own.

I passed the city of Novi Sad and once again crossed the Danube. The sight of the river gave me heart as I remembered Hans, whom I associated with the river from our lunch at Passau. My thoughts about love lightened my heart, and I started singing "Don't You Want Somebody to Love" by Jefferson Airplane in my head. God, was that a great song!

The long drive from Budapest had finally led me to the outskirts of Belgrade. I motored slowly into the heart of the old city. I'd driven 380 kilometers and was looking for a shower, a decent meal, and a comfortable bed after the experience in Budapest, and I was willing to spend some money for it. I soon came up to the Hotel Nobel, which had a fancy-sounding name, although the building itself was not in the best repair. I parked and went in to see what was available.

At the desk, I was pleased to find that the clerk spoke English. A room was fourteen dollars per night, breakfast included. Dinners ranged from six to twenty-five dollars, which suited me fine. I signed the register and went out to get my bags. A bellboy came with me, took the bags, and escorted me to the room. I wasn't used to this treatment, but I might as well enjoy myself. I had another long ride tomorrow. I remembered to give the little guy a tip.

After a shower and a change of clothes, I had a dinner of chicken, duck, or some kind of fowl. It was the cheapest thing on the menu and had a novel taste, which was pretty good. In the room after dinner, when I was checking the route for tomorrow, I discovered I had made a miscalculation. The trip from Belgrade to Salonika was 684 kilometers through the southern mountains, and I couldn't go more than forty-five kilometers per hour in a lot of places. It would take at least ten hours. How had I missed that?

Looking at the detailed Hallweg map, I could see from the terrain that the mountains of southern Yugoslavia were going to be the most difficult ride of the trip, as Alex had said. The A1 highway was the only road from Belgrade to Salonika, and there were mountains bordering the road that were over five thousand feet. The passes in the mountains were single-lane roads with steep grades.

I poured over the map to see how far I could reasonably go through the mountains in one day and where I would wind up. I calculated that I might be able to get to the city of Skopje, which was 520 kilometers, or nearly seven hours at a slow pace. That would be difficult, but doable. I didn't see any other place I could stay.

Breakfast was rolls, jam, and coffee, and I snuck a couple of rolls for the road in my pocket. Then I paid the bill, which came to twenty-two dollars in dinars, and the manager was nice enough to accept a twenty-dollar AMEX check as part of the payment, which left me extra dinars for the next night in Skopje. I asked the manager about the ride south on the A1.

"After the city of Nis, that is a bad road," the manager said. "There are mountains on either side, which experience rockslides.

The government cannot maintain it well. A river runs close alongside the road, which floods the road in spring, but that should not trouble you now, but there are no guardrails, so you must watch carefully for potential washouts.

"There are steep grades and blind curves, which are not signaled in advance. On a motorcycle, you should do better because there are no lane markings and you can get out of the way of cars coming from the other direction. You truly take your life in your hands up there. And there is no one to come to your assistance should you need it. Now tell me, where are you going to spend the night?"

"In Skopje," I said.

"Well, be sure you get there before nightfall. Do not drive at night. There are bandits in those mountains. They would love to get their hands on a motorcycle like yours."

"Bandits? Really?" I asked, hardly believing.

"Yes, they learned from being partisans during the war. Some never stopped being outlaws."

Holy cow! I thought. *What kind of country is this?*

"What's that weather like?" I asked.

"In the winter, it snows and is very cold. Now, in late spring, it is decent but cool. You shouldn't drive there in the rain because the roads will be slick. It will be foggy in the morning, but when the sun is up, it can be good."

I was less than thrilled to hear the manager's tale. The idea of bandits freaked me out, and I was sure there were no state police patrols. I tipped the manager and the bellboy as I went out to load up the bike. *This is really going into the mouth of the lion*, I thought. I gassed the bike up to the very top before leaving Belgrade and turning south on the A1. It was eight fifteen, and the road was good leaving the city, so I opened up the bike to a hundred kilometers per hour to get a good start on the day.

It was a gorgeous morning, and I decided that with the mountains further down the road, I would go as fast as I could to get to Nis. If I could make it there before noon, I could eat, gas up, and take my time getting through the mountains at whatever speed the road dictated.

Just then, my sunglasses almost got knocked of my head. I reached up and grabbed them just in time. When I stopped by the side of the road, I saw that a large bug had struck the right lens just off-center. It was a mushy mess. I got my water bottle and cleaned it off using my shirttail. This hadn't happened before. I wondered if it was an omen of the pitfalls the manager had spoken of.

As I approached Nis, I saw that the hills were getting steeper all around. Here were forested ravines along both sides of the road and mountains in the distance. The road itself took on more grade, and there were sharper curves. I took an exit for Nis, where I gassed up. Back on the road, I saw from the map that I was in the Morava River Valley, which passed between mountain peaks that it said were between twenty-two hundred to forty-five hundred feet high. I figured top speed on this road would be sixty kilometers per hour.

There were narrow bridges, which allowed the road to pass over the water, but none of them had guardrails or warning signs. If there had ever been a center line painted on the road, it had long since vanished. The road was paved; otherwise it was more like a country trail. I saw signs in Cyrillic, obviously meaningless to me.

I realized I was going to have to concentrate totally on the road, so I dialed the bike down to fifty kilometers per hour because I was about to enter a steep gorge with hills close on either side and the river just thirty feet below with no guardrail in case a car or truck should be coming the other way. This was rugged country.

I rounded a sharp curve and saw a tall mountain on my left, figuring it to be over five thousand feet when compared with the others. But I was forced to keep my attention on the edge of the road to my right where there was no guardrail or shoulder and a drop-off into the river of over a hundred feet. I kept the bike at fifty kilometers per hour because I wanted to get this stretch of road behind me as fast as I could. It wasn't that fast, but I realized that if I hit a stone in the road or a truck came the other way, I could be knocked off the road and down into the river.

I navigated a couple of sharp curves and then saw another meaningless road sign in Cyrillic, so I kept going. And then I was upon the entrance of a tunnel. And then I was driving in the tunnel at fifty kilometers per hour, and it was *pitch-black* all around. I was driving blind! I couldn't see anything ahead or on either side of me. My stunned brain processed the fact that the first thing I had to do was to stop the bike, so I slowly braked while disengaging the gearbox. I rolled to a stop and put my feet on the ground.

I took off my sunglasses and immediately saw that they were a part of the problem. Once my eyes adjusted to the darkness, I turned to see some light at the entrance of the tunnel when I turned my head. The tunnel was curved so that if you were inside it, you couldn't see the far end. Of course, in these mountains, there were no electric lights in the tunnel for safety. *Maybe that's what the sign was about*, I thought.

I understood that by staying cool, I had saved my life, but I also realized that I was still in imminent danger. My blind braking job had left me two feet from the wall of the tunnel on the *wrong side* of the road. Anyone entering the tunnel in that lane would have run me down in an instant. Further, I saw that I couldn't remain motionless in the tunnel on either side because cars entering either way wouldn't be able to see me and stop before smashing into me. I had to get out of the tunnel.

I was too stunned to drive the bike, so I turned the headlight on, put my sunglasses on top of my head, and walked it out of the tunnel. When I was out of it, I discovered the road was in the same condition as on the other side. There was no place to pull over and collect myself. I kept walking the bike up the road until I found a spot where I could see both ways, park the bike, and sit on a stone overlooking the river. I knew I could have been killed, and I kept repeating the hotel manager's words, "There's no one to help you out there."

I determined that I had stared death right in the face, and that face was pitch-black. If death had arms, it would have grabbed me, but either it didn't have them or I had evaded them. My legs were actually shaking as I sat on the stone. I didn't see how I was going to get on that bike again after this experience. For the first time, I saw the true danger in riding a motorcycle, and I wanted no more of it.

But then I remembered what the hotel manager had said about the bandits who would take the bike and probably toss me down the ravine into the river. This was not the time to lose my self-confidence. That could be just as fatal as driving on this road could be. So I made the choice to keep going, keeping the bike below thirty-five kilometers per hour, while passing through the shadows of two thousand- to four thousand-foot peaks as I drove.

I realized I couldn't get to Skopje before nightfall at thirty-five kilometers per hour, but I wasn't going to go any faster until I'd gone through the worst of these mountains. "Jesus! What a road," I grumbled as I sputtered along, watching out for any potential hazards.

Finally, the road widened slightly as I approached a town that had a two-alphabet sign that said "Vranje." My first thought was, *Why couldn't the sign for the tunnel have been in two alphabets?!* I pulled over to the side of the road and got off the bike to wait for the remainder of my anxiety and tension to subside. I looked at the road ahead, where the town of Vranje was situated under a menacing rock ledge that was probably five hundred feet tall. The rocks looked like a vulture waiting to fall on its carrion. I wondered how people could live there, given the nature of the geography in this wilderness. I had another thought: wasn't this earthquake country?

With that thought to spur me on, I got back on the bike, adding my near-death experience to a couple of others from the past caused by my speeding habit, but this one would top the list.

I checked my watch, two forty-five. I'd made good time to Nis, so driving slowly through the most hazardous part of the trip hadn't cost me too badly. I figured I was about one and a half hours from Skopje even if I had to go slow.

Shortly, I came to another section of road, which was as narrow as it was before I came to Vranje, and I had to keep to thirty-five kilometers per hour as I went up steep grades and around curves with no guardrails as the road wound along the river valley. I was passed by two cars going in the opposite direction. There was room to pass, but I sure didn't want to encounter a truck.

Thoughts of my destiny had become blurred as if a fog had descended over them. All I could think of now was how I could get through these mountains alive and make it to Greece.

19

Greece: New Friends

DRIVING A MOTORCYCLE THROUGH the mountains of southern Yugoslavia was proving to be as much of a challenge as I had ever faced. These could hardly be classified "roads" in my experience, and I had little practice driving the big BMW bike in any case. I remembered how cool I felt when I was forging the motorcycle stamp for my AAA International driver's license back home, never anticipating what I might be up against when I actually hit the road. I thought of my friend Hans. He wouldn't have a problem out here. He'd just hitch up his hoden and move on. Despite my feelings of disquiet, I had little choice but to do the same.

I rode on and in an hour the road widened and I could see further ahead into a valley where there were cultivated fields. I figured that this topography was leading toward Skopje, so I juiced the bike up to ninety kilometers per hour. In about twenty minutes, I came to a sign that said that Skopje was 12 kilometers to the right and Salonika was 178 kilometers to the left. I hadn't thought I could go five hundred kilometers through the mountains from Belgrade to Skopje, but I made it, sore, tired, and scared from riding the bike through the treacherous terrain. I definitely could not go further. Besides, I had a wad of dinars to spend, so I went into Skopje to look for a hotel to relax in as I had found in Belgrade.

As I drove into the city, I passed a large park and a hill topped by a medieval fortress and crossed a river. Down the street, I saw a funky multicolored archway with letters over it spelling out the entrance to the Ambasador Hotel with one "s." It was definitely a relic, but I figured that would make it cheaper. I parked right by the entrance and went to the desk, where the clerk got the manager, who spoke broken English. I figured that Skopje wasn't on the usual tours from the States. I'd never heard of it previously.

The manager said rooms were twenty-five hundred dinar, and that included breakfast. I checked my wad and found I had forty-one hundred dinar. Dinner was seven hundred fifty to nine hundred dinar. *Great*, I thought. *That leaves me with extra for gas and then some.* The bellhop got my bags off the bike and escorted me to a third-floor room. I remembered to tip him, but I resolved that this was the last time for this kind of luxury.

After dinner, I asked the manager if there were a laundry service. I wanted to go to Greece with a clean set of clothes. He said I could have my clothes washed overnight for one hundred and eighty dinar. The bellhop would pick them up, and they would be at my door in the morning. *Maybe there was something to traveling first class after all*, I thought.

———◆———

I slept for twelve hours, and some of the tension I'd been carrying from my experience in the mountains had been washed away with the sleep. I thought I might be passing into that dark tunnel again when I turned off the light, but I just flopped onto the pillow and passed out.

When I woke up, I knew the ride to Salonika was only three hours and I was going to finally get to see the Aegean Sea and the ancient land of Greece. I felt that Greece held a vibrant promise for me: in the ancient history and the monuments it had left behind that I loved the pictures of; in the foundation of Western philosophy that had come from there; and from the warmth of the sun and the attraction to people from all over the world who I might be able to find some common ground with.

I loved the stories of the pantheon of the ancient Greek gods and heroes and by the way the Greeks had used their imaginations to weave human and divine characteristics together in their guardian powers. Maybe some of that imaginative air was still there for me to breathe and grab hold of to augment the vision of my future. And what of Crete, the oldest of the Greece civilizations, the mystical island that Eva had discovered and directed me toward? I would go there soon to meet my own challenges.

In the morning I picked up the package of clean laundry from outside my door, packed my bags, went to pay the bill, and thanked the manager. I decided to have breakfast at an outdoor café and then gas up before heading for Salonika.

While looking for a café, I came up to the bridge where I had crossed the river near the fortress on the hill. There was a man selling souvlakis from a pushcart, and the smell was enticing. I pulled over and bought a souvlaki and a thick, dark coffee from his samovar and stood on the bridge looking at the fortress while enjoying my novel breakfast. I had another cup of coffee while I ate a roll. I had time to spare today, but I did want to see the Aegean soon.

I got on the bike and filled it up at a nearby gas station, giving all my remaining dinars to the gas station attendant, who was incredulous, but I was sick of all the different kinds of money I'd been dealing with since Vienna; I was happy to be rid of them. Once I got to Greece, I'd only have to deal with drachmae, and they traded at thirty to one on the dollar, an easy conversion.

As soon as I passed through the southern outskirts of Skopje, I picked up the A1 again, and I found myself hemmed in by deep ravines and bluffs as I wound along the valley of the Vardor River. I kept to fifty kilometers per hour when the road was crimped by a ravine and the river was just a few feet from the road, but there were stretches where the hills opened up and I could make ninety kilometers per hour. Every fifteen to twenty kilometers, I would pass through a village where I could see signs of farming. *This country is for farming rocks*, I thought.

I had been attuned to sudden changes, but now the road slowly widened into a beautiful ride in wild country. There were no villages and no vehicles on the road, just me biking the wilds of southern Yugoslavia. It was far out. The road started to angle slowly downward, so I had to think I was coming out of the mountains.

I started to see more and more cultivated fields, and when I saw a sign: Hellas—12 km, I smiled.. I had biked over seven hundred kilometers of unbelievably rugged country and made it to the promised land. But that trek was not yet my journey's end; I still had five hundred kilometers to get to Athens, however, I could now imagine the spirit of Athena watching over my shoulder and guiding me to my destination.

When I came to the border crossing, the Yugos were officious and feisty. They made me open the saddlebags, but otherwise gave me no trouble. The Greeks were fun-loving in contrast, readily stamping my passport and wishing me a great time in Athens with a few winks to give me the idea. It was two by the time I got going, and it was sixty kilometers to Salonika. I'd get there by three; there was no other town I could go to spend the night in. I didn't want to have to spend more money in a hotel. I'd enjoyed the rest and the meals, but I wanted the raw experience of the road. Maybe I could find a campground.

The terrain flattened out all around and was green with fields and marshes from the river. I went over a rise and saw the shining blue-green expanse of the Aegean Sea about six kilometers ahead. I stood up on my foot supports and shouted, "Here I am!"

I came to a roundabout at the end of the A1. Salonika was ten kilometers to the east; Athens was 515 kilometers to the south. I went toward Salonika, and as I got to the city's outskirts, I saw a campground. I pulled in and saw mostly cars with small trailers that had been converted into campers, which had quite a few children running around them. My intuition told me they were gypsies.

I found the office and asked if I could spend the night with my motorcycle and sleep there using just a sleeping bag. The proprietor said I could sleep anywhere for fifty drachmae. That was nothing, so I asked where the WC was and paid the man. I sought out an area where I could bunk down safely and found a spot under a light. I piled all my gear around me with the sleeping bag in the middle and tried to sleep, but had little success, as I had to watch out for the other campers who never seemed to sleep.

I got up and was on the bike by six thirty as I drove toward the A1 to Athens and found a café just opening. I had rolls, coffee, and a fruit bowl at an outside table while I checked the map. It was going to be a long ride of about six hours, but most of it would be along the seacoast, so that would keep me going. It looked to be a beautiful day too.

I was just finishing breakfast when I was approached by a hippie with blond hair tied in a ponytail. He had circular, rimless, wire-frame spectacles and wore a heavy khaki shirt, which was unbuttoned halfway down his chest, jeans, and a pair of heavy hiking boots. He was of average height; his eyes were as blue as the Aegean,

He put down the large backpack he was carrying and asked in German, "Guten Morgen. Is that your BMW?"

"Yeah, that's my bike. I'm about to hit the road. Long way to Athens."

"Holy cow! Fantastic," said the hippie. "You're American. I am too. My name is Charlie Kluszewski. I'm from Milwaukee, and I'm heading to Athens too." He had a pleasant smile and offhand manner, which made him seem amiable.

Where the hell did this guy come from? I thought. But I could guess why Charlie thought it was great we should meet up.

"I'm Jack Higgins. I'm from New York," I said in a noncommittal manner. "Where have you come from?"

"I've been traveling through Eastern Europe for the past three months. I'm Polish, and I came to see relatives in Poland. I got a visa extension so I went to Moscow. From there, I took a train to Sevastopol and then a ferry to Istanbul. I hitched a ride here with a trucker. I've been here for two days looking for a ride to Athens. You wouldn't have room on your bike, would you? I can pay for gas."

"Wow. That's quite some traveling," I said. "How did you get along behind the Iron Curtain? The commies gave me a hard time at every border."

"I speak six languages. Comes from being brought up in a third-generation Polish family. My grandparents got out before the war. They were Lithuanian and spoke Polish and German. I've got an ear for languages. I speak Polish, English, German, Lithuanian, Russian, and some Greek. I learned Greek in school, a little more difficult."

"You've got to be kidding. The different alphabets drive me crazy. I almost got killed by a Yugo road sign a couple of days ago."

Charlie laughed. He had a pleasant laugh, which evidenced an amusement in my predicament that was not judgmental. I was taking a liking to this well-traveled hipster. I thought about the problems carrying a passenger for five hundred kilometers would entail. With the extra weight, I would be forced to concentrate on driving more. I looked Charlie over. He probably weighed half of what Wild Bill weighed, yet I couldn't tell about the backpack and sleeping bag. But Charlie spoke Greek. That was a major plus, and it would be fun to have someone to share my journey with.

"Look, Charlie, I wouldn't mind giving you a ride. It's just that this is my first long ride on a big bike, and I had no idea of some of the problems you can get into that lead to real trouble so far. I mean the roads over here stink. Poor surfaces, no guardrails, no lighting. I've had one near-death experience already—no shit. Having to deal with the extra weight would be tough."

"Hey, Jack. Are you in rush to get to Athens? I'm not. We can go slow and enjoy the scenery. And I can read the road signs for you." He laughed pleasantly.

With that Charlie won me over. "Hey, sure. Why not? I'll take you to Athens. This could turn out to be a gas. And speaking of gas, I need a fill-up, and there's a gas station at the junction to the highway."

"Thanks a lot! Outstanding! You got it," Charlie said.

I showed Charlie the map and told him it was about a six-hour ride. I also hefted his pack to check its weight. "Holy cow! What've you got in here? Your rock collection?" I said.

I figured the pack weighed forty to fifty pounds, which would make Charlie and his stuff more than equal to Wild Bill's weight.

"It's all road essentials," Charlie said, not waiting for me to change my mind. "Ah, let's see. How do I get aboard this thing?"

I got on the bike first and then tried to let Charlie swing his leg up, but it didn't work. The bike almost fell over. I figured that Charlie was going to have to get on first while the bike was up on the parking stand. Then I could slip my leg over the tank and settle into the driving position and then let the bike drop off the stand with a thud. It worked, but I didn't like it. I hit the electric starter and thanked BMW again because I wouldn't have been able to use the kick-starter with Charlie aboard.

As I cranked the bike up to ninety kilometers per hour, we headed for the road junction to get gas, and Charlie let out a "Whoop!" I got it up to a hundred kilometers per hour, and the bike rode smoothly, but the weight made the steering sluggish. I dialed it back down to eighty kilometers per hour as we approached the junction and pulled into the gas station. As I pulled up to the pump, I realized the real problem the extra weight caused. The brakes were soft.

I tried to stop next to the gas pump, but I couldn't slow down in time so I had to roll past it, drive to the end of the lot, and tell Charlie to lean in the direction I wanted to go to get back to the pump.

When we got to the pump, Charlie indicated that he was aware of the problem. "Looks like we're a little overloaded," he said sheepishly.

"A little. Depends on the speed. You wouldn't mind leaving your backpack on the side of the road, would you?"

"Well, if you don't think it's going to work, I'll find another ride. I mean we don't want to wind up in the Aegean."

"I think we can swing it. I've got to be careful about the speed, and you're going to have to press yourself against my back when we go through sharp curves. You have to feel which way I'm leaning the bike and follow along. I've seen some other makes of bikes with disc brakes and they'd really help. But the BMW has drums, so we're going to have to make do."

I had to whistle for the guy to come fill the tank because I didn't want to go through the loading procedure again. Charlie paid the guy. The tank was three-fourths empty, and it only cost 180 drachmae to fill it. Greece was starting out cheap. I liked that.

"Thanks, Charlie. You've paid your fare to Athens."

"Hey, don't I get meal service on this flight?"

"Just leave your mouth open. You'll pick up some fine bugs on the way."

Charlie slapped me on the shoulder, and we took off.

I remembered from the map that the A1 was a secondary road for about fifty kilometers before it turned back into a highway running along the coast. The speed limit was seventy kilometers per hour, which suited me fine. Charlie hung onto my belt and looked at the scenery. When we came to the highway, it was right next to the coast, stretched out in its blue-green calm as far as the eye could see.

Charlie yelled, "Yahoo!"

I yelled, "Yeah, man!" thinking that this was the place I'd been in search of for a long time. I considered that it was a comfort to have a friend along, despite my resolve that I had come here alone for a purpose. Maybe Charlie had picked up some knowledge on his travels, and he seemed like a fun guy whatever.

We passed the town of Katerini, where the road widened and had been improved with shoulders and guardrails along the waterside. The speed limit was marked at ninety kilometers per hour, but I was hesitant to put it up that high at first. I dialed it to seventy-five kilometers per hour to see how the bike behaved. That was all right. I was just about to go to ninety kilometers per hour when we went around a curve and there, straight in front of us, was an enormous mountain with a snow cap.

Charlie yelled, "Holy shit! Look at that!"

I was awestruck. I knew it was Mt. Olympus, the tallest mountain in Greece and the home of the gods. "Mt. Olympus!" I yelled back at Charlie.

I carefully braked the bike to a stop, slid off the seat, and held the bike while Charlie got off. We just stood and stared at the sharply defined peak, which stood a thousand feet taller than the mountains that flanked it.

"Where else could the gods have lived?" I asked.

Charlie asked to see my map. He saw that Mt. Olympus was marked at 2,911 meters and made the conversion instantly. "Mt. Olympus is 9,550 feet," he said. "And that's 9,550 feet above sea level because there's the sea right there."

"You made that conversion fast."

"I learned how to connect to the metric system long ago because of family. Comes in handy."

I continued to gaze at this spectacular treasure, which I never thought I would see, while Charlie crossed the road to look out over the water. In a minute, Charlie came bounding back across the road and shoved me on the shoulder.

"Look what's coming," he said, pointing up the road toward Salonika.

I turned and saw a motorcycle coming toward us with both a driver and a passenger. The passenger was whooping and yelling for the driver to stop. He had obviously seen Mt. Olympus. The driver pulled the bike up next to the BMW, and the two guys got off. The passenger was going nuts about Mt. Olympus, although he wasn't quite sure it was the real deal. I assured him it was by showing him the map. The guy was ecstatic; the other guy showed hardly any interest. He poked around his bike, a red Norton 750 Commando.

I went over to the guy with the bike and said, "Hi. I'm Jack. That's a nice bike. British, isn't it?"

"Yeah. I've been having some problems with it though. It's been burning oil, and I don't know why."

"If you're going to Athens, I'll bet you can get a tune-up there. You know, that's Mt. Olympus over there ..."

The guy just shook his head and muttered something. He was obviously American, but he didn't mention his name. He had close-cropped hair like a soldier, dark-brown eyes, and a thick nose, and he wore a perpetual scowl. He had on a light-brown leather jacket and pants and what looked like expensive motorcycle boots. I thought he was a sourpuss. How could someone be scowling on a day like this in the shadow of Mt. Olympus?

Charlie had better luck with the passenger, an Australian named Nigel Crowe. I introduced myself. He looked like a wild man from Borneo. His blond hair was long and disheveled. His bright blue eyes flashed with his frequent bursts of enthusiasm. His clothes were torn and filthy. He wore a pair of Converse high-tops, which had strings for laces. Like Charlie, he had a backpack and a sleeping bag, but Nigel's looked a lot smaller. I figured he was a pure hippie, but also a genuine road warrior. He was so funny in how he waxed rhapsodic about Mt. Olympus, as if he hadn't seen anything like it in his year on the road.

"You've been on the road for a year?" I asked him.

"Yeah, mate. I've been hitchhiking all over Europe and the Middle East for about a year. To see anything like this is fantastic. There's only one Mt. Olympus, one Persepolis, one set of pyramids, and one Petra, and I've seen 'em all."

"Wow. That's quite a tour," Charlie said.

"I've seen the Alhambra, the Eiffel Tower, the Tower of London, you name it, and they're all fantastic. Every one of them represents a part of human history. And the people I've met and had a beer with everywhere…All fantastic."

I had heard that Aussies had a wild streak in them, and Nigel was proving the rule. He was totally upbeat, as opposed to the American he had hitched a ride with.

We had walked away from the bikes to get a better look at the mountain, so I asked him about the guy he was riding with.

"Dunno, mate. I just got a ride with him out of Salonika this morning. He doesn't have much to say except he curses that lovely machine he's riding. I could make do with a bike like that.".

We agreed to go to the next town on the map. We could all grab a beer and lunch and see if we wanted to drive to Athens together. so we saddled up and drove the twenty kilometers to Litochoro, a small village off the road that had a taverna and a terrific view of Mt. Olympus.

While we waited for the beers, Charlie asked everyone who they were. I was primarily interested in to finding out who the owner of the Norton was.

When it came to his turn, he said, "I'm Pete Elkins from Hartford, Connecticut. I just got out of the navy after two years. I enlisted because my draft number was ten, and I knew I'd be humping a rifle in the jungle the minute I got out of college.

"I came to Europe three months ago to figure out what to do with the rest of my life."

I thought I might have found a kindred spirit, but Pete evidenced a kind of inner anger that made him unapproachable.

That didn't put Nigel off. "Have you seen anything of Vietnam?" he asked.

Pete deferred the question. "I wanted to see more of the world like the navy said I would if I joined up. Big joke. So I'm doing it on my own now.

"After my discharge, I went to the south of France where I figured it was a hot spot for chicks, but I kept striking out. So I bought the Norton, used, from a dealer. The chicks went crazy for the bike. It was like a magnet. I was getting laid every night. But soon I figured there was something wrong with the oil pressure, so I might have gotten screwed there.

"I saved plenty of money from the navy, but it was too expensive on the Riviera. One of my girlfriends told me I should go to Dubrovnik on the Dalmatian Coast. She said it was beautiful and inexpensive there, and I could see Venice on the way. I thought she wanted to come with me, but I'm strictly on my own, so I left her flat when I took off from St. Tropez.

"Venice was amazing and the ride down the Yugo coast was gorgeous, although the roads were dangerous in places. Dubrovnik was cool, too, but after a week or so I figured out I was at the end of the line. There was nowhere else to go with a bike. Finally I figured I'd go to Athens, and I started out over the mountains of southern Yugoslavia."

"Hey," I said, "I came through those mountains and nearly got myself killed. The roads are totally primitive."

"You ain't shittin'," Pete said, "It was like four hundred kilometers of goat track the whole way from the coast to Skopje. Potholes everywhere. No guardrails where there are two hundred-foot drop-offs. But it turned decent from Skopje to Salonika."

"I came from Belgrade to Skopje. That's where I almost got killed. We must have taken the same road from Skopje to Salonika."

By now, we were working on our third round of beers. I wondered if the Aussie had money to pay his tab, given his appearance. Charlie said we should have lunch while we were in the presence of the gods. A few of the townsfolk had begun to gather at the taverna for their lunch in what was likely a daily ritual. We bikers had disrupted them; they gathered around the bikes to stare and comment.

The proprietor came out and took everyone's orders. I was woozy from having three beers on an empty stomach. I needed food. Soon, a woman brought out a large platter that had a plate of braised lamb, sliced tomato, greens, and feta cheese with a basket of thick-sliced bread on the side.

We dug into the food as if there were no tomorrow. Charlie said he hadn't had breakfast. We had to keep Pete from eating half of everything. He apologized, saying that in the navy you had to eat fast because you never knew when general quarters was going to sound. Nigel guzzled a fourth beer without batting an eye.

We stared at him, and he just said, "Hey, mates, four beers is just wetting my whistle."

When we paid the tab which came to 320 drachmae, or just over ten dollars. We all marveled at how little the meal and the beers cost.

I saw that Nigel had a roll of bills, so I wasn't going to worry about him paying for his beer habits.

"If all Greece works out to cost like this, I could spend a year here," I said to Charlie as we headed for the bike.

"Amen to that," Charlie said.

It was one thirty, and we still had over three hundred kilometers to go to reach Athens. That was five hours, which was a long way in our condition, so I said we should probably camp out on the way to Athens. Everyone agreed, so Charlie pulled out his guidebook of Greece and looked for a campground on the route.

"Hey, look at this," Charlie said. "There's a spa and hot spring at Thermopylae. That's where the three hundred Spartans made their stand against the Persians in 480 BC. That would be a cool place to spend the night. From there, it's only two hours to Athens."

We headed down the coast, sometimes winding inland around some smaller mountains, but always coming back onto the coast. We were riding in tandem, Pete and I matching speed at eighty kilometers per hour. Charlie and Nigel were yelling at each other on the backs of the bikes and having a great time with their hair flying out behind them. We passed through two towns that had mile-high mountains behind them.

I couldn't believe the beauty of the scenery with the blue-green of the sea and the white-blue of the sky sparkling around us in the warmth of the sun and the mountains occasionally cooling us in shadow as we motored down the dreamscape coast of this ancient land. I smiled inwardly. I was happy to have found some fellow adventurers to share my journey, although I could see that the others might not be there for the same reason I was.

Charlie shot his arm out over my shoulder, pointing to a sign and yelling that I should turn right at the next road. Pete saw him and gave a thumbs-up. In one kilometer, I turned onto a dirt road, which led up an incline and then leveled off under a mountain ridge that looked like it was about a thousand feet high. The road led to a paved driveway, which I followed to the front of a fancy hotel with Pete right behind me.

We stopped under a portico, and everyone dismounted. The front of the hotel was all glass, which had gold lettering in Greek on them. Charlie told us that it said, "Thermopylae Hotel and Spa."

"Must be the right place," Nigel said.

Abruptly, the front door opened, and a liveried hotelier stepped out and asked a question in Greek. Charlie answered in Greek, but made it clear that English would be preferred.

"Gentlemen," he said. "Do you have a reservation? We only take guests who have reserved in advance. We do, in fact, have a waiting list. This is an internationally known spa."

I thought that this guy was looking down his nose at us four bikers, who were pretty grimy, and may not have been the usual clientele of a four-star hotel, if that's what this place was. I exchanged glances with the other guys and saw that they were thinking along the same lines.

"We don't want to spend the night," Charlie said. "We just want to use the spa. We've been on the road all day."

"I'm afraid that's impossible," the man said. "The spa and hot spring are for the exclusive use of our guests."

"But the hot spring comes from deep in the ground," Pete said. "Your hotel can't own it unless you own this whole mountain." I saw that Pete was getting pissed off at this guy's attitude.

"The hot spring has been here for millennia, as have the mountains. The hotel has been built over it to take the best advantage of it. It has become famous, and we serve an international clientele. Now I have duties to attend to. Enjoy your stay in Greece." And he went back into the hotel.

"What an asshole!" Pete said.

"I say, an excellent choice of word," Nigel said, laughing.

"So what are we going to do?" I asked. "It's too far to go to Athens. There was a town back up the road about twenty kilometers we could check out."

"No way," Charlie said. "I want a bath in that hot spring. I saw a little sign just before we pulled into the hotel that said the actual hot spring was up the road two kilometers. Let's go check that out."

We drove the bikes further up the hill until we came to a sign that said we were at the hot spring. We left the bikes and followed a path to a pool of water about twenty feet square, which was surrounded by rocks. The rocks had a white, crusty substance on them at the waterline; the water itself had a greenish tinge and bubbled occasionally. I could feel the warmth of the water from a few feet away. The source of the water could only come from inside the earth, spilling out through gaps in the rocks and then tumbling down the hill toward the hotel as a swift-flowing stream.

"Boys, our bath awaits!" Nigel said as he stripped off his clothes and prepared to jump in the pool. Charlie was right behind him. I figured these two hadn't bathed in weeks.

"Hold on a sec, you guys!" Pete yelled. "You don't know what's in the water or how hot it is. You're taking a risk here."

"Ok. I'll stick my toe in first," Nigel said, sitting on a rock and dangling his leg over the water. He put his foot in. "Oooo! That's delightful." He jumped into the spring.

"Listen, Pete," Charlie said. "If the temperature is ok, then I can't think that anything would be wrong with the water. That guy at the hotel said that people come from all over the world to bathe in this water. It's got to be good. I'm going in." And he joined Nigel in the water.

I looked at Pete and shrugged. I could use a high-priced spa for free so I started to undress.

"Hang on a sec, Jack," Charlie yelled. "Could you go up and get my shampoo and soap out of my pack? Might as well do this right."

I gave him a thumbs-up and got his stuff. By the time I got back, Pete was in the water.

"Man, this is really fine," Pete said, floating on his back. "So relaxing. Gets the kinks out from riding the bike."

I stripped and climbed slowly into the water, which I found to be between warm and hot. It definitely relaxed my muscles. I gave Charlie the soap and shampoo and floated on my back for a while.

"Jeez, look at this," Charlie said, disturbing my reverie.

I looked over at Charlie and saw he was covered in a mountain of bubbles, which seemed to be multiplying out of nowhere.

"What the hell? Did you use the whole bottle?" Pete asked.

"I only used the usual amount. I wanted to clean my hair. There must be something in the water."

"Give me some of that," Nigel demanded. He proceeded to lather up, causing the same effect as Charlie had. By now, more than half the spring was covered in bubbles.

"I'm next," Pete said, and Nigel tossed him the bottle.

By the time we all had a good wash, the entire spring was two feet deep in bubbles. When I tried to climb out, I was still covered in bubbles and wanted to rinse off but couldn't. I pointed this out to the guys, and Pete, who had taken a real dislike for the snoot at the hotel, came up with an idea.

"Let's get a couple of branches off the ground. We can use them to corral all the bubbles and push them down to the stream. Maybe they'll wind up in the spa and screw that asshole over. At least we can get rinsed when we get out of the pool."

That set the guys in motion, and before long, we had cleared the surface of the pool. We watched with glee as the mounds of bubbles roiled down the stream toward the hotel. Then we rinsed and went back to the bikes to dress.

"Nigel, you actually look like a human being now that you've got all that dirt off you. You aren't really going to get dressed back in those rags you took off, are you? I mean, no offense, but you stunk even when you were sitting behind me on the road," Pete said.

"Well, I was going to get some new clothes when we got to the city."

"Tell you what. I can give you some underwear and a pair of shorts. Can either of you guys give him a shirt?" I dug a shirt out of my saddlebag, figuring I could replace it in Athens.

The sun had gone down behind the mountain ridge, which towered behind us, so the question remained as to where we were going to spend the night. We decided that since we all had sleeping bags, we'd sleep under the stars on the mountain. There was still enough light to follow the dirt track up past the hot spring. It took a hairpin curve and then paralleled the ridge for a half kilometer until we came to a treeless fifty-foot-long flat rock outcrop, which overlooked the bay beyond Thermopylae.

We were all speechless as we got off the bikes and walked over to the edge of the rock and watched the sun burnishing the mountains on the island across the bay in gold and azure as it set on them, leaving the waters below an iridescent light blue.

"I don't think the blokes in that fuckin' hotel have got it any better than this," Nigel said.

No one disagreed with that statement as we unpacked our stuff and laid out our sleeping bags. Nigel had the drill down best as he went into the surrounding brush to get bedding to put under his sleeping bag. We all followed his lead. Charlie then got some kindling and some small logs and started a campfire.

With the darkness descending, I said, "The ancient Greeks might have camped on this very spot twenty-five hundred years ago to look out for the Persian fleet."

"That's a nice thought, mate. But right now I'm much more interested in current affairs, like with the ladies," Nigel said, getting full agreement from Pete.

I was embarrassed for a moment but decided to take advantage of the opening Nigel provided.

"Hey, I'd like to run something by you guys," I said. "I just broke off with someone. I admit it was my first real relationship, but I don't know how well I handled it. She was French and fourteen years older than I was, but I wasn't really sure what I was doing."

"Hold on, mate! You're telling us that you had your first affair with a Frenchie who was fourteen years older than you? I'd say you were doing a lot right just to get in her pants!"

Nigel, Pete, and Charlie burst out laughing, leaving me flustered at what I considered to be a somewhat sensitive matter.

"I wasn't going after her or anything. It just happened," I said. "Maybe having the bike might have helped move the situation along."

"You ain't shittin'," Pete said. "All you have to do is stand next to your bike and the women come crawling all over you."

"One at a time was plenty," I said. "She sort of had control of the situation. She showed me quite a bit of stuff, I guess, but it seemed to be on her terms."

I thought a moment before revealing more to these guys whom I had only known for a few hours, but I figured that it might be better to talk these things out while the subject was open and with guys I might never see again. This was my journey. I might not get the chance again.

"I mean, I didn't have any real knowledge, so I didn't know what to ask for. She asked me to do stuff for her. Then she got me off, and that was pretty much it. Should there have been more?"

Nigel and Pete snorted indulgently, and Nigel said, "Yes, indeed there should. Let me ask you: did you lick her pussy?"

"Yeah, she liked that."

"And did you get a blow job in return?"

"Only once. I didn't ask again."

"You should have. After all, fair is fair, right?"

I saw the point, but I wasn't sure how to bring up the subject. I could imagine the girls I knew back home being horrified at the suggestion.

"Look," Nigel said. "Here's what you do. Girls love to have their pussies sucked, so while you're doing that, just maneuver your body around on the bed so your cock is in front of her face. Any decent girl will get the idea and start sucking on you. Fair is fair, right?"

"I guess so," I said, lacking conviction as to what I thought was a somewhat primitive maneuver.

"And if she doesn't, screw her at your pleasure and move on to the next one 'cause she ain't the right one. You can't be tenderhearted with women. You'll let them ruin your life if you are."

Pete decided to chime in. "I learned a few things about women in school and a lot more in the navy, although those were mostly hookers. Still, lessons learned: One, treat 'em nice and make 'em laugh and they'll give it up. Two, all women want it as much as we do. You've just got to tease it out of them. They all want to be called the most beautiful girl in the world, although sometimes you've got to be pretty drunk to say it."

That got a roar of laughter.

"Three, have something they can't get from the next guy, like our bikes. These machines are like magnets for women. You can't fail to get laid."

Pete lay back with a snug smile at having resolved the universal problem of how a guy gets a girl in the sack. Nigel nodded at his sagacity. Charlie, like me, looked a little perplexed.

Finally, I said, "These tales make for good stories around the campfire, but there still has to be an element of engagement. Like, how do you break the ice? You guys have been all over the place. You know American what women are like. They can freeze you out before you even get started. How do you get around that?"

"American women want to get married," Pete said. "They're trained from birth."

Everyone laughed.

"No, seriously, from what I've seen, most American women won't give it away without the promise of a ring," Pete said. "That's one of the reasons I'm over here now having fun. I've got some sorting out to do, and I sure as hell don't want some bitchy girl hounding me about marriage when all I want to do is get laid while I'm figuring out my life. I mean, is that too much to ask?"

"Sounds reasonable to me," Nigel said. "The shielas back home and the women here in Europe are sophisticated about sex. They know everyone needs it. It's live and let live. If it turns into an *affair de coeur*, well, that can be another story. I've never had one of those, although I came close once. I realized it just in time and made my escape."

There was more laughter all around. I lay back and looked up at the stars. I'd absorbed more practical knowledge about the pragmatic mores of sex in two hours than I'd known in my life. There was something about hearing these stories told around the campfire as in ancient times that resonated with me. What Nigel and Pete said probably wasn't universal truth, but their stories had opened my thinking toward sex as a simple human reality. By imagining too much around the subject, I had allowed the simplicity of male-female interaction to overcome the basics. Pete and Nigel had found a simple approach to it, and that was enough. I'd have to strip away my past trepidations and revisit what I'd learned from Eva.

I didn't think when I was with her. Things just happened.

20

On to Athens

THE SUN WOKE US, first rising with fingers of intense rays over the mountain ridges of the island off the coast and then shimmering off the Aegean all around and illuminating the bay between the island and the mountains and the mainland as a dark-blue abyss. I was entranced by the scene, the colors, and my awareness of the moment. I looked over at my companions as they grumbled out of sleep and wondered what they thought about their place in this extraordinary setting.

"Fuck! I'm hungry," Nigel groused, bringing my thoughts down to earth.

I was hungry too. We had split up what snacks we had for a communal dinner, but my stomach was growling now. It was five thirty in the morning, and I hadn't eaten since lunch yesterday.

"Let's get going," Nigel persisted. "There has to be a spot within a few klicks where we can get something to eat."

I let Pete lead the way down the rocky path past the hotel and spa and back to the main road. In about fifteen minutes, we pulled into the main square of a village that was just waking up. We didn't see a taverna, so Charlie asked one of the locals if there were a place we could buy something to eat.

After a brief discussion, Charlie came back and said, "The baker will have the first loaves of the day ready soon." Then he pointed to a house where a woman sold fresh strawberries and yogurt.

"Sounds like breakfast to me," Nigel said, so he and Charlie went to buy the strawberries and yogurt, returning with a large bowl of each with four spoons. There was enough to feed eight people.

"I'm beginning to love Greece," I said as I bit on a wonderfully sweet strawberry and then took a spoonful of the thick, white yogurt. I'd never had yogurt before. Its slightly bitter taste complimented the sweetness of the fresh strawberries.

The baker's wife called out to the villagers that the first bread of the day was ready, so Charlie and I joined the line to get some. The smell of the freshly cooked bread just out of the oven was delectable. Each loaf was the size and shape of a football, only flat on the bottom, dark brown, thick and crusty, and piping hot. The women who bought them held them in their aprons. Charlie took off his shirt to hold two of the hot loaves. I figured two loaves would be enough, but Charlie spotted some jars of raw honey on a shelf and asked if they were for sale.

We left the baker's shop with two jars of honey and four loaves of bread. When we showed Nigel and Pete our haul, they were flabbergasted. It all had cost three hundred drachmae, ten bucks, for a huge breakfast for four.

We took our time enjoying our food, sitting in the shade on stones that circled an old cypress tree in the center of the town square. I poured honey on chunks of bread and munched contentedly. Nigel mixed some honey in his yogurt to sweeten it, and soon we were all doing it. Pete kept saying he hadn't had a better breakfast in a restaurant in three months. We were relaxed and content. I couldn't imagine a more peaceful scene.

Then I wondered why there had to be so much discord in the world, as the memories of the obstacles I faced contrasted with my current setting. I knew that this idyll was just a respite. I had a long way to go with the draft hanging over me, and even if I got out of that, my life path was still undetermined. I had picked out Pete as someone who had made choices and was working out his future, so I went over and told him that I was waiting out the draft here in Europe.

"Good decision," Pete said. "I sure got fucked with my draft number, but it clarified things. I had to enlist in the navy. I hope you don't get sucked into that meat grinder of the army. One time when we pulled into Cam Rahn Bay, we saw these Starlifters land and belch out whole companies of raw recruits. Once they'd cleared the area, they'd load the planes up again with coffins. It was really depressing. Then we'd go get drunk and go find some pussy. If they call your number, stay here." That was all he said.

What Pete said was a real bummer. I'd guessed it was bad in Vietnam, but here was a firsthand account of what the body count meant. I had toyed with the idea of not going back home if I were going to get drafted. Now Pete was advocating for it because he'd seen what it was actually like. But I didn't know if I could live my life as an exile, which would probably be permanent. Jesus, what a bind.

The only possible saving grace I could see was that Nixon was lowering the draft number each year because the draft was a political liability for him in an election year. But his decision to invade Cambodia showed that Nixon could not be trusted, so where the hell did that leave me?

Well, I was here now, and it was a beautiful place. And I was on a mission to discover more about myself, so I'd have to wait out my draft call-up number. But the pressure of waiting for that was squeezing measures of joy from my life despite my immediate surroundings.

We left the village with full bellies and anticipation of seeing Athens in a couple of hours. Nigel and Charlie were really whooping it up. We'd gone about sixty kilometers down the highway, which got more improved as we neared the city when suddenly, we heard sirens go off behind us. I saw two motorcycle cops in my rearview mirror waving at us to pull over. I couldn't think as to why. We certainly hadn't been speeding the way we were loaded up, but Pete and I pulled off the road and waited for the cops to come up to tell us what their problem was. I sure was glad Charlie was there. He took charge and surprised the cops by speaking Greek at them. There was a brief discussion, and the cops then mounted their bikes and went back the way they came. Charlie sauntered back with a self-satisfied look on his face.

"What the hell was that all about?" Pete asked.

"Apparently, it's against the law for motorcyclists to ride in tandem," Charlie told him.

"Oh, fuck that," Pete said, starting up his bike.

"I totally agree," I said. "But let's give them a couple of minutes to go back around the curves where they came from before we go on."

"Good point," Nigel added. "We've only got fifty kilometers to go to get to Athens. No sense in courting trouble."

Pete turned off his bike, disgustedly. While we waited, we talked about where we wanted to go once we got to the city. Charlie and I were up for the Plaka, the area just below the Acropolis where there were hotels for ten drachmae per night and lots of cafés. I had a passion for seeing the Acropolis.

Nigel and Pete wanted to go to Piraeus, where the women were. It was Athens seaport and known to be the sleaziest port on the Mediterranean for hookers. Charlie said we should probably split up once we got to the city and maybe we could catch up later. We agreed as we mounted the bikes and drove in tandem toward Athens.

In a half hour, we turned a curve and saw the Acropolis with the Parthenon crowning its height. Everyone except Pete let out a "Whoop!" We drove down a hill until the highway ran into Patission Street. We watched the Parthenon looming larger as we neared the center of the city at Omonia Square, where we stopped at an outdoor café in the square for a few parting words, and I noticed again that here in the city the big bikes attracted attention. The silver BMW and the red Norton were not common sights.

Nigel suggested that a beer was in order if we were going to part company. I couldn't believe how that little guy could pour down the suds. We pulled the bikes up onto the sidewalk next to the café tables and spread out to discuss our trip down the coast. Once the beers came, Nigel had a few swigs and started laughing about the soap bubbles going into the spa. We all started laughing, and the people walking on the street looked at us in some apprehension, as if we were the Scythian invaders of ancient times.

I had the best view of the Acropolis from my chair. I could hardly wait to go up and look around. I was ready to let Nigel and Pete go cruising for women in Piraeus. They sure were on a different path than I was; Charlie too, from what I could tell. How could they come to Athens and just prowl for sleazy women? Everyone to their own tastes, I guessed. Soon they loaded up Pete's bike and went their way to Piraeus. Charlie and I took Ermou Street from the square and made a quick right turn into the Plaka.

The Plaka is an ancient neighborhood that clings to the bottom of the Acropolis as a young child clings to its mother's skirts. It encompasses only a quarter of the base around the hill of the Acropolis. Most of the streets angle down from the high walls of the Acropolis. There are cross streets, which connect to them to make a cobweb of neighborhoods, with some streets passable by cars, others are pedestrian walkways.

The buildings were painted blue, ochre, and yellow with shutters of red and orange. There were cafés with outdoor tables and many tourist gift shops around the lowest level nearest to the gate, which led to the stairs to the temples on the top of the hill. Almost every street led up toward the Acropolis, but ended at the cliffs, which were ninety feet high. These cliffs had barred entry to the temples on the sacred ground on top for millennia.

As we cruised slowly around looking for lodging, I saw that the lower level of the Plaka was a tourist trap, but as I drove higher, I was charmed by the colors and the irregular layout of the streets. People lived here much as they had for centuries. Charlie had been directing me to take certain streets, as he had seen signs for various possible lodgings. Finally he called a halt and told me what he had seen.

"There are two small hotels and two houses that have rooms to rent. I'm thinking that if the prices here are like what we've seen so far, maybe we can handle a hotel."

"Sounds good to me," I said.

So we drove to a hotel, and Charlie went in to check the rates. He came out and said that a single room was one hundred and twenty drachmae per night (four dollars) or eight hundred drachmae per week (twenty-four dollars). There was a communal WC and shower on each floor.

I said that sounded good, but Charlie said we should check the hotel that was further up the hill. He thought it might be cheaper because of the walk up the hill. We had the bike, so it wouldn't make any difference to us, so I drove up to the next hotel, which was smaller and truly overshadowed by the cliffs above.

"Quite a spot. I hope nobody throws anything off the top," I said.

Charlie went in and came out with a grin on his face. "We can get single rooms here for six hundred drachmae per week (twenty dollars) or a thousand drachmae (thirty-three dollars) for two weeks. There are only four rooms on the third floor, and they're all empty. We'd get a shower and a WC to ourselves, at least for now."

"That's great," I said. "Sign me up for two weeks. I'm heading for Crete at some point, but I might as well take advantage of these prices to have a place to stay."

We unloaded our stuff, and on the way up the steps the proprietor, Yiannis, came out to help us. Yiannis was probably in his mid-twenties, I guessed. He had dark hair and olive-colored skin like many Greeks. He tried to be helpful and do everything at once, but mostly got in his own way.

In the front hall, we met Arianna, Yiannis' wife. She was clearly at least six months pregnant, yet she was about to tote all the towels and bedding up to our room. We looked at each other and shook our heads. Charlie explained to Yiannis that if we needed anything from downstairs, we would come get it ourselves. Yiannis protested, but Charlie said it was nothing. We both paid for the two weeks in advance, and it was settled. Yiannis looked very pleased.

We took the two rooms that overlooked the street we had come up, which gave us a great view of the Plaka and north into the commercial district of the city. Just down the street, there were two sidewalk cafés and flowering trees, which overhung the street and clung to the walls of the mustard-colored buildings. The pink flowers gave beautiful highlights to the buildings.

I stuck my head into Charlie's room next door, but Charlie hadn't come upstairs yet. I figured he was chatting with Yiannis and Arianna. Charlie was out-going like that, good to have along. So I made up my bed and unpacked. By the time I got all my stuff out and squared away, I realized I hadn't been at home since Berlin. My saddlebags had kept the road dirt off the packed clothes, but I needed to have my riding gear washed, and I had to buy a couple of polo shirts and at least one pair of shorts because it was warm in Athens at twenty-five degrees Celsius (seventy-seven degrees Fahrenheit) and it was only late May. So clothes were on the to-do list, but if the prices in Greece held up, this was going to be a lark financially.

Charlie came upstairs and was similarly impressed by the view. He said that Yiannis had taken over the hotel from his father who had died suddenly. He had been learning the business and was just getting used to being in charge. Yiannis was very happy that we had paid in advance and would take care of getting anything we needed. He thanked Charlie for not having Arianna to worry about walking upstairs.

"Well, ask her to do a wash for me," I said, "but don't tell him that the room rates are ridiculously low."

We both laughed, and Charlie said he'd put his wash in with mine and take it down to Arianna. I showered and dressed in street clothes, as did Charlie. We went downstairs, leaving the wash, and went to explore the city on foot.

It was bright, sunny, and full of life as we walked down the hill. I wanted to see the Acropolis, but when we reached the gates, we found that it was closing in an hour, so there wasn't enough time to go up and really see it. I resolved to go up in the morning the next day.

We followed the map back to Omonia Square, where we found a book shop, and each of us bought guidebooks that had maps of the city center and descriptions of points of interest. I bought a history of the gods and heroes of ancient times to refresh my memory. Then we returned to the Plaka by a different route so we could get oriented to the area. We settled into a taverna near a church for some Fix Hellas beers and dinner.

I was glad of the walk to stretch out after driving the bike, but I was tired by now. When the first beers came, I told Charlie to have the waiter take his time because we would be here a while to learn the city. Charlie agreed; he'd had enough of the road too. He said that while the spot they had slept last night had incredible views, the granite mattress left something to be desired. I started laughing at the reference to the granite mattress, but then I remembered the soap bubble attack we made on the spa, and the two of us went off in gales of laughter. That was sweet revenge.

When we finally got it together, I told Charlie I was glad I had picked him up. I felt like we were kindred spirits. I was also really lucky I'd picked up someone who spoke Greek. What were the odds?

Charlie felt the same. "Sometimes you just know," he said.

We sipped on our beers and found some places we wanted to see from the guidebooks. We could relax and enjoy Athens with our rooms paid for two weeks in advance. We both said it was a luxury. I wanted to visit some key places, but I also wanted to have some time to stretch out on my bed to read and think.

That brought me back to Charlie. While we were companionable, I didn't know anything about him or what he was thinking about as far as getting on with his life was concerned. It was the end of a long day, but I always wanted to know what a guy's draft number was. It was the elephant in every guy's pocket. My elephant had tusks that poked at me constantly.

So during our second round of beers, I asked him, "Charlie, what's your draft number?"

"Two ninety-six. I was so happy when that number came up. I got stoned for three days."

"What's yours?" he asked.

"It's 166," I said, dejectedly.

"Hey, the call-up number has been coming down every year for the past couple of years, so it might work out ok for you"

"I've already had a physical, which is not a good omen, but the number hasn't been drawn for this year, so I'm on tenterhooks. That's one reason I came over here, to beat the stress."

"Look, you are here, so put the damn thing out of your mind and enjoy the moment you've created for yourself." Charlie said.

I really liked the sound of that and resolved to do my best to follow Charlie's advice.

Charlie had a way of projecting calm about himself, which I thought I could learn from. It seemed like it came from within Charlie, like the tranquility Siddhartha personified. It just seemed to be a natural mindset. Right now, it was too heavy a subject for me to want to consider, so we ate our dinner and walked back to the hotel, said good night to Yiannis, and went to bed.

When I started to sleep, I thought about Charlie and his easygoing approach to life. I slept a long time, very deeply, but just before I awoke, I had a dream about falling into a dark hole where there was no light. I couldn't tell what the situation was, but I remembered just falling forever into the darkness. Maybe it had something to do with the tunnel in Yugoslavia. You never know about these things.

21

In Athens

WHEN I GOT UP and looked out the window, the lovely street scene was playing out down the street in the midday sun. I looked at my watch, eleven forty-five. I needed that sleep. The bike really ate up my energy, but now my body felt relaxed and refreshed. I went to the shower to give myself a clean start on the day.

I noticed that Charlie's door was still closed. I didn't know what the perils of hitchhiking were like, but I figured a hitchhiker might be lucky to get one good night's sleep in ten, so Charlie likely needed his rest more than I did.

I was getting dressed when Charlie stuck his head in my door. "Whew! That was some sleeping. Over twelve hours. Good for the body and the soul," Charlie said.

"I needed it too. The only problem is that we've missed the Acropolis for today."

"We'll figure out something else. Let's get some breakfast."

We went out into the bright sunshine. We both added new sunglasses on the to-do list, as we walked down the street squinting against the sun. We reached Ermou Street, the first large street below the Plaka. We soon discovered it to be a major retail shopping drag and were about to retreat back up into the friendlier confines of the Plaka to find some breakfast when I spotted a Lacoste store. I loved the croc shirts for their colors, so we went in and couldn't believe that they cost less than a third what they did in New York.

I bought two of them and a pair of shorts. Charlie bought a shirt and shorts.

We walked a little further down the street and saw a rack of Foster Grant sunglasses outside another store. We tried on a half-dozen pairs before settling on a pair each. I found some wraparound glasses that hugged my ears.

"Essential equipment for biking," I said.

"And cool enough to mingle with the tourists," Charlie said.

We sat at an outdoor table at a café on the edge of the Plaka and ate pastries with honey and yogurt and drank coffee. After brunch, we wandered off into the less-populated areas of the Plaka to see what we could see. We explored the cross-streets, where there were few gift shops and eateries. There were alleyways connecting streets where tradesmen made leather goods and women sewed shawls and traditional skirts.

As we walked down a particularly gloomy alley, Charlie stopped, his eyes transfixed by a strange-looking, two-foot-tall object in the small display window. I looked at it and saw that it was an extraordinarily ornate crown mounted on a pedestal. The crown itself was well over a foot tall, rounded on top, bulbous in the middle, and tapered at the bottom so it would fit on a person's head. It was elaborately decorated with symbolic eagles all around with a larger one in front. There were stars made up of what appeared to be diamonds and rubies all over, and on top was a cross made of gold encrusted with diamonds. The background color was crimson silk, which showed the gold off to stunning effect.

I nudged Charlie. "What is it?"

"It's a Greek Orthodox Patriarch's crown. I've seen a couple at home. It's like a Protestant Archbishop's mitre, only much fancier. I wonder why one is here in this window."

There was a passageway leading to a door with a small sign on it, and Charlie went to see what it said. I didn't like the narrowness of the alleys we had already traversed, so I waited for Charlie to come back. I watched as Charlie knocked a couple of times on the door and was surprised when it opened. After a couple of minutes, Charlie waved at me to come join him. I walked down the alley where Charlie introduced me to George.

George was someone like I had never seen. He stood about five-foot-five, thin to the point of emaciation. His skin was almost translucent. It didn't appear that he had been out in the sun in years. The skin on his face was pulled taut so that his cheekbones and chin showed prominently and caused his eyes to rest deep in their sockets. He was a living skeleton from what I could see. However, George turned to speak to me, and that was when I looked in his eyes and saw a twinkle of life there, but there was also sorrow and heart-rending pain.

I repressed an expression of shock, thinking the man might have a terminal illness or something. George invited Charlie and me into the shop. The room was about twenty feet square with a low ceiling and no windows. There were three main tables where several crowns were in various stages of assembly with dozens of boxes of decorations like the ones on the crown in the window on them.

There were three stools for the workbenches, and George went slowly about arranging them in a circle. He placed the stools in a circle and shut off all but one of the lights. When we were bid to sit in the circle, I had the feeling that we were sitting in a cave in prehistoric times as the one light cast weird shadows like a campfire on the walls all around.

"George told me he is the only person in the world who makes these crowns for the Greek Orthodox Church," Charlie said. "When I told him my grandparents were Orthodox from Lithuania and I would like to put one of the crowns on my head, he asked me if they had died in a concentration camp in WWII. I told him they had escaped before the war, but some of my other relatives had not. That's when he said I could come in."

Charlie spoke briefly to George and pointed to me. He told me he would translate George's story to me verbatim as he spoke. I was mesmerized already. George began to tell his story. His voice seemed to become separate from his frail body as he invoked the past.

I was fourteen when I began to work with my father and brothers against the Germans in the Eleftheria, the Greek Resistance. This was in 1942. I was used as a courier taking messages from town to town on my bicycle. I was small, and a child would not be suspect. One of my brothers was caught and executed in 1943, and the Nazis burned our entire village. That's what they did to stop the Resistance. They burned more than fifteen hundred towns in Greece, and the people had to live in the hills and the mountains. Many starved, but my father was a cell leader, and he hated the Germans so he kept up his resistance work, killing officers, blowing up trucks full of soldiers and supplies. By the summer of 1944, everyone was half-starved, and word came that the Nazis were being beaten by the Russians and would have to pull out of Greece at any time. We were very happy to hear this, and we let our guard down by coming out of hiding to steal some food from the Nazis. The SS caught us and executed my father, whom they had been searching for years. My mother, sisters, and I were sent to concentration camps.

I don't know where they were sent. I never saw them again. I was sent to Birkenau and made to do forced labor. They first made us move rocks from one place to another to exhaust us before gassing us. But in the winter of 1944, I was selected to a special squad called the Sonderkommando. Our job was to take the bodies of those who were gassed from the gas chambers and put them into the ovens to be burned. This was important work for the Nazis to have done, so they fed us more. That's how I survived. However, some of the men in my squad told me they knew that the Nazis rotated Sonderkommandos every ninety days, bringing in new ones and shooting the old ones. This was because they didn't want any witnesses to the act of taking gassed people direct to the ovens. I began to count the days, but before I reached seventy, one day the guards burst into our room and started shooting everyone. I fell under someone who was shot and stayed there a long time.

When I got up, I saw that another man had survived. We went to the door and went outside. The first thing we saw was that there were no German guards. The prisoners were walking around freely. Then we saw the Russians come in riding in vehicles and a couple of tanks. Some of the people got down on their knees before the Russians to thank them, but they didn't wait around. They left the gates open and took off after the Germans. My companion wanted to go east because that was where the Russians would be coming from. I wanted to go home to Greece, so I went south.

Of course, there was no doubt about what we were, wearing those striped pajamas, so I had to stay out of sight and travel at night.

I managed to steal some vegetables from a farm. And one time I waved down a passing Russian officer's car. He was horrified by my looks, but I learned I was in the south of Poland. He then threw me a coat and some bread and drove away. HPPSdr.exe

That was how I traveled for many days. I had no shoes, but my feet were used to that. Once I stole a skiff to cross a river. I would find refugees on every road, and some would share food. I finally came to Macedonia, where I could hide from the Nazis, by then it was spring, and only the partisans were there. They fed me and took me toward the Greek border. From there I made it to Athens. The Nazis were gone, and the war was over.

But everyone was starving. There were relief attempts, but black marketeers stole a lot of the food. You needed money to survive. I looked like a ghost. I had run out of strength. I sat on a curbstone in front of a church and looked up at the Parthenon. I had a delusion that Athena would come down and help me.

But it wasn't entirely a delusion. An old man had stepped in front of my view and asked me if I would like to have something to eat. He put his arm around my body and led me to this very shop where we are sitting now. He fed me broth and some cheese for strength and let me gain strength for what seemed like a long time as I lay on a cot over there in the corner. I would hear people come and go sometimes.

When I was finally well enough to get up, I learned what he did here. It looks much the same now as it did then. The old man told me he had a son, but he was in the Eleftheria, and the Nazis caught him in the hills and executed him. He had hoped that his son would take his job of making crowns for the church when he died. He had the appointment from the Patriarch of Constantinople himself. He was getting old and needed someone to succeed him, so he asked me if I would like to learn his trade. I fell on my hands and cried in thanking him. I was just eighteen with no home, no family, and no food, and life looked to be at an end, and this man found me and saved me.

Tears flowed down George's cheeks. My eyes were unabashedly brimming with tears as well. So were Charlie's.

We all took a few minutes to recover. Then George said, "I pledged to this man that I would continue this work as long as I live. The church is in need of these regalia of authority. He taught me the trade for eight years before he died. Now I am only forty-two, but I fear that my deprivations will bring me to an early end. So be it. I have lived my life well on a path that was chosen for me."

Charlie had been translating for me all along and was in need of a break. I was drained from this story of horror. I knew about the concentration camps, but I never imagined I would be listening to the firsthand tale of a survivor.

Then George did something surprising. He stood up and smiled at us and then said to Charlie, "Thank you for listening to my story. I tell it poorly, but it is good to have it told."

Charlie asked George if he could put a crown on his head. George hesitated. I thought it might be a sacrilege or something. George got up and gave Charlie a crown, which was not quite completed. Charlie took the crown and gently put it on his head. It was much too big and slid down over his eyes. He pushed it up with his thumbs and said, laughing, "That what I get for being curious."

George took the crown from him with a stern look and put it back.

"Thank you for your hospitality," Charlie said to George. "Your story is one we will never forget."

"It has been years since I have had visitors who were not church officials, so I was pleased to have you stop by," George said.

I was astonished by George's story. I couldn't get my head around it. When I was fourteen to eighteen, I was sent away to prep school and had hated it. I once had referred to it as a concentration camp, but after hearing George's story, I'd never say that again. George's experience of those years in his life was beyond my imagination. George lived with death either staring him in the face or looking over his shoulder that entire time, while his home and family were torn from him. And then, at the last when he had given up hope, he found his path, or had it found him? It was inconceivable. Did life work that way?

George's tale had taken the gaiety out of the bright Athens scene for both Charlie and me. We had nothing to say as we walked back to the more populated parts of the Plaka. I said I'd like to return to the hotel to do some reading; Charlie wanted to walk around the city, so we split up.

When was back in my room, I sat on the edge of the bed and stared at the floor. I took my head in my hands and softly began to weep. I tried to determine a cause for my breakdown, initially thinking that it might have been triggered by the horrors of the story George had told. But while I grieved for George, I came to realize that my sadness was caused by my personal angst.

I had come to comprehend my own story in a more complete sense. I had a painful childhood, however privileged, and was now actively seeking for those things within myself that would break me away from the bonds of childhood and define me as a man. I was set on living life as my own man, not defined by the lives of my parents. And whether I succeeded or not, in the end I would die.

In these terms, life seemed so pointless, and the journey to get there was so hard. I didn't want to die, but I would, and for what? Some sort of self-determination? At that point, I stopped weeping. I was man enough to know that that was how life worked. Death was the end point you couldn't get around.

I needed to change my mindset, so I picked up the *Tropic of Cancer* and propped myself on the pillow. I liked books, but I didn't know what to expect from this one with its savage reputation. I knew that Miller's books were banned in the United States as soon as they were published. *Tropic* had been published in 1934. What had Miller written that caused all the ruckus?

I read the short preface to this edition, which was written by Anais Nin, one of Miller's many lovers, where she stated that what drives the book is "an obedience to flow." In reading that, I was reminded of Siddhartha and the river. But then I read Nin's warning that,

> *Here is a book which, if such a thing were possible, might restore our appetite for the fundamental realities. The predominant note will seem one of bitterness, and bitterness there is, to the full. But there is also a wild extravagance, a mad gaiety, a verve, a gusto, at times almost a delirium...*
>
> *In a world grown paralyzed with introspection and constipated by delicate mental meals this brutal exposure of the substantial body comes as a vitalizing current of blood ... We need a blood transfusion.*

I finished the preface and paused. *This was going to be a wild ride,* I thought, as I delved into Miller's expatriate life in Paris in the 1930s. On the first page, Miller began his theme.

> *We are all here and we are dead... There will be more calamities, more death, more despair. Not the slightest indication of a change anywhere. The cancer of time is eating us away... There is no escape.*

This was mirroring the thought in my own head when I picked up the book, so I read on. And in the next paragraph, I was brought up short when Miller wrote,

> *It is now the fall of my second year in Paris. I was sent here for a reason I have not yet been able to fathom.*
>
> *I have no money, no resources, no hopes. I am the happiest man alive. I no longer think about it, I AM. Everything that was literature has fallen from me. There are no more books to be written, thank God. This, then? This is not a book. This is libel, slander, defamation of character. This is not a book in the ordinary sense of the word. No, this is a prolonged insult, a gob of spit in the face of Art, a kick in the pants of God ...*

As I read about Miller's chaotic circumstances. I was lifted from my somber mood. Nothing was sacred to Miller; everything was profane. Sex oozed everywhere as the most normal of human interactions. Miller's emotions ran riot on every page. His paragraphs consumed whole pages. He disgorged his story comingled with his opinions and his feelings. The prose swept me along, through the streets and cafés of Paris, into the business and the beds of the Parisian whores. Miller seemed to have an obsession for whores, describing their activities in graphic detail, in particular one called Germaine who craved only one thing in life, a man between her legs!

I had to take a breath after Miller finished his exposition on sex by describing the need for sex as dominant and unrelenting for both men and women. I felt that Miller was being authentic to *his* beliefs in such expressions, but I thought that Miller was also being his wild, animalistic self when he tried to make a universal case for such stuff.

I started to skim the book, both fascinated and repelled by Miller's episodes, finding that Miller's wanderings, enforced poverty, and need to find food and shelter to be a bit tedious after a while. I was about to close the book when I came across a more developed argument.

> *On the meridian of this there is no injustice; there is only the poetry of motion creating the illusion of truth and drama ...*
>
> *And so what I think what a miracle it would be if this miracle which men attends eternally should turn out to nothing more than these two enormous turds which the faithful disciple dropped in the bidet. Somehow the realization that nothing was to be hoped for had a salutary effect upon me. For weeks and months, for years, in fact, all my life I had been looking forward to something happening, some extrinsic event that would alter my life, and now suddenly, inspired by the absolute hopelessness of everything, I felt relieved, felt as though a great burden had been lifted from my shoulders...*

I read on a couple of pages to learn that Miller was going to use the release from his burden to become even more of a ravaging beast of prey than he already was. Miller knew what women were for, as far as he was concerned. I got the picture and closed the book.

Lying on my bed after experiencing the feeling of hopelessness I had felt for myself and reading that Miller had felt the same thing, I felt enlightened. Miller just wanted his soul to be free so he could act on his instincts. *Primitive instincts,* I thought. Siddhartha wanted to free his soul so he could experience Unity with all other souls, as nearly as I could determine, which was a more elevated pursuit.

But Miller's revelation that there might not be anything more at the end of life than two *"enormous turds"* gave me a feeling of release too. My life had been lived under restrictions ever since I was born, primarily because of my parents' slavish devotion to the strictures of the social conventions of their class. They were so uptight that they had to pay lip service to the notion that America was a classless society, no matter what they should have thought if they had freed their minds. But I knew better by the way they conducted themselves in daily life and expected me to do, by the exclusive company they kept and expected me to keep.

I thought of how my father supported the war because it was what his circle of friends did. He went along. Was America the Land of the Free? If I got drafted, would I be free? If I got killed, would my father go along with that? In fact, all he would have would be two enormous turds: one would be my death, and the other would be his own guilt that he had supported a pointless war that I had been killed in.

This reasoning had made me angry. I got up off the bed, no longer depressed. I hungered for something more, some wild adventure to split me away from my former life. I felt like I had been infected by Henry Miller's passion to a certain extent and that I needed to bust out. I put on my biker gear and was heading down the stairs when I met Charlie.

"I'm going for a ride. Want to come along?"

"Sure," Charlie said. "Where to?"

"I'm thinking about going down to Piraeus to pick up a whore."

"What?! Where'd you get that idea?"

"That's what Nigel and Pete have been doing since we got here. I think it's a rite of passage. You don't have to come if you don't want to."

"Boy, I could understand it better if you said you were really horny and didn't try to intellectualize it. But I'm not interested in venereal diseases. Count me out."

"You don't have to have a whore. Just come with me to check them out. They hang out at the seaports for the sailors."

"I don't think this is a good idea, but I'll come along for the ride."

I drove the five kilometers to Piraeus in fifteen minutes, but the time it took to get there didn't begin to measure the moral distance between the shining whiteness of the hallowed seat of democracy and the dull-grey commerce of the modern-day seaport. I went down to the water's edge and passed marinas for pleasure craft and docks for shipping, which were mostly gated and locked.

By this time, my heated state of mind had dissipated, and I decided that this was a useless errand, so I started to head back toward Athens when we passed a taverna and someone shouted at us. Charlie told me to stop. It was Pete and Nigel, who were having beers at an outside table. I turned the bike around, and we joined them and had beers ourselves.

We compared notes on the lodgings we had found. Nigel said they had taken a couple of rooms short term because they were still looking for women. They'd given up on the whores because they had been told that the whores in Piraeus were the filthiest in the Mediterranean. Charlie looked over at me, but I just put on a sad look and shook my head. Charlie caught my drift and didn't follow up on why we had come to Piraeus. Charlie said we'd taken rooms for two weeks in the Plaka, which were really nice.

The others were still stuck on Piraeus and looking for easy women, but Pete said they had scored some very good hash. "Would you guys be interested in buying some?"

Charlie and I looked at each other and quickly said there may be some interest.

"How much is it?" Charlie asked.

"How about a half gram for four hundred drachmae?" Pete said.

"That seems like a lot," I said, remembering the cost of the hash in Berlin. "How fresh is it?"

"It could have been made this week," Pete said as he pulled a packet out of his pocket and opened it. I could smell it from across the table. It was very fresh. Charlie and I split the cost.

Nigel asked if we wanted to troll for women with them, but I said we had just taken a ride to check out the waterfront. Maybe we could explore the city together sometime? Nigel said "maybe" without meaning it. Charlie and I went back to the city figuring these guys had done us two good turns: telling us about the filthy whores and selling us the hash. I figured we wouldn't see them again. They were walking their own paths.

When we got back to the city, we were hungry for dinner, so we found a place at the base of the Plaka that had souvlaki, which we ate with sliced tomatoes drenched in olive oil and fresh-baked bread and beer.

I said we really had to do the Acropolis tomorrow, and Charlie agreed. He told me there was a monument on a hill across from the Acropolis, which he thought would be a great place to smoke some hash and view the Parthenon. I said that sounded cool.

We went back to the hotel into our separate rooms. I thought of reading some more of *Tropic of Cancer*, but I had enough of that. I'd gotten some unexpected bits of wisdom out of it, but Miller was a different kind of animal from me. A beast with too much appetite for life. I picked up my guidebook of Athens to prepare for going back in history tomorrow.

22

Love at First Sight

AFTER BREAKFAST, WE WENT to the Acropolis and walked up the stairs that the people of Athens had trodden for over three thousand years. We went through the Propylaea, the spectacular entrance building to the sacred ground. Once we passed through the Propylaea, the brilliant-white Parthenon stood before us against a soft blue sky. Its symmetry and beauty enchanted me, even in its somewhat ruined condition.

Recalling my reading, I had to accept the fact that time, war, and history had taken their toll on this magnificent structure. Still, it was glorious.

"You know, the columns on the Parthenon were painted red in ancient times," I said to Charlie.

"You're kidding," he said.

"Nope. And back then there was a roof, and the Athenians placed a fifty-foot statue of Athena inside, all covered in gold."

"Wow. Cool!"

"Yeah, but the Greeks were fractured in city-states. The Athenian' Golden Age only lasted fifty years. They thought they were superior, and so they had too much hubris, which was a sin the gods couldn't abide. They got into a thirty-year war with Sparta, which they lost. Both city-states were weakened, which set the stage for Philip of Macedon to come down and begin the conquest of all Greece, which his son, Alexander the Great, finished."

"You're really into Greek history."

"Yeah, it grabs me. We were taught about the Greek gods and heroes in elementary school. I thought they were terrific. I read quite a few books about ancient Greece, one of my favorites was *The King Must Die*, which was about the legend of Theseus who killed the Minotaur in the labyrinth in the palace of Knossos in Crete. I'm going to see Knossos when I go to Crete."

"So you really are going to Crete," Charlie prodded.

"Yeah, I am, although I'll admit I feel that I'm being directed there rather than making a conscious choice of going. This girl I got involved with in Berlin put the idea in my head that there is something important for me there. Maybe it's mystical, I don't know, but when she went there, she had an experience that changed her life, and I've picked up on her vibe. It's kinda weird, but Crete is a special place anyway. It's ancient. The Greeks believe it's the home of Rhea, the mother of the Olympian gods.

"Since having Christianity crammed down my throat in prep school, I've rejected that. I think of the Greek gods and heroes as more divine, bearing a closer relevance to real people with the human characteristics the Greeks imbued them with. Christians call that paganism, but Christ established an impossible ideal for people to follow, so what good is that if you're looking for solace? I think there is something to be said for looking up to Athena," I said.

Charlie looked over his shoulder. "I don't want to have to dodge a lightning bolt because of your blasphemy." And we laughed at that.

We meandered over to the Erechtheion, where we gaped at the beautiful porch of the Caryatids. The six marble columns were carved in classic Greek style as women in flowing gowns, which support the roof of an extension to the main temple. After millennia, their forms were still beautiful.

As we walked down the Sacred Way past the Parthenon, I told Charlie how the British had stolen the beautiful friezes from the Parthenon and put them in the British Museum. The Greeks wanted them back, but the Brits wouldn't give them up. We then looked down the side of the rock that was opposite from the Plaka and saw the two Greek theatres where the plays of Aesculus and Euripides were still performed every week.

As we left the Parthenon, I thought, looking back at the six Caryatids, *There's something to be said for paganism.* This place was a jewel of history in my mind, and I was so happy to have had a chance to see it firsthand.

Going down from the Acropolis, Charlie pointed out the monument on the hill in a park across the street where we could get stoned and get a great view of the Acropolis. We crossed the street and bought gyros and Cokes from a street vendor and walked up the hill to the base of the monument. We learned that this was the tomb of a Roman consul, Philopappos, erected in the second century AD. It was three stories tall with a large statue resting on a marble base. The statue had been partially destroyed, but it was still impressive.

I was disappointed because it was a Roman tomb, but one look across the quarter-mile distance to the Acropolis brought me back to the Golden Age of Athens in a heartbeat. The view was fantastic because we were at the same level as the Parthenon itself with nothing to obstruct our view. I couldn't imagine anything more spectacular.

Charlie nudged me with his elbow and offered me a poke on the tiny hash pipe he had just lit up. It was a weird-looking thing, but he said it was easy to hide in his belongings when he crossed borders. I laughed and took a poke, knowing not to take too much because it was so fresh. I held it in as long as I could, but had a coughing fit despite my precaution. Charlie had a coughing fit too; this fresh stuff was brutal.

When I caught my breath, I could see little colored lights dancing around the periphery of my vision. Charlie said he could see them too. I looked over at the Parthenon, and it seemed closer than it was before. I sat on a rock and looked at the Acropolis more intently. The ground between the hill we were on and the Acropolis started to wave slowly like a flag. I was stupefied.

Charlie sat next to me, still clutching the pipe as if he were a statue. "What's wrong with the ground? It's moving."

"I think it's the hash."

"Uh, I guess. Want another hit?"

"Well, I don't know. If we have more, maybe we'll watch the Parthenon fall down or something."

"Let's just finish the pipe," Charlie said as he took a poke and handed it to me.

We both coughed like crazy again on the sweet, fine smoke and started laughing uncontrollably. When we stopped, there were tears on our cheeks, and I was dizzy.

"I haven't smoked anything like that in my life before," Charlie said.

"I had something like it in Berlin, but this is turning my brain into an amusement park ride," I said, and we started laughing again.

I lay back on the rock and looked up at the tomb of Philopappos and asked Charlie, "What does a guy do in life to get people to put up a monument like that for him? I mean, whoever heard of this guy? Genghis Khan maybe, or Napoleon, or Abe Lincoln, but who was this guy?"

"Maybe he invented the gyro or souvlaki or something."

"He was a Roman. Maybe he invented the pizza."

That got us laughing again.

We had our lunch, which helped quell the munchies, but we were too stoned to walk down the hill, so we sat and gazed at the Acropolis for the better part of an hour. I was getting a tan in the glorious sunshine and measuring time by the feeling of coming down from being stoned.

But I realized that while getting high was fun for the moment, it was a real time-waster. It made me nonfunctional in terms of moving ahead with my life. Smoking a lot of pot in college had almost cost me graduating on time. It was time for me to come to terms with this disrupting influence. This was something that I determined to leave behind as I walked down my path.

Finally I stood up and asked Charlie if he were ready to move on. He said his head was clearing, so we got up and started down the hill. I looked across the city and saw a tall hill with a funicular railway about a mile away and said to Charlie that we should check that out sometime.

We came to the Plaka and entered Pandrosson Street market, one of the more touristy streets on the lower half of the Plaka. One shop after another offered imitation Greek pottery, Greek flags, sandals, and peasant costumes all under the banner of "traditional Greek products." At each shop, someone was sitting in a chair making sure the tourists didn't walk away without paying for something.

Suddenly I found that I was frozen in place. I looked ahead and saw the most beautiful girl I had ever seen sitting in a chair in front of one of the shops. The sun fell full on her golden hair. Her forehead was broad with dark eyebrows nearly meeting above her straight, proud nose. Her sunglasses were on top of her head as she spoke to a customer, so I could see that she had emerald-green pools for eyes. She wore a white, wide-sleeved shirt open down to her bosom. She wore a traditional Greek skirt of the type that was sold on the racks at the front of the store.

I looked at her face and could only see a warm, simple sincerity that contrasted with the girls back home I knew who could be cynical or fatuous. I guessed she was about my age. She was *so* gorgeous.

Charlie had walked ahead, not realizing that this beauty had transfixed me. He came back and asked me what the problem was. I turned so I wasn't staring so blatantly at the girl, but I pointed her out to Charlie and told him I was in love.

Charlie turned to look at the girl and said, "She is particularly exquisite, but I must remind you that you are still partially stoned and have been out in the hot sun for a while. You should take some time to get your shit together."

"OK. I may not be in the best condition to declare myself, but I swear to you that I am absolutely in love with that gorgeous creature, and I will be back when I've cleaned up my act."

Charlie laughed. "Ok. I'll come along to watch the carnage. "Or maybe she has a friend. Ha, ha!" he said.

On the way back to the hotel, I didn't say anything. The sight of this girl had burnt a hole in my consciousness and inflamed my hormones. I felt that this was serious, although it was as sudden as if Eros had come down off Mt. Olympus and shot me with one of his arrows. I was suffused with a flood of emotions I had no control over.

I had only experienced women of surpassing beauty in the pages of *Playboy* or *Sports Illustrated* swimsuit issues, and these had become my ideal of womanhood during adolescence. It was hard for me to fully engage with normal girls my age when I knew there were these ethereal beauties out there.

I had met girls whom I liked, who were attractive, warm, and cuddly, but I had always been conflicted by the knowledge that there was a female Xanadu, which harbored in my dreams and desires between the pages of these magazines. It seemed as if the jolt of seeing this one beauty had even disrupted the reticence I had adopted toward girls since the days of my sisters' cruelties.

I was in a state of dazed euphoria. I wanted to talk with her. Charlie saw the change in me and tried to rally me out of it. "Hey, Jack, next time we light up some hash, it should be on a desert island, ok? I mean, you've sort of fallen off a cliff here, and you haven't even spoken to her yet."

"Sometimes you just know about people. You said it yourself, *love at first sight.* I never thought of it happening to me."

"Man, you have a problem. You better go figure out who this goddess is, where she came from, and, most importantly, if she has a boyfriend, which I would be amazed if she didn't."

The thought of a boyfriend punched a hole in my reverie. Yeah, that was a possibility I hadn't had time to figure on. I never knew what to do about boyfriends back home. I'd just bug out to avoid complications. But this time I was really inspired. Yet, Charlie was right. I was going to have to quell my raging hormonal urges and see where I stood before falling off the cliff, as Charlie had said.

Charlie and I walked through the end of the Plaka to the National Gardens and sat on a bench, exchanging thoughts about girls.

"Girls just seem to be difficult for me," I said. "I love their looks, and I like to talk to them, but when I get together with one, they always want to get closer. They're always wondering if you'll make the move. They put the onus on you. They just make hints and signs. In the meantime, I'm all scrambled up inside. I know I just freeze. But it seems to me that that's how they take the measure of a man, and I don't think that's fair. There should be a halfway point or something."

"Well, you're not a girl, and I'd say you're bucking a lot of human psychology." Charlie punched me on the shoulder. "No, seriously, girls want to know what men are made of on a primeval level. When it comes to a guy, they're looking for a guy to kiss them and sweep them off their feet. Then they figure he's attracted to them, and that's something they need for their self-esteem. It's kind of like you and your bike. The bike shows everyone you've got balls, especially the girls."

"I guess it's the psychology that's got me tied up. I think about it too much; then I blow it. But as far as the bike is concerned, I can't ride it up to that shop. That's a pedestrian street. I've got to meet this goddess as just me. That's the worry."

"Look, we'll just walk down the street together, and she'll be sitting there. I can check out some postcards and then disappear while you say hi. Ask her where she's from. She sure doesn't look like she's Greek. Then take the conversation from there. She can't run away. She's got to mind the shop, so you can make the connection or not. Easy."

That sounded reasonable to me, and it loosened the knot in my stomach. I figured I'd better stop thinking of this Aphrodite or I'd get tongue-tied when I tried to speak to her.

"Ok, Charlie. Thanks for the advice. Let's go get a beer and some dinner."

We went to a taverna in the Plaka and had moussaka with our beers and split a baklava for dessert. We followed some new streets back to the hotel, where we said good night to Yiannis and Arianna before going to bed.

I found it hard to sleep that night. I envisioned that beautiful woman until she became an obsession, and I allowed my imagination to take me places where I could not go. I turned on the light and read through some of the stories in the book of Greek gods and heroes. That was no help because the gods had powers that would allow them to appease their desires at their whim. I began to wish I had these powers myself.

23

Enter Dimitris

FORTUNATELY, SUNRISE CAME AND with it the noises in the street and then the familiar knocking about of Charlie in his room. I had already been in action. I had shaved my beard again, and my hair had grown just long enough to tie it back behind my neck, which I did after washing it thoroughly. I dressed in one of my new Lacoste shirts and shorts, which looked nice, but I thought my sneakers made me look like a dweeby tourist. I was going to try to make an impression for this girl that I was as cool as possible, and it made me uncomfortable, just as always. I wished I could bring the bike along as a prop.

Charlie and I had breakfast at our usual café just down the street from the hotel. We lingered because the tourist shops didn't open until later. I told Charlie I was nervous, but Charlie repeated the strategy he had laid out the day before and told me not to worry. "Just be natural," he said. But that was my problem.

We walked up Athinas Street to Omonia Square and went through the lobby of the five-star Hotel Grand Bretange, which, at a hundred years old, was one of the great old hotels of Europe, still retaining the opulence of another era.

"What we're paying for two weeks in the Plaka would get you ten minutes in the men's crapper here," Charlie said. We looked at some postcards in the gift shop, but they were twice as much as in the Plaka, so we passed.

I remembered I was running low on drachmae, so we went over to the AMEX office, which was in Omonia Square. The interior was more utilitarian than the fancy one in Vienna, but the basic layout was the same with tellers and advisors helping the clueless American tourists. I went to the teller station and changed $150 for 4,500 drachmae, not knowing what I might need on Crete or where I could change money there. If I had extra, I could use it when I got back to Athens.

Then we started back for Pandrasson Street, and by the time we got there, the shops were open, and the market vibe was in full swing. I saw my Aphrodite as she was encouraging a woman to look at a skirt for sale. The two women jabbered for a while, and then the tourist left without having bought anything. The girl sat down on her chair. It wasn't bright enough for her to put her sunglasses on yet, so I could fall into the green pools of her eyes from as far as twenty feet away as I started to walk somewhat mechanically toward her.

I heard Charlie say over my shoulder, "Loosen up, pal."

Charlie stopped to check out postcards while I went to the shelves that held the pottery and picked up a couple of pieces and put them back.

Then I turned to the girl and said, "I'd like to have one of these as a souvenir, but I drove to Athens by motorcycle from Berlin, and I don't think one of these would survive a trip on the bike in one piece."

She turned to me with a warm smile. "You came all the way from Berlin? But you sound like an American."

"So do you. How do you come to own a gift shop in Athens?"

"Oh, I'm Canadian, from Winnipeg. And I don't own this shop. I'm minding it for my boyfriend, who is the owner. He owns four shops and a restaurant here in the Plaka."

I paused, dispirited, and looked over at Charlie, but Charlie kept fooling with the postcards.

"Wow," I said, mustering up what self-respect I could, having found out she did have a boyfriend, and trying to climb out of the emotional abyss I had fallen into. "Did you just come here as a tourist and wind up with a job? That's pretty unusual."

"No. I'd been planning to get away from the cold winters and the empty spaces of the prairie for a long time. I waitressed during high school and afterward until I had enough money to come here. I had it all picked out from pictures in magazines. It's more beautiful than in the magazines."

"I agree with you on that," I said, trying to find some common ground and learn about the boyfriend. "By the way, I'm Jack."

"I'm Candace," she said. "How long have you been here?"

"Just four days. I'm staying at a hotel up the hill in the Plaka. It's really nice. I saw the Acropolis yesterday. How long have you been here, Candace?"

"Almost a year. When I got here, I came right to the Plaka too. The magazines said it was the cheapest and most fun place in the city. I took a room, and in two days I met Dimitris while I was looking around in one of his other shops. As soon as he heard me speak English, he asked me if I would like to work for him minding one of his shops. He wanted someone who could speak English for the tourists. It was something to do, and it paid money, which meant I could stay here longer, so I said yes. It's been fun. Later he became my boyfriend. He's shown me all over Greece. I never expected that when I was reading the magazines in cold, snowy Winnipeg."

"I'd say you got lucky," I said, reflecting that *I* wasn't likely to get lucky this time. I looked at a few other souvenirs while parsing the path that Candace had described she had taken.

> *A single, beautiful girl, she created a dream she had made up based on pictures in magazines, left home on her own, and went to a faraway place with a completely different culture, and she found a guy in two days who gave her a real job and became her boyfriend of a year. Everything worked out perfectly.*

I didn't know everything that went on in the world, but I had to think that this girl was really lucky, like she'd been dropped on her head on a pile of horseshoes out in Winnipeg.

I could see that my initial efforts were only going to go so far as to make friends, so I called Charlie to come over and introduced him. Charlie immediately started up a conversation with Candace, even testing her Greek, which pleased her.

I was about to re-insert myself back into the conversation when an imposing man stepped out of the shadowy interior of the shop. The guy was about six-foot-two with a barrel chest and hams for forearms sticking out of a loose-fitting shirt, which was unbuttoned to show a rich growth of black chest hair. He was so physically arresting that I didn't look at his face right away, but when I did, I saw the image of Zeus as it was painted on the pottery paintings that were on sale at the store. He looked to be about thirty with a curly black beard that matched the curly ringlets of his hair.

"So, Candace, you are making some new friends?" he said, moving behind the girl and putting his hands on her shoulders.

Candace explained what she had learned about Charlie and me and then introduced the giant as her boyfriend, Dimitris. I had a hollow feeling pass through me as it registered in my mind that my hopes of getting to Candace would have to go through Dimitris, and that was never going to happen. But my heart was still captivated by her. I didn't know what to do. My insides felt as empty as the northern Canadian plains and about as cold as they were in winter.

Dimitris talked with Charlie and me for some time. He was quite voluble, being proud of the tourist shop chain he had built. He was even prouder of his former place on the Greek Greco-Roman Olympic wrestling team at the 1964 Games in Rome, but he had torn a shoulder muscle just after the games, and it never healed, so he had to give up the sport, his passion. He had raised money from friends and family and bought a gift shop five years ago, and now he had four gift shops, a leather goods shop, and a restaurant on the backside of the Plaka called Gargareta.

Dimitris was being expansive. He asked Candace if she would like these American boys to join them at the party at his restaurant this evening. Candace thought that would be nice. I could see he was a friendly guy who had made his way in world and was lucky enough to pick up a beautiful girl on his journey, and he made sure we knew that the girl was definitely his.

"That didn't go quite as hoped for," Charlie said as we headed back to the hotel.

"No, it didn't. Boy, that guy is huge. He could break someone like me in half. The problem is, I can't get her out of my mind. In talking to her, I get the idea that she's not the smartest girl in the world either. Am I in love or what?"

"Could be, but it could also be infatuation. Infatuation wears off. Time will tell," Charlie said with a sagacious undertone.

"Thanks for nothing, Sigmund," I said. "In the meantime, I'm left with this feeling of hopelessness, like I'm empty inside."

"Let's do something to fill the time, get your mind off your problem," Charlie said. "Why don't we check out that hill with the funicular railroad on it?"

I needed to back off my obsession with Candace, so we went and got the bike and drove to Mount Lycabettus. We took the railroad to the top, which, at three hundred meters, was the tallest point in Athens. It was located in the center of the city so we could see everything, looking past the Acropolis down to Piraeus and the Aegean and up north into the hills. At the back of the mount, we saw the new performing arts theatre where a sign was posted that said Bob Dylan, Ray Charles, Joan Baez, Chuck Berry, Jerry Lee Lewis, and many other current greats had performed here.

From this fantastic perspective, I tried to envision how the Greeks had fought off the Persians under Xerxes at the walls of the Acropolis twenty-four hundred years ago, but I was distracted by the vision of Candace. I imagined her as a latter-day Helen of Troy whose face could easily launch a thousand ships. I mentioned this to Charlie, who pronounced me certifiable, so I decided to keep my thoughts about Candace to myself.

We explored the city on the bike for the rest of the afternoon, off the tourist trail, soaking up the sunshine and living for the moment. We both must have started to get hungry at the same moment because Charlie asked, "Where is this party?"

"Dimitris said it was at the Taverna Garagareta."

"I know where that is. It's ten minutes' walk from the hotel at the back of the Plaka."

I drove to the hotel and parked the bike. When we got to within a block of the taverna, we could hear the noise coming from the party.

"Sounds crazy," Charlie said.

We stood in the doorway for a minute and saw that the place was filled with people, yelling above the din, some singing to an accordion player, men arguing about something. Dimitris spotted Charlie and came over to put his huge arms around our shoulders.

"Everyone, these are my new American friends, Jack and Charlie. They came to Athens from Berlin by motorcycle."

Everyone cheered and quickly put copper mugs full of wine in our hands. Dimitris told Candace to introduce us around. I was a bit mortified but smiled and went along. Candace was more beautiful than ever. Her golden hair was swept back in a curl, from which a flowing stream of locks cascaded over her right shoulder. To complete the effect of a Greek goddess, she had entangled shiny golden ribbons in her hairdo. She was wearing an embroidered white shirt, open at the neck down to the bust. I couldn't help but notice that she wasn't wearing a bra.

She introduced me to a few of Dimitris' friends, whom I promptly forgot. She was the only one I wanted to get to know better. As we passed through the crowd, I sipped on the wine, which was called retsina. It tasted more like the copper mug it was in than wine. I mentioned this to Charlie, who gave it a thumbs-down. But everyone was guzzling it like champagne, so we joined in and had a couple more mugs. After that, the retsina tasted better, and we made a few friends.

Dimitris then ordered the men to take all the tables and put them in one long line down the center of the room with the chairs on either side. I guessed there were seats for forty people at the table. This done, the women brought out forks and knives and candles and set the table for dinner. Then they brought out huge platters of roasted lamb chops, piled a foot deep, equally large platters of sliced tomatoes covered in olive oil, plates of feta cheese, bowls of olives, and big baskets of sliced freshly baked bread.

I had never seen such inviting food, which my stomach was aching for. The platters were passed around, and everyone took as much as they pleased. There wasn't enough to go around, so more platters were brought out. The crowd fell to, the noise level dropping as the food was being eaten, but not by much.

A couple of women kept going around the table filling everyone's mug with retsina, which I thought was pretty good at this point. Charlie and I were sitting next to each other, matching the number of chops each had eaten. I said it was a food orgy. Charlie just nodded and chewed.

When everyone had been sated, Dimitris stood up and made a speech about the friends for whom he was throwing the party. Then the women kept pouring retsina, and the noise level just kept going up.

———•••———

I didn't remember stumbling back to the hotel. I thought I'd been with a crowd of people, but when I woke up, I was alone. I could feel my head throbbing like voodoo drums were beating inside it, and it hurt too. I got up and opened Charlie's door to see if Charlie had some aspirin, and I got a shock when I saw Charlie sprawled out over his bed with a naked girl sprawled out on top of him. They were both asleep, so I closed the door quietly and went to the shower to soak my head in cold water for a few minutes to see if that would bring me back into the land of the living. I felt a little better, but I still wanted aspirin and coffee, so I dressed and walked down to our usual café and explained a hangover as best I could to the proprietor.

He mixed up a coffee that was eighty-proof. I was hesitant, but the owner kept pushing it at me, so I sipped on it, and sure enough, it started to dispel the evil vibes in my brain. *I guess this is what they mean by hair of the dog*, I thought. *And how about that Charlie? He's a fast worker*.

I remembered that everyone was getting very friendly by the time the party was breaking up. I also remembered that I'd been staring at Candace more than I should have, but in the general melee I didn't think anyone noticed. I ordered a regular coffee and baklava and thanked the owner for his concoction. I ate slowly and ruminated about my situation.

I'd been in Greece only five days, and some amazing things had happened, mostly because of the people I'd met: Charlie, Nigel, Pete, Candace, and Dimitris. I'd always gone my way alone, although I'd had Wild Bill to bounce around with for the past couple of years, and Chris was my best friend from way back.

But I now began to see that I should widen my circle of friends to get along. I knew quite a few people; it was a matter of staying closer to them, which would turn acquaintances into friendships. That's where life happened. Girls were social and created those relationships for guys, but there was so much surface palaver and tittering to put up with from them; it got under my skin. And then there was the sexual agenda with its emotional roller coaster. Still, this scenario needed consideration for the future.

I finished my coffee and saw that it was now late morning. My head was coming around, but I'd remember that retsina: snake oil juice. I strolled through the Plaka, passing the shops and the cafés where the tourists were poking around looking like dumb tourists and saw myself in a shop window wearing my new Lacoste shirt, a pair of shorts, and sneakers. I saw in myself another dumb tourist.

Then I came to Pandrasson Street and saw Candace sitting in her chair outside the shop. She had on her sunglasses and did not appear to notice me until I said, "Hi, Candace."

Startled, she looked up. "Oh, hi, Jack. I must have dozed off. That was quite a party last night."

"The party was great. I think it was the retsina that got me. I've never had it before."

"The retsina does take getting used to, but we stayed up late talking with Dimitris' friends. I really could have slept this morning, but Dimitris is very keen on keeping the shop open. Lots of competition, he says. I told him to mind the shop himself this morning, but he kicked me out of bed, so I sleep on the job."

Just then, Dimitris came walking up the street, holding his arms out. "I almost didn't recognize you, Jack. You look like a tourist with those sneakers. Hey! You enjoyed the party last night?"

"Definitely, but I should have been warned about the retsina."

"I have a cure for that."

"Oh, the owner of a café we go to fixed something up for me. I'm fine now."

"But this one could use something, eh, Candace? Let me make you one of my specials so we don't get robbed today. Ha! Ha!"

Dimitris went into the shop and came out in a minute with what looked to me like an eighty-proof coffee. "Drink it all down. You'll feel better soon." He kissed her on the forehead.

"Jack, I saw you as I walked up the street. If you are going to spend any time in Greece, you can't look like you just got off a tourist boat. Come, we will change your image."

Dimitris put his huge arm around my shoulder, steering me into the shop, and told me to sit down while he pulled out a few pairs of Greek sandals for me to try on. I didn't know how to refuse and felt a little like I was being intimidated into buying Dimitris' sandals, but I found a pair that fit and that I actually liked.

"How much?"

"I charge these tourists six hundred to fifteen hundred drachmae for them, and they think they are getting a bargain. But I will sell them to you for my cost, three hundred drachmae."

That was a pleasant surprise. I'd never had a pair of sandals before, and these were cool on my feet and pretty sharp-looking. I paid Dimitris and thanked him, wondering why he was being treated so kindly.

"And Jack," Dimitris said, "I did see you staring at my Candace last night. Take care, my friend."

I walked back to the hotel in my new sandals, carrying my sneakers by the laces and thinking about the threat Dimitris had mentioned. I peeked into Charlie's room, but the girl was gone. Charlie was lying stretched out, face up. When he heard me come in the room, he lifted his head for a moment and then dropped it back, groaning.

"What the hell happened?"

"Oh, bullshit, Charlie. Don't you remember you got laid last night?"

"Oh, yeah. I remember that alright. She was really fine. But what the hell happened to my head? It feels like a marching band is going through it."

"That was the retsina. Filthy stuff. C'mon. Get dressed. I know where there's a cure."

"Lead on, Dr. Schweitzer."

I took Charlie to the café, where the owner mixed me the eighty-proof coffee that helped diminish the effects of the retsina for me. Charlie drank it down and also had a cup of coffee and baklava at my suggestion.

"Dimitris and I had a conversation about Candace this morning," I said.

"And…"

"He said he saw me staring at her a lot during the party, and he wasn't pleased about it. At the same time, he sold me a pair of sandals as a cover-up from Candace who was outside the shop."

"That doesn't sound good, but the sandals look great."

"No, it doesn't, especially since I'm having trouble keeping my eyes off her. I do like the sandals, but I'm thinking that maybe I should be shoving off for Crete sooner rather than later."

"Oh, man. That would be a bummer. We're just getting into the swing of things here."

"You may be, indeed. Are you going to hook up with that girl, what's her name?"

"Yeah, we thought we'd have dinner at Dimitris' place tonight when it's more civilized. Her name is Katerina."

"So you're set with her. I've got a date with some sort of destiny in Crete, and the longer I stay here, it looks like I could wind up being turned into a pretzel by a jealous wrestler. I should get on the road."

"When are you going to go?"

"Tomorrow. I'll have to find out when the ferries leave for Crete. Want to take a ride down to Piraeus to check them out?"

"Yeah. Sure."

Charlie and I took a quick bike ride down to the docks where we found the ferry office and the daily schedule. There were two boats for Crete each day, one left at eight thirty and another left at four thirty. The trip was thirteen hours. There were general passage tickets where you slept wherever you could, and there were shared cabins that had four berths. I paid 150 drachmae for a cabin on the four thirty ferry the next day.

We went back to the hotel, where I told Charlie I wanted to start packing up. I'd find dinner on my own. Charlie insisted we have a beer together before he went to meet Katerina. I said, "Absolutely."

I put my saddlebags in front of me as I sat on the bed and just looked into them, not fully grasping the meaning of my need to go to Crete. The bags were empty now, but I had to find something in Crete and bring it back with me to make my journey complete. I didn't think it was something that was meant to go in the saddlebags. I remembered again that Eva had said I would find what I was seeking if I went to Aigia Galini, but she couldn't know what it was. I had to go there to face a challenge, not knowing myself what it was, and master it.

I methodically packed the bags, which were spacious enough to handle all the new things I'd bought. I needed room for food so I figured to leave Henry Miller behind. Charlie might be in need of some enlightenment given his present situation so I'd give it to him. I still had *Siddhartha*, *The Odyssey*, and the book of Greek gods and heroes. I would gas up the bike, buy some sandwich material for the ferry ride, and say goodbye to Candace and Dimitris in the morning.

I sat back and began to read up on ancient Crete when Charlie came in the room. "How about that beer?" he asked.

"You got it, pal."

We went to our usual spot down the street and ordered a couple of Fix Hellas.

"It's been a lively five days," Charlie said.

"It's been a whirlwind of the human experience. I can't imagine how people live to be old in this country."

"They probably get pickled from the retsina."

"You might have something there. The Fix Hellas is excellent, however. Compares with Coors back home."

"Say, Jack. I haven't got a handle on why you have this compulsion to go to Crete. Can you let in me in on it?"

"Well, I was just thinking about that, and I'll tell you I'm not completely certain. It's sort of like when you've been looking for something for a long time and you just run out of time and space, except for this one place, and that's the place you have to go if you're going to find it. It may or may not be there, but you have to go because if you don't, you'll never know if you missed your chance to find it. I've come a long way, and I think Crete is where I'm going to find it. So I've got to go."

"And if you don't get out of Athens, you're going to have the Minotaur eat you up."

"You're so dumb. The Minotaur was in Knossos in Crete."

"Just kidding. I was referring to Dimitris. Candace is too tempting for you. He's a bear. Don't want to rile him."

"Yeah. That was a strange circumstance running into her. But maybe my being struck by love was intended as some sort of omen. Now I need to get moving. How about you and Katerina?"

"Hey, who knows? She's turning into a two-night stand, which is nice. She's friends with Candace, so I'm in with the in-crowd."

"Don't do something that's going to piss off Dimitris."

"Not on your life!"

Charlie said he had to get to the taverna to meet up with Katerina. I said I'd be leaving Athens around noon tomorrow, so I'd stop by to say goodbye to everyone on my way to the ferry.

Then I went back to my room, where I picked up the book on ancient Crete. The Minoan culture of 1500 BC had built Knossos, the fabulous palace that had so many rooms and levels that it was called the labyrinth even in ancient times.

King Minos was the most famous of the Minoan kings. Legend had it that his wife, Pasiphae, had lusted after a white bull and had a device made so she could mate with it, giving birth to the Minotaur, which was half-bull, half-man. Theseus killed the Minotaur, which was part of the story of "The King Must Die." I'd have to read that again.

I also read about Rhea, the wife of Cronos and the mother of Zeus and other Olympian gods. She was the Great Mother god of Greece whose seat of worship was in Crete. Rhea sparked my imagination. I had a feeling that my challenge would come in the form of a woman and that I would master the challenge, although my experiences with women had not been inspiring so far.

BOOK III

24

To Crete

I WASN'T IN A rush the next morning, having decided to take the afternoon ferry. When I got up, I looked in Charlie's room, but he wasn't there. That was strange. Charlie wouldn't have left his room without saying anything to me. Maybe he had slept elsewhere with Katerina. I left my copy of Henry Miller on Charlie's bed. I was sure he'd get a kick out of it.

My bags were packed, so I went down to our café and ordered a Greek breakfast of bread, yogurt, fresh fruit, baklava, and coffee. Then I went further down the street to a market where I bought bread, meat, tomatoes, cheese, and beer. When I got back to the hotel, Yiannis said Ariana would be happy to make the sandwiches for me. I asked him to have her wrap them well because they were going in my saddlebags.

Then I loaded up the bike, putting the sandwiches on the very top of the bags, and thanked Yiannis and Ariana for their help. I drove down to Pandrasson Street and wormed my way through the tourists, drawing some stares for driving on the pedestrian street. When I got to Dimitris' shop, I found that neither Candace nor the displays were outside, although the shop was open. I got off the bike and looked inside, calling for Candace.

"Who is that?" came a call from inside. I recognized Dimitris' voice.

"It's Jack. You're opening a little late today. Do you know what happened to Charlie? He was at your taverna last night."

"We had a small party. It lasted late. We got into drinking ouzo. Charlie got very sick. We took him to my house where we could look after him. Candace isn't feeling well either, but they'll both recover. It seems that retsina and ouzo don't agree with non-Greeks." He started to chuckle but stopped abruptly and put his hand to his temple. "Of course, no one should drink too much ouzo."

"So you're minding the shop today. That's too bad. I wanted to say goodbye to both you and Candace, not to mention Charlie. I'm taking the ferry to Crete today."

"You are going to the island of the Mother Earth. Some of us still think of her that way. It is a different place. Very old. Be sure to visit Knossos."

"I will. Say my goodbyes for me. I have to come back through Athens, so I'll see you all again soon."

"Good luck," Dimitris said before turning around and going back into his shop.

I hopped on the bike and weaved down the street to Ermou Boulevard, which led to Piraeus Avenue. I was in Piraeus in the usual fifteen minutes, so I scouted around for a gas station to top off the tank and check the oil.

With three hours before boarding, I figured to have a nice lunch at a café, take stock of my cash, and look over the map of Crete. I found a taverna with outdoor tables overlooking a marina and ordered a broiled cut of lamb with couscous, sliced tomatoes, and a basket of bread with a Fix Hellas. I looked in my wallet and saw forty-one hundred drachmae and my ticket to Crete. *Greece had been great to my finances, so that should suffice*, I thought.

My assessment of the map of Crete was more worrisome. I'd be getting off the ferry in Heraklion and going straight across the island a mere eighty-four kilometers to get to Aigia Galini. However, I'd be going through mountains that were five thousand to eight thousand feet tall, the tallest peak being Mt. Ida at eight thousand feet. I saw that the roads were marked on the map in the same manner as the roads in southern Yugoslavia were, and remembered what Hans had said about the terrain on Crete. I figured it was going to be a difficult ride, but I was anxious to get to my destination to see what awaited me.

I finished lunch and went down to the dock to watch the ferry from Crete pull into the slip. What I saw was a working ship that had seen better years. The paint was peeling in various spots, showing rust underneath. The crew and the longshoremen had two hours to unload, clean, fuel, and load it before departure at four thirty, but it didn't seem that long before I was told to get in the queue for boarding with trucks, cars, motorcycles, and bicycles.

When I got to the cabin, I found that having a load of gear was a distinct liability. The cabin was about ten-by-twelve and only had room for two bunk beds. This would be fine if there were a spare bed to put my stuff on, so I chanced it and dumped it all on an upper bunk. I sat on the one beneath it and waited to see if I were going to have roommates.

In about fifteen minutes, my three roommates arrived, and I saw right away that these guys were pure dirt farmers because they hadn't washed, shaved, or changed clothes in days. As soon as the three of them were in the cabin, the space was filled with their stink. They immediately started squawking at me for putting my gear on one of the bunks.

I didn't waste a minute: I grabbed all my gear and went out on the deck, putting my stuff in a pile by the bulkhead while gulping down fresh air. I figured to stay on deck as long as I could or, if the crossing were smooth, maybe all night. If it got cold or wet, I'd look for a bench inside, but the polluted cabin was not to be considered.

The ferry left on time, so I calculated it should get to Heraklion around six in the morning. I was lucky that it was a gorgeous late spring evening, and I reflected that the weather had been on my side for most of the journey. I got up and leaned over the railing and watched the ship carve its way through the waters, sending the white-foamed waves rolling away from its bow. I was on the starboard side, and since the trip took the ship almost directly south, I was bathed in the late afternoon sun. I found a chair up forward, brought it back to my spot, put on my sunglasses, and watched the sun set below the rim of the Mediterranean as the hours passed and the old ship rumbled on.

After sunset, I ate one of Ariana's sandwiches and listened to the passengers in the main cabin where the benches were, singing and dancing to an accordion. They went on and on. *Must be fueled by retsina*, I thought, realizing that the deck outside was going to be my berth for the night. I made myself as comfortable as I could, staying awake until the party petered out around midnight. A couple of times a man or a woman rushed out to the rail to heave their drunkenness over the side. I was lucky that there was little breeze and no blowback of vomit onto the deck.

When all was still and the only sounds remaining were the splash of the bow waves and the rumble of the engine, I got up and pissed over the rail. I was getting sore from lying on the deck and down from being alone. The proximity of the raucous party reminded me of my usual state of isolation, which had been temporarily stayed in Athens by all the people and the goings-on around me. But once again I was on my own on a quest to find myself.

It was something I had to do alone, but I thought of Wild Bill, Charlie, and, most of all, Eva. I had a sudden longing to share the thread of my life with her. In the short time we had together, I had revealed more of my intimate self to her than I had to anyone else, and I thought that she may have done the same with me. That made me feel vulnerable in a way I had never felt, and it triggered an emptiness in me not being with her. Yet I knew I had to leave her behind because this was my time of self-discovery. Ironically, she was one of the things I had discovered. Maybe I could reconnect with her sometime, but now I had to master my emotions and forge ahead. It was funny, but my thoughts of Eva were stronger than those of Candace, whom I thought was *the one*. I guess I was infatuated, as Charlie said. She really bowled me over with her looks, though.

The splash of the waters and the rumble of the engine kept such a steady drumbeat that these sounds accentuated the silence around me. Maybe in Crete, Rhea, the Mother Earth, would define my destiny, but I insisted it wasn't going to be what my parents were like. I watched the stars drift by until I finally dozed off.

The sky was just beginning to brighten when by some passengers who had come on deck woke me. I looked at my watch to see that it was just under an hour until we landed. I stood and stretched, feeling sore and unrested from spending the night on the hard deck of the ferry. I consoled my aches by thinking it had been a warm, dry night, and then I pulled a sandwich out of my bag and munched on my breakfast.

I saw the island ahead, first the tall mountains in the distance and then the shoreline. The ferry passed a cape, and then we were in Heraklion harbor. A horn blew, and all the people with vehicles were told to go down to the vehicle deck in preparation for disembarkation.

Driving into Heraklion, as much as I wanted to get going over the mountains, I needed to use a WC and have a cup of coffee. I cruised around through the center of the city looking for a café that might be open early, getting a bit desperate until I finally found an old man arranging outdoor tables and chairs at a café on the road leading into the mountains. I asked for a cup of coffee, and while the man was getting it, I used the facilities. I scanned the mountains as I drank the coffee and saw some tough terrain ahead.

I hopped on the bike and went about four kilometers down a straight road through olive orchards where the farmers' houses were made of whitewashed stone. All the window frames and doorjambs were painted bright colors, rich blue, crimson and bright yellow. I passed a sign on the left that read "Knossos—5km." *I can see that on the way back to Athens*, I thought.

The main road was narrow and unimproved. This wasn't a good sign. Although it was only eighty-four kilometers to Aigia Galini, I could see that it would probably take a couple of hours to get there at fifty kilometers per hour. I wasn't sure what would happen if a bus or a truck came from the opposite direction; the road was that narrow.

I went through a small village and stopped in the town square where I got my first full look at Mt. Ida, which still had a snowcap. I was only nineteen kilometers out of Heraklion, and the road ahead was getting steeper as I entered the mountains. I might be facing the same kind of road conditions as in southern Yugoslavia, so I tried to focus my vision on the road, although I was tired from the all-night ferry ride.

As I wound my way up the mountain, the road began to perform multiple switchbacks like a snake in motion. I had to carefully maneuver through the 180-degree switchbacks at walking speed with one leg dangling off the side of the bike for balance or support, as needed. The road became steeper as it clung to the mountainside like a creeper vine. It was no more than twelve feet wide in any place except the deepest part of the switchbacks, where it might be fourteen feet deep. I figured that was where cars would stop and let opposing traffic pass.

Higher and higher the road went, but I didn't look over the edge until I came to a switchback where I had to stop the bike to walk it through the curve. When I stood with the bike between my legs, I saw that I was less than five feet from what had to be an eight hundred-foot drop-off. There were no guardrails. I stared, amazed at what I saw over the edge of the road below: a pitch of sixty degrees strewn with rocks and boulders of all sizes and the snaky road behind, which I had just navigated, and a whole lot of empty space until the next mountain a few kilometers away. And this road kept going up!

I resolved to drive as close to the wall on the inside, away from the drop-off as I dared from here on, but I was worried that another vehicle might meet me head-on due to the narrowness of the road. I had not passed any cars since I started climbing the mountain road, but the morning was progressing, and a car could come along at any time. I didn't like to think of the irony that I had come almost three thousand kilometers to be run off the road into a canyon when I was a mere fifty kilometers from my destination.

At last, I reached what seemed to be the highest part of the road; the switchbacks would be downhill from this point. But I found that going downhill was harder because the bike tended to accelerate under its own weight and momentum, and I had to steer, brake, and shift to keep the machine going where I wanted it to go while concentrating on the quirks of the road.

It was at a moment when I had a brief lapse in concentration as I entered a switchback that a bus appeared square in front of me, going up the mountain. The bus driver and I must have seen each other at the same time because as soon as I saw the bus, the bus driver leaned on the horn, and my heart skipped a beat. My flight instinct had the effect of forcing me to act. I saw that the bus was going very slowly because it was going uphill as it entered the radical curve. I was going downhill and on the inside of the curve, shielded from the horrific drop-off of the cliff by the bus, and I knew the bike was more maneuverable than the bus, so it was up to me to get out of the way.

I accelerated the bike at a slow pace at a sharp angle across the front of the bus and toward the mountain wall on the inside of the curve and hoped there was enough room between the bus and the rock face for the moving vehicles to pass when I turned straight to let the bus go by.

I made it to the wall and then made the turn to parallel the bus. The bus driver had slammed on his brakes, which caused the rear end of the bus to slew toward the inside of the curve, cutting off my exit. But the bus stopped, and I stopped the bike, positioned in a triangular wedge between the bus and the rock wall. I was astonished that the bus hadn't hit me.

There was a lot of screaming inside the bus. The next thing I knew, there was a hand on my shoulder, which grabbed and spun me around while I was still sitting on the bike, and a large, irate, black-mustachioed Greek bus driver was yelling in my face what could only be multilayered strings of abuse.

I just looked at the guy with a stupid expression on my face, which was all I could muster, considering that I had almost been run over by the guy's bus in the preceding ten seconds. I looked at him and shrugged my shoulders and shook my head, trying to show I was sorry but didn't understand what he was saying. My legs were shaking as I straddled the bike.

I noticed that the bike was so closely confined by the bus and the rock wall, the only way I was going to get it out was to back it up, but the bus driver was still standing in the way, fuming. The driver saw that I didn't understand Greek, so he threw a few more invectives at me and went back into the bus and started the engine. That wasn't good. I could see that if the guy didn't drive the bus on a certain line as he pulled away from this spot, the bus would clip the handlebars or the cylinders of the bike, so I quickly started walking the bike backward to widen the space between the bike and the bus.

I looked up at the bus and saw a dozen faces of Greek peasant women with shawls on their heads looking out the window at me. The bus driver completed his uphill turn, missing the bike by a couple of feet, and the bus continued its way up the mountain.

I got off the bike at the scene of the near-accident and walked it to the deepest angle of the curve where I could park and observe any traffic coming up or going down the mountain. Then I walked over to look at the road where the bus had skidded to a stop. I was alarmed to see that the right front tire mark was less than two feet from the edge of the road; if it had gone any further, it would have gone over the side.

"Holy shit!" I said out loud, remembering the screams from the people inside the bus. I understood the driver's anger; maybe the bus wasn't going fast enough to go over the edge and plunge down the eight hundred-foot drop, but the driver could have stepped out the door of the bus and taken that fall. I felt a sense of shame and accountability for this incident. Further, I was a raw amateur biker, driving on an illegal motorcycle license. I'd be up the creek if something had really happened.

I stood on the road thinking and getting pissed off. *What happens when a car or truck meets a bus coming the other way on this ridiculous goat track? This road is marked on the best maps as one of the 'primary' roads on this island, for Chrissake! That driver handled the situation as if he'd experienced other such encounters before. Is this the way people live around here? Do they never leave their houses, unless they're riding donkeys, or what?*

I admitted to myself that I was transferring the blame, but I was scared shitless. The bus driver seemed to take the incident in stride. I walked back to the bike. I figured to wait a few minutes to settle down before continuing down the mountain, consoling myself that I was more than halfway to Aigia Galini.

When I started rolling through the switchbacks again, I couldn't help but think of the grille and the headlights of the bus coming at me. They looked like the face of death, the headlights being its eyes and the grille being a wide-open mouth. In the same way, the blackness in the tunnel in Yugoslavia showed me a portent of what death was, blackness. In my mind, I was accumulating a list of instances with increasingly dark consequences that I had managed to evade. *The bike is fun, but it really is dangerous. How many of these incidents can I dodge?* I thought.

Soon, I turned a corner on the mountain and saw a sweeping view of the entire Mediterranean and the south coast of Crete. The road flattened out at the village of Aigia Geka, where it turned west before becoming a dusty, dirt road shaded by overhanging trees. I opened up the bike to fifty kilometers per hour and kept an eye on the surface for potholes. I passed several whitewashed stone dwellings, but there was little sign of life beyond the town.

How the hell did Eva find this place? I asked myself. *She must have taken that bus that had nearly flattened me on the mountain. At any rate, this is as far out in the world as I've ever been. Maybe some mysticism is involved here after all.*

I had gone a few kilometers before I saw a small sign pointing down toward the sea on my left. This had to be the way to Aigia Galini. The road was rutted, so I eased the bike slowly down toward the village. I could imagine carts pulled by animals as being the best way to get up and down this track and came at last to the village square on the water with a beautiful view of the sea. I put my feet on the ground, straddling the bike, feeling a sense of relief and accomplishment.

I surveyed the scene: there were five of the typical whitewashed stone buildings set at odd angles to each other, forming an ellipse facing the sea. The ellipse itself formed the town square, which had a circle of white-painted stones in the middle. The houses all had doors that were painted crimson with window frames in yellow and blue. There was a rocky beach, and a river flowed down from the mountain into the sea on the right. To the left were fishermen's shacks and two derelict fishing boats pulled up on the shingle.

Driving slowly around the square, I saw that there were a couple of paths leading up the hill between the houses. I drove up one path to find that the village had a second level of buildings, and here I found a hotel, a two-story building with a whitewashed stone first floor and a wood frame second floor with an extension out back. I parked the bike in front and went into the hotel where it took me a moment to adjust my eyesight from the bright sunlight to the cool, darkened interior of the stone-walled reception area.

There was no one about, so I looked around to find that the lobby was comparable to a New England country inn with a sofa, stuffed chairs, a fireplace, and a coffee table with various magazines piled on it. Some of them were in German, which surprised me. I turned when I heard someone come into the room from a door on the far side of the entrance.

"Hello," I said. "Could I have a room for a few nights?"

I was looking at a woman of no more than five feet tall, but heavy-set, broad in the shoulders. She had greying hair, and her skin was weathered, but she had fire in her dark-black eyes. She just looked me up and down without saying anything.

I thought at first she didn't speak English, and I certainly couldn't communicate with her in Greek, but then I realized that it might be my appearance that was affecting her. I must have looked a filthy mess, covered in dust and dirt from the ride over the mountain. So I went to the front door, opened it, and showed her the bike.

"I've just come from Heraklion," I said.

She seemed to get that and nodded her head positively. She said, "Eeenglish?"

"No, American." I pulled out my passport.

"Ah. Amerrrika," she said. "Amerirrika girl here." She pointed to the back of the hotel where the rooms were.

My mouth went dry, and I felt a lump in my throat when I heard that. I'd been wondering what was at the end of my journey, and an American girl was staying in the same place I had been directed to.

Don't lose your cool, I told myself. *This could be circumstance. Don't go back to being the klutz you used to be. Take what you've learned from Eva and see what develops. Now that you're here, at the end of the earth, you aren't going anywhere for a while, so let's see what happens.*

While these thoughts were racing through my mind, the woman brought out some papers for me to sign into the hotel. She stood in front of me holding the papers with a look of curiosity on her face. I shook loose from my musing, took the papers, and filled them out. She asked me how long I wanted to stay by holding out a sheet that laid out the rates by the week: six hundred drachmae for one week, a thousand for two weeks, and so forth. These were better rates than in Athens so they were fine with me.

I asked her in pantomime about the showers, which she thought was funny, and motioned for me to follow her to the back of the hotel. We went upstairs where there was a balcony extending the full length of the hotel with the open side facing up the hill. I counted five guest rooms in all. The woman opened the third door, and there was the shower. The WC was next to it. The woman then took me down to the end of the building and opened the door, indicating that this room was for me.

I was enchanted. My first thought was of the picture Van Gogh had painted of his room in Arles. The room was bright and sunny with an open window overlooking the fishermen's shacks and the sea beyond. White lace curtains were blowing in from the sea breeze over a table and two wooden chairs beneath it. Next to that was a double bed with a headboard and white sheets. On the other side of the room stood a nightstand with a bowl and a pitcher of water and two folded towels. The room was painted a light shade of blue, and the door was crimson on both sides in the Cretan theme.

I turned to the woman and held up two fingers to signify that I wanted to stay for two weeks. I figured that thirty-three dollars for this piece of paradise was next to nothing. The woman was pleased, so we went back downstairs where I paid a thousand drachmae and handed over my passport. Then I moved the bike down to the end of the building where I could unload it easily. I brought all the stuff up and unpacked it all over the room to see what I had and what condition it was in. There was some road dirt that had to be wiped off, and my road clothes definitely needed washing.

But nothing needed washing more than I did. I could feel the dirt from the dusty roads everywhere, so I stripped and wrapped a towel around my waist, grabbed my soap and shampoo, and spent the next fifteen minutes in the shower. When I was done, I had washed away the dirt from the road, but the sight of that bus heading for me and the women's screams in my ears was still with me. I supposed that it would be for some time. That was a total freak-out.

I shaved and combed my hair, which was long enough for a ponytail, but I combed it over the top of my head for the first time in my life. I needed a barber to make it work right, but I'd seen my father and his business cronies using this hairstyle for years. It was a power look. I looked at myself in the mirror and didn't think it looked so bad. It gave me some gravitas. I liked that word. Nothing like a trip to the end of the earth to make some changes. And I wanted to look good in case I ran into the girl, so I put on my Lacoste shirt, shorts, and the sandals I got from Dimitris.

My thought about Dimitris brought me back to my failure with Candace. It didn't matter that Dimitris stood in the way; I was too flustered by her beauty to make it with her anyway. And now I was preparing to meet some American girl, the likes of which I could only imagine from past experiences, none of which bolstered my confidence. What was this American sweetie going to be like? Maybe she'd be standoffish, a games player who you couldn't get close to. Perhaps she'd be a San Francisco free lover who would just open her legs for me like a flower. Or possibly she'd just seduce me like Eva had, putting all questions aside. *Jesus, women are so complicated*, I thought. I'd never known a woman as a friend and doubted the possibility. Sex always became a part of the agenda sooner or later, and that changed things.

And if the girl were ready for it and I wasn't, she'd be offended and dump me. I remembered the signal Eva would give me to let me know she was ready: she'd stick her hand in my pants. I preferred that to the pussyfooting around of the American females.

I caught myself up; I had to snap out of this daydreaming about all the past failures I'd had with women. That wasn't what I had made this journey for. I wanted to change myself to be successful in the future. I might think of Eva as a cornerstone, but I had to move ahead, not look back on my mistake-filled adolescence. I couldn't be down on myself because of what I didn't know in the past or what my hang-ups had kept me from doing.

Since I'd come to Europe, I had experienced and learned a lot, but I had a ways to go yet. And I knew myself well enough to know that these meanderings about the past were just an excuse for not going out that red door and finding out what this American girl was all about. Besides, it was mid-afternoon, and I was hungry and could use a cold beer. So I left the room in a mess and went down to the lobby to ask the hotelkeeper if there were a taverna or café in the village.

When the woman saw me in the lobby, her eyes went wide, and she put her hands on her cheeks in a mock expression of shock at my transformation. I got it, and turned around 360 degrees to give her the full effect. We both laughed. I was happy to make a new friend. Charlie had been doing all that in Athens. Now it was my turn to enjoy the feeling. I said the word *taverna*, and the woman took me to the door and pointed across the square to the furthest building on the circle. She also pointed to her wedding ring and said "Nikolas." I figured that the taverna was run by her husband, Nikolas.

I pointed to myself and said that I was Jack. The woman said she was Thea. I shook her hand, noting she had a warm smile coming out of that face that had been weathered by the sun and hard work. I figured that she might have been a teenager when the Germans invaded Crete. If so, she'd been through tough times.

I walked across the square in the bright sun. The breeze coming off the water cooled my arms and legs after the nerve-wracking ride over the mountain. My new sandals were a lot more comfortable than the motorcycle boots. When I reached the red door of the taverna, I felt the cool solidity of the interior that was imparted by the thick stone construction. Although it was dim inside, I saw two old men smoking and talking at a corner table as I walked up to the small low-slung bar that had three wooden stools in front of it. Behind the bar stood a stout, dark man with black hair, parted in the middle, and a large, thick salt-and-pepper mustache.

I sat on a stool and said to the man, "Hi, I'm Jack. I'm staying at the hotel. Are you Nikolas? I spoke with Thea. She told me I could get something to eat and drink here."

Nickolas said nothing for a moment, staring at me curiously. Then he handed me a menu, entirely in Greek. I looked at it and told Nikolas I didn't speak Greek. Then Nikolas laughed and snatched the menu from me.

"If you don't speak Greek, how did you get my wife to tell you my name and where the taverna was? She speaks no English."

I took this for a friendly sally, so I showed Nikolas the pantomime I used for Thea.

"That's very good. What would you like to eat? Maybe some calamari, tomatoes, and feta cheese with pita bread?"

"That sounds great. And a Fix Hellas."

"Good, because that's all there is left from lunchtime. Ha, ha! I'll bring it to you on the terrace. It's too nice a day to eat indoors."

I said ok and turned to see the terrace, which opened onto the sea from two French doors on the far side of the room. As I walked toward it, I could see that the opening had been cut fairly recently; the frame was painted a bright blue, and the window glass was clear. I also saw that the terrace itself was larger than the main room of the taverna and had more chairs for dining. A sunscreen of posts and boards about eight feet high covered half of it while the far end was left in bright sunshine where there were several lounge chairs for sunbathing.

The girl was stretched out on a lounge chair reading a book. She was facing the sea so she didn't see me. I saw her in profile; her bronzed legs seemed to stretch out forever. They attached to a pair of tan mini-shorts, and above the shorts was a flat, bronzed midriff, which flowed with small waves of muscles. A skinny, purple bikini top covered her small breasts. Her arms were long and slim, but her shoulders indicated strength. Her dark-blonde hair was clipped up in back, revealing a long, thin neck and the small but beautifully proportioned head that rested on it. She was wearing a large pair of Foster Grant sunglasses.

I realized I was girl-watching without engaging, so I started to step toward her, and just then Nikolas came out to the terrace with the food.

"Ah, I see my American guests have met already," he said as he put the plate and the beer on the table nearest to the girl's lounge chair.

The girl was slightly startled by this disturbance. She closed her book, using a bookmark, and swung her legs around to see what Nikolas was talking about, eyeing me warily as she did so.

"Oh, you haven't met yet," Nikolas said with a mischievous grin on his face. "Miss Kara, this is Mr. Jack. Mr. Jack, this is Miss Kara. You are both Americans. I will leave you now. Ha! Ha!"

I said hi to Kara somewhat sheepishly, knowing I could have stepped up sooner, but Kara didn't know that. Kara lifted her sunglasses onto her head and revealed a pair of light-blue eyes, which were highlighted by her bronzed skin tone.

"Nikolas thinks he is being very funny sometimes," she said. "So you are staying at the hotel? You must have just arrived."

"I drove my motorcycle over the mountain. That was a memorable experience."

I couldn't help puffing myself up in the face of this beautiful girl. When she stood up, I saw that she was almost as tall as I was. I could now look at her oval-shaped face with its thin, regular nose and bow-shaped mouth. Her lips were inviting, but her voice was terse, evincing some annoyance in the manner in which she had been interrupted.

"Motorcycles are dangerous," she said and stretched out again to continue reading her book.

Here we go again with a bitchy American girl, I thought, as I sat down to eat my lunch. Right now I was hungry enough to let this calamitous introduction pass. From what I had seen, Kara and I were the only guests at the hotel, so there was no rush. My experience had led me to believe that women were the ones who were more needful of socialization. The food was delicious, so I allowed myself to enjoy it. I finished eating and turned my chair so I could see the water better while I sipped on my beer.

My patience was rewarded in a few minutes later when Kara asked me, "Where did you drive the motorcycle from?"

"Berlin," I said without looking directly at her.

"You mean you drove a motorcycle all the way here from Berlin?" Kara asked incredulously.

I turned to face Kara. "All the way from Berlin. And I have to agree with you. Motorcycles are dangerous. I was nearly killed on the mountain road from Heraklion just a couple of hours ago."

"My God, that is a dangerous road. I was petrified taking that ancient bus. There isn't room for two cars to pass each other. Our bus driver made cars coming the other way back up until there was a place where the bus could go past. And no guardrail! I couldn't believe it! I can't imagine going back."

"Yeah, well, that's the kind of problem I had. I'm glad the bus drivers have experience in driving that road, although I bet they have ulcers."

Kara laughed softly, almost as if she'd forgotten how, I thought. Maybe it was me, a guy being there all of a sudden where she had the place all to herself. Still, it was a strange sound to my ear, incomplete somehow.

I wanted to know more about her so I asked a nondisruptive traditional question, "Where are you from?"

Kara didn't answer for a minute, and that started me thinking that maybe she didn't want me to know, so she would spin a lie and everything would be a mess from the beginning. There were some people at college like that. Really weird. I thought they came from broken homes.

Finally, Kara looked out over the water and said, "I'm from Lake Forest, Illinois, on the North Shore of Chicago."

I knew a guy who went to college at Lake Forest, but I just said, "I'm from Westchester, New York, just north of the city. It's a tony suburb; sounds like we're from the same kind of neighborhood."

"What do you mean?"

"Rich, straightlaced, and a social pressure cooker," I said disgustedly. "Just the way the parents want it."

Kara sat up straight and looked me in the eye. "That's exactly it! And they want us to be that way too. To be just like them. I can't stand it! That's why I came here. To get away and try to figure out what to do. Is that why you came here?"

I knew I had touched a nerve, and the girl had opened a part of her heart to me. We had common ground we could talk about, and that meant that I could relax and maybe make friends with her, something I had never done with a girl before. I could tell her about my journey and what I was looking for inside myself. But I didn't want to get ahead of myself. I'd let her take the lead and see where things went.

"I absolutely had to get away from the parents," I said. "Since I finished college, they've been driving me crazy about starting a career, their kind of old-fashioned career. I'm draft-eligible this year, so starting a career would be pointless if I'm going to get hauled off to some jungle and get shot. They just don't get it."

Kara sighed. "You guys have that war hanging over your heads. I forget that sometimes because it doesn't affect me directly. But I've gone out with boys in college who were really eaten up inside about it. My problems are kind of small compared to that."

I wanted to get off the subject of the war. From where I was sitting right now, it couldn't be further away. "How long have you been here?" I asked.

"Almost a month," she said. "The dollar goes a long way in Greece, which is why I picked it when I made the decision to run away from home. I mean, I'm over twenty-one, so I can go where I want, but my situation at home makes it feel like I ran away."

"Ha! Me too! I just blew out of the house on New Year's Day. I left the parents a note."

"Gosh, you've been gone a long time," Kara said.

I saw that Kara had brightened up. I hoped it was because she had found some company. "I prepared for a six-month journey, but I had some help. A friend was living in Berlin, and I lived with him for free for almost four months. He had to go home suddenly, and things fell apart fast, but by then I had the bike, which saved me. I'll tell you about it sometime. Totally nuts. Then I went to Vienna and down through Yugoslavia to Greece. I picked up another biker and two hitchhikers going into Athens. That was wild. And then I came to Crete."

"Why Crete?"

I didn't want to answer the question directly, so I said, "I heard that Crete was a beautiful, ancient land and I want to see Knossos. A friend in Athens told me to go to Aigia Galini to relax for a couple of weeks. I said I figured to go over the mountain first and see Knossos on the way back."

Kara seemed to accept that, so I asked, "How did you come to Aigia Galini. I mean this is just about the end of the earth from where we come from."

She looked out over the water. "I'd been thinking of getting away for at least six months. I'd finished at college, but I was two courses short of my degree. I was on the swim team, and it just ate up time traveling all over the country. I was the NCAA two hundred-yard freestyle champion in my junior and senior year."

"Holy cow! That's cool!" I said.

"So now I'm done with college, and I'm sitting around at home, but without a degree. My mother insists that I be married. That's the way it is in the Midwest. My younger sister is married to the son of my parents' best friends and is pregnant already! My older brother is in law school. And I'm a lay about and an embarrassment to her in front of her friends. I told her I needed a break and definitely wasn't interested in getting married, and what business was it of their friends anyway?!"

Her voice rose as she said this. I understood where she was coming from and said nothing.

"My father runs the office of a large insurance company in Chicago. Every year around May 1, the company rents a country club and throws a big bash for their clients, partners, and wives; that's when I planned my escape for. I knew I wanted to come to Greece because it was warm, far away, and inexpensive. I had taken money out of my savings and bought AMEX travelers' checks the week before. When they were gone, I left them a letter, took a cab to O'Hare, and bought a flight to JFK and from there a nonstop flight on Olympic to Athens.

"I'll have to admit I was scared of just taking off like that without a real destination, but I got lucky on the Olympic flight because all the stewardesses were Greek. The flight was ten hours, so I spoke with them about what I should do and where I should go. The girls all thought I should go to the islands because they were the most beautiful and the least expensive. One of them had a boyfriend from Crete and had been to Aigia Galini and said it would be perfect for me. The only problem was the thirteen-hour ferry ride, which was full of stinky peasants. I should buy a ticket for the main cabin and hold my nose, and they all laughed.

"When I got to Athens, I spent the night in the airport hotel and took a taxi to Piraeus the next morning and caught the ferry. Then that incredible bus ride, always thinking we would go over the edge at any moment until I finally got off here. I've been swimming, sleeping, walking up the beach, and reading ever since. It's been so peaceful I've almost forgotten what it was like back home."

"Until I got here and disturbed your serenity," I said almost under my breath.

"Oh, no. Don't worry. I know I can't stay here forever. It's just been such a relief. No parents, no television, no riots, no Nixon, just blissful quiet."

"I have to say that what you've just said describes my situation pretty well, although I have some other issues I needed to address.

But let's make a pact: let's not bug each other about stuff back home if we decide to hang out. That way we can keep the bliss."

Kara turned her head toward me and pulled her sunglasses down over her nose so she could look me in the eye. "Deal," she said.

I would have liked to have another beer and keep talking with Kara, but I didn't want to push my luck. There would be time. "What do you do for dinner around here?"

"Well, there are two ways to get food here. One, you can let Nikolas cook it for you. He does breakfast, lunch, and dinner, and he's a really good cook. But some days he takes off, and the taverna is closed. So, two, there is a small market next door. I think his brother owns it. You can get bread, cheese, yogurt, fruit, and things that will tide you over until Nikolas comes back."

"So what are you doing for dinner tonight?" I asked, cocking my head to one side and making a silly grin.

Kara laughed. "I thought we could continue our conversation. I'll see you back in the hotel in a couple of hours."

"It's a date." I went inside to pay for lunch, which came to ninety-five drachmae, or about three dollars. *Good ol' Greece*, I thought to myself.

As I walked back to the hotel, I felt a feeling of delight and anticipation. It seemed that I had found a kindred spirit and she was actually a beautiful girl! She ran away from her parents just as I had done and for the same reasons.

I had to catch my breath and sort this out. I reasoned that I should allow Kara space to express herself if I wanted to get closer to her, and that need was beginning to percolate in me. She had earned my respect. An NCAA swimming champion! And she had the guts to take off from home alone, and she was a girl! I remembered the angst I had gone through before I took off, and I had a destination in Berlin. She had just taken off.

I didn't know where this was leading because it was unique in my experience, but that was what I was on the road for. I'd have to be patient and see how things developed, and I knew all too well how patient I could be with girls. Too patient for the most part, but that was because of circumstances and inexperience. I told myself that this time it would be different.

25

First Touch

I wanted to take a nap when I got back to the room, but I'd left it in such a mess. I had to pick up and sort out everything. Some things needed washing; other things need wiping down from the road dust. I used one of the bath towels for wiping and then sorted clothes into a clean pile and a wash pile that I hoped Thea would clean for me.

My riding jeans and jacket had not been washed since Yugoslavia, and they were so laden with dust from today's ride that I decided they were too much to ask Thea to work on without putting them in the shower for several minutes to get the top layers of grime off. Since I had trashed the towel from the hotel, I put that in with the jeans. Then I rung them out and hung them over the balcony of the hotel to dry, figuring to deal with those tomorrow. Finally I flopped on the bed and fell asleep in a moment.

In a dream, I heard knocking. Three knocks, then nothing, and then three more knocks. Then someone shouted "Jack" from a long way off, but I realized it wasn't that far away. I woke and sat up. I heard three more knocks.

"I'm coming," I said, shaking the sleep out of my brain.

When I opened the door, Thea was pointing to the laundry hanging on the balcony.

"No good!" she said as she wagged a finger in my face and grabbed the towel and my clothes and headed downstairs. I didn't have time to say anything.

"Well, where were you?" asked a voice behind me.

"Huh?!" I said, startled after my encounter with Thea. I turned around and saw Kara, her blue eyes wide, staring at me with her arms crossed on her chest.

"I took a nap. Wh—what time is it?" I asked, still foggy from deep sleep.

"It's six thirty, and I've been waiting for you. I finally decided to have Thea knock on your door to see if you were all right." Kara turned up her nose. "She certainly didn't like your laundry arrangements."

"I'll have to fix that up with her tomorrow. I am sorry that I kept you waiting. I had a long night sleeping on the deck of the ferry, and that crazy mountain road scared the bejeezus out of me. Let me wash up, and we can go straight over to the taverna. Do you know what's on the menu?"

Kara playfully changed her tune. "I suppose the combination of the ferry ride and the mountain road deserves a nap, so you're forgiven. Nikolas always has lamb and fish. He can cook lamb in a dozen ways. The fish is the catch of the day, and I saw a fisherman bring some in when I came back to the hotel. There are always greens, tomatoes, and cheeses. It's simple fare, but very good."

"I'd love some fish. I've been gorging on lamb in Athens. I love it, but I'd like a change."

I was happy that Kara hadn't given me grief for getting Thea to wake me up or making her wait for our date. Back home, girls would go into a pout if things didn't go as they expected. She seemed to be more relaxed in general. Maybe the month in Crete had mellowed her, but I didn't know what she was like before, so I'd have to see over time.

We sat indoors as the breeze off the sea had freshened. The tables had checkered tablecloths and a bottle with a candle in it in the middle. The two old men I had seen in the afternoon were still at their table playing cards. Before I pulled Kara's chair out for her to sit down, I told her how pretty she looked in her white blouse and Greek skirt. I thought that all the girls looked great in that outfit, especially if they had a tan, so the compliment rolled off my tongue easily. She looked at me and smiled, obviously appreciative. She said she'd bought the skirt at the airport.

Nikolas came over and lit the candle in the bottle. I thought about having a Fix Hellas, but I wanted Kara to join me in a drink, and this wasn't the time for a beer. I asked Nikolas what kind of wine he had, other than retsina. He recommended a bottle of white Vidiano, which was a Cretan wine, very good but not well-known. I didn't care what it cost, given my experience with the drachma, so I asked Nikolas to bring a bottle. When it came, I tasted it and let Kara taste it too. I could see that she was pleased with the gesture. The wine was good, so we toasted our new acquaintance with filled glasses and asked Nikolas if there were fish on the menu tonight.

He said that today's catch was bonito, which he could filet and serve with a light sauce with tomato, onion, and peppers. We both wanted that; Nikolas suggested a half filet for each of us since the bonito that were caught today was quite large. We could start with sliced tomatoes, greens, and sliced bread to dip in olive oil.

I stared into the candle, not quite believing in my good fortune at having found this place and these people, especially Kara, at the end of my journey. Kara gave me a nudge with her foot under the table. I woke out of my reverie and looked at her, my first thought being, *Who is this girl, and how can she be so different and so cool?*

"You were drifting off."

"Oh, wow. I'm sorry. I'm really bushed, I guess. The months in Berlin were intense. And then I was on the road like I never could have imagined. I was almost killed in a tunnel in Yugoslavia. Athens was crazy. The last two days have been a blur. I was almost squashed by a bus earlier today, and then I run into someone like you. I need to regroup."

"And who is someone like me like?" Kara teased.

I looked at her past the candle with the flame flickering its light on her bronzed face and golden hair. I felt I wasn't up to crossing wits with her right now. I was really tired, so I said honestly, "I don't know yet. But I'd like to, if only because you kicked me beneath the table just now. Let me get a night's sleep and we can start again tomorrow."

"Too late. It's already started." And she rubbed her foot on my leg again, which made me tingle despite my fatigue.

Nikolas brought the food and poured some more wine. "Enjoy," he said.

We ate in silence for a while, savoring Nikolas' light touch with the sauce on the bonito. The taste of the fish came through pleasantly. I savored the moment as well. I didn't want to disturb the mood that Kara had created with her flirtations. I was a klutz at flirting. I never had any experience and had little self-confidence at it, so I had rationalized it away as being unimportant. All of a sudden, I was discovering its pertinence and struggling to join the game that Kara said had already started.

I resorted to honesty again. "Sometimes it takes me a little while to get into the starting blocks." After which, I looked away.

Kara didn't answer for a minute, but then she said, "You know, that's a nice thing to hear from a guy. I'm used to having to fend off aggressive advances from guys. But I'd have to say you really do need some sleep." She paused and looked at the candle. "There's a lovely little cove down the beach where we can have brunch tomorrow. You sleep tonight, and we'll start again there."

I nodded with a sheepish grin. That sounded like a safe proposal, sleep now and brunch on the beach tomorrow. We said little else as we finished dinner. The rest of the bottle of Vidiano just about put me to sleep on my feet as we walked back to the hotel. I sort of remembered giving Nikolas three hundred drachmae for dinner and the wine and not believing it was just ten dollars for a great meal.

We went upstairs and Kara stopped at her room, which was next to mine. "Tomorrow then," she said and then wound her arms around my neck and kissed me full on the lips, inserting her tongue into my mouth and entwining it with mine for a long time. She pulled away and said, "Pleasant dreams." Then she went into her room and softly closed the door.

I stood on the balcony in bewilderment. I wasn't as sleepy as I had been a minute ago, but I knew I was exhausted and had to have sleep. I went to the WC and found it difficult to take a piss until the hard-on Kara had given me subsided. Having accomplished that, I went to my room, undressed, pulled up the blanket, and fell into a dreamless sleep that lasted until the sun flickered into my eyes in the late morning.

26

On the Beach

WHEN I WOKE UP, I rolled over and buried my head in the pillow. God, it felt good to have slept like that without a bunch of craziness going on around me. In my own room on a comfortable bed and no obligations. Wait! I checked my watch. I had slept for thirteen hours! I remembered Kara saying something about brunch on the beach, and it was past eleven. I got up, dressed quickly in a bathing suit, a Lacoste shirt, and my sandals and went to Kara's door and knocked. No answer. I went down to the lobby. No one there. The only place left was the taverna where I found Nikolas tidying up. Nikolas just pointed out to the terrace, and I saw Kara in the same position I had first seen her, only this time she was wearing a stunning, royal blue-and-white diagonal-striped bikini as if she planned to go swimming.

I walked out and said, "Good afternoon."

Kara looked up at me without raising her sunglasses. "Good afternoon indeed. I was thinking about having brunch today, but I've already had breakfast to keep from starving. Did you really just get up?"

"I'm afraid so. I was totally exhausted. But I feel completely refreshed after that sleep. I could use something to eat."

"Nikolas prepared a lunch for us. Can you hike a mile before eating?"

"Sure, but maybe I can get a piece of bread to munch on while we walk."

"Ask him. We need to get cold beer from him anyway."

We got our things together, and I carried the sack of food over my shoulder and chewed on the bread as we headed down the beach past the derelict fishing boats that were there. The sandy beach changed into a shingle of small stones after about sixty yards from the center of the village. I was glad I had my sandals on, but I was slipping from time to time because of the leather soles. Kara had on sneakers so she was fine.

It seemed to me we had gone more than a mile when the shingle ended abruptly, and we had to turn onto a path to avoid some brush that grew right down to the water. There were trees on the upslope overhanging the rude path. Then we came to an opening where there was a small sand beach about fifty feet long beyond which the trees and brush continued, leaving a cove in an isolated semicircle of greenery.

"Isn't it perfect?" Kara asked as she walked to the middle of the beach with her arms spread out, turning round and round.

"It's fabulous. Does anyone else come here?"

"I found it two weeks ago and have been coming almost every day for a tanning session and a swim, and I've never been interrupted. Why don't you get the blanket out of the bag and we can get comfortable?"

I was laying out the blanket and looking for food in the bag when I looked up and saw Kara standing next to me without her bikini on. I noticed right away that she had no tan lines on her body; she was perfectly bronzed all over. She helped me to finish laying out the blanket and put her bikini in the bag.

All I could say was, "So this is where you get your perfect tan, in your secret hideaway."

"But it's not a secret anymore," she said as she came over to me and pulled off my shirt and shorts. Then she put her hands on my shoulders, pushed me down on my knees, went to her knees, and caressed me around my eyes, finally finding with my mouth and kissing me just as she had last night. I kissed her back as hard as I could but decided that being on my knees wasn't going to do it, so I dropped her onto her side and then rolled her on her back and started reaching for her body.

Kara was doing the same to me, digging her fingernails into my back until it hurt and I said "ouch." She only panted and dug her nails into my shoulder. I figured that the only thing I could do to turn down the heat was to screw her with everything I had so I entered her and started going a mile-a-minute, and she really responded. But then I thought I should make it last, so I backed off and did it slower, but just as hard.

Kara groaned and writhed and said, "Faster!"

I said, "No," and I lifted my upper body off her to look at her eyes.

Kara looked me in the eyes and said, "Please ..."

"You want it to last, don't you?"

"You're strong," she said, still looking in my eyes.

With that, I gave her what she wanted, and we both lay panting for a while until I rolled off to her side and said, "I'm sorry I wasn't ready for you last night."

"I didn't sleep very well." After a pause, she said very softly, "I'm not that kind of girl, although I haven't given you a reason to think otherwise. Before I came here, I was so uptight and depressed. I had to get away from home. And the solitude of this place has renewed my spirit, but I've been really all alone, and that's not something I've dealt with before. When I saw you on the terrace yesterday, I didn't want you to see how much I needed someone, but you showed me you're a nice guy, so I let my feelings go last night. I'll admit you disappointed me. I thought you'd follow me into my room, but you've made it up to me now. That was wonderful."

She put her hand on my cheek and kissed me. I rolled on top of her, and we made love again. Afterward we held hands as we splashed into the water to cool off. I always liked to skinny-dip, whether it was at Chris' pool when his parents weren't around or in a mountain stream at college after soccer practice. But after sex, when my body was fully alive and I was with this beautiful, lithe nymph splashing about me, it was a feeling of ecstasy. I could see why the ancient Greeks thought that Zeus would come down from Olympos and snatch away maidens like this for his pleasure.

We went back to the blanket and shared Kara's towel to dry off. She then got the food out. I delighted in the lamb, tomato, and olive oil sandwich that Nikolas had made. I popped the tops off the beers, which were lukewarm by now but still delicious. We sat on the blanket and just looked at each other while we ate.

I had only seen scenes like this in movies, or maybe it was in my imagination. I was shattered by the beauty of her body, its silky skin, and the way it moved. I dug into the sandwich to try to pry myself away from the thought that women had such a tactical advantage over men because of the beauty of their bodies. I believed that the feminists were right in fighting against men objectifying their bodies, but I couldn't help being caught up by Kara's physical form. She must have seen me staring at her, so she kicked me again, one of her favorite amusements.

"You don't have picnics in the nude very often," she teased.

"Actually this is my first."

"I've had lots, except I've always been by myself down here."

"So you were hoping someone would come along?"

"I already told you that."

"So you did. But now that you've gotten what you wanted, what do you plan to do?" I teased. *Maybe this was flirting*, I thought.

"Oh, don't be mean. We can talk about things and be friends, and we can make love too. This won't last forever. We should make the most of it."

I saw that I had stung her. That wasn't flirting; that was hurting. I saw my mistake. She had apparently been sitting out here in Crete harboring hopes that a guy might come along who knew the answers to her questions, and along I came, who was looking for answers to my own questions. I had never thought that *my* answers might be delivered through a relationship with a woman.

"I'm sorry. That was a cheap shot. I apologize. I'm not used to a whirlwind of sex like this. I didn't have sex while I was in college. People were just bed-hopping like they were rabbits. All about bodies. It made the whole thing meaningless to me. I came from a boys' prep school so I didn't know anything about girls anyway, so I just smoked pot, played sports, and stayed on my own. I've just come from Berlin where I had a relationship with a French woman who was fourteen years older than I was. That was my first relationship, which I just fell into. I learned a few things, but I still need to learn a lot, and you're the most beautiful girl I've ever seen, and I can see no reason why we can't learn together."

I watched as a couple of tears rolled down Kara's cheeks. I bent towards her and kissed them away.

"That was so beautiful," she said.

She pushed me back onto the blanket and kissed me all over as I ran my fingers through her hair. Then she mounted me and used her supple body like an elastic pump to bring me to ecstasy. After that, she put her head on my chest and said, "I guess we have a few things to talk about."

"I guess we have."

For the rest of the afternoon, we lay in the sun and rubbed Kara's tanning oil on each other. When we got too warm, we went swimming again. I wasn't a great swimmer so I didn't venture too far from the beach, but Kara was intrepid, swimming far out to the point where I lost sight of her around a point of land, and I began to worry. But I remembered that she had said she was a champion swimmer, so I went back to the blanket on the beach to wait for her to come back. Finally, she reappeared, exhibiting a strong, smooth stroke and not showing any sign that she had been out for a half hour.

When she got out of the water, all she wanted to do was dry her hair and put on the tanning oil. She wasn't even winded. I was impressed. She reminded me of the Amazons in ancient Greece, but I couldn't say that to her because the term had taken on a different meaning over the centuries.

"Your body has glory in it," was what I managed to say, remembering what Kamala had said about admiring one's lover.

"What a nice thing to say, Jack. I enjoy my body, and I love exercise. You have a nice body too. I can see you've been an athlete. We must keep fit, or our bodies will become a burden to us when we grow old. My mother told me that when I was young, and I didn't want to listen, but when I started swimming in middle school and saw that I was good at it, I took the responsibility of keeping fit upon myself. I guess that's the way you learn best, when you hear the lessons in your mind and act on them when they become relevant to you."

Yeah, that was true. I hated having the parents dole out adages and advice from their past, although every so often I had found truth in them once I had come to a point in my life where they could be tested and proven.

We dressed, packed the sack, and walked back to the village. We didn't say much on the way. I was absorbing what we had done on the beach, how our bodies had meshed together outdoors under the Cretan sun where the Minoans had probably done it six thousand years ago like it was depicted on the ancient vases.

We got back to the hotel, and I asked Kara if she would like to shower first. She suggested that we shower together, to save hot water, as she said, with a wicked grin. I had no problem with that, so we put our stuff in our rooms, got soap and towels, and washed each other down. I thought it was almost as good as having sex, and I presented Kara with a large hard-on to wash, which she did with glee.

We dressed for dinner and went to see what Nikolas had on the menu. I ordered another bottle of Vidiano. It was good wine that pleased us both, and one bottle was enough. Nikolas announced that we were in luck. His brother had procured a couple of chickens, which he could broil and make a sauce from eggs and goat's milk. He hadn't had chickens for quite a while. Kara and I were content to accept anything he offered, so he went off to the kitchen humming a tune and rubbing his hands together.

"It's nice he has a new challenge for his cuisine," Kara said.

I nodded, but I was thinking of the challenge Kara presented to me. She was beautiful, smart, athletic, and friendly. I'd never encountered such a girl. She threw off all my prior notions of females, and I needed to know more about her. She said we had some things to talk about. We'd better get to it.

"Tell me more about your situation with your mother. I mean, it's unusual for a girl to blow off her parents and go to Greece. What's going on?" I asked.

"I don't mind telling you, Jack. I see something in you that I haven't seen in other boys before. I've dated quite a few guys, and it doesn't take me long to find out if they were jerks or at least not right for me. It's been a long, discouraging journey through all that with my mother hovering over me waiting to hear when the chapel bells are going to ring. At this point she wants me to get married or finish college, preferably in that order and soon. Where I'm from, girls are sent to college to find husbands. At least 95 percent of them are. When I got on the swim team and then won the NCAA championship, that was nice, but it showed her I wasn't concentrating on getting a man. And then it took away from my class time, so I didn't graduate. I'm two courses short."

"Winning an NCAA championship is *nice*?! It's fantastic! I can see you have a problem there," I cut in.

"She's a real Mrs. Beaver Cleaver, a 1950s housewife with an attitude. And my father is as conservative as they come. Guys with long hair drive him crazy, and he supports the war, although I think he's starting to hear it from some of his friends who've had their sons drafted that it might not be in the country's best interest."

"Wow," I said. "It sounds like you've got it worse at home than I do, the difference being that the draft is still hanging over me."

"I guess that's worse. You could be killed or maimed before your next birthday. How old are you, if you don't mind my asking?"

"Why should I mind? I'm twenty-three."

"I'm twenty-three too. Gosh, we do have things in common. That's kind of nice."

We sat in silence for a while, staring at the candle. I thought about having things in common with a twenty-three-year-old girl. Before I met Kara, I would have said I could have nothing at all in common. But she was from the same kind of background as I was, and she was in the same kind of bind I was in and had reacted the same way I had. I figured her mother was to her like the draft was to me, a wicked institution. I could see she had guts, and I liked that.

Maybe it was time for me to put trust in someone who could help me get to the root of my issues and help me come back. Who knew? What did I have to lose? I had come to the end of the earth; this had to be the time.

So I decided I would open up to her in a way I'd never done before. She had given herself to me and had revealed her problems. No one else had done that, except Eva, and she was much older than me. I had been knotted up inside for a long time looking for answers, trying to find out who I was. Kara was my age and seemed to be on the same journey, although she was on a shorter timeline.

"My mother and father are like a corporate team," I finally said. "They work together and put their energies into the business my father works for. All the men in the business do the same thing to make money, to climb the ladder, and all the wives give parties to promote their husbands, and they all stick together like a tribe. It's all programmed out in advance. It's what their fathers and mothers did. No one dares to think for himself or drop out and do something different. If he does, he becomes a pariah and is never spoken of. It's fucking unbelievable."

I saw that Kara was going to say something, but she held off to let me continue.

"I want to know Who I Am," I said emphatically. "What is my path? What am I supposed to do with my life? The reasons I want to know are pretty simple: I do *not* want to live my parents' lives. And what is it that I should do that will give *my* life meaning? That's it. I see all these people our age back home running around protesting everything and saying they are going to follow Buddha and find peace, and all they're looking for is their next joint. They're full of shit. They have to get out and find some real answers for themselves. That's what I've tried to do, to gain real experience from life and people. And you know what? I think you're about as close to a real person as I've come across because you're out here doing the same thing as I am. Am I wrong?"

So I had said it all out loud and was thinking maybe I had said too much. I hadn't noticed that Nikolas had brought the chicken during my soliloquy, but when I stopped talking, I noticed that Kara hadn't touched her food.

"Oh. We should eat," I said stupidly to change the subject. We started in on the meal, and both of us went "mmmm" because Nikolas had prepared another epicurean achievement.

Kara had been listening intently, waiting to make sure I had said my piece. Then she said, "What you just said put all my fears and anxieties and all the obstacles that have been put in front of me preventing me from finding happiness into two categories: parents and social conformity. I have been crushed by the pressure inside to know myself and break away from the crowd, but not having the experience to make a beginning. I was happy as a child. Now all that seems to be so far away. Bob Dylan says, 'There's no direction home.' It all seems so overwhelming."

Kara put her elbows on the table and held her head in her hands as if the weight of the discussion had made it too heavy for her neck to hold it up. I looked into Kara's eyes and saw the weariness that I had felt for so long. It was born of too much contemplation and the inability to react to circumstances that constrained our needs and desires. Frustration had driven both of us from our homes to find life experiences and resolve the issues we faced.

Kara had jogged a flashback to my childhood, which held happy memories for me. I remembered when I won a prize in elementary school for reciting a poem in assembly, I recited,

> Tyger, Tyger, burning bright,
>
> In the forests of the night:
>
> What immortal hand or eye
>
> Could frame thy fearful symmetry?
>
> In what distant deeps or skies
>
> Burnt the fire of thine eyes?
>
> On what wings dare he aspire?
>
> What the hand, dare seize the fire?

"Sorry. That's all I can remember."

Kara's mouth was open when I finished, and I reached across the table to touch her chin so she would close it. She grabbed my hand and kissed it. 'The Tyger,' by William Blake," she said.

"You're right. I didn't know what it meant when I was young, but we studied Blake in college. It's from *Songs of Innocence and Experience*. In 'The Tyger,' Blake is glorifying experience where each man must go out and resolve his own existence in life. That's what we're doing."

"That was wonderful. I've been here a month trying to collect my experiences and make sense of them, and you come along and recite a poem that sums it all up for me. Thank you."

"And as Dylan said, 'There is no direction home,' so it's every man and woman for themselves."

Kara's features fell when I said that. We had finished dinner, so she just got up and went out the door, leaving me to settle up with Nikolas. In doing so, I noted I was getting a little light on drachmae. I'd have to check again in my room.

Outside the taverna, Kara was nowhere to be found. I looked at the beach area and around the square, but she had disappeared. *Maybe she needed to use the WC,* I thought, so I went to the hotel and up the stairs and saw the door to the WC open. I was perplexed. I knocked on Kara's door. No answer. Now that was strange. I started to go back down the stairs when I heard a door open and saw Kara step tentatively out onto the balcony. I turned and walked toward her and saw something that unnerved me. She'd been crying.

My mind was flooded with the emotional impact it had cost me when I had to deal with women's tears in the past. My experience was that when I saw a woman cry, I caved in. Whatever she wanted, I'd try to get it for her. I was a sucker for a damsel in distress, although this time I had no idea what the problem was.

I slowly approached her. She had crossed her arms on her chest and looked at me wistfully. I saw no anger or accusation in her eyes. I drew on my experience and newfound self-confidence while I thought of what the right thing to say might be. We stood in silence for a minute like chess pieces waiting to be moved, but I wasn't going to let Kara move me. That was in the past.

"Why did you say that?" Kara finally said.

"Say what?"

"That it's every man and woman for themselves."

"You quoted Dylan, 'There's no direction home.' I was just following that thought. We all have to find our own paths."

"But he didn't say we all had to do it by ourselves, alone. I think that you've been out in the wilderness by yourself for so long that you've forgotten how to connect with other people." With that, she went back into her room, but she left the door open.

I stared at the open door for a minute. I reflected back and knew that Kara was right, but how did she know that? I could see that I had just begun to connect with people since I had come to Europe. In the past, I would isolate myself. Now I realized that my interactions with Wild Bill had changed me. Eva had a strong influence on me. So did Hans and Charlie. And now I was getting completely entangled with Kara, whom I had only known for two days.

I had taken the leap and liberated myself by leaving home and was emerging from the self-defense cocoon I had erected to shield myself from the onslaughts of my sisters and my parents and the mess that was the United States. I had dropped my guard with these people and, in so doing, had learned more about myself than ever before because I could now look into a mirror and see my real self.

I felt there was more to it. That was why Kara had left the door open. I pushed at it, and it swung open. Kara was stretched out on her bed with a pillow propped up behind her head.

"Took you long enough. What were you doing out there?" she asked.

"Thinking about the wilderness."

"Come sit by me."

I closed the door and sat on the bed next to Kara.

She took my hand, "Have you been lonely?"

"To tell the truth, I'm always lonely, but I've conditioned myself to it so it doesn't hurt too much. I 'm always battling someone or something and always by myself."

"Have you ever cried?" she asked.

"I have cried sometimes; just lately I cried in Athens, thinking how hard it was trying to find my way by myself."

"That was why I cried tonight. I thought I might have found someone who could help me find my path. Then you had said that everyone had to go it alone, and that upset me."

By now, I had stretched out next to her on the bed so I could look into her eyes and know that she was speaking from the depth of her soul. I felt that she was drawing me out of myself from that same depth, but my usually cautious nature still held on to a need for self-defense. Yet I didn't want to hold on anymore. I needed to be free of myself. The paradox was that I had to give myself to someone else to be free of myself.

We talked about many things: our childhoods, my awful sisters, our parents and the old ways they clung to, our lives in college, and our friends and how they were dealing with life.

"What about your girlfriends?" Kara asked.

"I'm serious when I said that Eva was my first sexual experience," I told her.

"I'm surprised. I would have thought you had had a dozen girls," she said and giggled.

"What about your boyfriends," I asked.

She shot me a look, but she said, "I admit I used sex to rebel against my mother, and I've had a few casual boyfriends since high school. I knew they were after my body, and I like sex, but that got me a reputation. I had never found anyone I could fall in love with, except Paul McCartney. But that didn't work out."

That made me laugh, but I was curious about her sexual adventurousness. Making the assumption, I asked her, "When did you start taking the pill?"

"I started taking it at sixteen because the doctor said that I needed to make up a hormone imbalance. My mother was not pleased, but that's when I got my license to screw," she said.

I laughed so hard at that that I fell off the bed. "You're a witch," I said.

"A sex witch," Kara countered. "Come up here and I'll prove it."

I bit my lower lip as I undressed. Kara had already shown me how aggressive she could be. I had never heard of a woman doing what she did to me when she was on top of me on the beach. And now she wanted to prove to me she was a sex witch.

I clambered onto the bed with her, and she climbed on top and gave me a long, loving kiss. Then she used her hands and her mouth in just the right ways, at just the right moments, to drive me almost crazy until I couldn't take it anymore. Then she got on her back and offered herself to me, and we did it twice before I dropped down on her in complete surrender.

"Where did you learn all that stuff?" I asked.

"Believe it or not, there's a lot of girl talk that goes on when you're traveling to swim meets. Swimmers are really good athletes, you know."

I thought of myself as something of an athlete, but sexual athletics were beyond me. I didn't realize I could get tired out so fast that way.

"Come here," Kara said. "You should know something about how to please a girl. Don't worry. I can see you need a rest. I only need your hands for a while."

She showed me how to touch her in ways that made her squirm and moan. She told me to go faster or slower after I learned what to do. Then she put her arms around my head and kissed me savagely and said, "Now you have to learn to finish with your tongue." She took my head and drew it down between her legs and told me to lick her all over. I was flustered at first, but I did what she wanted and got the idea that I was on the right track when she started to scream between her teeth and her body jerked convulsively.

Finally she pushed me away, rolled on her side, and said, "You're a great lover, Jack."

27

Bike Ride

I LAY ON THE bed staring at the ceiling for a long while. I wasn't sleepy at all. I could still smell the musk of her hair. Kara was sleeping lightly beside me so I pulled the blanket over her and thought about what she had said. I never thought I'd hear any woman say I was a great lover. She must have been talking out of passion. I felt I had lived a half a lifetime in the past several hours and at a much faster pace than I was used to.

The room lightened as the sun began to rise, so I got up, took a shower, and went down to the taverna to get some breakfast. When I got there, it was closed. I figured it was one of the days we'd have to buy food at the market, which I could see was doing good business as the fishermen were buying their day's rations before putting out to sea. There was some jostling and joking going on as they filled their boxes with food and drinks, which stopped when I came up to the door.

I put oranges, a lump of feta cheese, a loaf of bread, and a jar of honey on the counter. I asked Nikolas' brother if there were any yogurt, but he told me it was being prepared and I could come back later. I paid for the food and went back to the hotel, where I found Thea in the lobby. She confirmed that Nikolas was away and that the taverna was closed for the day. I showed Thea what I had bought and indicated to her that I needed knives and plates. She nodded and got them from a cupboard.

I asked her for coffee, but she pointed up the road and said "Taverna. Tymbaki." I remembered that Tymbaki was the last town I had passed before I came to Aigia Galini. Maybe Kara and I could make a coffee run on the bike.

I got back to Kara's room to find her curled up under the blanket, sound asleep. I didn't want to wake her, and I was sleepy too, so I left the food on the table and went to my room to take a nap.

I took off my sandals and stretched out on the bed and started thinking about what happened last night and fell asleep in a moment. It didn't seem as if I'd been sleeping for very long when I discovered that I was living in the dream I'd been dreaming. Kara was pulling down my shorts and stroking my groin, for real. She was still naked, which meant she had come from her room that way and was eager for sex. She got on top of me, pulled off my shirt, and began to slowly grind on me, kissing my mouth, my eyes, and my neck.

I actually had wanted to have something to eat when I woke up, not to be eaten. So I grabbed her torso and flipped her under me, whereupon she let out a little squeal, and pumped her for all she was worth. When I was done, I was done, and I told her, "That's enough of that for a while. I got up to get some breakfast, and what I get is a sex witch. Didn't you see the food in your room?"

"Yes, I did, and I thought it was so sweet that I decided to come and thank you in a special way."

"You're very welcome. C'mon, let's eat. I'm hungry."

I put my clothes back on, but Kara went back to her room naked, just as she had come. I shook my head, but I couldn't help thinking how beautiful she was.

We sat and ate breakfast, both remarking on how delicious the raw honey, which had bees' wings in it, was on the freshly baked bread. I lamented the lack of coffee, but Kara said she had been living without it since she got to Greece and was calmer for that. I told her that I'd really like to have some coffee, and since the taverna was closed today, we'd have to venture out for meals anyway. I said that Thea had mentioned there was a taverna in Tymbaki, so I went to my room to check the map. It would take about twenty minutes to get there by bike, going slowly.

I knew Kara thought bikes were dangerous and she might not ride with me, but I didn't want to eat yogurt and fruit all day, and I had an ulterior motive for going back toward Tymbaki. On the map, I had seen that there were ruins of an ancient Minoan city called Phaistos, which was only six kilometers from Tymbaki. I'd love to see it.

When I went back to Kara's room, I found her getting dressed for the beach and her usual routine. She had put on the purple bikini top, only this time with the matching bottom, which was barely there, recognizable only from the small bows on the sides. *How can she walk around in that outfit?* I thought while relishing the sight.

But I was up for getting on the bike again and to get real food and see the historical site, so I was forthright about making my proposal. "Listen, I have an idea, Since Nikolas is away, we can go to the taverna in Tymbaki for lunch, and I found this ancient Minoan city I've never heard of, which is only five kilometers from Tymbaki. I'd really like to see it."

Kara squinted at me, expressing disapproval. "How far is this Tymbaki?"

It's about ten kilometers, which is six miles, not a long way. It would take fifteen to twenty minutes, going slowly."

"Oooo, I don't like motorcycles," she said. "I really want to swim."

"You swim every day. Nikolas is away, and we have to eat. Let's do this for today. We can swim the rest of the week. You need a little culture to go with your sex."

"Very funny. Tell me you aren't having a good time since you met me."

"I've been having a terrific time with you, and you know it. I think you should know a little more about what I like. The ancient Greeks fascinate me, and having come here, I want to find out more about them. It's part of who I am. Doesn't that interest you?"

"Oh, yes. It does. Really." She hugged me. "I'll even risk my life on a motorcycle for that," she said mockingly, her eyes wide.

"I don't think you'll be going that far," I said with a frown. I told her to put on a shirt, shorts, and sneakers and to tie her hair in a ponytail.

I asked her if she had any laundry for Thea, but she didn't, so I got mine. I needed a rag to wipe down the bike and wasn't sure how to ask Thea for one after the laundry fiasco of the other day. We went downstairs and found Thea out back of the main building. I held out the clothes, which Thea took, understanding them to be laundry. Kara saw a pile of rags in a box and took one out to ask if she could have it. Thea said she could while shaking her head at me.

I had to spend a few minutes wiping down the bike, which had picked up a lot of dust coming over the mountain. Kara was getting bored, so I wiped off the seat and told her to get on while I finished up. I checked the tank and saw that it was well over half full. Then I slid in front of Kara. I told her to put her feet on the folding footrests and to hang onto me around the waist and to sit still. Then I started the bike and slowly made the climb up the track from the village to the dirt road above.

Once on the road, I felt the familiar rhythm of the bike in motion with the gentle thirty kilometers-per-hour breeze in my hair. Having Kara hanging onto me reminded me of days in Berlin and Vienna with Eva. I hoped she'd gotten home all right, but squelched those memories in favor of Kara, who was becoming a person of major consequence on my journey. I really liked her.

"How are you doing back there?" I asked.

"I'm fine. Could you go a little faster?"

"Ha!" I said. "And this coming from the motorcycle-hater!"

I juiced the bike up to fifty kilometers per hour, which was fast enough on the dirt road. The dust started flying out from under the front tire, and I slowed to forty kilometers per hour.

"Too much dust. Got to slow down."

By the time we got to Tymbaki, the road was paved. There was a main street, which had some shops; a taverna in the middle of town; and whitewashed dwellings behind these buildings on both sides of the road with olive groves behind them going up the mountain on one side and down to the sea on the other. I drove slowly through town and saw another taverna at the end of the main street.

"Looks like we have a choice."

"Let's ride some more," she said.

I noted that people were stopping what they were doing and looking at the bike. Or was it Kara or both? I smiled, remembering what Wild Bill and every other guy said about bikes and girls, and here it was happening again. I saw that the road ahead was straight and in reasonable condition, so I yelled back at Kara to hang on tight, and then I flicked my right wrist and jumped the bike from forty to eighty kilometers per hour in a heartbeat. Kara squealed, but she lifted her head from behind my shoulder to get the full effect of the rush of air as we sliced through it.

In two minutes, we passed a sign that said Phaistos in Greek and English.

"There's Phaistos."

"Keep going!"

So I drove all the way to Aigia Daka, which was eighteen kilometers from Tymbaki. I had to slow down as the road became curvier and then stopped in Aigia Daka because there the road started to climb the mountain. I pulled off the road in front of a honey stand and turned to look at Kara, who looked back at me, wide-eyed.

"These things are dangerous," she said, straight-faced. She grabbed my face, kissed me, and said, "But they sure are fun!"

I started laughing to the point that I almost let the bike tip over, scaring Kara. "Yeah, they're fun, but they're serious business. You have to concentrate on what you're doing all the time or you can really screw up," I said as I steadied the bike. "Ok, let's stop at Phaistos on the way back and see what that's all about. Then we can get some lunch."

Kara agreed. It seemed to me that the bike ride had made her day. She'd been cooped up in the village for too long. I was happy that she was going to indulge me in a little Minoan culture. I drove back to Tymbaki a little slower so I wouldn't miss the turnoff to Phaistos. When I found it, it was a well-paved road of less than a half kilometer, which led directly to the site. It was apparent that it had been extensively excavated and was well kept up. We went into the ruins through the propylaea, the ceremonial entryway. I explained to Kara that the most famous of these was on the Acropolis.

I was surprised to see how big the city was. Although only the walls of the first floor remained, they covered a large area in which there were palaces and smaller dwellings, large ceremonial staircases, courtyards, a theatre, and the remains of columns in various places. Kara was amazed that all this was built by a culture that thrived two thousand years before Christ.

We went into the gift shop on the way out where I showed Kara souvenir statuettes of the Cretan Snake Goddess. I told her she was the principal deity of Crete, which was a matriarchal culture. Kara said she approved of that arrangement. I bought a guidebook of Crete, which included the early- and late-Minoan periods.

Then we drove back to Tymbaki, where we chose the taverna in the middle of town, and I was delighted to see that they had souvlaki. So I ordered two sticks and a Fix Hellas. Kara had a Greek salad with feta cheese and a glass of red house wine.

While we were waiting, I thumbed through the guidebook. I read that Phaistos was the second city to Knossos in Minoan times. The palaces had been destroyed by earthquakes three times in three hundred years and rebuilt each time.

"No wonder they called Poseidon 'The Earth Shaker,'" I said out loud.

"What on earth are you talking about?" Kara asked.

"I told you that ancient Greece is a hobby of mine. The Minoans, the Athenians, the gods, and heroes. I'm sorry to bore you."

"You're not boring me. You're neglecting me."

That remark stung me. I felt that it was something a spoiled princess back home would say, and I was at the point of making a sharp rejoinder when I thought that maybe I could use Kara's own attitude to enlighten her as to how she had changed the mood with her words. After all, she had said she could use some help along her path, so what the hell?

I just stared at her for a minute to see if the thundercloud on her brow would dispel itself. She stared back at me, but as the seconds ticked by, her expression slowly softened. I continued to say nothing, and then the cloud blew away in a flood of tears.

"Oh, Jack. I'm so sorry! I was being a bitch. I don't know what came over me. I hate bitchy girls." She had to catch her breath and wipe her eyes.

"You know, I had been thinking I was here long enough by myself when you showed up. I was getting worried about my parents. They must be beside themselves with me disappearing. I've been troubled about my problems, and I didn't have anyone to talk to about them. And you come along, seemingly solving your problems as you go. I need some help with my future direction. You might have noticed I was getting kind of horny too. Jesus. While I like sex, I'm not that wild, but that's a problem you've solved for me nicely, thank you."

She looked over at me, although her expression remained clouded. I smiled but still said nothing. I wanted to hear everything she had to say, and I didn't think she'd made a clear breast of it yet.

"I'm going to have to go home soon, and I think my mother is going to be really angry at me. I have no idea of what I'm going to do. I don't want to fall into the same spot I was in when I left, but I haven't been able to put a plan together that's going to change things. What am I going to do?"

The look on Kara's face told me that she was done talking and pretty much at the end of her rope. I figured I could step in and make it a discussion at this point.

"You got under my skin with that princess attitude, I'll admit. Better that you drop tone entirely. The only guys who put up with that are the jerks you want to avoid. If you want to be your own person, people are going to have to respect you, and to make that happen, you have to respect yourself. That's what I've found out.

"I was really hung up about women, and that did a number on my self-esteem. I was good at sports and made grades in the subjects I cared about, but everyone else was making out sexually. That's what mattered on campus, and I was left out. I needed to break out, and since I've been over here, I have. When I combine that new self-esteem with what already comes naturally to me, like my ability to organize things, I'm starting to see who I am and where I could fit in life. Before it was just a blur. Nothing was connected."

The waiter brought the food, and I dug into my souvlakis before Kara could reply. She nibbled at the salad, poking at the cheese with her fork. I could see that she was thinking.

"You've used your time over here better than I have. You must have seen what you needed before you came here and then went after it. I just escaped what still looked like my fate for a short period of time. When I go home, I'll still be trapped."

"I used to think that way too, but I don't think that anyone with brains and guts has to be trapped in life. I can see you've got brains and guts. What you need is a plan to get you to an alternative objective from the one your mother is steering you toward."

"Jack! Do you think that's possible? How do I start? You said you can organize anything. Can you help me make a plan to get me out of my trap?"

I was flattered by the question, but also taken aback by the thought that she was so readily willing to rely on me to help her chart her way forward. I hardly knew her, and yet I felt inside that she was what I was supposed to find at the end of my journey. She was the challenge and the reward. I felt an instinctive attachment to her, and I had a responsibility to help her. After all, I had done more or less the same thing for Eva, so why not for Kara too?

I reflected on how I had come to the answers to my questions that I was starting to resolve: through talks with Wild Bill and Chris and the trip across the United States. Reading *Siddhartha*, Henry Miller, Hemingway, and other writers had provided me with a foundation of knowledge. But I had learned that there was no substitute for experience. Sleeping with Eva was a release. Meeting Hans was a godsend. I needed to learn about life by living it, and I had organized a plan to do that for myself. I had more to do when I got home, but I had laid a foundation already.

"Listen," I said, "everyone's journey in life is ultimately a plan that is unique and personal to themselves. I've read a lot of books that conveyed that message. Siddhartha would be a prime example. Maybe we can put together a short-term plan for when you get home so you can show your parents you've been doing a lot of soul-searching over here and have found a path that *you* want to go down rather than the one they want you to go down. Do you think that would be a good start?"

"Yes! That's exactly what I need, to get out from under my mother's constant needling. The parents only know their way. If I could show them that I have a different path, one that would work for me, it would give me space to breathe and work things out."

"You have the right idea. That's exactly where I was coming from. We do have things in common. Let's go for a swim, and we can discuss some details later."

We finished lunch and went back to Aigia Galini, where we bought food for dinner, changed, and walked to the cove where we stripped, made love on the beach, and went swimming. Kara was out a long time, but I didn't worry about her. I figured she was thinking while she was swimming, feeling that swimming was one way she set herself free.

When we got back to the hotel, we shared a shower and went to our rooms. Ever since I had talked to Kara about helping her make plans, my mind had shifted into its pragmatic mode. I found that being with Kara was a pleasant diversion from my own issues, but now there were practical issues to be attended to, not just love affairs.

"Is this a love affair?" I asked myself.

Yes, it might well be because our attraction for each other was strong, but I didn't want to fall head-over-heels in love right now. It churned my emotions, as I had found with Candace. I thought I could help Kara out better if I kept my head clear and then see where things went after we got home and set our plans for the future in motion.

28

To Spili: Making Plans

BACK IN MY ROOM, I counted my drachmae and saw that I'd been spending faster than I thought, likely because I'd been paying for Kara's meals. I figured I had four days more here in Crete. Kara said she had to leave pretty soon, so that was going to be it anyway. I'd given Thea enough for six more nights at the hotel, but I wasn't going to hassle her for the extra two. It was the daily expenses that were the trouble. I had a round-trip ferry ticket. I absolutely had to visit Knossos. Otherwise, I could make the money last three days, realistically.

I had to tell Kara about this situation, so I went to her room and saw her dressed in a red polka-dot bikini top with large white dots and a pair of tan short-shorts. I figured that bikini tops were her favorite because she was a swimmer and because she looked so fabulous in them.

She was in the process of laying out food for our meal, but I told her to hold off for a bit while we talked about practical matters. She was up for that, but why not have a glass of wine while we talked? So I pulled the cork on the red Vidiano we were trying out and sat down for a conversation. Kara said she had five more days left on the room and a little more than five thousand drachmae ($170). She had bought a round-trip ferry ticket too. She had her flights back to O'Hare all paid for, but she thought she'd have to spend the night in Athens before she caught her flight. She had a hundred dollars in AMEX checks for that. I told her to spend wisely because that was just enough money. She had to figure in food too.

I told her about my diminishing supply of drachmae and that I would have to leave in three days. She wasn't happy about that, but I said that was my limit. We looked at each other with the forlorn expressions of those who knew they had little time left together. Kara put her hand in front of her eyes to hide the tears that were welling up. I reached out to touch her, and she grabbed my hand as if it were a lifeline.

"So where do we go from here?" she asked.

"We're looking toward the future, right? I think that the best thing for you is to finish your degree. Then you will be employable in a career-oriented job. It doesn't matter what just yet. Otherwise, you're just a high school grad, one of the millions. I once heard my father say something about hiring women who said they could type just so they could get a job. They never get out of the typing pool. Never say you can type. Remember that.

"Also, if you are finishing your degree, you can fend off your mother trying to get you married for six months. That's reasonable. Hopefully, if you can get into courses at Lake Forest College that meet your degree requirements and can be transferred, you can get your degree by Christmas. You can live at home to save room and board, if you can stand it. Your father will pay the tuition, won't he?"

"I suppose so. I can ask him."

"Taking two courses isn't a big deal. You should also audit a literature course to get some perspective on the life issues we've been talking about. I'll give you my copy of *Siddhartha*. Start reading it so we can talk about it. It's a book about self-discovery."

"I'd like that. I'm all out of reading material, and what I've been reading is so trashy. I don't know what is good to read."

"I can give you a list from my English courses. There are some amazing books out there."

"So I get my degree. Then what?"

"We'll have to think some more about that. I'm still working on the next step for myself. Your problem is to pacify your mother by showing her you're moving forward and don't need a husband to keep you occupied."

We ate dinner and went for a walk through the village square, down to the beach, and watched the last of the fishermen return and haul their boats up on the shingle. The breeze was blowing across the water all the way from Africa, but the sea was fairly flat as far as we could see in the gathering dusk. When we got back, I gave Kara my copy of *Siddhartha* so she could get started on it. We kissed and went to our separate rooms. I got on my bed and read the history of the Minoans, hoping Kara would take to Siddhartha.

When I got up in the morning, my first thought was about how hungry I was because of the makeshift meals we'd had the day before. My second thought was that this was my next-to-last day in Aigia Galini with Kara. I thought about getting Nikolas to take an AMEX check for the meals to extend my money supply, but we had arranged things, best not to go back. I was ready to get on the road again anyway. I had a long journey home, and I didn't know how I was going to get there. Yugoslavia wasn't in my travel plans.

After dressing, I knocked on Kara's door, and she told me to come in. She was dressed in bikini top and shorts and stretched out on the bed, reading *Siddhartha*. It appeared that she was at least halfway through it.

"Oh, Jack. This is an amazing book. I didn't think I'd like it at first. I'm not much for Eastern culture, but the writing is so easy to understand, and the idea of what Siddhartha is trying to accomplish with his life is more or less what we are doing."

"He's trying to find his true self. Don't want to spoil anything, but he finds a lot more."

"Gosh. I'll be interested to find out what."

I said I could really use some breakfast, so we went to the taverna, where Nikolas greeted us and apologized for not being there yesterday. He said he'd gone to Rythimno for supplies and promised that he would have a tasty meal for us tonight. He said he would bring us breakfast right away with coffee he had gotten in Rythimno.

He came back with a tray full of fresh fruit, yogurt, bread, and jam and a carafe of coffee. Kara and I told him that we loved the hotel and Nikolas' cooking. We also had to tell him that I was leaving in two days and Kara soon after. Nikolas was sad. He could see that "his Americans" had grown close in Aigia Galini.

We wondered what we were going to do with our last two days, figuring in time for swimming each day, so we asked him where we should go. Nikolas told us about the beautiful village of Spili, which was on the way to Rythimno, about thirty kilometers to the west. He said it was situated in a valley beneath a mountainous cliff. The town was at nearly a thousand meters, so it was quite a bit cooler than on the seashore. There were two nice cafés and some lovely fountains. We thought it sounded perfect.

We went back to get long pants and jackets. Thea saw me and brought my clean laundry. I put the clothes in my room and slipped into the newly washed jeans jacket. Putting it on reminded me of being on the road and why I had come all this way. I had the idea that I had accomplished everything I could, resolved questions, and found my reward in Kara, so I was eager to get back on the road to return to answer my last question: what I was going to do with my life.

I had been thinking about where I could go to get closer to home than from Greece. I thought there were ferries across the Adriatic from Greece to Italy, which would cut the mileage, but I had no idea of the time and cost of such a trip. Or maybe there was a ferry to Venice. I could drive across northern Italy like Pete had done. I'd have to see when I got back to Athens.

I heard a noise, turned, and saw Kara standing in the doorway, looking me over. "You were contemplating again," she said.

"Yes, I was. I think about things. It's part of who I am."

"There are worse things to be than a thinker." Kara came over and planted a kiss on my mouth. "I'm ready to go for a ride."

We drove the hill up to the road across the south side of the island. I turned west toward Rythimno. Right away I could tell that the road was curvier and had more hills than the road to Tymbaki, so I stuck pretty much to forty-five kilometers per hour with no bursts of speed to titillate Kara. As we went up the valley, the scenery of the mountains became more appealing, so a slower ride turned out for the best.

After forty minutes, we arrived in Spili and stopped in front of a café, which faced an eight hundred-foot wall of grey stone mountain, which the village had wrapped itself halfway around at the base. On the other side of the valley to the northeast was a ridge that led to Mt. Ida. Clouds perched on top of the ridge like white icing on the edge of a grey-green cake, but most of the valley was lit up in sunshine. The white stone buildings gleamed a warm presence from the little village.

"Oh, Jack! What a beautiful village!" Kara said.

We sat at an outdoor table at a café and had some tea and a sweet snack while taking in the scene. When we ordered, Kara asked the waiter where the fountains were. He said they were just down the street to the right. We sat in the sun in an idyllic trance with the cool air flowing around us until I started to feel my face getting warm. I asked Kara if she were getting a sunburn, and she laughed and said no, but I was. She had been tanning for weeks. I was still white by comparison. Up in the hills, the sun was stronger, so she said I'd better cover up.

I paid the bill, and we started motoring down the main street looking for the fountains. Kara saw them first and pointed to the right, so I drove over and dismounted to view thirty carved lions' heads spewing water in a row out of their mouths into a trough about sixty meters long, which backed onto a rough stone wall. Bushes were growing at an angle to the fountain at one end where a ninety-degree angle extended the fountain another fifteen meters and gave a stereo effect to the softly splashing sound.

I stayed near the trough because there was shade there, but the melody of the waters attracted me. I was reminded of the river in *Siddhartha* and how it spoke in a thousand ways and helped Siddhartha reach his soul. I sat on the edge of the trough and listened for what the waters might tell me when Kara came over and asked me for a coin to toss in the fountain. I regarded this practice as nonsense, but I tossed her a coin without saying anything and went over to start up the bike.

All of a sudden, it seemed like things were getting too complicated with Kara, which gave me an urge to get back on the road. I wished I could talk to Eva about what I was feeling about

Kara. I was going to do my best to help her out, but Kara was too caught up in her own dilemma to help me see my way forward. Man, she'd certainly gotten under my skin. When she got back to the bike and hopped on, I had it running.

"I'm sorry I was short with you back at the fountain," I said. "Throwing coins in fountains for luck just isn't my thing. It amounts to nothing and wrecks a lot of good fountains."

"Jack, you have no sentiment whatever!" Kara snapped back at me. "When you toss a coin in a fountain, a wish goes with it. Did you know that?" She glared at me.

"Well, that's the hope, but what are the chances the wish will come true? Isn't it sort of a futile gesture?"

"You're a lunkhead! It's a gesture of hope. We can't live without hope. It keeps us going. Tossing a coin in a fountain reminds us of that. You have to see things on a human scale sometimes and not just from where you sit on your motorcycle like some knight on a quest to solve the mysteries of all of humanity."

I felt my eyes open wide as she made this pronouncement. I turned off the bike. When she said she wanted a coin to throw in the fountain, I felt she had slipped a notch in terms of intellect, but she had just jumped up a few notches again with this speech. I looked back into her eyes and saw that what she said was heartfelt. I also saw it had saddened her to say it. Why?

The answer came quickly. "Oh, Jack. I'm sorry I said that. You hurt me back at the fountain, and I didn't want to hurt you back. I just got frustrated. Want to hear my wish, for what I hoped?"

I nodded.

"I wished we could get back together when we get home. I know we have to part, and it would be easier if I thought there were a chance we could meet up again. Do you think that could happen?"

I looked away because I didn't want her to see my growing feelings for her. Then I turned back and said as truthfully as I could, "'We've got miles to go before we sleep,' if you remember Robert Frost. It's so true in our cases. You've got to get back to Chicago and finish your degree. I've got to get back to New York and work on my parents to buy me a car because I'll be pretty much broke when I get back. And I'll be working on a career plan that suits me and one that my parents will buy into. Until we do these things, we won't be free and on our own. So the answer to your question is: Yes, we could meet up again, but we've got a lot of work to do before we can make it happen."

Kara listened to what I said, and then her face stiffened. "Practical Jack. That's what you should be called. You're right, of course, and we've discussed this. I was wondering if you actually *wanted* it to happen."

I had to take a moment. I sensed that if I said that I wanted to see Kara again, I might be making a commitment I couldn't keep. I wished I had more experience with women. I bit my lip involuntarily.

But I had reached a point in my journey when I knew who I was and couldn't hide it anymore. I had gained sexual experience from Eva, and I had felt the irrepressible surge of love that Candace had engendered in me. Now I had to tell Kara, who had combined sex and love for me in one woman, how I felt about her.

"Of course I want it to happen, Kara. I've never met a girl like you. It seems like we are meant for each other. And meeting here in this place because of our common circumstances is almost mystical. I have to believe I'm in love with you, so that in itself wants me to get back together with you again. I'd say that you are my destiny. I've been thinking about it, and it seems to be the case more and more. I can't see that changing. But we have obstacles in front of us that we still have to overcome. We still have to get back home and put our plans into operation. What happens if I get drafted? I'm a dead man. What happens if you can't get your degree for some reason and your mother goes ballistic and forces you to marry the boy next door?"

Kara stared at me, and tears welled up in her eyes and started rolling down her cheeks in a continuous swell. She did nothing to conceal them or wipe them away. She wasn't even sobbing, which freaked me out. Finally she took a napkin and wiped off her face.

"I'm in love with you, too, Jack Higgins. I guess we both will have to stay out in the wilderness for a little longer, but we can't forget we said that we love each other because, while a lot can happen in a few months, that won't change."

I had nothing to say to that. I gazed into Kara's wet eyes lovingly, having been assured by her love. I would return it from my heart. I was flabbergasted, delighted, curious, and amazed. I had had the immature rumbling of love coursing through my adolescent brain and body for years past, but it had always dissipated, and I had never had the sexual experience to solidify it.

The course of my life had been in doubt for so long that I always had to assess my emotions. This was new. It felt real, mature, and I didn't want to let it dissolve into juvenile memories as the others had. *Damn*! Kara made me *feel* like a man! That was what I'd been looking for!

"Kara, I've been edging my way along by myself for a long time, in the wilderness, as you put it. I've never been in love with anyone, and I've never had anyone love me. I'm in love with you, it does feel real, and it sure feels fine."

That put a smile on Kara's lips. She reached over and touched my face. Then she sat back and looked at me. "Jack, I've known a lot of boys over the years. I've slept with a few of them, too, but they all fall away because I've never known one who is so basically honest with himself as you. That speaks to me. It tells me that you will be honest with me. You also make plans and are willing to help me make a plan. No one has been willing to take my part before when I needed guidance. You have, and for that I love you. Even my parents just want to shunt me off on the same track everyone else is on. I will follow your plan because it makes sense for me. I do worry what becomes of us in a couple of months back home because of what we know can happen. And I'm sure it will break my heart if we don't get back together soon."

We hugged each other as if we would never let go.

29

I Leave Kara

WE ORDERED TEA AND baklava to share instead of lunch and drove back to Aigia Galini. On the way, I noticed that the clouds that were in the mountains had followed us down to the coast so that the village was shrouded in a misty gloom by the time we got back in the late afternoon. Having scrimped on lunch, we both were hungry, so we changed and went to the taverna for an early dinner.

Kara first mentioned the clouds to Nikolas. "This is the first day since I've been here that I've seen clouds."

"That is so," Nikolas said. "Usually at this time of year the sirocco winds from the desert blow across the sea and keep the cooler weather from coming over the mountains, and we stay nice and warm. But sometimes the sirocco fails, and we get cool, wet weather."

That caught my attention, but Nikolas continued, "This is better than when the sirocco blows too strong. Then it picks up the sands and dumps them all over us."

I broke in, "You mean it could rain here soon? I've got to drive over the mountain in two days, and I can't drive the mountain road if it's a sea of mud."

"That would be dangerous on a motorcycle," Nikolas said. "You will take the young lady with you?"

"No, I'm not a good-enough driver to take that road with a passenger. Besides, we have too much luggage."

"So the young lady will stay with us?"

"Just for a day or two," Kara said. "I have to get back myself."

"In that case, I will have to prepare a special meal for you. It will take a little while, so I will bring toasted pita, some sliced tomatoes, and feta cheese and a bottle of white Vidiano. Will that be all right?"

We both said yes at the same time and laughed.

I told Kara that I'd have to see what the weather looked like in the morning. If it weren't raining, I might have to go then. I couldn't chance it raining on the south coast. That would mean it was raining all over the island, and the road would be a disaster because the wet weather would come from the north.

Kara looked glum, and I apologized for being practical, but I was afraid of that road even when it was dry. To counter the mood and my own fears, I said everything would turn out for the best. I still had money for some time in Europe, but I'd have to sell the bike to get home. Kara had planned out her return to Lake Forest, so we'd be fine until we got home. Things would work out, and we would get back together. I conveyed this to Kara, and it pleased her, but she still said she didn't want me to leave. We talked about times to come at home while we finished the hors d'oeuvres, waiting for Nikolas' meal. When he came out of the kitchen, he was bearing a tray with a steaming casserole dish on it.

"My famous moussaka," he said. "Careful. It's very hot. Just out of the oven." The moussaka smelled heavenly as the aroma circled the table.

"What's in it?" Kara asked.

"It is a secret recipe," Nikolas teased, "but I can tell you that in it is eggplant, lamb, tomato, potato, and spices. You might smell the cinnamon. The topping is a simple béchamel sauce with some feta added to make it truly Greek."

"It looks fantastic,' I said, not remembering when I had last seen such a special meal. My first taste proved me correct. Each bite revealed a different layer of taste: eggplant with garlic and cinnamon; minced lamb with onion and allspice; and potatoes with a cheesy topping. It was a festival of taste. I looked at Kara, and she looked back. We both smiled and kept eating.

When we were done, the dish was three-fourths empty, but we were full. We thanked Nikolas and apologized for not being able to finish. He said he would take the dish to Thea for her dinner. She loved his moussaka.

I asked Nikolas about the potential for rain. He said the sirocco could stop blowing for a week, but it was never certain. I decided I would leave early the next morning if it weren't raining. I asked Nikolas if he would make me two large sandwiches to get me back to Athens on the ferry. Nikolas said of course. I could pick them up at breakfast tomorrow.

Kara and I walked back to the hotel to find Thea and settle my bill, but I owed nothing. Kara told Thea she would be leaving when the time she had paid for was up in three days. We both told her we had a wonderful time, and she smiled and hugged Kara.

We went upstairs to my room. Kara had wanted to go to her room, but I said, "Not yet," because I had to pack for an early departure.

"Practical Jack," Kara said and went to her room while I got ready for the road, dreading the mountain road and wishing the rain away as I packed. When I was done, I gave my gear a last look and went to Kara's room, I knocked on her door to be polite and then went in.

"You know you don't have to knock on my door, Jack. It will never be closed to you."

"I was just being polite. I mean, it could have been the bogeyman," I teased.

"That's sweet, but come over here and I'll show you what I do to bogeymen," she said, getting up on her knees on her bed. I went to her, and she wrapped her arms around my neck and head and kissed me all over my face. I was being besieged, so I just held her waist until she took one of my hands and placed it on her ass.

"Squeeze here," she whispered.

I was willing, but I wanted to say something about getting at least some sleep tonight. In a moment, I realized that resistance was futile, and I surrendered completely.

We made love and talked and made love again. Kara was doing most of the lovemaking and the talking. She wanted me to know how much she wanted me and to be sure I would come back to her, and this was her last chance to express her feelings. I sensed her anxiety and gave her as much comfort as I could muster. At one point in the middle of the night, I got up and went to my room for a piece of paper, on which I wrote my name, address, and phone number. Then I tore off a piece of it for Kara to do the same. We were surprised we hadn't thought to do that before.

"Thank goodness for Practical Jack," Kara said as she folded the paper with my number and put it in her passport case. I went back to my room to do the same. Then we slept together on Kara's bed, holding each other until the sky brightened.

I got up to see what the weather was like and found it to be unchanged from the past evening. I told Kara, telling her I would take my chance to go over the mountain now. She hugged me and buried her head in my chest.

I could feel the tears trickle down my naked body. "I've got to get dressed and pack up the bike. Will you have breakfast with me?"

Kara hesitated and then said no. She wasn't hungry. She would come say goodbye when she heard the bike start up.

I dressed quickly and brought all the gear down to the bike. It was damp from the mist, but that wasn't a worry. Once the bike was loaded up, I went to the taverna where Nikolas was serving breakfast to the two old men. He spotted me and came over right away.

"There was a small rockslide on the mountain last night right below Aigia Varvara. That's about fifty kilometers from here. The bus left for Heraklion a little while ago, so they may have gotten word that the road will be cleared. I will get you some coffee and baklava. I have made your sandwiches too. You must eat and go while there is a chance the road is still good."

I sat and waited for breakfast. *I would need the coffee for this ride*, I thought. When Nikolas brought the food, I stood up and put out my hand. Nikolas shook it warmly and said, "Thea and I were happy to see the young lady find a nice young man. She had waited a long time. You make a handsome couple."

That wasn't what I was expecting to hear, but I acknowledged the thought and thanked Nikolas for his wonderful cuisine and Thea for her hospitality, which I said I knew was a tradition dating back to ancient Greece.

Nikolas was surprised and happy to hear me say this about Greek traditions. He told me that Crete was the home of Rhea the Earth Mother, and I surprised him by saying I knew that too.

Again Nikolas was surprised. "Here, we learn to listen to our hearts. I hope you have listened to yours."

He insisted that I not pay for the breakfast or the sandwiches. I was embarrassed, but Nikolas was adamant. He gave me a warm bear hug and wished me a safe journey.

After I had breakfast, I went to the bike and put the sandwiches in the saddlebags. Then I hopped on and started it up. And there was Kara. She must have been waiting in the lobby. I didn't tell her about the rockslide; I was eager to get going. She came out and hugged me fiercely, and we kissed. She then held my head and whispered in my ear, "Remember," and went back into the hotel, looking back just once as she passed the doorjamb.

30

Back to Athens

I GAVE THE BIKE a little gas and slid and slipped up the muddy track to the main road. When I got to the top and turned right, I looked back and thought I had lived a lot of my life in a week in this small village. I might never come back, but here at the end of the earth, I had come across a piece of life that made me more complete. The journey to this place had provided me much of what I had come for, fundamental answers to my questions about life because there was Kara.

But this was no time for contemplating. I had to get over the mountain before the rain started. The mist was thick as I drove slowly through Tymbaki. It may have already rained on the other side, which would put me in a perilous situation.

I came up to the rockslide about eight kilometers past Aigia Daka. The bus was parked on the road behind a couple of large rocks. People had gotten out of the bus, and ten men were engaged in levering the rocks over the side of the road. I figured they had been at work for some time because they had stripped to their waists and were sweating. I thought about helping them, but just then, they sent the first rock over the edge. I could hear it crash down the slope; the sound muffled by the dampness. The men went to work on the second rock and quickly dispatched it since the first one had been blocking it.

The men congratulated each other, and people started filing back into the bus. There were two cars behind the bus, but I didn't want to deal with any other vehicles being in front of me all the way over the mountain, least of all the bus, so I took the inside track by the rock wall and wiggled past the cars and the bus and started up the road in front of the traffic. I didn't care what people thought of this move. I wanted space, room to negate my miscues or those of others as I negotiated this fearsome road.

I knew I had open road ahead going up the mountain because the bus had blocked the traffic. I still had firmly in mind my encounter with the bus on the way to Aigia Galini, but it was morning, and I was sharper, despite being kept up half the night by Kara. No time to think of her, I reminded himself, but it was difficult. She was unforgettable, a part of me now.

I found the switchbacks going up the mountain to be passable. The weight of the bike didn't generate momentum, so it was easier to control using the accelerator.

As I went up, I penetrated the lower level of the clouds, so visibility became murky. After a time, I couldn't see two hundred feet ahead, but at least it wasn't raining. By the time I reached what I thought was the highest point of the road, I was deep in the clouds and couldn't see fifty feet ahead. There was no way I could see a car coming my way and vice versa.

But now I had to start going down, and the five hundred-pound weight of the bike started to generate its own momentum. I had to control the turns in the switchbacks using mostly the brakes, down a straight, around a 180-degree turn, down another straight, and repeat at least ten times. I also had to use my legs because the road was slippery in the wet. My arms and shoulders were getting sore from this routine. But no cars came up the mountain. I figured the locals probably knew better than to drive in these conditions.

At last I broke out of the cloud bank. It wasn't sunny, but the mist had diminished, and there was still no rain. My riding clothes were damp with the mist, but they weren't soaked through. I only had to go nineteen kilometers to Heraklion, and it wasn't quite noon yet. I was sure the ferry left in the late afternoon, but I wanted to make sure of the boarding time, so I went to the dock and found that it boarded at three thirty and left at four thirty, just like in Athens. The ferries must pass each other in the night. Now I had an urgent errand and three hours to spend on it.

I bought a cup of coffee and ate Nikolas' delicious sandwich with it. Then I got on the bike and headed for Knossos. I could have wished for better weather, but it wasn't raining, and this was something I had looked forward to in coming to Crete all along. At this point in my journey, it was just a tourist attraction, compared to what else I had found on this island, but it was a place of wonder that I had to see.

I motored the eight kilometers to Knossos, which was east of Heraklion, and pulled into the site where there was very little activity, likely because of the weather. I drove the bike past the gravel parking lot and around to the sides and back of the site so I got a complete view. The thing I noticed first was that Knossos was truly a ruin. I'd read that even during its centuries of glory, it had been destroyed by earthquakes and tsunamis three times in three hundred years, from 1900 to 1600 BC, but it had always been rebuilt. Now only ruins and partially rebuilt remnants remained.

I saw that a few columns had been restored around the palace grounds and repainted the same deep-red color as on the doors of the hotel in Aigia Galini. But only four columns had been restored to give an idea of the originals instead of the twenty or more columns on each level, which had supported five floors. I found King Minos' throne room with the throne embedded in the wall to project permanence and the room with the painted dolphins, swimming as realistically along the walls as if they were in the water. I went down stairways into dark areas, which were likely storerooms where I imagined the Minotaur had lived in the labyrinth.

Coming back out, I drove the bike down to the end of the ruins, which extended hundreds of yards where excavating was still being done. I went to the visitor center and saw a model of what the palace may have looked like at the peak of its dominance of the Mediterranean trade, which lasted a thousand years. The model showed the palace as being over five stories tall with a couple hundred of red columns substituting for walls in many places. The palace looked spectacular. When I left, I bet that when Knossos was in full flower. It could have rivaled Schonbrunn Palace in Vienna, or even Versailles, for its opulence, but the times were too different for real comparison. *I had a bias anyway*, I thought, and smiled. It was great to have seen Knossos finally.

I drove back to the city to wait for the ferry, and when I got to the docks, I looked out to the north and saw the sun on the water in the distance. It wasn't going to rain after all. I had left Kara a day early, but that was the choice I had made based on what I knew. I'd always done that, and for the most part, I'd been right. 'Practical Jack,' Kara had called me.

"Yeah, I guess so," I said out loud.

After boarding the ferry, I went up to the main passenger area and picked out a spot on one of the benches. I didn't even consider checking out a cabin after the last trip. I stuffed my gear under a bench after putting on a dry jacket from one the bags. I hung the damp jacket over the bench to dry. My pants had dried out enough, so that if I didn't have to spend the night on deck, I'd be ok.

After the ship cast off, I saw that I'd have a lot of room because less than half the passenger area was occupied. I took out my stuff and made a pillow of the sleeping bag and stretched the length of the bench. I went through the guidebook of Knossos again just to remember what I'd seen while eating half of my dinner sandwich and settling in for the thirteen-hour trip back to Athens.

I thought about Kara and hoped she'd get home all right, get back into school, and be able to manage her parents. 'Manage the parents' was the term. I'd been through that scene plenty, and I still had a hurdle to jump. I didn't know exactly when that would be, but I couldn't wait to call Kara as soon as I got back.

I also thought about the changes I had adapted to my old self and those that had been grafted onto me during my journey. I felt different, more self-assured, especially around women, but also in my ability to see life on a larger scale. I had helped two women through their difficulties and hoped that what I had proposed for them would work out. I cared about them, which was new to me too. And I knew that Kara had a hold on me, which I sensed was a pleasant feeling. "She was some girl," I kept repeating. I wondered why I had never come across a girl like her before.

But it was just as well that I had some time to put some space between us. I had some things to figure out, like how did you know if love would stick? I was hoping Charlie might answer a question or two, and I had an idea of visiting Eva on my way back to an embarkation point for home, draft or no draft. I had abandoned the idea of being an exile. I didn't think I could live that life. I'd just chance the numbers game that the draft was and enlist in the navy like Pete, if it came to that.

Around midnight, the passengers quieted down so that I fell asleep and only woke up when the ship's horn above the cabin blew, signaling the ship's entry to the harbor at Piraeus. I went out on deck to see the sun just rising over the islands to the east of the harbor. It was six in the morning. I thought about having the rest of my sandwich for breakfast, but I figured that if I waited till I got off the ferry, I could drive up to Athens and get a hot breakfast at a café.

My bike was first in line to get off the ferry, so it took a mere fifteen minutes to get to the Plaka, where I found that the owner of my favorite café was starting to put the tablecloths on the outside tables. I drove up and asked if he had any breakfast ready yet, and he said he had baklava and coffee right now. I said that would be fine, so I sat and had the sweet and the stimulant and tried to figure out what to do next. It was too early to look people up, but I needed a shower and a change of clothes, so I went up the street to the hotel.

Yiannis was there but was somewhat wary at seeing me. He said he had let out all the rooms on the top floor since Charlie and I had left. He said he could give me back the money for the time I hadn't used, but I told Yiannis that all I wanted was to use the shower. Yiannis said that would be fine, so I cleaned myself up and changed. I wondered where Charlie had gone, but I could ask Candace later.

Then I went to the AMEX office to talk to an advisor about the best way to get to Western Europe from Greece, hopefully taking a ferry to cut off driving through Yugoslavia. I was early, so I sat on a bench in Omonia Square to wait for the office to open. At eight sharp, the doors opened, and I went in and was the first in line to speak to an advisor. I was directed by the concierge to a good-looking, Middle-Eastern young man, dressed in a suit. He occupied a desk behind a partition much like in the AMEX office in Vienna. He introduced himself in perfect English as Amal El Khoury and asked me what he could do for me.

I was impressed by Amal's manner and sophistication. I gave him a quick synopsis of my travels on the motorcycle and told him that I wanted to get from Greece to France the shortest way possible.

After hearing my tale, it was Amal's turn to be impressed. "You have traveled far by motorcycle through countryside, which I would think is less than suitable for that machine. I am not persuaded that motorcycles are particularly safe in any case, so I hope I can help you find a safe way to the West. Please wait. I will check with one of my colleagues."

Amal went over to the desk of an older man, and I watched as they spoke somewhat animatedly in Greek before the older man pulled a folder from his desk drawer and gave it to Amal. Amal looked at a sheet of paper in the folder, smiled, and walked back to his desk.

"Mr. Higgins, you are in luck. Yesterday we received notice of a luxury ferry boat that leaves from Patras on the west coast of Greece and travels nonstop to Genoa, Italy. The ferry line calls this a 'shakedown cruise,' and it is not open to the general public. However, rather than sail with the ship entirely empty, the ferry company has alerted AMEX and Cook's Travel to see if they might notify some of their customers to this sailing, possibly to defray costs. I must say that this would be ideal for your purpose, as it takes you all the way around Italy and leaves you about two hundred kilometers from Nice in France."

"That would be fantastic!" I said, knowing that Nice was only a hundred kilometers or so from Aix-en-Provence, where Eva lived.

"There might be a slight problem," Amal continued. "The ferry company just sent this notice yesterday, and the ship sails today at three."

"How far is Patras from here?" I asked.

"About two hundred and ten kilometers with a driving time of about two and a half hours. I warn you that this road is dangerous. There is construction, and the people drive like maniacs."

"I can make that easily," I said, brushing off Amal's warning. "After my experiences so far, I'm not going to worry."

Amal gave me a quizzical look that indicated that he thought I might be slightly deranged.

"It says on the notice that tickets must be purchased at the terminal, but I think we could give them a call to let them know you are coming. It also says the fare will be accepted in drachmae only."

"How much is it?"

"One thousand two hundred and fifty drachmae."

"That's about forty-two dollars," I said. "I can cash sixty dollars in travelers' checks here. I can get gas in Patras and food on the boat. And I'll also cash some checks for French francs. Oh, I'll need maps of northern Italy and the south of France. Do you have them?"

"Yes, I have the maps in my desk. They are thirty drachmae each. I do advise you to be careful on that road. While you are cashing your checks, I will call the ferry company."

When I came back to Amal's desk, he told me the company was expecting me at the shipping office no later than two thirty. There were very few passengers on this trip due to the late notice. I shook his hand and thanked him very much for his service.

Amal said once again, "Be careful on that road," as I left his office.

I left the AMEX office and considered going to say goodbye to Candace and Dimitris, but I didn't want to get involved in any conversations that would take up travel time to Patras. Besides, they didn't even know I was in Athens. I would have liked to see Charlie once more, but he was a will-of-the-wisp, one of those guys who just come in and out of one's life.

Patras was two and a half hours away. It was eleven thirty now. The ferry boarded at two and sailed at three, so I'd be cutting it close if I had a smooth ride. I had to find the ferry dock in Patras when I got there, so I'd better get moving.

I wasn't worried about the drive, no matter what Amal said. The map showed a four-lane autoroute, the A8. There was a smaller road that followed the edge of the Gulf of Corinth. That looked like it could definitely be dangerous.

I hopped on the bike and checked the gas. I had plenty to go 210 kilometers. I started up and went through Omonia Square, where I saw the sign for the A8 to Corinth and Patras. I'd be in France in two days. I couldn't believe it.

31

Patras to Genoa Ferry

I PICKED UP THE A8 about three miles out of Athens, and right away I noticed that the drivers were using this new road to its best advantage, speeding. I quickly got the bike up to 120 kilometers per hour and realized I was one of the slower vehicles on the road. I knew that if I went all the way to Patras at 120 kilometers per hour, I'd be there in time, but driving at a higher speed for two hours could be tiring. It was 88 kilometers to Corinth and 135 kilometers from Corinth to Patras. I figured I'd go like hell to Corinth and then gas up and see where I stood.

I juiced the bike to 130 kilometers per hour all the way to Corinth. That was really biking like I hadn't done since Austria. The wind whipped my hair straight back. I'd bought the wraparound sunglasses in Athens, hoping they would flatten against my face at speed, and they seemed to be working. The sun was glorious, and the road was smooth. I was passed by cars from time to time, and the drivers and passengers waved at me. The Greeks liked to have fun on the road.

I pulled into a gas station just off the road in Corinth. It wasn't twelve thirty yet. I'd done that stretch in less than an hour. That gave me almost two hours to go the 135 kilometers to Patras. I asked the attendant how the road was to Patras, and he told me there was construction for about fifteen kilometers just out of Patras. I didn't like the sound of that, so when I got back on the road, I kept the speed at 130 kilometers per hour. After another half hour, I began to feel the strain of handling the bike at speed in my muscles.

But the reward for my labors came when I found the construction zone after only forty minutes from Corinth. I'd have plenty of time to find the dock and get aboard the ferry. I had to slow to forty kilometers per hour and even slower as I passed through the construction. The road was being widened, and a barrier separating the lanes was being added. I could see that this stretch of road could really be dangerous, especially at night the way these people drove. I was frustrated by the slow pace, so I checked the time, one fifty.

Finally I came through the construction and took off at a hundred kilometers per hour. I pulled into the center of Patras at two sharp. I'd knocked a half hour off Amal's estimate. Now I had to find the ferry dock. As I motored through the city, I realized I was shaking a little from the effort of driving at speed. I drove down a main street and saw a mountain on the other side of a bay in front of me, so I was headed toward the water. When I reached the waterfront and could go right or left, I chose left and went all the way to the end before I saw the sign for the ferry company. It was two ten, which meant boarding had started.

I stopped the bike in front of the shipping office and saw a brand-new gleaming white ship with gold trim and a dark-blue smokestack with a golden griffin painted on it docked next to the building. I went into the office to a desk, where I was greeted by a tall, beautiful, black-haired girl with olive skin, black eyes, and a generous mouth, who looked at me with some disdain. I could see that she was a true Grecian beauty, but I was hardly a street urchin, so why should she regard me so?

I wasn't going to let it ruin my day, so I asked bluntly, "Do you have my ticket for the ferry to Genoa? It was booked by AMEX earlier this morning."

The girl's eyes flashed open. "You have come from Athens just now?"

"Yes. By motorcycle."

"Oh, so that explains it. You should see yourself in a mirror."

I realized I must have picked up a lot of road dirt traveling at speed, and then there was the construction dirt. Well, I got here on time and in one piece, which was what mattered.

"You did get the call from AMEX?" I asked again.

"Oh, yes. Mr. Higgins, isn't it? I can process your passage as soon as I see your passport and vehicle papers."

I handed over my papers.

"Here is your ticket, Mr. Higgins. The fare is one thousand two hundred and fifty drachmae for a berth in a four-berth cabin. There will be one other passenger in the cabin with you. Boarding has already begun, and I think you should board right away so you can shower as soon as possible."

Duly chastened, I paid the fare and asked how I should board the bike. She told me I could wheel it up the side loading ramp, which led to the vehicle deck. No cars or trucks were going on this initial voyage. She picked up the phone and spoke to someone, and turned to me, saying I could board now and have a bon voyage.

I went out and wheeled the bike toward the loading ramp, where I saw a ship's officer waiting for me. As I walked along the pier, I asked myself why I had ogled the babe in the office when Kara was my love. Maybe it was just in the nature of men. But what if I'd been with Kara? She enjoyed kicking me, I remembered. I'd have to check this habit going forward.

The officer was wearing a white uniform with short sleeves and gold pinstripes down the sides of his pants. He had on a dark-blue cap, and a golden griffin was emblazoned on his shirt pocket. His name was on a plaque attached to the pocket.

"Good afternoon, Mr. Higgins. I am Lieutenant Alexopoulos, the second officer. I have the pleasure of welcoming you as the second passenger on the *Hellenic Spirit* steaming from Patras to Genoa. In fact, you are the only other passenger we have for this voyage, this being a shakedown cruise for the ship and the crew. If I may see your papers, I will have one of my men board your motorcycle and secure it on the vehicle deck. You can take off your baggage, and an attendant will show you to your cabin. I hope you have a pleasant voyage."

I thanked the officer and let a husky crewman wheel the bike on board. I took the bags and gear off the bike and turned to see a beautiful blonde attendant in a dark-blue uniform waiting to escort me to my cabin. I just followed her, trying to tamp down the sense of euphoria I was feeling at the thought of having found this dream ship, which was going to take me to France in just two days. I was also coming down from the high of the high-speed ride, which had gotten me to the ship just in time.

When I got to my cabin, my sense of wonder increased. Everything about the cabin was new, from the rich, dark-blue, deep-pile carpet to the furniture, two stuffed chairs and a table, to the new bunk beds with blankets that had the griffin symbol on them. The walls were white, and there was a closet with mirrored doors. There was a second door, which I figured was the bathroom, and I heard a booming male voice singing in the shower. I looked around the cabin, and sure enough, I saw a backpack and clothes scattered all over one of the lower berths. I was, indeed, the second passenger on board.

I wasn't going to complain, however. The accommodations were superior, and if the guy I were going to share the room with was taking a shower, then he wasn't going to stink like the Greek peasants on the ferry to Crete. I plopped into a chair and laughed out loud, "All this and a trip to France for forty-two dollars!" I was incredulous.

I got up and unpacked, realizing that there should be plenty of room for two in the four-berth cabin and waited my turn in the shower. Shortly, the bathroom door opened, and out came a rugged man of about thirty, five-foot-nine, swarthy with a ruddy complexion with a balding, egg-shaped head that had a few scars on it and a well-trimmed beard that offset the baldness. His thick body was muscular with a barrel chest that had several scars on it as well. I decided I wouldn't want to get in a fight with this man.

The fellow was taken aback by my presence, especially since he was naked coming out of the shower, but he must have been told he was going to have a roommate.

"Well, who have we here? Ah, yes. I seem to remember something about a roommate," he said. "It's not as though there isn't enough empty space on this barge for them to let us spread out."

"You would think with the whole ship empty, they could give us separate cabins, I said.

We both laughed and shook hands.

"I'm Jack and I'm American," I told him.

"I'm Paul, and I'm a Scotsman." my roommate said. "Been out traveling for pleasure this summer. How about you?" He dried himself with his towel and began to dress. I heard the Scottish accent in Paul's speech.

"I came over to Berlin in January and stayed until spring when I bought a motorcycle and drove it to Athens and then to Crete. I've just come from Crete, like this morning. It's been a crazy two days."

"Blimey, I've had some adventures, but you sound like you could top 'em. A motorcycle, I'll be damned."

"Where are you from, and where have you been?" I asked.

"I play on club rugby teams in Glasgow. We make money when we win and when the bets go right. It's a living." He smiled.

"I'm always short on cash, but it helps when you love the game. I've been hitchhiking for a vacation this summer. I hitched from Glasgow to Southampton and from there took a ferry to Dieppe. The Frenchies weren't so sporting about giving me a lift, but a trucker finally took me to Paris. I found a lovely lady there and spent two weeks with her, and she drove me to Nice where she has a grandma. She didn't want the grandma to see me, so we parted ways.

"I got rides to Venice, and then worked my way on a steamer to Istanbul, and then down to Athens. Beautiful places. Always wanted to see them. I saved up enough to travel and made my chance.

"I've always had a way with the ladies, so that usually helps for a bed, although not so much in Istanbul. I've been slumming around in Athens for the past ten days with two American girls in a hostel. That's been a bit of all right, but they had to go home.

"So I called my French lady from the Cook's office and asked her if she'd like some company. She said she was going back to Paris soon and she would love to see me. How about that? But I had no idea how to get to Nice 'soon', as she put it. So I asked the fellow at Cook's, and he told me about this ferry. That was yesterday. I had to sleep in a park in Athens and catch an early bus to Patras, six hours, and what a stink! The people here don't wash, you know. But here I am, on my way to Nice."

I thought that was a great story and told Paul I would fill him in on my adventures after my shower. That brought me back to thinking about Kara and our showering habits, which started to bring me erect, so I cooled the shower to keep from walking into the room in that state.

I backed out of the bathroom, but needn't have worried. Paul was sitting in one of the chairs studying the brochures of the ship.

"I've found the bar. That's our next destination," he said.

As I was finishing getting dressed, I told Paul that I had a couple of encounters with women myself during my journey and wondered if Paul could comment on them. I wanted to begin my queries with my complete infatuation with Candace, which had been a crushing and still-unresolved experience for me.

Paul said he'd be happy to, but it was a subject that was best discussed over some frosty beer, and he headed out the door, holding the ship's plan in front of him as a guide. We found the bar, but it was closed.

"The bar closed! I'd say we should mutiny!" Paul roared. "But we can find out what's up. A lovely female attendant showed me to the cabin. I suggest we sally forth and see what awaits our pleasure."

We went out onto the deck and saw that the ship was getting ready to sail. The lines had been cast off, and the officer at the engine controls was skillfully using the forward and reverse thrust to pull the five hundred-foot ship away from the dock and turning it west toward the open sea. We watched as the ship motored out of the harbor, leaving the mountainous, ancient land behind. We went below decks, and this time we found the bar open with a bartender cleaning its surface of mahogany and glass.

"We'll have two Fix Hellas," Paul said.

"We're not open until six, sir," the bartender said.

"Now, laddie, you have two desperate travelers here. This fine young man drove a motorcycle from Athens in record time to make this sailing, while I was consigned to a pigsty transport for six hours to get here. Truly, only beer will save us."

The bartender couldn't help but laugh at Paul's story, so he opened an ice chest and produced two bottles of beer.

"I can't thank ye enough, my good fellow, only as it's now four and you don't open until six. I'm sure you can appreciate that just one bottle apiece just won't do for us. Would a larger gratuity persuade you to add another bottle apiece to our salvation?"

The bartender gave Paul a frown, but he pulled out two more bottles. "Please take them to your cabin so I don't get in trouble," he said.

"We thank you kindly. We'll see you at six sharp. Jack, please pay the gentleman." And Paul started off back to the cabin with the haul.

I paid the bartender, who was still shaking his head at Paul's chutzpah. I followed Paul to the cabin, where he took out an eight-inch knife from a sheath which was strapped to his leg, and popped the tops off two beers. Then he propped his feet up on the table and took a long draught, followed by a loud belch.

"Now that makes things better with the world," he said. "I remember you were seeking some advice about the female sex …"

"I've just come from what are my first three attachments to women, and they were really complicated. I had sex with two of them, but the one that really fried me was the most beautiful girl I ever saw, and she was totally committed to a nice guy, who was also a giant who could have broken me in half if I tried anything, so that was a flame-out. But she was so beautiful that every time I saw her, I just melted. I can see how the beauty of Helen of Troy caused the Trojan War. Beautiful women can be like dynamite."

Paul laughed at my consternation. He had a deep, booming laugh that was sincere in its humor. It came from that barrel-shaped chest, which gave it a worldly resonance.

"Now, now. There's nothing wrong with dynamite if it's treated right. It's the men who go around with lighted matches that cause the trouble. By that, I mean they've got their dicks hanging out of their trousers all the time. You see how that can be a problem for the ladies?"

I admitted that, but my problem was their physical beauty. It captivated me, and I'd freeze up and say stupid things and lose out.

"Well, laddie, you just need more experience with the fair sex. Engage with them and you'll find they don't bite. You're a good-looking fellow who seems to have his heart in the right place. That's what the ladies are looking for, but they have to sort out the bad lot before they can find someone like you."

I thought that this sounded very sensible. It was a high-level view of sexual dynamics from a guy who seemed to have plenty of experience in the field. I remembered that this is what Kara had said to me, in effect. I was wondering if I should continue this conversation.

"I have a sandwich we can split, if you're hungry," I offered.

"Now that is a friendly gesture. I'll take you up on it."

I reached into the saddlebag and pulled out the last of Nikolas' sandwiches. Paul grabbed his knife and quickly sliced it in two. I stared at the sheath of the knife strapped to Paul's leg.

Paul saw me staring. "One can't be too careful out on the road by oneself. Your motorcycle can move you out of scrapes fast. All I've got is my feet and this."

"You've been in a lot of scrapes then?"

"A few, and I'll admit it's the company I keep sometimes. But the lads back home prefer the fists when they get under the influence, and it's pretty much in fun, if you follow me. I bring the knife along when I'm on my own because, although I can take care of myself, in foreign lands a companion is a good thing to have."

I didn't disagree, although I knew if the knives came out, I'd be in worse trouble than if someone wanted to punch me out. I wasn't into this line of thought, so I checked the time. "Hey, it's a quarter to six. Let's get back to the bar."

"I'm for that."

We strolled through the corridors of the ship and didn't see anyone. We hadn't expected to see passengers, but we thought there'd be crew members doing their jobs somewhere, but there wasn't a soul around.

The barman already had the bar open when we got there. He said he'd been expecting us. Paul ordered two bottles of Fix Hellas, downed one at a gulp, and then sat at the bar and sipped the other. I had one beer and sipped it contentedly.

"Y'know, laddie, we're not exactly pleased with the food and beverage arrangements on this voyage," Paul said offhandedly to the bartender.

The bartender looked Paul squarely in the eye. "You can take it up with the management. I just do my job."

I was afraid a confrontation might be brewing, so I said, "We walked through most of the ship just now to get here and didn't see any crew. Where are they? At a training session or something?"

The bartender said nothing and turned to wipe off some glasses.

"Well, it would be nice to know if this scow is running on autopilot all the way to Genoa," Paul said with some menace in his voice.

I could see that Paul was trying to provoke the barman, so I suggested we should go sit at a table by the window. Paul wasn't interested. He downed his second beer and asked for another. The barman hesitated in bringing him one, and Paul was about to reach over the bar to grab either a beer or the barman, when a small door at the end of the bar opened and a cabin attendant came out and said, "Oh, you must be our two passengers. It must be a boring trip for you. The crew is having a party down below. Why don't you follow me and join in? Alexi, please bring down some more beer, and then you should close the bar and come too."

The noise bursting from behind the little door confirmed what she said, so Paul and I slipped behind the bar to follow her through the door.

32

Genoa to Aix

PAUL AND I GLANCED at each other excitedly as we went through the little door and followed the attendant down the narrow flight of stairs.

The girl turned and said, "I'm Anna from Denmark," before the deafening noise reached up to make conversation almost impossible. When we got to the bottom, we were engulfed by a roaring mob of partygoers, all of whom were dressed in the livery of the ferry line. Everyone had a drink in their hand.

"Here is my friend, Elke, from Stockholm," Anna shouted. "The crew are all just getting to know one another. The captain said we could throw a birthday party for Elke tonight because we have no duties to perform. She is twenty-two today."

I saw that we were in the crew's mess. Tables and chairs had been stacked in a corner of the room to make room for a dance floor. There were probably fifty crew members, mostly women, standing around the edge of the dance floor, watching couples doing the twist, the mashed potato, and variations of other popular dance moves, as a boombox blasted out mid- to late 1960s tunes. Quite a few women were dancing with each other as there seemed to be a shortage of men.

Paul noticed this fact right away and stepped up to fill the void. He went over to a stunning black-haired girl who was on the sidelines and asked her for a dance. She complied, and they soon blended into the whirling group on the floor.

I stood sipping my beer and watching the scene. The crew was a polyglot crowd, obviously from different regions: blonde, fair-skinned Scandinavians and dark-haired, olive-skinned Mediterraneans from Italy, Greece, or the Middle East. I figured this could be a great way to make some money for a summer while exploring the Med, but it wasn't for me. I needed something more solid, and I thought again of Kara.

I finished my beer and was thinking of going back upstairs to get out of the noise when an attractive, dark-skinned girl took my hand and pulled me onto the dance floor. I could hardly refuse, and could she dance! The song was Wilson Pickett's "Land of a Thousand Dances," a real mover. Holding her hands clasped above her head and shaking her hips to the beat, I had no move to follow along with that, so I did a deep-dive twist and looked up at her once in a while.

The song ended, and everyone let out a cheer while my partner disappeared back where she came from. I couldn't tell where she went because everyone was dressed the same, so I went over to a table that had cases of beer on it and grabbed one to quench my thirst. I had just taken two swigs when another girl came over and asked me to dance. I said to myself, *What the hell*. And the boombox lit up with Dave Clark's, "Can't You See That She's Mine," which was a great dancing tune. This girl wanted to dance a sort of jitterbug thing to it, so she grabbed my hands, and we spun around together, bouncing off each other to the rich bass tune. It was a lot of fun, but when the song ended, she just said, "Grazia." And she vanished, heading into the crowd like the other one. At least I could tell she was Italian.

The room was getting hot from all the bodies and the energy. I looked for a beer, but there were none on the table. But there was Alexi, the bartender, hauling a couple of cases across the room with some bottles of booze on top. I went over and grabbed a cold one before they were gone. Just then, the music stopped, and everyone turned to a double door, which had opened across the room.

Two officers were standing in the doorway. One of them had four stripes on his sleeve so I knew he was the captain of the ship. He smiled and called out in Greek and Italian, and everyone cheered. The he waved and went back out. I asked a guy next to me what that was all about, and he said the captain wished Elke a happy birthday and for everyone to enjoy themselves.

The party really took off from there. The music was louder. I was starting to get into it myself. I had a dance with another disappearing girl who rubbed her ass against me at one point, and I started to wonder if I were just being used, but it was a pleasure, and I thought, "So what?"

I went over to see what kind of booze Alexi had brought down. Both men and women were throwing down shots from plastic cups and challenging each other to match them by slamming down the cups on the table after they had taken theirs. This was a rowdy group, and I thought I'd pass when someone shoved a cup in my hand and said "Go!"

This wasn't my thing, but I figured I could take one shot and make an escape afterward, so I fired down the liquor in a gulp. Right away I wished I hadn't, as the fiery, licorice-tasting fluid filled my nasal cavity and made me swoon.

Alexi laughed in my face and put another cup in my hand. "Let's see how well this one can handle the ouzo," he sneered.

I didn't want to look like a wuss in front of the crew, so I fired it down and almost fell down after I swallowed it. I heard the people laugh as I staggered past the dance floor and up the stairs to the door by the bar. I fell prostrate on a couch and let the world spin around inside my head until I slowly passed out.

❖

When I came to, I didn't know how long I'd been out, and I honestly couldn't figure out what was going on inside my head. I thought I might have been poisoned, but I slowly grasped that I was suffering from the most vicious hangover I'd ever had. As I tried to sit up, I realized that I didn't have control over my balance so I lay down again. It was still dark out over the waters, and I couldn't hear any music from the party, so I guessed it was early morning.

All I could hear was the hum of the engines and the splashing of the waves as the ship cut through the water. I concentrated on that to get my bearings and got up. A ferocious pain was in the upper part of my head. I could stand if I kept my head still, but the motion of the ship made me wobble so I sat down again. This was agony. I needed water and aspirin, but I'd have to get back to the cabin for that. So I stood up and made for the bulkhead, which I followed, hand over hand, down a flight of stairs until I came to the cabin door.

There was a towel draped over the doorknob, which I knew to be the universal signal that someone was getting laid inside. I couldn't have given a rat's ass! I started pounding on the door, yelling. "Paul, let me in!"

I didn't hear anything for a few moments, but then Paul opened the door, standing there buck naked, and said, "Well, you were a good lad to give me so much time. The young lady is dressing in the washroom. She should be out in a minute. You look like hell itself. What have you been up to?"

"I had a couple of shots of ouzo on top of a few beers. I've never felt like this in my life. I need aspirin." I started digging in my bags for some pills.

"You never heard that ouzo is to be taken very lightly and always with food?"

"No, I only heard of ouzo once, and that was a warning in Athens. I was partying and forgot. Damn stuff hit me like a pile driver."

Paul started laughing with that booming laugh of his. "I'll bet you were set up by that devil bartender. I knew he had a mean look in his eye."

Just then, the bathroom door opened, and the girl, who was only partially dressed, came out and asked, "Paul, what's going on out here?" Then she saw me and slammed the door.

Paul started laughing again. I found the aspirin and downed four of them, plopped on a lower bunk, and told Paul to shut up, saying that my head was splitting.

Paul put on some underwear and knocked on the bathroom door. "Time to go home, lassie. My roommate has returned, and he's sick as a dog."

After a minute, I saw the girl open the door a crack. She saw me stretched out like a corpse and tiptoed across the cabin, but before she could get out the door, Paul grabbed her ass and told her she was gorgeous. She smiled and disappeared. I took a deep breath and fell into a tortured sleep, feeling like Alice in Grace Slick's version of "White Rabbit."

At some point in my dream, things got violent, or that's what I imagined. I was being shaken and yelled at. I didn't want to open my eyes because I was afraid my dream would become reality. My head felt like a pumpkin that sensed its pain as it was being carved out. But the shouting persisted, and then I could definitely feel a hand on my shoulder. I couldn't remember where I was until I opened my eyes and saw Paul grinning at me.

"So you *are* amongst the living. I was giving up on you for lost. Come. We must go on deck. A wonderful sight."

I looked out the porthole to see that it was daytime and that the ship was passing near land.

"Hurry! This won't last forever," Paul urged.

I was already dressed, so I stumbled up onto the deck to see that the ship was passing through the Straits of Messina. To the southwest, we could see smoke rising from Mt. Etna.

"That's a sight for you, eh, laddie?" Paul said. "Remind you of drinking ouzo on an empty stomach? Ha, ha, ha!"

I told Paul to "fuck off," but the mention of an empty stomach told me that I needed to eat something. I said to Paul that we had to find some food, and Paul was all for that, so we went to the bar, but it was closed. Paul cursed mightily, but I went to the door where we had gone down to the party and found that it was open.

We went down the stairs and saw that the tables and chairs were set out as a crew's mess normally was. A few crew members were eating breakfast and drinking coffee. Paul went up to one of the girls and asked in his usual persuasive manner where they might find some breakfast. The girl smiled pleasantly and told him that breakfast was officially over, but took us through a door into the kitchen and showed us where all the food was kept and the cooking utensils were stored. She instructed us to help ourselves.

We gaped at each other. "Mother McCree," Paul said.

We found eggs by the dozen, pounds of bacon, loaves of bread, two large urns of coffee, and more. We divided up the chores. I cooked a half-pound of bacon on the grill while Paul whipped up six eggs for scrambling, cut large slices of bread, and buttered them to be grilled while he cooked the eggs.

We had to wait for the bacon to cook. When it was done, he browned the toast expertly and poured the eggs onto the grill, turning them quickly so they would remain wet, French-style, and put them on a platter with the rest of the breakfast. We each refilled our coffee mugs and headed to the dining room to indulge. The girls who were still at the table were shocked at the amount of food, but Paul gave them a "do not disturb" look, and we fell to. Soon there was nothing left on the platter.

"Can't say I've had a feed like that since I left Glasgow" Paul said, loosening his belt and stretching his arms above his head.

"I've been eating pretty well this trip, but not a breakfast like what we've just put down. Now I'm due for a nap."

"Well, now we still have fifteen hours till we reach Genoa, and I won't be begrudging you on your nap, but I would be asking you for a favor."

"What's that?"

"A ride to Nice since you said you're heading through there."

"I don't see why not. Is the backpack all your luggage? That's the main problem."

"It's just me and my pack, and I'm grateful to you. You can have the cabin. I'll find a lassie who can't resist me and find other accommodations for a while."

I walked back to the cabin, amazed at Paul's single-minded determination to get girls into bed. Paul said that he had a way about him with women, but I'd never seen a guy so focused or so successful in practice. He reminded me of a benign Henry Miller. I took a shower and rolled into my bunk.

When I woke up, it was six thirty, but I remembered there was an hour time shift between Athens and Genoa, so I moved my watch back to five thirty. We would be landing in two hours. I was feeling the need for a snack, so I went up on deck, but the bar was closed, and I saw the crew practicing their landing drills. This was their first landing in Genoa, so they had no time for us. I went back to the cabin to pack up, and Paul was there.

"Here you are, lad. I've managed to scrounge something for us to eat, in case the cafés are closed when we dock." He gave me a large ham and cheese sandwich on a roll with tomato and lettuce hanging out on the sides.

"Where have you been, and how did you get this?" I asked in astonishment.

"A lovely lassie was appreciative of my attention. She led me back to the kitchen after we had some fun."

"You're incorrigible. You wouldn't mind if I ate half of mine now?"

"Be my guest. You can cut it with my knife."

I got a glass of water and downed the half sandwich. Paul showered while I ate. Then both of us changed into riding gear and packed our stuff. It seemed to me that Paul had a larger pack than I had originally envisaged, so when Paul finished, I asked if I could check the weight. It was heavy, maybe fifty pounds, which, when added to Paul's weight would make roughly 240 pounds, which was more than Wild Bill weighed.

I'd have to hope for good roads and not too many curves, but this was the civilized part of Europe, not the backward Eastern side, so I guessed we'd be all right. As the ship neared the shoreline of Italy, we went forward to see the lights of Genoa. The ship steered straight for them. Soon the engine slowed, and I could see the ship being steered into the harbor, which was guarded by a long breakwater. There were many docks on the landward side.

A claxon went off, which was the call for vehicular traffic to prepare to disembark. We went down the stairs to the empty vehicle hold, found the bike, and loaded it up. A seaman was standing by the bike. He asked to see my papers and then undid the restraints. There was a significant bump when the ship hit the pier and was tied up. Then the side door opened, and a ramp was placed for me to wheel the bike up and onto the dock. A ship's officer was standing by to tell us we had to go through immigration and customs.

I parked the bike and walked to the immigration desk where the sleepy official stamped both our passports. Then he asked us if we were carrying any cigarettes, liquor, or contraband. We both said no, and he marked our bags with a C in chalk and waved us along.

"Now, was that really necessary? I mean, the fuckin' bureaucrats," Paul said as we got on the bike, the same way we did when Charlie was riding with his pack.

Right off, I didn't like the balance of the bike. After the first few turns through the city, I could tell that Paul created more tilt because he didn't know how to lean into turns. He and his pack weighed more than Wild Bill, but he was a novice when it came to biking. I had to compensate for Paul's lack of experience by using my strength, which I couldn't do over the long haul. I stopped and told Paul to lean forward and put his arms at least halfway around my waist so he could feel how to lean through the turns.

He seemed to pick up the drill in the three kilometers before we picked up the A10, which went all the way to the French border. When we got to the entrance, I checked my watch. It was just after nine. I was rested, and the bike was gassed up for about two hundred kilometers. The traffic was light, so I figured we could go for an hour or so before needing to stop.

The A10 was a superhighway like the interstates back home. There were lane markers, lighting poles, shoulders, and clear international road signs, and the curves were smooth and banked where necessary for fast travel. After ten kilometers, I hadn't seen any speed limit signs, so I guessed the rules were like the autobahn in Austria. I was cruising along at 120 kilometers per hour, certainly not too fast, and Paul was having a great time and said so. I loved having the wind whip my hair and press against my face on a road where I wasn't going to go into a blind tunnel or worry about falling off the edge of the road into a three hundred-foot gorge. Driving at this speed at night was a new experience too.

The road turned west for a kilometer away from the coast and then straightened out onto an elevated section linking some ridges, which went down to the sea. We had just hit the straightaway when the first supercar blew by us going more than twice our speed and causing a draft, which almost knocked the bike over.

"What the bloody hell was that!?" Paul yelled.

"It looked like a Ferrari," I said. "He must have been going 160 miles per hour or 270 kilometers per hour."

I kept going and got almost to the end of the straightaway when another supercar roared by, causing me to nearly lose control of the bike.

"Fuck this," Paul yelled. "Let me off. I'd rather walk."

"I can't stop out here. It's too dangerous. I saw signs for a tunnel up ahead and a town called Terrarossa, three kilometers. We'll stop there."

Paul said nothing as I took off my sunglasses and slowed down, preparing to enter the tunnel, which I saw had lighting all along the ceiling, mercifully. In a few minutes, I pulled the bike into a turnoff at Terrarossa, a village hard by the road. It was now nine thirty, and the village was closed for the night, but the only thing that mattered to me, and especially Paul, was that we were off the autostrada. I motored a short distance away from the exit until we found a wooded area where we got off the bike. Paul was shaken, but I was strangely calm. I'd been through a lot on the bike and was used to being out there with my life on the line.

"We were damned nearly killed out there," Paul said.

"I'm not going to deny it," I said. "The fact is that with your weight, I can't control the bike when those cars blow by us. I don't think I can take you to Nice with all that weight. I've got to leave you here."

"You're bloody well right," Paul said. "I can get a ride somehow. Always have. Do you think you're going to make it all right?"

"I can control the bike with less weight and if I get into a more aerodynamic driving position. Anyway, I don't have a choice. I'll have to keep an eye out in the mirrors for those supercars. These roads were built for them and everyone else beware."

"You've got real bollocks, Jack, my lad. I wish you luck. We can bed down here, and I'll buy coffee in the morning."

I pulled the bike into an enclosure in the woods, pulled out my sleeping bag, and lay on it while Paul just flopped under a bush.

———•◆•———

Awakening with the dawn, we got on the bike, drove around the village square, and waited for the only café in town to open. We had coffee and rolls. Paul asked the proprietor if he knew where he could hitch a ride, but the guy made out like he didn't know what Paul was talking about.

"I'll bet he's just putting me off," Paul said. "That's how they jerk off foreigners. Well, Jack, it's been a time. I'm not for sentimental farewells. If you're in Glasgow, come see the rugby and you'll find me. You'll do fine with the lassies. I can see from how you handle that machine that you've got what they're looking for. Best of luck, lad."

We shook hands, and Paul started to walk toward to A10 to look for a ride. In a minute, I passed him and waved. Then I carefully turned onto the road, gunned the bike up to 130 kilometers per hour, and tucked myself into the wind-resistant position with my chest atop the gas tank. With Paul gone and the speed increased, I figured I wouldn't be buffeted about so much by the draft when the supercars passed me.

My theory got its first test in about five minutes. I just barely saw a yellow Lamborghini in the mirror before it screamed past me, going at what I guessed was 290 kilometers per hour or 180 miles per hour. I had the bike at 140 kilometers per hour, which was 90 miles per hour, nearly as fast as it could go. The draft did punch me around a bit, but it was nothing like when Paul was on the bike. A hundred and forty kilometers per hour was an exhilarating experience. The road was a blur beneath my feet. The scenery, when I could look at it, was spectacular. This was the Rivera.

It was early morning. I had to deal with a couple more supercars, but as the day progressed, ordinary folk began to use the road and then trucks, and the danger of the supercars faded as the traffic slowed everyone down. Paul might have stuck around, but I found that even to keep up with the general traffic, I couldn't back down from 130 kilometers per hour. Italians as a whole seemed to be fond of driving fast.

I crossed the Verbone River and then entered a tunnel, at least a kilometer long, which had a curve in it so I couldn't see the end. It reminded me of Yugoslavia, only this one had lights in it. I soon crossed the Nervia River and entered another long tunnel. Then it was the Roya River and another long tunnel. I accepted that this was the way of things on this coast, but the lights in the tunnels meant everything to me.

I saw a sign in Italian, French, and English that said I was approaching the French frontier before I came to the last tunnel. After I passed through that tunnel, I had to stop for customs and immigration. I checked the time, eight thirty. I had made the ride from Terrarossa in an hour. That was really moving. I was in France, only a half hour from Nice.

There were few cars at the border, and the Italian guards were very casual. They told me I should have bought a Moto Guzzi, an Italian make. I countered by saying, "In Berlin?" They got a laugh out of that. The French guards were more circumspect and asked me to open the saddlebags, but they didn't go into them and passed me through.

I pulled over into a parking lot to stretch my legs and shake off the road. Riding at speed was demanding. It required complete concentration. And those supercars; holy shit. They didn't write about them in the guidebooks. They just came out at night like banshees.

I got back on the bike and noticed right away that the traffic was going twenty kilometers per hour slower than in Italy. Were there police patrols here? Maybe the French drivers were just more civilized. Anyway, it was a relief from having to drive at 130 miles per hour and being at risk all the time.

After a half hour, I passed north of Nice, which I could see was a big city. Then I went through some ridges to the Var River and turned south down to the coast. The day was sunny and warm, perfect for biking. I unbuttoned the top buttons of my jacket to take in the air. I could see the Mediterranean to the left as I passed the exits for Antibes and Cannes. After Cannes, the road turned away from the coast and into the wooded hills. I knew I was less than an hour away from Aix, so I juiced the bike back up to 130 kilometers per hour.

On the way into Aix, I had to throttle back several times to go through construction zones, which was frustrating when I was so near my destination. When I slowed to a crawl, I looked around at the countryside and saw a mountain that dominated the landscape. I knew it was Mt. St. Victoire, the favorite subject of Cezanne's landscape paintings.

I bore my irritation with the traffic as I approached the center of Aix and had an embracing thought about all I'd been through on the bike in the past couple of months. I started thinking about Eva. I was sure she'd gotten to Aix all right. I wanted to tell her about Aigia Galini and how I'd found Kara there, as some sort of mystic confirmation of her guiding me there. Would she be freaked out to see me? I had to cogitate on this, to think back to how we'd parted. Surely she understood I couldn't have taken her on that crazy ride through Yugoslavia. But then, she didn't know how crazy it would be.

I wanted to tell her that I had changed in the few weeks since she had last seen me. Or would she be angry and not care? She could be like that. It wasn't like I wanted to get back together with her. That brought the image of Kara back to me again. I had poured my soul out to her; she knew who I was more than Eva. Still, Eva had set me on my course, so I'd like to hear what she thought.

I took the exit that led me into the inner part of the city and found myself motoring slowly up a beautiful, tree-lined avenue bordered by fancy shops and beautiful, late-nineteenth-century houses. I crossed the main rail line and reached what I was sure was the heart of the city, a traffic circle in the center of which was a broad fountain on three levels. I drove around the circle and saw a wide avenue that was totally shaded by overhanging trees. I spotted a street sign: Cours Mirabeau. This was obviously a central artery. I went around the circle again and saw a large café called Le Festival that had dozens of outdoor tables and a bike park next to it.

I was starving and sat at a table where I could watch the bike. A waiter came up, and I thought I'd try out the French I studied in school for five years. I ordered a "jambon et fromage en rouler et un biere." I was a little rusty, but the waiter smiled, sort of giving me credit for the effort.

When the waiter returned with a ham and cheese on a roll with a beer, I congratulated myself on my French and then put away the sandwich in short order. I sat at the table looking at the fountain and down the Cours Mirabeau as I finished the beer. When I got up to pay the bill, I noticed across the street from the fountain a sign on a building that said, "Office de Tourism."

"This must be my lucky day," I said to myself.

I wanted to find out where there was a cheap hotel and get a guide of the city, so I drove over to the tourist bureau and parked next to it. I went in and found it to be fairly crowded. There were waiting lines for different languages: French, English, German, and Spanish. The French was the shortest one, so I joined that one. When my turn came, I asked where I could find "un chambre peu couteuse," which meant an inexpensive room. I struggled with the clerk's response for a moment, "pendant combien de temps?" But then I figured it out, "for how long?"

"Une semaine," I said, meaning a week.

The clerk, who seemed annoyed that I wasn't really French, looked through her brochures and pulled out three. Two were for hotels, and the other was for a youth hostel. I asked for a guide to the city, which the clerk gave me along with a map. Then I went back to Le Festival, ordered another beer, and studied the map and the brochures. I found that although the hotels were centrally located, they cost three times what the hostel did. The hostel was on the Rue Albert Einstein, which was two kilometers out of the center of town, a small inconvenience compared to the price. I could spend ten days there for forty dollars.

I finished the beer, made sure of where I was going, and drove out to the hostel, which turned out to be fifteen minutes from the center of town through the traffic. When I got there, the manager told me that a large group had just left and the rooms had to be cleaned. There were two dorms with eight bunks each, four rooms with four bunks, and two rooms for counselors with two bunks. Prices ranged accordingly. Remembering the ferry ride to Crete, I asked for a two-bunk room. The cost was one hundred forty France or thirty-five dollars per week, which I paid in advance. I asked if I could shower while I was waiting.

The manager led me down the hall to show me the room and the facilities. I went out, brought in my gear, left it in the room, and took a hot shower. By the time I was done, the room was ready, so I unpacked, dressed in my Lacoste shirt and shorts, and combed my hair back on my head. Looking in the mirror, I knew that Eva would be pleased to see me. I then propped myself up on the bed and looked all through the guide of Aix to get the lay of the land.

I read that the University of Aix had just merged with the University of Marseille, which now had an enrollment of twenty thousand and was considered second only to the University of Paris in France. The old town of Aix was founded in the thirteenth century and, as part of Provence, had once been ruled by its own king.

In the seventeenth century, the city was apportioned, using the Cours Mirabeau as the dividing line. The old town was thirteenth century. The new city was eighteenth-century baroque. There were open-air market days on Tuesdays, Thursdays, and Saturdays in all the main squares in the old town and along the Cours Mirabeau. One would be tomorrow. I had to see this traditional means of commerce, which the book said went back six hundred years. So I decided to call Eva late tomorrow to see if she would see me the next day. As for the rest of today, I'd go back into town and get some dinner and then have a decent night's sleep.

I drove back to the fountain at the center of town. The circle was called La Rotonde, as I learned from the guidebook. I parked the bike and walked up the Cours, where I discovered that the girls gave me the eye assertively, even without me being on the bike. I would nod at them and smile, but didn't wink because I wasn't tuned in to this kind of social aggressiveness. Paul had said I had more to learn, and the French social style was proving him correct. These girls were obviously a few levels ahead of me. They all were attractive. They knew how to dress and move their bodies. Even the ones with men had what my mother called "a roving eye," but the men didn't seem to care. It was the practice here.

I concentrated on the different stores on both sides of the Cours and the series of fountains that were situated in the center of the street. I saw a large department store called the Monoprix that I figured could be of use at some point. Then I came to a restaurant called La Bastide de Cours, which had a menu outside that listed a salmon steak. I hadn't had a fish dinner since Crete, so I went in and was seated in a glassed-in patio area on the sidewalk where I could watch the passing crowd. I ordered the salmon and a glass of white wine. It was early, so there were no other patrons on the patio.

Having the place to myself and effectively isolated from the outside world, I had space to think of myself as I was now compared to six months ago.

I knew that in the past I was immature, not complete as a man. I had to answer basic questions to let myself know who I was and what I was going to do with my life. Six months ago, the only thing I could do was initiate change. I was trapped by my parents, social upheaval at home, and the draft. I had broken away from those shackles to find that I had the courage, the life skills, and the determination to impress people whom I was impressed by. This had a self-reinforcing, cumulatively positive effect on my self-esteem. I had lost my virginity to a beautiful woman who was fourteen years older than I was. I had made friends with a German WWII veteran. I had made friends on the road in Greece, sticking with Charlie and having fun with him while letting Nigel and Pete go because I sensed trouble there. I had fallen desperately for Candace, a new sensation for me, but I had been disciplined enough to control my emotions when I found out she was Dimitris' girl. I looked down at my sandals as a reminder of that.

I had gone to Crete because of some mystical energy that made me feel that my destiny lay there. I had met this beautiful girl who was undergoing the same struggles for independence and understanding in her life as I was. We had made love, and she had told me I was a great lover. After I had worked out a general plan for her to free herself from the trap she was in, I realized she was what I was looking for: it was she who was my destiny. She had told me that she was in love with me. That was still sinking into my consciousness, but the thought of it brought me to another level of awareness of the meaning of life in that it established a true bond between the two of us, something I'd never experienced before. I was in love with her and had to get back to her soon.

On the ferry from Patras, I'd met Paul, whom I thought of as a man among men. Paul had told me that I had a big set of balls for being able to handle myself on the bike in dangerous circumstances. I had driven that bike through more trouble than Paul knew and came away unscathed, so he was right.

I knew that all these things were true. Wild Bill may have called me into coming to the place where I would experience this adventure, but Bill had crashed out, and I had pulled myself through and had come away with a sense of myself I didn't have before.

33

Eva and Emile

THE SALMON WAS DELICIOUS. I sometimes ate in high-end French restaurants in New York when I went out with my parents, and the food was always superb, but my father had always paid, probably on an expense account. The waiter asked if I would like to see the dessert tray. I said, "Absolument." When I looked it over, I chose a framboisier, which was a raspberry mousse cake. Raspberries were my favorite.

The bill was not inexpensive, but the meal was so good! I collected the bike at the Rotonde and drove slowly through the old town. Some of the streets were so narrow they were virtually impossible for cars, but they made great outdoor venues for cafés. The squares where the markets were to be held in the morning were filled with overflow crowds from bars making merry on a warm summer evening. A couple of girls holding wine glasses came up to me and asked for a ride, but I managed to beg off. I'd come back tomorrow and see more, but now it was time to rest.

Back at the hostel, I decided to count out my remaining money. That certainly had a bearing on my next move. I came up with two hundred and eighty dollars in AMEX checks and twenty-two dollars in francs. I'd have to change for some more francs tomorrow to pay for meals in the short term. The remaining two hundred dollars hopefully would pay for food and incidentals for the ten days. I'd already paid for at the hostel, but I wasn't thinking of traveling any further anyway.

All my questions were answered except for what my path forward would be, and I figured I'd have to go home to find out the answer to that. Seeing Eva again would bring me full circle here in Europe. I'd need money for airfare; for that I'd have to sell the bike.

And what about the draft? I paused in my train of thought and said to myself, "These are discrete issues, some of which you can resolve and others of which will be resolved for you. You came to Europe to learn how to deal not so much with issues, but how to deal with yourself. Now you've learned that you can work things out."

———•◆•———

In the morning, I washed, shaved, dressed, and checked the guidebook one last time to plan out my day. I needed breakfast and francs, so I drove to the Cours to find a café, but the entire boulevard was closed because the open-air market was being set up all along the boulevard. So I drove around the Rotonde and up a street, which paralleled the Cours until I saw the statue of King Rene of Provence at the top of the Cours at the other end from the Rotonde. I parked the bike and sat at a table at a café called Cagnina, where I could watch the stalls being set up and all the vendors' wares were being displayed.

For breakfast, I ordered a big glass of fresh orange juice, two croissants with preserves, and coffee. There were several banks on the Cours, and I changed a hundred dollars for four hundred and fifty French francs, figuring I wasn't going any farther than France. I asked for fifty-franc notes so my wallet wouldn't bulge.

On coming out of the bank, I decided that today I wanted to be as free of the bike as possible. People were starting to flood the market, so I would go with the flow, and that meant on foot. I chained the bike to a post near Cagnina and walked around the town, going from square to square through the small connecting alleys in the old town.

For lunch I stopped into a sandwich shop for a ham and cheese and a Coke to munch on as I toured the markets, but then the markets started to unfold, closing time being two. I figured it was time to call Eva. "Crunch time," I said to myself. I went back to the bike and drove down the Cours to the Rotonde and the Tourist Bureau, where I had seen two phone booths outside.

This call to Eva was going to be a cold call on both ends, certainly hers. I had to be as casual as possible, so thinking of Paul and his smooth ways, I picked up the receiver and dialed her number. Before any connection was made, the operator told me to deposit two hundred centimes. I didn't have that many coins, so I hung up. The banks had closed, so I'd have to go into the Tourist Bureau to get change for a fifty-franc note.

I went up to the lady in the English-speaking window and asked her, "I have to make a local call, and I don't have change. Could you please break a fifty-franc note for me?"

"Oh, my. That's a large note. We probably don't have enough change for that. Is it a call right here in Aix?"

"Yes, it is." I showed her the number.

"If you make it a short, local call, I suppose you can make it from one of our office phones. Go to the desk over there."

I thanked her and made the call.

"Allo?" the voice answered. I could tell it was Eva.

"Eva. Hi. It's Jack. I wanted to know if you made it home all right. I went all the way to Aigia Galini, and I'm on my way back."

"Jack? From Berlin?" Eva was flustered, obviously not expecting to hear from me.

"Sure. I was thinking about you and your train ride from Vienna. You gave me your number and said to call if I were passing through Aix sometime."

"And you are *here*? In Aix? Now!?" she exclaimed incredulously.

"Well, yes. I got here yesterday. I've had quite an adventure in the past few weeks. Could we talk over a glass of wine?"

There was a long pause before Eva said, "Perhaps. Yes, you did send me back home, and things have changed for me. Maybe I should tell you about them. If you are still riding about on your motorcycle, you are most likely free at any time?"

"Absolutely," I said, although I sensed that Eva was being guarded in her conversation.

"Well then, I am meeting someone for dinner this evening at seven at the Café Jeanne in the Place Ramus. It is in the center of the old town not far from the Hotel de Ville. We can talk then. A bientot." And she hung up the phone.

I wasn't sure what to make of Eva's attitude, but I was pretty sure she was being guarded. I started thinking: *We'd had a good time in Berlin. I'd gotten her out of a bad situation with her boss. I helped her skip out on her rent. I paid for her trip from Vienna to Aix. Why could she be sore at me?*

I thanked the clerk for letting me make the call and asked her where the Café Jeanne was on my map. With the directions, I decided to make a trial run to find it since the old town was really a warren of small, curvy streets in what was a community that hadn't changed its layout since medieval times.

At six forty-five, I drove the bike back to the Place Ramus and stood waiting by the small fountain for Eva and her friend. I waited quite a while, looking at the small restaurant at the end of the dead-end square fill up with the evening's patrons. There were dim electric lights strung across the square, which gave it a romantic flair.

When I turned back to look at the street, I saw Eva arm in arm with a tall, handsome man walking toward me, talking and laughing. Eva was wearing a white blouse, pulled far off her shoulders and tucked into a billowing, brightly colored skirt with Moorish designs running all around it. Her loose hair was flowing all about her, only corralled by the Foster Grants he had on the top of her head, her golden-red hair highlighted by her deeply tanned skin. She looked ravishing.

The man, *her man*, as she was making it clear, looked to be about forty. He was wearing a white linen jacket over a dark-blue sea island sport shirt. He had tan trousers with a knife-edge pleat and wore black Gucci slip-ons with gold buckles and no socks. He was also deeply tanned and had wavy brown hair combed back over his head. He had a pair of Foster Grants balanced on the top of his head too.

Eva broke off her conversation with her escort when she saw me and gave me a wave with a smile as she said, "Bonsoir, Jack." When she did not offer me the traditional French kisses on the checks, I figured that she wanted to maintain a distance between us, probably because she was making a serious move for the fashion plate on her arm. *Why shouldn't she?* I thought and bit my tongue so I didn't crowd her act.

Eva introduced the guy as Emile Larocque, a professor of economics at the University of Aix. We exchanged pleasant bonsoirs, and Emile told the maître d' that they had a reservation. The maître d' was very cordial to Emile, whom I suspected was a regular customer. We were seated at a quiet table by a wall where ivy was growing up and over the sign of the café. There was a candle in a red-colored glass in the center of the table that cast a flattering light on the diners.

"Please understand that I called Eva just to say 'hello.' I didn't mean to intrude on your evening," I said.

"It is no intrusion to have an old friend to join us for dinner. C'est bien, n'est-ce pas, Emile?" Eva said soothingly, but with an edge in her voice.

"Pas de tout," Emile said. "Jack, Eva tells me that you came to Berlin from the United States to live in a commune with six people. This is unusual. How did it happen?"

I thought I should be careful with my answers so as not to upset Eva's relationship with this professor, so I decided to be as broad as possible.

"I got sick of what was going on with the war protests in the States. Also I'm waiting to hear if I will be drafted into the army, so I thought it would be good to get away and go to Berlin to visit with a friend who was living in the commune. It was really a fortuitous experience and a good one overall, but it almost turned out to be a calamity in the end when the landlord pressed me for back rent. Then I had to leave post-haste. Eva helped me get away."

"Eva tells me you bought a motorcycle."

"That's it, parked right over there."

"A BMW. Those are beautiful machines. I would like to look at it later, if you don't mind."

"Not at all. It has done very well by me."

"You are eligible for duty in Vietnam then?"

"Yes, unfortunately."

"France had its debacle over there, and now it is the United States' turn. No good will come of it, I'm sure."

"I can't see how."

"Aside from all the protests, which we have a lot of over here, you know, what caused you to take on such an adventure, if you don't mind my asking?"

I looked over at Eva, but she was looking at Emile, content to let him carry the conversation, especially because she knew the answers to these questions already.

"I have questions about myself I needed to find answers for. The trip on the motorcycle wasn't part of my original plan, but it proved to be an essential part of finding the answers."

"And what answers have you found; may I ask?"

I thought this guy was getting a little too personal and wanted him to back off. "The answers would depend on the questions, wouldn't they?"

Eva now jumped into the conversation. "Jack is doing what so many of his contemporaries are doing in the United States. They are trying to find themselves after being pampered by their parents for their first twenty years. Now they have come up against the realities of life, which include the mess in Vietnam, and they can't find a way forward. They have to survive on their own, and they are finding it difficult."

So that's what she's sore about, I thought. *She made her choice, and she had to struggle. Now she's throwing her experience of that pain at me in some sort of misdirected revenge.*

Emile saw that she was getting heated up and wanted to keep things civil. I guessed that he knew Eva had slept with me, but he sure didn't show any emotion about it. That's the way Europeans treated sex, detached and very civilized.

"Eva, I teach classes every day to students who are perhaps a bit younger than Jack. They are perplexed and have questions about life they will need answers for. I can only teach them economics, but the large pool of people in that time of life remains at a crossroads, which are in many instances defined by the questions they must find answers to."

Eva stewed on Emile's mollifying answers for a moment, but she wasn't done with me yet. "You said you were going to Budapest, Athens, and then Crete. Did you go to those places?"

"Yes, I did. All the way to Aigia Galini."

"Then how did you get back to Aix so quickly? You put me on the train in Vienna only four weeks ago."

"I went to all those places, and I met some wonderful people, especially a girl in Aigia Galini. I would like to tell you about what I have found with her. But if you are wondering how I got here from Crete so fast, it was an amazing piece of luck. I stopped in Athens on my way back, and the AMEX office booked me on a brand-new ferry from Patras to Genoa. It took two to three weeks off traveling from Greece to France by road."

Emile sat back in his chair and looked at me as if he were quite impressed. Eva looked at Emile and frowned.

"So what answers do you get for yourself from driving around like that? Are you going to do that for the rest of your life? Surely you must see there is more. You can't be satisfied with that."

I was stunned and deflated. I had wanted to tell Eva about my journey in the spirit in which I had made it. There was depth in the adventure itself. It had meaning for me, and I had wanted to tell her something about Kara, but I couldn't mention my feelings for her in this heated atmosphere. I saw Eva as trying to show me up in front of her man, that she could convey that she thought she had completed her journey and maybe settle down after all her years of wandering by snagging a man.

Once again, Emile stepped in, seeing things from a broader viewpoint. "Eva, it would seem that Jack has made an arduous journey, starting from a place of asking and arriving at a place of knowing. This has value, although it might not be his final destination. Jack is here in Aix with his motorcycle. I am sure that if you asked him, he would tell you that he does not intend to stay in Aix with his motorcycle. His journey will take him further, likely back to the United States, hopefully not to Vietnam. So he isn't going to be satisfied by coming here. He will move on, and that will be fine."

I thanked Emile for his kind words with a nod. I did my best to avoid Eva's eyes, but she had cooled off. She'd said her piece, I figured. Then the waiter came for the order.

Before making an order, I said, "I should probably be moving on and let you two enjoy your dinner together."

"Pas de tout," Email said, again. "You are my guest, and that is final. And I think we might have some more conversation, no?"

In looking at Eva, it was apparent that she would comply with whatever Emile wanted, although I wondered what more Emile wanted to discuss.

Emile ordered a bottle of red wine and asked if I liked lamb. I didn't mention the piles of grilled lamb I'd had in Athens; I just said I loved lamb. Emile ordered souris d' agneau and told me it was the best lamb dish in the south of France. He had the same for himself. Eva ordered grilled chicken and potatoes gratin.

With Emile having taken charge of the conversation, I thought I'd venture to ask Eva about her trip from Vienna. She said under her breath that it was uneventful but tiring and would have left it at that, but I wanted to know how things went with her mother.

When I asked the question, Eva's eyes went wide, and she looked at Emile. Then she bowed her head and began to sob. I was horrified that I had ruined everything, but Emile just patted her hand and nodded. The two of us let Eva express her emotions to herself until the storm had blown itself out.

Then she took her napkin, wiped away her tears, and looked me straight in the eye and told her story.

"It had been fifteen years since I had seen my mother. When I came to her front door, I was afraid she wouldn't recognize me, but she opened the door, and it was just as if I had come home from school. We hugged and kissed and cried and cried. It was so joyful but so painful. We sat on the couch and talked and talked for hours. Then we ate and talked some more. She had missed me so much, and I didn't realize how much I missed her. She said that my father never truly forgave me, but now, well, he isn't here anymore, so I have a new life living with her.

"And two weeks ago I am shopping at the market by the Hotel de Ville, and Emile comes up and asks me if he has met me before. Of course, I say 'no' to such a line." Eva smiled at Emile. "But he is charming and invites me for a glass of wine at a café. Well, he is charming…" Emile smiled at Eva and took her hand.

"The little bird finally flew home," he said. "I have been to see her mother and her home, a lovely cottage just outside the Boulevard Jean-Jaures."

Eva looked at me and held my eyes for a moment. "Merci, Jack," she said softly.

I felt the same feeling I had when I worked out the plan for Kara.

Dinner came, and it was truly delectable. I decided to tell the story of the piles of lamb chops at the party in Dimitris' taverna. But, I said, the French have a delicacy with their cuisine that is unsurpassed. Emile was delighted to hear the compliment, and Eva was surprised at my sophistication. Emile suggested they have some dessert so I could experience some more French cuisine. He called the waiter to order tartelette aux fraises et noisettes. I had to ask what that was, and Emile explained, strawberry and hazelnut pie. I loved it.

By the time dinner was over, night had fallen over the city and was leaving a luxuriant cooling air over what had been a warm day. Emile and Eva talked quietly in French between themselves.

I thought about Eva's initial reaction to my reasons for coming to Europe. I had told her about myself in Berlin when I was still floating with no foundation, but now I had changed. Now her circumstances had changed, too, so she came down on me as though I was still a seeker without hearing my whole story. Emile must have made a journey of discovery himself; he understood. He made Eva understand in very few words too. I admired him for this.

Just then, Emile broke away from his conversation with Eva. "Jack, I have been talking with Eva about you. You are a fine young man, and I think I might have an idea or two for you. Would you be interested in having a chat?"

"Absolutely," I said.

"Please take my card. I will be in my office at the university from one to two tomorrow. If you come at one, we can have some coffee and talk."

"I'll be there," I said. "Merci, and thanks for the dinner. It was delicious."

I said bonsoir to Eva, and she came up and kissed me on both cheeks. I walked over to the bike and started it up. Emile and Eva were walking down the street when I rolled slowly past them. Emile called for me to stop. Emile wanted to look at the bike, as he had said. I got off to let him have a thorough look.

"This is a beautiful piece of machinery. You must have had a wonderful time driving it."

I said I did but didn't elaborate.

"A demain," Emile said.

I knew that meant "see you tomorrow." It was an appointment I meant to keep.

34

Emile's Advice

THE NEXT DAY I rolled over and slept until almost eleven. When I woke up, I jumped out of bed remembering my appointment with Emile, but I had two hours, so I caught my breath, cleaned up, and drove to the university where I had two croissants and coffee for breakfast at a café while I waited for one o'clock to happen.

At twelve forty-five, I drove to the building listed on Emile's card, and I went in and found Emile's office. I was early so I waited in the hall. Shortly, I saw Emile walking with two students in tow. Emile said, "Bonjour," to me, unlocked his office door, and went inside. Emile asked me to wait by the door while he went to his desk to get some papers for the students, which he handed over, and dismissed them. I saw that they didn't look so happy as they looked at the papers.

Such is the life of a student, I thought. Emile was writing something in a notebook, so I took a quick look around the office, which was a bit cramped with a desk, two chairs, a file cabinet, and shelves filled with books lining the wall behind the desk.

Emile said, "Please sit. I have been busier this morning than I had anticipated. Do you mind if we talk here? I cannot provide coffee."

"I had coffee with breakfast, thanks. I slept late."

"Tres bien. Well, in speaking with Eva last night, she told me that she would be pleased if I could help you in your journey in some way. She and I met only a short time ago, but we have become close. She has told me her story about marrying against her father's wishes and how she has had to live on her own for a long time. Despite her being angry with you last night, she has come to realize that you changed her life by sending her back to her mother. She has a future now. She is a survivor and is free to walk her own path."

"To be honest, I couldn't sit by and let her be exploited by her boss in Berlin, but all I could do was tell her to get away. She did that by herself. When she came to Vienna, I had already made plans to leave and couldn't take her with me. It was because I had to call my parents from Vienna that I thought she might do the same. She needed a safe harbor."

"That was very mature and considerate of you. You have affected lives by what you have done. At least Eva's and her mother's. One can never be sure where *des affaires de coeur* will lead, but Eva and I seem to have a certain rapport. If she had not come to Aix, rien, nothing. I have le logique; she has la passion. Maybe there is something here. Time will tell."

Emile turned his swivel chair so he could look out the window. "Eva was wondering where you are going next. She has a concern for you, although she let her passion get the better of her last night. So, if I may ask, what is your plan?"

I took a breath. Emile's question had backed me into my past where in the short term I was facing the draft and in the long term, my parents' insistence that I live my life as they lived theirs. In the past, I would have become frustrated, angry even, because I didn't have the experience or the self-assurance I needed to confront such obstacles in life. I realized my journey in Europe was ending, and it was because I had acquired knowledge of myself through experience of life, which would provide me with answers that I could take home with me that I could answer Emile directly.

"For the short term, I have to wait to see what happens with my draft status. There is a chance that my number will not be called. If it is called, I will enlist in the navy for two years. If my number is not called, I have determined that I will leave my parents' way of life behind and find a way to make a living in another part of the U.S. All the protests that are going on in the U.S. aren't just about the war. There is a movement of some people my age to break away from the past and create lives of their own. I know some of them. When I get back home, I'm going to contact them and see what they are doing. Also I met a wonderful girl in Crete who is from Chicago. She wants to break away from her restrictive family too. I am in love with her, and I want to get back with her again."

Emile turned to me slowly. "I think Eva was concerned about the Jack she knew in Berlin. From what I have just heard, you have learned much from your journey. I will tell her that she need not worry herself further about you."

"Thanks for your confidence, but I'm still up in the air about the draft over which I have no control. It's got me dangling in the breeze."

Emile became very professorial, or so it seemed. "Everyone sees on the TV the involvement of the U.S. in Vietnam. We French have had the experience of being humiliated there, so it is astounding to us that your country has been sucked into it to such a degree. But here is what logic tells me is going to happen. The U.S. is not winning the war, and the people want it over. Nixon does not want to be the first U.S. president to lose a war, but he wants to be reelected this year even more. So what will he do? After making the mistake of going into Cambodia, he now understands how angry the people are, so he will start a pullback of the U.S. engagement to show the people he is going to get out of Vietnam. He won't remove troops, but he has already started a reduction in the drafting of new troops, which is most unpopular with the voters. Do you think this could affect your situation?"

"You know, you're right. Two years ago they drafted number two hundred and twenty-five. Last year it was one hundred and seventy-five. This is my year, and I'm one hundred sixty-six."

"So you could have been passed over this year. Do you know what the number that has been called for this year is?"

"No, I don't. I've been over here since the first of the year, and I haven't been in touch. But I'm sure they've drawn the number by now."

"Perhaps you should find out."

"You bet I will. I'll call home today!"

"Good. Call me when you have any news."

I thanked Emile and practically flew down to the bike. I couldn't believe I'd forgotten about the draft number drawing. I wanted to get to a phone while the parents were at the house. It would be almost eight in New York. They were probably having dinner.

I drove quickly but carefully through the winding streets of Aix until I got to the Rotonde where I parked on the sidewalk next to the phone booths. I got in a booth, closed the door to the traffic noise, and placed a collect call to my parents, whom I figured would be at home. After the operator made the connection and got acceptance for the charges, I heard my father say, "Jack? Is that you? Where are you?"

"Hi, Dad. It's me. I'm in Aix-en-Provence in France. I've had a terrific time over here."

"Why are you calling? Do you need money? Are you in trouble?"

"No. I'm fine. I've got enough money, and there's no trouble."

This was so typical of the old man, I thought, *first thinking about money and then concerned about his reputation.*

"I'm calling because I have a very important question to ask. What was the highest draft number they called up this year? They should have announced it by now. I've been on the road and haven't kept up."

"Yes, indeed, they did made this year's call-up. It was very irresponsible of you not to have been on top of that. And taking off the way you did without leaving a way to reach you compounded the problem."

My heart sank, and I became somewhat dizzy when I heard that. It sounded like I'd been drafted. I had to ask, "What number did they call, Dad?"

"They called up to one hundred and twenty-five." My father paused. "Your mother is very happy you will not have to do military service. And I suppose you think you're a lucky young man."

I was completely stunned and couldn't say anything. I was elated, but my father had managed it so that I was whip-sawed from the depths of despair to the heights of elation in an instant. I was free, and maybe my father didn't like that. Well, too fucking bad! I was free! Holy shit! I was stupefied.

"Jack, are you still there?" my father asked. "When are you coming home?"

"Yea. I'm here, and I'll be home soon. I'll let you know," I said as I hung up the phone.

Boy, can he be a dick, I thought.

When I opened the door of the phone booth, I could begin to feel all the pent-up tension of the years of waiting for the draft melt away from me. It was as if I had just poured myself out of the confinement of a sealed container of rules and restrictions into the bright sunshine of a Provencal afternoon where light and color were not even boundaries, just suggestions. I left the bike and walked up the Cours, only half-seeing the tourists, the shops, the fountains, and the statues. I could breathe the air freely with no constriction in my lungs. I had a new life to live.

I remembered that Emile wanted him to call with any news, so I went back to the phone booth and called. Emile answered, sounding rushed.

"Emile, it's Jack. I called my father. Guess what he said?"

"Jack, is this really the time for guessing games?"

"Maybe not. Sorry. The fact is that I will not be drafted."

"Oh, I am very happy for you. That is excellent news. I believe it calls for a celebration. We should get together with Eva and toast your return to your country where you can begin your new life."

"Emile, you've done a lot for me already."

We agreed to meet at Le Festival at lunchtime the next day for a quick farewell toast as Emile and Eva were heading out of town.

I wasn't waiting to celebrate, so I drove to Le Festival and ordered a split of champagne. *If ever there were a time for champagne*, I told myself. I wasn't sure how to feel now that I had been given control of my life back, plus a chance of living a full life. I was sorry for the poor bastards who hadn't made the cut, but I was out of it, which was what mattered.

I was angry at my father for presenting the facts the way he did, but I would need him for one more thing before I could break away completely. I could sit on my anger; it wasn't that big a deal. My father was who he was; he'd never change.

The champagne gave me a nice buzz as I watched the crowd walk by. A pair of pretty French girls gave me the eye, and I smiled and gave them a mock salute. That wasn't how it was done. *I really was out of tune with women,* I thought, but there was Kara. "Remember," she had said to me. I wasn't going to forget. I just had to get my ducks in a row first.

I left the bike parked at the tourist bureau and walked across the street into the old town, strolling aimlessly, my feet following the pattern of my thoughts that were scattered and dreamy. I had a sense of being truly on my own now. I had escaped Big Brother. I would move past the parents and have a vista open up before me where I could see a path I could choose for myself. There was nothing to fear from the past and only challenges to meet in the future.

I walked up to the Hotel de Ville square and sat on a bench under the trees. The sun was casting late-afternoon shadows through the trees onto the buildings around the square. I saw people filing out of the Hotel de Ville where the day's work had ended. That made me turn my attention to the one question I had not answered: What will I do with my life?

I wasn't frustrated or panicked when I thought about it now. I saw that the answer lay on one of the paths that I would find before me. All I had to do was choose one, make a plan, and act on it.

I suddenly felt that the fact of my deliverance had taken something out of me. I was tired and needed something to eat, so I walked back down toward the Cours and came across a pushcart man who was selling pizzas made on baguettes. Cheese, tomato sauce, and a choice of toppings, heated in a metal box with a Bunsen burner underneath it, for six francs. I chose sausage topping, had a Coke, and sat on a bench on the Cours to eat. Then I walked to the bike and drove to the hostel. As I prepared for bed, I felt that a long, wearisome chapter in my life had come to an end.

35

Selling the Bike

NEXT MORNING, AS I got ready for the new day, I felt lighter, unburdened. It was as if I'd been put in a plaster cast after an accident and now the cast had been broken away. I had less weight to deal with and actual freedom of movement. The twist was that this applied to my mentality. *What a change*, I thought. *And it happened so fast!*

I drove all the way up the Cours past the statue of King Rene and went to Cagnina where I sat inside by a window and had my usual breakfast of orange juice, two croissants with raspberry jam, and coffee. I had told Emile that my journey was over, but I had to have a plan going forward. I knew all my questions weren't fully answered; now I would drive myself forward to answer them in my own time.

I was going home. That was decided. In the short term, I had to give up the bike for airfare. In the midterm, once I was home, I had to settle differences with the parents. Leaving a rift would do me no good, and I needed a favor from my father in the form of cash for a car.

In the long term, I had to find out where I could land a job far away from the New York-suited crowd. No country clubs for me. I had to contact guys I knew from college to see if I could make a connection. There were precious few of them, but I was in solid with the guys I liked.

I drove to the Hotel de Ville square, where the central post office was, bought six postcards from a souvenir shop, and sat at a table and wrote out a synopsis of my journey to the guys I knew in school. I said I was coming home in a couple of weeks, having escaped the draft, and that I'd like to call them to see what they had been doing since graduation a year ago. I tried to frame the adventure on the cards as a teaser to pique their interest. I only had the addresses of three of the guys in my folder so I filled those in and mailed them from the post office. I hoped they'd enjoy the French stamps. The rest would have to wait until I got home.

I got to Le Festival for the toast Emile had suggested and waited for Emile and Eva to arrive. They drove up in Emile's convertible Mercedes 190SL, which he parked nearby, and said they had to run to get to their luncheon in Cassis, which was on the coast. They were spending a couple of nights on a friend's yacht. *So that's how they get so tan*, I thought.

Eva looked radiant, dressed in a fanciful outfit with golden harem pants, a deep-crimson blouse, and a wide, gold belt. She was wearing flip-flops of dark-brown leather. She had on no jewelry and didn't need it. Her hair was left loose and flowing. I thought she could have been twenty-one. I could tell that Emile was very proud of his lady. He was dressed in a light-blue, sea–island, cotton shirt and tan slacks that were pinched at the waist, which gave his legs a wide look. He wore a brown alligator belt and a Movado watch with a gold metal strap. I thought these guys would make out just fine together, if only based on their love of fashion. I hoped Eva would stick with this guy after all she'd been through because I liked Emile too.

Emile once again congratulated me on my good fortune. Eva kissed me on both cheeks, so I figured all was forgiven. I thought Emile had been beyond nice to me; given the circumstances, I guessed that Eva was behind some of it. Maybe she really did like me in the end.

I told them I had taken the first step in making my future happen by contacting friends at home whom I had known in college, and I would call them when I got back to see what they were up to. I'd given them a hint of my motorcycle tour of Europe and let them know I was not going to be drafted.

"Jack, that is an excellent first step. In fact, it is the very advice I was going to pass along to you. When you have friends at your back, the road ahead smooths itself."

"I figure there must be a few guys whose plans haven't come together yet after college. Or maybe a couple have found something and I can join up with them."

Emile agreed. Then he added, "One last thing, Jack. Whatever it is you decide to do, make sure it is what you truly want to do. Listen to your heart. Your inner voice will guide you so that everything else you have learned will make sense. I wish you bonne chance."

I heard something of *Siddhartha* in what Emile said and realized that Emile was speaking from his soul. The things he had been telling me were things he himself had hard-won in life. He had found his place and, with it, contentment. I wondered if Eva were going to fit in with that, but as Emile had said, 'Time will tell.'

As we were sitting down to the table, I asked Emile, "Do you know the best way I could sell the motorcycle? I need the money to get home. I was just getting used to being a biker," I said, not without feeling. "I survived the roads in Eastern Europe and the autostradas in Italy. Now that I'm driving civilized roads, I kind of like it. But driving a bike in the States is too dangerous, so it's got to go."

"Sometimes you must make a sacrifice of something you like to get something you need more," Emile said.

"The ancient Greeks were always sacrificing animals to the gods to have their needs met. It might be the case with me here."

They laughed at my purposeful misappropriation of history.

"So we are left with one more issue to resolve, but since this is a material problem, I think it will resolve itself in a simple way. You need to find a buyer with ready cash, n'est-ce pas?"

I said, "That would be the solution to the problem," feeling the handlebars figuratively slipping from my grasp.

Emile replied, "You should go to the Tourist Bureau and find out where the nearest BMW dealer is. You could find out how much the bike is worth there. They also might buy it or know of someone in the market for a used BMW."

"I will do that tomorrow."

Going to the Tourist Bureau could also provide me information on the cost of getting from Aix to Paris by train and from Paris to New York by plane, with a possible hotel stop in Paris.

Emile ordered a split of Taittinger champagne and three glasses. When the wine had been poured, we raised our glasses to wish me success and bon voyage. I thanked both Eva and Emile with a heartfelt remerci.

We parted on the sidewalk like old friends. As I rode back to the hostel, I considered how lucky I had been to find Emile, who was a genuinely decent person who had taken an interest in me, just as Hans had done, even more than my father, which struck me as being somewhat twisted. Emile had apparently taken a life journey of his own and so could relate to my quest. I reflected that if I hadn't done the right thing by Eva, I would never have met Emile, which made me feel that I was charting my own course and going in the right direction. I would figure out a way to sell the bike myself, just as I had done with the bus.

I got up the next morning and drove through the puddles to Cagnina for breakfast. If there had been a storm last night, I didn't hear it. I had been sleeping like a log since I had become a free man.

I liked being a regular at a café, whom the owner knew and greeted with a friendly bonjour. I had the usual orange juice, two croissants with raspberry jam, and coffee. Afterward, I drove down the Cours to the tourist bureau. I asked the lady at the desk if she knew if there were a BMW motorcycle dealer in Aix, but she said she did not. I asked where the nearest one might be, and she looked in the Provence phone book and found one in Marseilles. She wrote down the number and address on a slip of paper. I asked her for a city map of Marseilles, and she pointed to a rack on the wall.

Next, I went to the lady at the international travel section who had train and flight schedules piled on her desk. I told her I wanted to fly to JFK from Orly in the next day or two. I'd need to get to Paris first, of course.

As far as the trains were concerned, she said I could go to Paris any day. Second-class tickets were seventy-eight French francs (nineteen dollars). I would want to take a morning train, leaving at seven. The trip took six hours.

I asked for some sample airfares, and she looked up the Pan Am schedules from Orly to JFK: $197 for a night flight on a Saturday or $441 for a Monday morning flight. It was likely that I would have to spend the night in an airport hotel to make a connection, which would cost thirty dollars. So now I had something to work with. I'd need at least four hundred dollars to get home.

I didn't have that much at the moment, so I'd have to get as much for the bike as I could and fairly quickly. Every day spent in France cost me money. I figured the best way to sell the bike would be through the BMW dealer. If they wouldn't buy it, maybe I could network through them for a sale. I didn't speak French well enough to arrange a sale on my own; nor did I know what all the proper paperwork requirements were. I'd have to go to Marseille, and there was no time like the present.

I went back out to the bike and looked up the length of the Cours. Here in Aix I had been a tourist at leisure. I couldn't remember a time in the past several years when I hadn't been striving to find something in life: my identity, my purpose, or the meaning of my life itself. While constrained by the draft, I'd been in a backwater, an eddy in the flow of life, while I had to wait on chance so I could move on. Now that I had learned that I was free to live a full life, I wanted to move ahead.

Thinking of selling the bike reminded me of what it would be like to be a full-time pedestrian. If I sold the bike while I was at the hostel, I'd have to walk to town or get a cab. I needed to make necessary changes now while I had transportation.

I drove to the Monoprix department store to look for bags I could put my stuff in. The saddlebags would be useless; I'd sell them with the bike. I had dumped the duffle bag in Berlin because it took up too much room in the saddlebags. I was coming full circle.

I found a duffle-type bag that had two handles that straddled a zipper down the middle. It was about the same size as my other duffle. Getting rid of the boots would give me more room. I bought a pair of comfortable slip-on canvas shoes to replace them. I also bought an over-the-shoulder bag for books and food. When I paid, I asked for lots of change so I could call the BMW dealer.

I was stalled on the street by a very pretty girl with a guitar who had attracted a crowd to listen to her singing. The singer didn't look anything like Kara, but I felt she triggered the same primal response. This brought Kara to the forefront of my mind, and I wondered what her trip home was like, how she would manage her mother, and if she were able to work our plan, or if she had been trodden down by her mother's pressure. I wouldn't know till I got home, of course, but I had to chase down and solidify my own plan before I could find out.

I went to the phone booth in a state of resignation. I had to sell the bike, and I would demand top dollar for it. When the connection to the BMW dealership was made, I spoke first to a receptionist and finally got her to transfer me to a salesman by saying that I wanted to "vend un moto," which meant "sell a motorcycle." The salesman started speaking in French, but I asked for an English-speaking person, and the guy switched to English without a pause and asked what he could do for me.

"I'm an American," I began. "I have a 1972 BMW R60/5 that I bought at the factory in Berlin. I have just completed a journey of forty-six hundred kilometers, which is what the odometer reads, and I want to sell the bike before returning to the United States. I am hoping you could look at the machine to tell me how much it is worth." Then I had to put in more coins.

"But of course. We do that sort of thing all the time. We will need to see the machine. When can you come by?"

I told him I was in Aix and could come by in an hour or so. The man gave me his name. I repeated the address I had, and the man said it was correct. I then drove to the hostel, where I left my purchases and dressed in my driving gear. I emptied the leather bags Bill had found in Berlin. I figured they had to be worth something toward the sale.

Getting to Marseilles was the easy part, and I made good time getting there. I was on the A55, driving straight toward the sea, and since I figured this might be my last ride, I opened it up to 140 kilometers per hour, feeling the wind as it tried to peel me off the bike at that speed. The things a biker experiences puts his body on the line on the road, and I gloried in those feelings for what might be the last time. I passed every car on the twenty-nine-kilometer route, having a great time.

Finding the dealership in the city itself, which the map said was the second largest in France, was more complicated. I had to backtrack a couple of times before spotting a black sign with the white-and-blue BMW logo hanging over a sidewalk. I parked the bike right in front of the store and saw a row of shiny, new BMWs lined up inside

When I went in. I was greeted by a salesman. "Are you the American who had called about selling an R60/5?"

"Yes, I am," I said.

"Please bring the bike around to the back of the store where we have the workshop and can examine it."

I wheeled the bike down the narrow alley and into the shop where two mechanics were working on bikes. The salesman went to get a guy out of the office up front, who I supposed was the service manager, because he was wearing a coverall smeared with grease and oil. The salesman told him my story.

Then the service manager looked at the bike and his eye widened slightly. My car instincts told me these guys were looking at something they didn't see very often, an almost-new, low-mileage bike in excellent condition. I was thankful for the rainstorm last night, which had given the bike a good cleaning.

The service manager walked around the bike and finally got on it and reached for the key. I had to show him the electric starter, which let him know he had a hot item. These guys hadn't seen this feature yet. The guy started the motor and revved it, listening carefully for knocks, but it was purring smoothly as usual. He asked me if he could drive it, and I said, "Certainement."

The guy drove the bike out the narrow alley and was gone for about fifteen minutes. When he drove it back, I noticed that his face was expressionless, which made me realize that this might mean that the guy liked the bike but didn't want to show it so he could lowball me on the price.

I knew that, at retail, this bike would be worth twenty-five hundred dollars, or ninety-five thousand French francs. Because I had bought it at the factory for thirteen hundred dollars, I was already ahead by twelve hundred dollars if I had to sell it myself, but I wanted to hear the dealer's price so I could back that up. Actually, I knew I couldn't sell it myself and I needed to get as much as I could for it.

The service manager spoke with the salesman for a few minutes. They spoke in rapid-fire French, which left me completely out of the conversation. Then the salesman came over and said, "You have full papers for this machine?"

Right then, I knew the dealership wanted to buy the bike for itself. "Of course. Sales documents, title, insurance, everything."

"We would be prepared to offer you forty-four hundred francs for the machine if the sale is made now. We wouldn't want to see it damaged if you kept it for a few days, you understand."

I knew the exchange rate was 4.65 francs to the dollar, which meant that all they were offering was nine hundred dollars. That was way too low. A new bike sold off their floor would cost more than twice as much, and my bike only had four thousand kilometers on it.

"I'm sorry. Forty-four hundred francs is not what I had in mind. I was just looking for an idea of a price I could sell it for. I wonder if you have taken these beautiful leather saddlebags into consideration. They are worth at least three hundred francs each. I am thinking that sixty-five hundred francs is a more accurate figure," I said with complete resolve. I was sure they could sell the bike at the dealership for at least that much.

"But the motorcycle has to be fully inspected, cleaned, and tuned up before we could sell it. That costs money," the salesman wheedled.

"The first tune-up at five thousand kilometers includes an oil change, new spark plugs, and a check of the timing, the wiring, and the brakes. That doesn't cost much. It might take a mechanic a half hour," I countered.

The salesman gave me a look, which indicated that he knew he was dealing with a more seasoned biker than he supposed. He said he would have to speak with his boss and went to the front office.

I had decided that this was as good a place to sell the bike as any, but I wasn't going to be shortchanged. I might have to give a little, but this was probably my best shot if I wanted to sell the bike soon.

The salesman brought the sales manager with him this time. *Things are getting serious*, I thought. The manager greeted me with a friendly "bonjour" and proceeded to closely inspect the bike. He looked carefully at the saddlebags. He called for the guy who had driven it and asked him a few questions. Then he spoke tersely to the salesman and went back to his office.

The salesman looked me over with an appreciative look on his face and said, "The manager says this machine is worth more than we originally had thought. We will offer you fifty-five hundred francs for an immediate sale, no more. Is that acceptable?"

I made a quick calculation. Fifty-five hundred francs was fourteen hundred dollars, which meant I had used the bike to take me on my journey for a net cost of almost nothing, except for gas. I couldn't argue with that. I accepted the offer, with two conditions: I had to have a cash payment because I was leaving for the United States in a couple of days and had nowhere to cash a check. Next, I needed a ride to the train station to get back to Aix. The salesman said these were not problems, and I was shown into the manager's office to fill out the paperwork.

Two hours later, the paperwork was winding down. The manager ordered coffee and macaroons for lunch while the secretary typed the transfer papers. The manager had wisely sent to the bank for the cash before it closed. The only hitch had come up when they had to call the BMW factory in Berlin to verify the sale. The French were not cordial with the Germans, I noted, so despite working for the same company, there was a holdup.

In the end, I stood on the train platform waiting for the six fifteen train to Aix with fifty-five hundred French francs in my pocket and a small hole in my heart for the sacrificial bike that had brought me to a new situation in life. When I got to the station in Aix, I picked up a schedule of trains to Paris. I saw that the seven o'clock train took six hours. I would have to spend the night in a hotel at the airport to catch a morning flight to JFK.

I walked from the station to the Rotonde up the Avenue des Belges. It was a warm evening, and I was hot in the biking gear. All that stuff was going to have to go. I wasn't a biker anymore. That part of my adventure had played out.

I sat at a table at Le Festival and ordered a beer and asked for the menu. I really wanted a hamburger. It had been a long time, and I was feeling the pull of home. When I saw the menu, I was not surprised to see there were no hamburgers, so I ordered an entrecote, a small steak. I asked for pommes frites as a side. There were two things American that just get into your blood, meat and potatoes. As I enjoyed the steak, I reflected that I had been exposed to a much wider variety of foods in Europe than I had been used to. That was something I would carry forward.

After dinner, I went to the taxi stand at the Rotonde and took a cab to the hostel.

The manager saw me come in. "Where is your moto? he asked.

"I sold it because I am returning to the States in a day or two. I have four days paid for at the hostel left, but you can keep what I don't use."

"Tres bien. Merci." The manager shrugged and said, "Bon voyage."

I went to my room, stripped, and showered. *This has been one hell of a day*, I thought. I had given up the bike, but at the same time, I was free of it. Wild Bill had talked me into buying it, and it had served a purpose I could not have imagined when I bought it. It had made my journey an adventure, and it had helped to make me a man.

If I doubted that, I need only remember the tunnel in Yugoslavia and the bus on the mountain in Crete or the way Eva and Kara had clutched me around the waist on our rides. And it had come at a net cost of almost nothing because I had stood my ground at the dealership.

But I didn't need the bike now; it was time to move on.

36

Heading Home

I SLEPT A LONG time and woke lazily. Although I was hungry for breakfast, after getting dressed, I made time to see how well my clothes and possessions fit into the new bags. Satisfied that there was plenty of room, I asked the manager if I could call a cab to bring me to town. The manager said, "A votre plaisir." After all, he was keeping two nights' payment of mine for nothing.

I had the cab take me to Cagnina for a late breakfast. I told the baker that this would be my last petit dejeuner in Aix because I was going home to the States tomorrow.

The guy said "bon voyage" and kissed me on both cheeks. That custom always made me uncomfortable, but I smiled and ordered my usual breakfast. When I was done, I asked the baker which of his pastries would keep and be good for breakfast the next day when I was on the train. The baker scratched his head and said he baked fresh every morning, but he thought linser tortes might keep. I told him I loved linser tortes, to give me three of them and put them in a box so they would travel well. We shook hands, and the baker said "bon voyage" again.

I walked down the Cours to the Monoprix, where I had seen a sign for a barber in the basement when I was shopping for luggage. I figured it was time to go all the way with my new swept-back look. My hair was long enough for a short ponytail when it was combed over my head, which was what Kara liked, but it was basically unruly.

The barber spoke little English, so I had to use gestures to show him what I wanted. The barber showed me a picture of a coif on the wall, and I gave him a thumbs-up. The barber said it cost sixty francs, which was fourteen dollars. *The end of the biker image comes with a price*, I thought, but when the barber was done, I looked in the mirror and said out loud, "I can live with that." I gave the barber a nice tip.

On my way out of the store, I saw a white Lacoste shirt and a dark-blue windbreaker, which would go with my faded jeans. I was ready to go home, but first I had some calls and arrangements to make.

I went to the Tourism Bureau to have the lady at the international desk book me a hotel room at Orly. She did so, and told me the train from Aix would arrive at the Gare de Lyon in Paris. I could take a taxi from there to the hotel. I thanked her, and she said, "Pas de quoi. Et bon voyage."

As I left, I realized how my journey had been facilitated by the people of the AMEX offices and this Tourist Bureau I had been to. I appreciated their services, even Alex Morgen, who had sent me behind the Iron Curtain. I'd be telling that story for a while.

I wanted to call the parents to let them know I was coming home and ask if they could pick me up at JFK. I'd have to call from JFK once I arrived because I didn't have a flight time yet. I went to the phone booths. It was seven in New York, so I figured I had a chance to reach my mother. After the connection went through and the charges were accepted, she came on the line.

"Jack? Is that you? Are you all right?"

I always had to adjust myself to my mother's inclination of assuming that anything out of the ordinary, like a phone call from me from Europe, had a portent of doom.

"Yes, Mother. It's me, and I'm fine. In fact, I'm flying into JFK the day after tomorrow, and I wonder if you can pick me up."

"You're coming home? Oh, that's wonderful! Oh, but that's the long Fourth of July weekend. We won't be home. We are going to Martha's Vineyard for a party at one of your father's biggest clients. Why does it have to be then?"

I almost came back with a crack, but I bit my tongue. *These people are what they are; they can't change*, I thought.

"Well, that's when I'm flying in. But don't worry. I think there's a bus from JFK to Grand Central. I can get a train and take a taxi from the station."

"Oh, that sounds good. I'll make sure there's things in the fridge for you to eat. But Jack, you really should give us some notice of this sort of thing. Anyway, we'll be home Sunday afternoon and looking forward to seeing you. It's been a long time."

"Yes, Mother. See you Sunday." I hung up the phone, thinking it would be nicer if it would be even longer before I saw them again. I paused and slowly shook my head. What did I really expect from that call? I needed to massage my father to get money for a car, something that was vital to my future plans. A ride from the airport was inconsequential by comparison. I'd manage.

I figured that since I would be on my own when I arrived at JFK, I could book whatever flight I wanted, so I went back to the Tourism Bureau to get phone numbers for the airlines. I could make a reservation for myself. The lady at the international desk looked at me querulously when I showed up again. I asked her for the reservations desk numbers for PanAm and TWA. She sighed, wrote the numbers on a notepad, tore off the slip, and handed it to me. I thanked her and left quickly; I figured I'd worn out my welcome there.

I walked up the Cours and got a fistful of change from the bank. Then I booked a flight on TWA the day after tomorrow leaving Orly at seven in the morning and arriving at JFK at six thirty in the evening. The ticket cost $295. I needed $19 for train fare, $30 for the hotel, and roughly $25 for food, which came to $370, or 1,700 francs. I had 5,500 francs from the sale of the bike, so I went back to the bank and changed 3,300 francs for $710. That's what I had left after six months of traveling. I'd done pretty well, remembering I'd lived for free in Berlin all that time. A rough calculation showed that I'd lived on about fourteen dollars a day for six months and I had owned a motorcycle and driven it through seven countries. This was a feat I could not have contemplated when I started out.

I folded the bills and stuffed them in my front jeans pockets, francs on the right, dollars on the left. No way a pickpocket could get at them there unless the guy wanted to give me a hand job at the same time, I figured with a smile. Now I was set to travel.

I strolled through the old city of Aix, looking up at the pink/ orange buildings with their blue shutters closed to keep out the heat. I saw a huge vine flowing over the pink walls of an enclosed yard, with its green tendrils reaching down to the sidewalk and providing an added splash of color to the ancient scene. It must have looked like this in medieval times. I reached the town hall square with the plane trees and the fourteenth-century clock tower that tolled the quarter hour, and then I went down through the medieval Passage Agard, one of my favorite places, and back out onto the Cours. Someday I'd have to come back here with Kara.

I stopped at the Monoprix to look at the books. I'd need something to read for the trip. There was a display for *Tai-Pan* by James Clavell, an adventure best seller that suited my taste. Then I went to the taxi stand to get a ride back to the hostel and realized I needed a ride to the train station in the morning.

I gave the cabbie a ten-franc tip when he left me off at the hostel. I told him I would pay the fare and give him another twenty-franc tip if he picked me up and took me to the train station tomorrow at six. The guy promised to be there.

In the morning, I was waiting at the door of the hostel when the cab showed up. I had repacked everything before I went to bed with my box of linser tortes in the shoulder bag. Aix was a beautiful town, but in the end, I had started to feel cooped up after being on the road for so long. When I sold the bike, I was like a shark on a beach: the ultimate creature of mobility out of its element. The cabbie left me at the station, and I looked around for a café where I could get some coffee, but it was too early.

The train came, right on time. I boarded and found an empty second-class compartment where I left the bags. When I passed a conductor in the passageway, he punched the ticket, and I asked him where the concession car was. I bought two cups of coffee and went back to the compartment to enjoy them with my linser tortes from Cagnina. I sat by the window, looking forward, so I could see the French countryside zip by. Because I had to concentrate on the road when I was on the bike, I had missed some of the scenery of the countries I had gone through. I would have seen more if I had been driving a car, but I would have missed the thrill of being a part of the country, exposed to the wind, whipping my hair and pulling at my face.

And the danger, was that what made riding the bike so thrilling? I had foiled near-death situations in the tunnel in Yugoslavia and in the face of the bus in Crete. I had to brush off these near-death episodes simply because I had to keep going. If I could look death in the eye and move on, what couldn't I do in life? I had dominated my fear with aptitude and agility. I could use those attributes to help build my future.

The train went north through central France with major stops and Lyon and Dijon before turning west to Paris. It pulled into the Gare de Lyon at one forty-five. I took a taxi from the station to the hotel near Orly, where I checked in and asked for a wake-up call at five in the morning. On the way to my room, I saw that the hotel had a small restaurant, so I could have dinner on the premises. I settled into the room and stretched out on the bed and began to read *Tai-Pan*. I was soon immersed in the sweeping saga of the rivalry between two Scotsmen who hated each other and were building trading empires in the newly colonized Hong Kong of the mid-nineteenth century. It was a long book, and I was happy that it would last through the flight home.

For dinner, I had a beer with some fish and chips. I had to start watching my money now. I'd done well and had seven hundred dollars left to spend, but my big move forward was going to need more financing from the parents, and I needed to save cash. I felt that my formative plan would pass muster with them; still, the more I had of my own, the better.

The phone rang at exactly five. "Bonjour, monsieur," the operator said.

I washed, dressed quickly, and went to the lobby to get the shuttle bus to TWA. It seemed to take a long time to come, but when it did, I was relieved that TWA was the second stop. I went to the desk and gave the attendant my passport and told her I had a reservation for JFK on the seven o'clock flight. She asked for payment, and I pulled out my remaining French francs. She counted them, gave me the ticket, and said, "Merci, monsieur. Bon voyage."

I walked down the open, high-ceilinged corridor to the gate. None of the little shops were open this early, but I did find a coffee vending machine, got a cup, sat down next to the gate, and pulled out the last of the linser tortes. After forty-eight hours, it was still pretty good. *That baker knows his business*, I thought, relieved I wasn't going to have to wait for breakfast until the flight took off.

As flight time neared, I was surprised at the number of people gathering around the gate, and after boarding, I looked around and saw that the plane was nearly full. *No exercise on this flight*, I thought, but it was only a seven-hour flight, and I had *Tai-Pan* to keep me occupied. After takeoff, a breakfast of croissants, jam, cut fruit, and coffee was served. After that, I used the WC and descended into the world of *Tai-Pan* until the announcement that we would be landing in a half hour. It was six twenty in the evening, local time.

I went through customs and immigration in about forty-five minutes and figured to call Chris to see if he would meet me at the train. Chris answered the phone.

"Hey, Chris! It's Jack. How're you doing, buddy?"

"Jack!? You've got to be kidding me! Where are you?"

"I'm at JFK. Just flew in from Paris. Have I got a few stories to tell you! But listen, my parents are out on the Vineyard for some corporate thing, and I've got to schlep my way to Grand Central and take the train home. I know it's kinda late, but I was wondering if you could pick me up at the station."

"Are you shitting me? You've been gone six months, and I want to hear everything! What terminal are you at? I'll drive down and pick you up in an hour and a half."

I was thrilled that my old friend would come through for me like that again. I said I was at TWA and would be waiting on the sidewalk from nine fifteen on. Chris said he'd be there. I went through the terminal until I got to the check-in counters at the front. I went out the front door into a steamy midsummer New York night that smelled of jet exhaust. I wasn't going to handle that for an hour and a half, so I went back inside and sat at a bench near the counters.

It seemed that this was where I had started my journey six months ago, waiting for the Icelandic Air attendant to show up. I looked over and saw a beautiful TWA attendant in her red-and-white uniform helping some customers. She was a knockout. *Where do these creatures come from?* I asked myself.

But I turned away to look outside, thinking of what a great friend Chris was to come pick me up and thinking of why I had to make such a big deal about attractive women. When I got back together with Kara, that would provide me with all I needed as far as an attractive woman went, and one that said she wanted me, no less. I'd discovered that women were a risk, but the right woman was a risk worth taking. I wasn't going to question my new knowledge about that.

Chris was coming, and I wanted to have my story ready to tell so it made sense. I was going to have to tell the story to my parents and others too. That there was a larger purpose to my journey, and I felt I had accomplished a lot of it, but I didn't want to come across as being pretentious. It was an exciting time: I should express it that way, and I had to admit that a lot of what happened on the way was random, so how could I make an operative framework for the story?

The more I thought about it, the more I understood what this time meant to me and my future. I felt so much more like a whole man than when I left, and I wanted to share that with Chris. I went back to the beginning and remembered Siddhartha, how he had given up his life as a Brahmin who searched for knowledge to gain experience of life in all its worldly forms, only to find love and unity in the ever-flowing river.

I thought about the feeling of release I had experienced in reading Henry Miller's declaration of his own freedom when he wrote that everything that might be served at the banquet of life could be two enormous turds. That would be an answer for my striving parents and all their crowd, although I wouldn't tell them that. In the end, wasn't life a lot of random events? And weren't the parents trying to eliminate as much of that randomness by casting rules over everything? They could never manage it, no matter how tight they drew up the rules.

I thought I might be tired and too much into my own head. I went to get a Coke. Maybe it was a stretch to frame my newly enlightened viewpoint with Hesse and Henry Miller. Maybe I needed to fill in some holes. Yet the argument seemed to make some sense. And at the end of the journey was Kara. I'd run it all past Chris to see what he thought.

I looked out the windows and saw Chris' car pull up. I ran out and jumped in, tossing the bags in the back seat. "Hey, man. Thanks for picking me up. It's great to see you."

"No problem. What are friends for? It's great to see you too. Wow! It seems like you've been away forever. You changed your haircut. You look more serious."

"'It's been a long, strange trip,' as *The Dead* say."

I told Chris the essence of the trip in the hour and half it took to my house, but there was a lot of the take on my illumination that needed more telling, so Chris spent the night. We played some of the tunes that I had been missing for six months and had a couple of beers, and as I spoke, I could tell by Chris' reaction to some of the things I said, that he was feeling left behind. Chris' old friend had transcended a barrier in life that he had not.

I tried to coax Chris into understanding the need for him to go out and discover himself, but Chris was resistant. He had just finished college, he wasn't facing the draft, and his father had set him up with a job in a big Wall Street bank. He couldn't pass up this kind of opportunity, he said. I could hear Chris' parents talking right through his mouth when he said that. I let it go. Chris would have to find out for himself, if he ever did.

We slept until ten and made a big American breakfast of scrambled eggs, lots of bacon, English muffins with jam, and coffee. I had almost forgotten how good all that was until I remembered the breakfast Paul and I had cooked on the ferry to Genoa. Chris was astounded in hearing that tale.

Chris pulled out a joint to complete my welcome home, but I said I had calls to make, and honestly, I was getting away from the pot. In college, it helped pass the time. Now I thought it was just a waste of time, I said.

Chris could hardly believe what he heard after the many ounces of pot he and I had consumed. I mollified his shock by saying I was trying to put together my own work situation and I needed to have my head on straight to do it. Chris understood. We embraced, saying we'd call each other tomorrow.

37

I Find a Future Path

IT WAS FOURTH OF July weekend. I hoped that some of the guys I had talked to at school about their future plans would be home so I could get an idea of what they'd developed since. I had to think a couple might have been snagged by the draft, but I couldn't remember which ones had the low numbers. I had the phone numbers of the ones I had sent cards to from Aix, so I'd start with those. But first, I owed Wild Bill a call to let him know what he'd missed, but no one picked up at Bill's parents' place, so I put that call off until later. Anyway, Bill had put himself in the past. It was time to move on.

I called Wally Hubbert, but his mother picked up and said Wally had gone to Vietnam six months ago. I said I hadn't heard and got off the phone as fast as I could. I had always thought of Wally as a nice guy, but a bit of a doofus. In Vietnam, he'd be someone the VNA would use for target practice if he didn't move fast enough. I hoped Wally made it out of the jungle ok.

I called Alex Simpson, whose father had inherited a company from his father. They made some sort of specialty paint for the marine industry, and they made a ton of money. Alex had the good fortune of being able to take life as seriously as he wanted and say screw the rest. He loved soccer, and so he put his full effort into it, being the center halfback and the team captain in college. I got along with him, so I wondered if Alex knew of people I could talk to about jobs. I would never work with Alex. His parents were more hung up socially than my parents were. There was no answer. They probably were cruising on their yacht.

I found Terry Short's number in the New York phone book. Terry and I had played some crazy pranks at college during our first two years but had drifted apart afterward. When I reached him at his parents' house, Terry told me he was starting his second year in medical school. Terry figured that a six-month bike ride through Europe sounded like something I would do, but he'd never consider it. When I pressed him for contacts, Terry told me that one of his roommates from senior year had started an insurance agency in our college town and might be looking for help. I said thanks and took the guy's number, and that was the extent of that call. Insurance was not for me.

I had some hopes for the next call. If nothing came of it, I'd have to mail out the other postcards I didn't have addresses for in Aix and wait a week to call them. My call was to Sam Duncan, with whom I had played on the soccer team for three years. Sam and I had remained close even after I was on probation from the team senior year. We played racquetball twice a week during the winter and became good friends.

Before graduation, Sam told me that his father, who was a state senator in Colorado and owned an Oldsmobile dealership in Denver, was in the late-planning stages of setting up a sporting goods distributorship. His older brother was going to help him run it, but Sam wasn't sure he wanted to get into a family business. He had actually come east to college to give himself some space from the family for a while. He had to wait out the draft with a middling number like me, but he might go back to Colorado to join the business if he weren't called.

When I called, the phone rang for quite a while, but just before I hung up, a woman answered. I asked if Sam were there, and the woman said he was and went to get him.

When Sam was on the line, I said, "Hi, Sam. It's me, Jack. I made it back from Europe. Did you get my card?"

"Jack Higgins!? Is that really you? Holy cow! I got your card two days ago and showed it to my father and my brother. We've been talking about you ever since. Where the hell are you?"

"I'm home in New York."

"Say, my brother and I think you have to have the biggest set of brass balls ever to go biking in Europe for six months. You didn't seem like that kind of guy in school."

"I had quite a time, Sam. You learn things on the road."

"I'll bet. Listen, we're in the middle of our big Fourth of July barbeque here, so it's a little tough to talk right now. I know my brother, Bob, would really like to talk to you though. Are you going to be around later tonight?"

"I'll be here. You got my number?"

"No. Let me write it down. Everyone should have left by nine our time. That's eleven your time. Can you take a call then? We'll still be pretty amped up from the party. Ha, ha!"

"No problem. Look forward to hearing from you. Have fun at the party."

"No problem there. Look, Jack, we've got some pretty big things going on here on the front range. Talk soon."

That went well, I said to myself, thinking that Sam was referring to the sporting goods venture. That would be great, but I knew better than to rely on just one contact to get where I wanted to go. I'd have to address and mail the other postcards tomorrow and keep thinking of other alternatives to strengthen my position. I wanted to be able to tell the parents that I had a job or at least was in a firm position to get one within a week or two at the most. That was crucial to my strategy of moving on.

On Monday, I could call the alumni office at college to get some more numbers. I'd be stretching things in some cases, but I'd learned from my father that was how you played the contact game. You kept calling, never knowing when you'd find gold. I had to admit, the old man knew a few things. For now, there was nothing to do but wait for the call from Colorado, so I grabbed a beer and watched ball games on the TV for the rest of the day.

The phone rang just after eleven. I was just starting a movie on *The Late Show*, but I quickly switched it off and picked up the phone. "Hi, Sam," I said, making the assumption.

"Hey, Jack," Sam said, sounding a bit breathless. "I've got my brother Bob on the line with us. Sorry to get back to you so late.

This shindig actually starts at lunchtime. We have square dancing and everything. We have about eighty people here for the barbeque every year, and they hang around for a while, especially my father's political friends. But here's Bob. He's the one who wants to talk to you."

"Hi, Jack," Bob began. "When I saw the postcard you sent, I asked Sam, 'Who *is* this guy? Is he doing this trip for real?' Sam said you were a good friend of his and told me what he knew about you. I'd like to know more. Could you tell me about your trip?"

I was glad I was prepared to tell the story, but I didn't figure why Sam's brother would be interested in the story of my bike ride. Nonetheless, I launched into the story, not omitting the reasons I had gone and some of the things I had learned. I even mentioned *Siddhartha*, hoping that Bob wouldn't be turned off by the esoterica. When I finished, I tried to direct the conversation toward my purpose of getting in touch with them.

"I got back home yesterday, and I'm trying to put together my next act. I'm looking for work, hopefully over the long haul. I'm free from the draft, and I don't want to live around New York where my parents are."

Bob didn't say anything for a moment. I heard him cover the receiver with his hand, likely because he wanted to talk to Sam privately. Then he came back on the line.

"Jack, here's what we're doing out here. We're building a sporting goods distribution center along the front range. It's called Varsity Sports, Inc. We have set up the warehouse in Denver, and now we need to build out a chain of stores that will service Denver, Boulder, Colorado Springs, and Fort Collins. We have just received bank financing to build out and start stocking up those locations. Do you know why we have chosen those cities?"

"No, I don't."

"Because in each of those cities is a major university: The University of Denver, The University of Colorado in Boulder, The Air Force Academy in Colorado Springs, and Colorado State University in Fort Collins. They are all within two hours' driving distance of our distribution center. All these schools need athletic gear, and using my father's connections, we can supply these colleges as well as many of the high schools in this region. We are also going to set up retail sporting goods stores in towns in Eastern Colorado.

"Sam tells me you're a smart guy with a head for organizing things. We've been interviewing candidates who can work in our distribution center, doing planning, organization, logistics, and such. Is that the kind of organizing you can do?"

"I think I'd be qualified at that," I said. "I'm really well-organized, personally, and have the ability to make plans to make things happen."

"I got that from what you said about your motorcycle trip. That isn't something that just falls out of the sky. You had a reason to go, made a plan, and pulled it off. We were impressed. As far as the inner workings of the company will go, my father will be CEO. He has put me in charge of operations. Sam is going to head up the retail end of things. We are going to hire some old pros who know the retail business to help us get off the ground; then they will become board members and let us run the business. We need someone whom Sam and I can trust to come in and learn distribution fast and not be afraid to speak his mind about what he thinks needs to be done. We'll all be learning on the fly. How does that sound to you?"

"It sounds like a really cool challenge."

"I like the way you put that. Would you like to come out here and let us get to know each other? I mean this would be on a trial basis, but frankly, we've been looking for a guy with some brains and creativity for quite a while and haven't found the right guy out here. Sam thinks you might be the guy."

My heart leapt into my throat. This was it! A job, one far away from the parents and their life, a chance to chart my own course in life. I forced myself to keep cool and formulate a measured answer.

"I'll be honest with you, Bob. I was looking before I left for Europe and didn't find anything that sounded anywhere near to what I want as what you are doing out in Colorado. I am an organizer and a planner, and I think I can bring what you want to the table. And I want to get started as soon as possible. It sounds like that's the time frame you're talking about?"

"Yeah. Right away. My father closed the financing for the build-out last week. Everyone was really happy about it at the barbeque today. My father wants to meet you. We need to put our slate of officers together for the bank as soon as we can, and we are missing a head of distribution. How soon could you get here?"

I was nonplussed by Bob's implicit trust in me and the hurried timetable he was proposing. As Bob had described it, this was a start-up business that had funding and solid prospects, especially with Sam and Bob's father's political connections behind it. I really wanted to join this enterprise.

"If it is absolutely critical, I could get on a plane on Tuesday," I said. "But there are two things that I'd like to ask you about. First, I'd need to get my car out there. I'm going to need it sooner rather than later. Second, I'd like to ask my girlfriend if she'd like to come. She lives in Chicago and is looking for work and a new situation, just like me. We have a history together. And she is a two-time NCAA swimming champion, which might help with your PR."

Sam burst in, "An NCAA swimming champion! Holy cow! She could be in marketing or sales for us. If you don't bring her out, all bets are off! Ha, ha, ha!"

"Your girlfriend is really an NCAA swimming champion, Jack? You *are* quite a guy. Yeah, sure. Bring your car and pick her up in Chicago on the way," Bob said.

I liked their attitude. They were smart and hard-driving; I knew Sam was friendly and bet Bob was too. I wouldn't let them down. I had lied about the car, but I was going to ask the parents to either buy me one or front me the money for one. If I had a job in hand, I figured I could talk them into that. It was their fondest wish, after all. Now I'd have to call Kara and see how she had made out.

"Great. Let me get in touch with her and get back to you. But, regardless, I'm going to take you up on this. It sounds like a fantastic opportunity. I am a planner by nature, and if my bike trip taught me anything, it was how to learn fast on the job. What's a good time to call tomorrow?"

"You can call me here at the house in the evening," Sam said.

"Ok. You'll be hearing from me."

We wished each other a happy Fourth and hung up.

38

Finding Kara Again

I WAS ELATED, TOTALLY pumped. I remembered driving through Colorado with Chris the previous summer. It was wide-open land with plains and mountains. The earth in all its glory, not a million parcels of land, all over-housed with pavements defining all the boundaries. It was a world I could feel and breathe in, and I was being offered a chance to make living there too. I was sure Kara would want to come with me. I had to talk with her.

The clock on the mantle said it was midnight, Eastern time, so it was eleven in Lake Forest, but it was a holiday. I was bursting to call her. Why not call? If one of her parents picked up the phone, I could say it was a wrong number. I went to get my passport folder to find her number and dialed.

I recognized Kara's voice on the phone as soon as she answered. "Kara. It's Jack. I'm back."

"Oh my God! Jack! I've been wanting you to call for so long. When did you get back?"

"Just yesterday. I got lucky when I got to Athens. I found a ferry that took me from Patras to Genoa. That saved me weeks of biking through Italy. I wound up in Provence for a while, where I called home and found out that my draft number wasn't called. I'm free!"

"Oh, Jack, that's wonderful!"

"Then I managed to sell the bike. I bought a ticket from Paris and got home last night. It was time to come home. I learned so much from being over there. It was so worth it. I've found what I was looking for in myself. And I found you too."

Kara didn't respond to what I said. I felt she was troubled. "How did things turn out for you?" I asked softly. She still didn't respond. "Did you get home ok? Were you able to sign up for any courses?"

Kara started to sob. "No. I called registration at Lake Forest College. They don't offer the advanced courses that would satisfy my degree requirements. I've been stuck here with my mother berating me for running away and scaring her to death. She says that now I have to get married and start raising a family. She's been asking her friends if they know of any good matches for me."

She paused to catch her breath. "Can you believe it!?" she shrieked. "It's like medieval times. I'm sitting here thinking of slitting my wrists!" She paused again. "God, I'm glad you called. What are you going to do?"

I was shocked to hear Kara talk like that. I hadn't realized it was quite that bad between her and her nineteenth-century Midwestern mother. She was desperate. I had called to tell her about the opportunity in Colorado. If she came with me, it would solve all her problems, but did she have the nerve to run away again? She'd be burning her bridges, maybe forever.

"Kara, hang on a sec. We said we loved each other, and you told me to remember you, right? And here I am, just home, and I'm on the phone with you, right?'

"Yes," she whispered.

"Well, I've always remembered you. I couldn't forget you since I left you in Crete. You've always been popping into my mind when I don't expect it. It's like you're part of me. I'm in love with you, but I'm still on my journey. I made a few calls to see if I could complete the last part of my journey, and I think I have found a spot. I had to find work to get away from my parents. So I started calling some guys I knew in college, and I struck pay dirt.

"The father of one of my classmates is starting a sporting goods chain in Colorado called Varsity Sports, and they've invited me to come out and see if I fit into a position they've been looking to fill. It looks like a fantastic opportunity, and they want me out there right away to see if I'm their guy. I'm sure I am, so I mentioned to them that my girlfriend was an NCAA swimming champion and asked if I could bring you along to see if they had a place for you. They thought that was terrific. They said you'd be great for sales. And all the stores will be in cities with major universities, so you could finish your degree in your spare time."

I stopped talking to let Kara have a chance to digest this news. She said nothing. "I'm going to drive out to Colorado. I want to be in Denver by next Tuesday. I can pick you up on the way, if you want to come with me. I want to be together with you. We can do this together. What do you think your mother would say to that?"

Kara didn't say anything.

"Kara, are you still there?"

"Yes, Jack. I'm still here," Kara said softly. "I can hardly believe what you've just told me. I was at the end of my rope, and now here you are with another plan for me. It's a bit overwhelming."

"I can understand that, and I'm sorry about the time frame. It's just that I've got to be in Denver by early next week come hell or high water. This is my chance. And I've got to talk my parents into giving me money to buy a car so I can get out there and have mobility. I'd love you to come with me. It would be a solution for you, but you might be burning your bridges."

"You're sounding like Practical Jack again."

"Ha. You know me. And that's just how I have to sell myself to these guys in Denver, as a problem-solver. I can do this."

"I'm sure you can. I just have to think about it. As you said, it would be a major leap for me. Give me a day. When will you leave for Colorado?"

"Not later than Thursday. I want to be in Denver early next week. I'll need a place to stay out there, but I'm sure Sam can fix me up with something short term."

"Ok. I'll call you tomorrow evening and let you know what I'll be doing."

"Kara, come with me, please. This will be our life adventure together. I promise."

"It sounds wonderful, dear Jack. I just need a little time. I have to say goodbye now."

I was really puzzled when I hung up the phone. At first, Kara sounded as if she were ready to run out her front door to get away from her mother; there was nothing at home for her but misery. I had come up with a plan for a way out, a new life for her. What did she need to think about? Holy cow! Women would forever mystify me.

I called Chris early the next morning to ask him to drive me over to the Jeep dealer so I could check out the Fourth of July Salathon. I wanted to get a four-wheel-drive car, which would be good in open country. I thought it fit my new image, somewhere between a VW bus and a bike. The dealer took us through the lot, and when I saw the Jeep CJ-5 Universal, I knew I'd found my car. It came with a canvas roof and a rollbar, but I could buy a hardtop in Denver for the winter. The MSRP was $2,895, but the dealer said there was an employee discount for the Salathon. I told the guy that I was a recent college graduate, so I got an additional 10 percent off. That got the price down to $2,325. I was sure I could persuade my father to give me $2,325 now that I had a job.

To celebrate, Chris and I went to the diner where I had sold the bus to the hippie to fund my journey.

"Do you think the babe was holding out the hundred dollars on that guy?" Chris asked, laughing, as we sat at the same booth where the sale had taken place.

"I'm not sure what women are thinking a lot of the time," I said, recalling my conversation with Kara yesterday.

I ordered a hamburger with fries and a Coke for the first time in six months. I found it strangely disappointing as a meal, but very American, greasy and filling. I reminded myself that I was going to expand my menu when I got to Colorado.

I decided to open up to Chris about my relationship with Kara. I told him I was in love with her. At first, Chris just grinned with a sexual undertone, but he changed his tune when he saw that I had real feelings for her.

"So what do you think she's going to do?" Chris asked.

"I've got to say that I was surprised that she hesitated when I asked her to come with me. Given what she's been going through with her mother, I thought she'd bolt. She could always come out to Denver later, but my guess is that the longer she stays at home, the more likely she'll cave to her mother's demands. It's an incredible situation. She said it was medieval."

"Sounds medieval. Boy, what a bummer for both of you."

"Yeah, but she's got to make the decision. I can't make it for her."

"No, I guess not. She's in a rough spot, but I figure one thing: if she decides to go with you, she's going to be your responsibility. She could be with you forever. Can you handle that?"

We didn't speak for a minute, and then I said, "Yeah. I think I can. She's a great girl, although I'm not an expert on the subject. I don't see how I could do better."

"Wow," Chris said. "That's really something. It's amazing how much you've changed since you went away."

"I think you're right. I feel it. But you know, I think you have too. You've made your decision about that Wall Street thing, and it's put you on course. My teachers at school would say we have gained gravitas."

"Ha. Heavy word. Makes us sound old. Are we ready for that?"

"Not sure, but I am up for making my own decisions and cutting my parents out of the loop."

"Fine for you, but I get along with my parents better than you do."

"No argument there," I said. "I hope Wall Street works out for you."

I asked Chris if he'd be around for a day or so. I'd need a ride back to the Jeep dealer if I could get the money. Chris told me he loved to buy cars and to just give him a call.

I had to wait for Kara to call and for the parents to come home. The job at Varsity Sports was a big fish for me to have on the line. I wanted to get on the road and get started with it, but I had to be patient and play my cards right with my parents. I could do that now.

It was Kara that concerned me. I wanted her; I really felt that, but she had to make a tough decision about her future. I remembered the tortuous mental and emotional state of affairs that had put me on my journey to Europe. Her decision now would be even harder.

I had dinner while watching the ball game. The game had just ended when the phone rang. I picked up and said, "Hello?"

"Jack, is that you?" said a voice in low tones.

I recognized Kara's subdued voice at the other end of the line. "Kara, are you all right? What's going on?"

"I can't talk too loud. I've had a huge fight with my mother over the past hour. I told her a little about getting a job in Denver and finishing my degree at the same time because I can't do it at Lake Forest. She blew her stack. She said no respectable girl would leave home and go live on her own. I said how the hell was I supposed to finish my degree if I stay here, and all she said was I won't need a degree when I'm married with children. I screamed at her and told her I would never get married. That was twenty minutes ago." She paused to catch her breath. "Now I'm ready to go with you as soon as you can get here."

My thoughts raced. *Right. Now you've got what you wanted. She's gonna be your girl. But think of the circumstances. You're gonna be responsible for her, as Chris said. She's running away from home for a second time, so she's burning her bridges. She's over twenty-one so she can make her own choices, but in choosing you, you bear the burden. And when you bring her out to Denver, they'll all be watching you to see how you treat her. So no turning back now.*

"All right, Kara. I'll be there as soon as I can, like Thursday or Friday. I've got to talk my parents into getting me a car, but I don't think that will be a problem. As soon as I get it, I'll be on the road. I will have to stop for the night somewhere because I can't make it from my place to Chicago in one hop. Will you be all right till then?"

"I've got to get out of here. I'll call a friend in Winnetka to see if she will pick me up when my mother is out of the house tomorrow. I can stay with her until you get here. She can drive me into Chicago, and we'll meet there. I'll pack as much as I can."

"Don't forget cold weather clothing."

"Practical Jack. Ha, ha!"

"Give me your friend's number. I'll call you Thursday night, and you can tell me where to meet you in Chicago."

I wrote down the number and put it in my wallet. "I'll remember to call."

"I know you will. Goodbye, my love," she said and hung up.

I couldn't wait to call Sam.

When I got Sam on the line, he said, "Sam, we're coming out and will be in Denver by next Tuesday. I'll be bringing Kara, and we'll need a place to stay."

"That's fantastic," Sam said. "My folks have this big Victorian house here in town, and I've been staying here to save money. Bob moved out to live with his girlfriend. There are six bedrooms, so there is plenty of room. I'm sure you'll love my folks. My folks really want to meet you, Jack, and Kara too."

I could think of no better way to get to know the boss than to move in with him, which made me somewhat uneasy because I'd be under a spotlight, but I was all-in now.

I said, "That sounds great, Sam." And it was settled.

I knew for sure that I would be on my way in a couple of days. After all the crap the parents had given me about getting a job, I had outdone them, and they had to come through for me. They couldn't accuse me of running away from anything this time. I was running toward my destiny.

I figured I might as well start packing my clothes too. I figured that Colorado had extremes of weather, so I'd better be prepared. I got my new bag and a couple from the attic and stuffed them with everything I'd need.

I was just finishing lunch when the parents pulled into the driveway. My mother was *so* happy to see me. I looked different. I changed my hairstyle. I looked older. My father was reserved, so I turned the conversation toward them by asking how their weekend went.

My mother said my father's firm had landed a big new account with more than a little glee in her voice. My father said nothing, but I knew that meant there would be plenty of money coming in soon, which suited my purpose. I relaxed and let them get unpacked from their trip. When they were done, I asked if they'd like to hear about my journey. My mother said, "Of course," and pulled on my father's sleeve to make him follow her down to the porch where we had drinks, and I spent an hour giving them a condensed narrative of my adventure, leaving out Eva and the life-threatening episodes.

I told them about going to Crete and meeting Kara from Lake Forest, knowing that was a community they would approve of. I didn't go too deeply into Kara. I stopped after telling them about taking the ferry to Genoa and then to Aix where I sold the bike and then flew home from Paris.

My mother was a bit dazzled by the itinerary. She said it sounded too frenetic for her. My father had finished his drink and leaned forward, putting his elbows on his knees and looking straight at me.

He said, "So now you're home. And you're free from military service. Now what do you propose to do with yourself?"

I told him about the calls with Sam Duncan, my classmate from college, and the business that his father was starting up in Colorado. I told him that their father was a state senator, who also owned an Oldsmobile dealership. The new business was in retail distribution and sales of sporting goods in four cities in Colorado. The distribution center was already set up in Denver, and the bank had just approved financing for four more outlets. I said that the Duncans had asked me to come out and join the business.

"So, you see, I absolutely have a good job in a place where I want to be instead of New York. But I'll need some help from you, in the form of a car, if I'm going to pin it down because I told the Duncans I would be in Denver by next Tuesday."

"You can't fly?" my father asked.

"I'll still need a car the minute I get there," I countered.

"Dear," my mother said, "we've been after him to get a job all this time, and now he has one. I think we should support him on this."

My father pondered for a few moments. "The father is a state senator?"

"Yes, he is."

"And he owns a car dealership?"

"Yes, he does."

"And they have secured funding?"

"Full funding for the rollout of the stores."

"And where will you stay?"

"At the family's house in Denver at first. They have a six-bedroom Victorian in town. Then I'll find a place of my own."

My father pondered for a few moments and then looked at my mother. "Well, it sounds like you've found your way, finally. All right, I'll help you out with a car, but only up to twenty-five hundred dollars. I think you can make do with that."

I suppressed a grin, knowing that I already had negotiated for the car I wanted at $2,325. I thanked my father by standing up and shaking his hand. I told him I was sure twenty-five hundred would be enough. I saw my mother wipe a tear from her eye.

I sat down again to remind my father of my timetable. I'd have to get the car tomorrow so I could get on the road right away. My father understood, went to his study, and came back with a check for twenty-five hundred dollars, and he wished me good luck in my new job. I thanked him again. My mother hugged me and told me she was proud of me.

Dinner that night was taken in a spirit of reconciliation.

39

Life Begins

The next morning I called Chris to ask if he would drive me to the bank where I could deposit my father's check and then close my account for cash to buy the Jeep. Chris said he'd be right over. I used the same bank as my father so the check would clear without a holdup.

After that, we went to the Jeep dealer, and I picked out an olive-colored, open-body CJ-5 with rollbars, black interior, and wheels. The salesman said the service department needed to set it up and it would be ready in two hours. In the meantime, we could do the paperwork. I told him I was taking it directly to Colorado, so I would only need a temporary plate. That made things easier. The salesman was surprised to be paid in cash, but he took it readily.

Chris wished me all the best as we hugged each other. I told Chris to make a million on Wall Street, and we parted, not knowing when we'd see each other again. I drove home with the Jeep's canopy top off so it was like riding the bike with the wind blowing in my hair. I dreamed of off-road adventures in the mountains of Colorado with my new four-wheel-drive capability.

My mother was noncommittal as to the Jeep; she drove a Lincoln. But when my father came home, he was enthusiastic about it, telling me he had driven a Jeep for several months in WWII. Sitting in it, he said this one was luxurious compared to the army version, but he congratulated me on my choice. He said he would put it on his insurance for a few months until I had gotten settled in Colorado. I thanked him; I hadn't expected that.

After dinner, I packed up the Jeep and told my parents I'd be leaving at sunrise. I left room for Kara's things, which I assumed would take up a lot of room. My mother said she would make sandwiches for the trip and leave them in the fridge. There were final farewells, and I went to bed early, but sleep was hard to come by.

I got up at dawn, ate a big breakfast, and left home for my new life out West. My mother had gotten up to wish me a safe drive. I took I-80, just as I had the summer before in the bus. I kept the Jeep under sixty miles per hour to break in the engine, but I made it to Cleveland by ten that night.

I called Kara from the Howard Johnson's motel I stayed at. She was so excited to hear from me. She told me to meet her in the lobby of the Palmer House Hotel, which was near Soldier Field where the Bears played. I said I'd be there around one.

When I got to the outskirts of Chicago the next day, I took I-90 into the center of the city and found the Palmer House. I saw Kara waiting on the sidewalk under the awning; when I got out of the Jeep, Kara ran and jumped on me, wrapping her arms around my neck and her legs around my thighs and kissing me all over my face. At first, I had to catch my balance so she didn't knock me over, but after that, all I wanted to do was kiss her on the mouth. Kara's friend was with her.

"Jennine saved my life," she told me and hugged her friend.

We went into the hotel lobby to retrieve Kara's things and load them in the Jeep. I was right; there was a ton of stuff, but she was leaving her home behind so it all had to come. When I produced several lengths of clothesline to tie everything down, Kara said, "Practical Jack," and kissed me again.

I thanked Kara's friend for her help, but when I saw them hug each other and the tears flow, I knew that no thanks were necessary. It was an old and steadfast friendship.

I got the Jeep headed west on I-80 after we left Chicago. We decided only to stop for food and gas, splitting the driving in two-hour shifts. I figured it would be a twenty-four-hour drive, including stops, and if we really got tired, we could spend the night in a motel. Kara didn't care; she just wanted to go.

We talked about Crete and how amazing it was that we had found each other there, at the end of the earth. We talked about Colorado and how this adventure might play out for us.

"Kara, I took a trip cross-country on this same road last summer and it had no meaning for me," I said. "Now, with you here and a future opened up before us, I can envision a life I could not before. I want you to share it with me."

"I want that too," she said. "And I'm not concerned about living with the Duncan's, despite the fact that they are the owners. We'll find time for ourselves." She grinned at me as she said that.

"And the Duncans sound like they are involved parents, willing to take their sons into their business. They're giving us a chance too. We could never expect anything like that at home."

I agreed with her and told her, "I reconciled with my parents before I left, and my father gave me the money for the Jeep."

This saddened Kara. She said she had taken the few hundred dollars she had in her savings account and left with nothing else but the proverbial shirt on her back.

"You have completed your journey of self-discovery," she said. "But mine is incomplete. I have found love with you, but I have cut myself adrift from my world. I have more to learn and a past to mend, which worries me."

I held her hand and told her my own journey was not complete. "Listen, Kara, I've just found a path to take and the courage to walk down it. Now that you have found a path, you certainly have the courage to walk down it. It's a long road, but we can walk it together."

"Forever," Kara said and as she kissed my hand, I could feel the tears streaming down her face. Her hand was shaking.

I smiled at her and squeezed her hand, concerned that she was still under the evil spell of her mother and had yet to make the break from home before she could be free.

Denver was only hours ahead, where a new world was going to open for both of us. So I drove into the future and let the past fade in the rear-view mirror.

Printed in the USA
CPSIA information can be obtained
at www.ICGtesting.com
LVHW051358091123
763364LV00048B/415